Oy, Caramba!

ANTHOLOGIES

The Norton Anthology of Latino Literature * Tropical Synagogues: Short Stories by Jewish-Latin American Writers * The Oxford Book of Latin American Essays * The Schocken Book of Modern Sephardic Literature * Lengua Fresca: Latinos Writing on the Edge (with Harold Augenbraum) * Wáchale!: Poetry and Prose about Growin Up Latino in America * The Scroll and the Cross: 1,000 Years of Jewish-Hispanic Literature * The Oxford Book of Jewish Stories * Mutual Impressions: Writers from the Americas Reading One Another * Growing Up Latino: Memoirs and Stories (with Harold Augenbraum) * The FSG Books of Twentieth Century Latin American Poetry: An Anthology

GRAPHIC NOVELS

Latino U.S.A.: A Cartoon History (with Lalo Alcaraz) * Mr. Spic Goes to Washington (with Roberto Weil) * Once@9:53am (with Marcelo Brodsky) * El Iluminado: A Graphic Novel (with Steve Sheinkin) * A Most Imperfect Union: A Contrarian History of the United States (with Lalo Alcaraz)

TRANSLATIONS

Sentimental Songs, by Felipe Alfau * The Plain in Flames, by Juan Rulfo (with Harold Augenbraum) * The Underdogs, by Mariano Azuela (with Anna More) * Lazarillo de Tormes

EDITIONS

César Vallejo: Spain, Take This Chalice from Me * The Poetry of Pablo Neruda * Encyclopedia Latina: History, Culture, and Society in the United States (four volumes) * Pablo Neruda: I Explain a Few Things * Calvert Casey: The Collected Stories * Isaac Bashevis Singer: Collected Stories (three volumes) * Cesar Chavez: An Organizer's Tale * Rubén Darío: Selected Writings * Pablo Neruda: All the Odes * Latin Music: Musicians, Genres, and Themes (two volumes)

GENERAL

The Essential Ilan Stavans

Oy, Caramba!

AN ANTHOLOGY OF JEWISH STORIES FROM
LATIN AMERICA

Edited by Ilan Stavans

University of New Mexico Press ✡ Albuquerque

© 2016 by the University of New Mexico Press
All rights reserved. Published 2016
Printed in the United States of America
21 20 19 18 17 16   1 2 3 4 5 6

Library of Congress Cataloging-in-Publication Data
Names: Stavans, Ilan editor.
Title: Oy, caramba! : an anthology of Jewish stories from Latin America /
Ilan Stavans [editor].
Description: Albuquerque : University of New Mexico Press, 2016. |
Includes bibliographical references.
Identifiers: LCCN 2015040297 | ISBN 9780826354952 (pbk. : alk. paper) |
ISBN 9780826354969 (electronic)
Subjects: LCSH: Short stories, Latin American—Jewish authors—
Translations into English. |
Latin American fiction—20th century—Translations into English. |
Jews—Fiction.
Classification: LCC PQ7087.E5 O95 2016 | DDC 863/.01088924—dc23
LC record available at http://lccn.loc.gov/2015040297

Cover illustration courtesy of Pixabay, licensed under CC0 1.0
Designed by Felicia Cedillos
Composed in Adobe Jenson Pro

CONTENTS

Introduction

– –

ILAN STAVANS

All that they do seems to them, it is true,
extraordinarily new,
yet it is part of the chain of generations. . . .
—FRANZ KAFKA

OCTAVIO PAZ, THE Mexican poet and recipient of the 1990 Nobel Prize in Literature, wrote in an essay entitled "The Few and the Many," included in his volume *The Other Voice*, that the world is intolerant of the particular. The majority, he claimed, overwhelms and does away with the minority. Perhaps nowhere is this assessment more apt than in Latin America, where the massive population is ethnically mixed but is generally known, both at home and abroad, as a society that is homogeneously mestizo, that is, part Indian and part Iberian. For more than five hundred years, waves of diverse immigrants beginning with the Spanish and Portuguese after 1492 and continuing with the Italians, Germans, French, Dutch, and Asians have created a mosaic of racial multiplicity. But the coexistence of different groups hasn't been a happy one, and pluralism has not survived without stumbling. The particular is continually being devoured by the monstrous whole.

The Jews are also part of the particular. Since the time of the Inquisition, in spite of all odds, they have stubbornly remained loyal to their faith and tradition. They have assimilated symbols of their environment and have contributed, albeit silently, to the cosmopolitanism of the region. They have often been the target of anti-Semitic attacks, even violence; left- and

1

right-wing regimes have used the Jews as a scapegoat, branding them a source of social and political distress. Yet their presence has also been valued by democratic, less aggressive forces as a reminder of how freedom can survive through the ages.

Political and economic turmoil has stimulated them to create a literature that bears witness to their deep historical transformation in the Latin American environment. That literature, more abundant in the last hundred years, is virtually unknown to North American readers. The reason for this neglect is easy to understand: as a Eurocentric country, the United States did not pay attention to what was written south of the Rio Grande until the 1960s, when a boom of fresh new literary voices from Mexico, Argentina, Peru, and Colombia began to renew the genre of the novel, exhausted after the contributions of Joyce, Kafka, Proust, and Robert Musil. But English-speaking readers failed to notice the less popular, more ethnically focused writers alongside Carlos Fuentes, Julio Cortázar, Mario Vargas Llosa, and Gabriel García Márquez. They saw the universal in Latin American literature but not the particular.

The twenty-eight stories included here belong to various nations and four languages—Spanish, Portuguese, Yiddish, and English. The purpose of collecting them for the first time in one volume for North American readers is to show how these Jewish Latin American writers think, feel, and nurture their dreams: thus the objective is at once anthropological and literary. Irving Howe and Eliezer Greenberg wrote in the introduction to their groundbreaking 1954 volume, *A Treasury of Yiddish Literature*, "We have no desire to make extravagant claims: Yiddish literature can boast no Shakespeares, no Dantes, no Tolstoys. But neither can many other widely translated literatures." Latin America has indeed produced extraordinary writers, and the writers in this anthology, no doubt, have as much talent as many of their better-known colleagues, along with a distinctive ethos and a remarkable style very much their own. Readers who have never before encountered their work are in for a feast.

The original version of this anthology was called *Tropical Synagogues*. About two-thirds of its content is featured in *Oy, Caramba!*, which is expanded with an assortment of stories originally written in Yiddish and others in Spanish and Portuguese. When released by Holmes and Meier in 1994, the previous edition was enthusiastically embraced, went through various printings, and was a staple of courses, book clubs, and other readers' gatherings. I used the image of the tropical synagogue in the title because it characterizes the collective personality of this literary tradition. Imagine—somewhere in Patagonia, the Amazon, or a rain forest on the border between Guatemala and Mexico—a forgotten Jewish temple celebrating knowledge and a dialogue with God. The climate is that of magic and revolution. The place is populated by ancestral tribes predating the Spanish conquistadores and the coming of Christianity. Frequented by Jews in search of a collective identity, this fecund temple mixes Hebrew paraphernalia and pre-Columbian artifacts, sometimes of Aztec or Quechua origin. Its indefinite age and improbable location, elusive to historians and topographers, speaks to its exoticism; probably founded by Sephardic immigrants escaping the Inquisition or by Ashkenazi refugees settling in the region before the Second World War, it has lost its place in memory. Yet the syncretism of its architectural style and interior design is proof of a religious and cultural encounter too rich to ignore. A crossroad linking fantastic surrealism and traditional visions, its enigmatic presence is a unique symbol of the cultural and social experience of Jews in Latin America—an intertwining of the Old World and the New, European and aboriginal, natural and spiritual, primitive and civilized, lo hebreo (things Jewish) and the gentile milieu.

Four essential concerns are mirrored in the work of these Jewish Latin American writers: assimilation and the struggle to retain the Jewish tradition in a modern, secular world; anti-Semitism and the difficulty of being considered distinctive and unequal, which ultimately has a strong impact on the collective Jewish identity; the violent political reality from 1910 to the 1990s and Latin America's passive response to the systematic destruction of 6 million Jews by the Nazis; and the supernatural, what critics like Tzvetan Todorov call "the fantastic." The very foundation of this last aesthetic approach may come from the surrealist movement in Europe, with its dreamlike images—but after a trip to Haiti in 1934, Alejo Carpentier, a Cuban musicologist and baroque writer, claimed that reality in the Caribbean was far richer, more colorful, and more imaginative than anything European surrealists could ever fantasize. In a 1984 interview in the *Paris Review*, García Márquez stated that he is nothing but a realist. "Foreigners may think I invent a lot in *One Hundred Years of Solitude*," he said, "but that is because they don't know Latin America." And indeed, several stories here can be taken as examples of this exoticism: a few are set in jungles or decaying cities, while others take place in Prague or Buenos Aires but have a supernatural twist, a "fantastic" aura. They deal with God not as an object of devotion but as a miraculous force that can suddenly stop the universe's pace. These texts, I foresee, will be retained longer by most readers precisely because this "supernatural" element is now the signature of all the literature produced in the region.

For this new edition, I benefited from the research and translations—even the headnotes—included in Alan Astro's volume *Yiddish South of the Border: An Anthology of Latin American Yiddish Writing*, released in 2003. The historical information and bibliography have been updated, as have the headnotes and authors' bios in the back matter. It is my hope that *Oy, Caramba!* will once again attract a generation of readers eager to explore the vicissitudes of Jewish life south of the US-Mexico border.

DEMOGRAPHICS

Jews are but a tiny fraction of the non-Native population in Latin America. Argentina and Mexico, two countries that became independent from the Iberian Peninsula between 1810 and 1816, and, later, Brazil entered the twentieth century by accepting Jewish immigrants from Russia and eastern Europe, who arrived with the hope of finding prosperity and adapting to a new culture. Most of them were uneducated, Yiddish-speaking inhabitants of the shtetl, poor and persecuted. Their odyssey to Latin America proved to be partially successful, at least during the first decades of collective life.

As Theodor Herzl was convening the First Zionist Congress in 1897, Baron Maurice de Hirsch was attempting to place human and financial resources in the agricultural region of La Pampa, thinking the zone would eventually turn out to be the true Promised Land. Actually, Argentina as Zion was for a while a real and concrete challenge to the Zionist dream of resettlement in Palestine. The very first immigrants who settled in colonies such as Moisés Ville in Santa Fe, near the border with Paraguay; Rajíl, in the province of Entre Ríos, at the northeastern border with Uruguay; and others in Rio Grande do Sul, may have both consciously or by pure chance chosen to travel to Palestine and even to North America, but they arrived instead at the River Plate with high hopes for an end to their diasporic wandering. The official census claims that in 1895 there were some 6,000 Jews in Argentina; by 1910 the number had risen to 68,000, and by 1935 it had increased astronomically, to 218,000. Compared to other parts of Latin America, the Pampas and Buenos Aires have always been the most populated centers of Jewish life. In 1910 Brazil had some 800 Jews and Mexico had 1,000; by 1930 there were about 30,000 and 16,000 Jewish immigrants, respectively, in these two countries. Although during the 1950s there was considerable demographic growth of the Jewish population in all of Latin America, since then political turmoil and violence have led many Jews to finally immigrate to Israel and the United States. According to the latest studies, by the late 1980s the Brazilian and Hispanic worlds outside the Iberian Peninsula had a total population of more than 450 million, of which only 1.2 percent or less were Jews. Argentina held the lead with a quarter of a million Jews, followed by Brazil with some 125,000 and then Mexico with some 40,000. Together, small countries like Guatemala, Costa Rica, and Peru counted barely 10,000. And compared to the world Jewish population, where the United States has 48 percent and Israel 26 percent, pushing the figures in the region doesn't make them reach 4 percent, indeed a minimal number. These figures have remained steady in the first decades of the twenty-first century. The Jewish population has neither grown nor shrunk significantly, as a result of stable birth rates as well as migration. Demographers suggest that in 2010 the entire region had approximately 250,000 Jews.

Although most of the original Jewish settlers in Latin America were of eastern European background, quite a few Sephardim, whose roots in the Iberian Peninsula predated the expulsion in 1492, arrived in the Americas with and after the four voyages of Christopher Columbus. They were secretly supported, both financially and with crucial cartographic information, by wealthy conversos (also referred to as Marranos) who practiced Judaism in secret and by New Christian entrepreneurs like Luis de Santanguel, the Genoese admiral's own economic backer and a close adviser to Queen Isabella of Castile, who had wholeheartedly renounced their original Jewish religion. Since 1492, the year of the so-called discovery of America, is also the date of the expulsion of the Jews from Spanish soil, a controversial theory supported by Oxford professor Salvador de Madariaga, Nazi hunter

Simon Wiesenthal, and historian Cecil Roth claims that the hidden agenda behind the search for a new route to the West Indies was the quest for new lands where the Iberian Jewish population could live in spiritual peace.

Be that as it may, a considerable number of Spanish emigrants escaping the cruelties of Torquemada arrived in the Americas and for a while tried to regain control of their ancient biblical faith. Such is the case, for instance, of the famous Carvajal family in Nueva Espana, later known as Mexico, portrayed in great historical detail and accuracy by Alfonso Toro. But the church didn't allow for much religious freedom in the colonies, and although researchers have found traces of their path in major capitals such as Lima, Buenos Aires, and Santiago, the Spanish Jews concealed their true identity and eventually vanished. By the time of the 1910 socialist revolution of Pancho Villa and Emiliano Zapata, south of the Rio Grande most of the original Sephardic settlers had disappeared. At most, in the New World, converso methods of secrecy managed to produce bizarre, anachronistic curiosities. In Venta Prieta, for instance, a small town near Toluca, Mexico, there is an Indian community that practices the Jewish faith and has a synagogue in which it keeps ancient scrolls—although its members cannot read Hebrew or Ladino—and most of the male constituency is circumcised. Discovered by a group of North American anthropologists a few decades ago, the Indians claim to be Jewish, although their lineage, as of yet not authenticated, has been put in question by the Ashkenazim.

Another wave of Jewish settlers from the Mediterranean (mainly Syria and Lebanon), many of Sephardic ancestry, arrived in Argentina, Mexico, Brazil, and Venezuela during the 1920s and onward. They chose Latin America because of the linguistic similarities between their ancestral languages (Ladino or Judezmo) and modern Spanish and because family cohesiveness meant more to them than the opportunity for upward economic mobility. Their contact with the Ashkenazim has not been easy: the two communities tend to live apart, attend different temples and schools, and rarely intermarry.

The demographics of Latin American Jewry began a trend of decline in the 1960s, as a result of dictatorial regimes and repression. The changes in the sociopolitical fabric made exile and aliyah—immigration to Israel—concrete options. (Some sixty-eight thousand immigrants moved to the state of Israel between 1948 and 1983.) As the Jewish community in Latin America is generally a small, insular, self-contained population, proud of its separation from larger society, its overall input into the cultural mainstream has inevitably gone unrecognized or has not gained the recognition it deserves. Voluntarily or not, their different skin color and non-Hispanic physical appearance, their unique religion, and their educational and economic status have turned Jews into outsiders. A few of the writers included in this anthology were activists opposing their national governments, imprisoned or forced into exile in Europe, the United States, or even Israel, distant from their native soil and language, dreaming of a return, writing in a tongue (Spanish) alien to their more intimate milieu. That component of extraterritoriality constantly marks their fiction. Even the inattentive eye can see how their stories repeat, almost in an obsessive manner, a handful of metaphors and images that have to do with alienation: a woman trapped in a bottle; an unloved mother-in-law who prefers to spend her days alone rather than join her estranged daughter and her daughter's new husband; a Jewish bride who runs away with a gaucho on the Pampas. Like that of Dr. Jekyll and Mr. Hyde, the identity of these Latin American Jews, judging by their fiction, is full of labyrinthine divisions, accompanied by guilt and anxiety. One gets the impression that a suffocating minority life has created a vacuum, a feeling of seclusion and exclusiveness. Borrowing the words of Danilo Kiš, the author of *The Encyclopedia of the Dead*, who himself was adapting a biblical phrase, these writers are "strangers in a strange land." They inhabit a tropical synagogue both as individuals and as a collective; they are the particular in a continent where only the universal matters—at least up until now.

Although the novel and poem are also favored genres (a bibliography at the end of this volume suggests further readings, including fiction, nonfiction, and criticism in Spanish, Portuguese, and English), this anthology presents a sample of the most memorable short stories created by Jewish writers in Latin America from 1910 to the present—a window through which we are offered a glimpse of their inner lives and cultural predicament. Although it is my belief that the Jewish experience in Latin America has been remarkably cohesive and interconnected throughout the continent, the particular context of that experience has varied in different countries. To suggest this diversity of environment and sensibility in the face of a generally cohesive ethnic identity, I have organized the volume according to the writers' countries of origin. Since my approach is at once historical and literary, the stories are arranged chronologically within this framework.

ALBERTO GERCHUNOFF

When talking about Jewish literature in Latin America, one needs to start with the magisterial figure of Alberto Gerchunoff (1884–1950). He is at center stage because he is to this minority literature what Mendele Mokher Sforim (Sh. Y. Abramovitsh) was to Yiddish letters—a grandfather and a cornerstone. Before Gerchunoff, one can find sketches, poems, vignettes, and chronicles of immigrant life, written by Jewish refugees in Russian, Polish, Hebrew, Yiddish, and at times a rudimentary Spanish. But it is his beautiful and meticulously measured Castilian prose in *The Jewish Gauchos of the Pampas*, translated into English in 1955 by Prudencio de Pereda, a book deeply influenced by Cervantes, that gave birth to the short stories included in this volume, as well as to novels by the same authors.

Gerchunoff's life and craft have to be understood in the context of the history of Jewish immigration to Argentina. In 1891, when the boy was seven, his father traveled from Russia to the Pampas, and the family followed him. Agriculture and cattle-raising were the jobs designated for the shtetl dwellers, and hard labor was their lot. As expressed in his 1914 autobiography, *Entre Ríos, My Country*, published posthumously in 1950, Gerchunoff admired the capacity for hard work of his fellow Argentines. His family was first stationed in the colony of Moises Ville, but when his father was brutally killed by a gaucho, or Argentine cowboy, they moved to the Rajíl colony. This tragic event and Gerchunoff's later adventures in the new settlement were the inspiration for his early work.

One of the admirable things about Gerchunoff is his polyglotism. Language, after all, is the basic vehicle by which any newcomer must begin to adapt to the new country. Most immigrants improvised a "survival" Spanish during their first Argentine decade. Gerchunoff, however, not only learned to speak perfect Spanish as a child, but by 1910, at the age of twenty-six, his prose was setting a linguistic and narrative standard. Reading him today, we discover in his writing stylistic forms that were later developed by his followers, among them Jorge Luis Borges. Simultaneously, Gerchunoff's brief biographical sketches of such writers as Sholem Aleichem, Miguel de Unamuno, James Joyce, Max Nordau, and I. L. Peretz, which appeared in newspapers and magazines, and his deep and careful readings of British writers such as G. K. Chesterton, H. G. Wells, and Rudyard Kipling, influenced future artistic generations on the River Plate.

Even if he did not fully belong to the popular *modernista* movement budding at the turn of the century in Latin America, many moderns welcomed his literature. The Cuban activist José Martí, the Mexican sonneteer Manuel Gutiérrez Nájera, and other modernistas dreamed of reviving all literatures written in Spanish. So did Gerchunoff, although he did not quite share the aesthetic and political values of these contemporaries. His objective was to help Jews become Argentines, to be like everyone else. Following Gerchunoff's death, after some two dozen books and innumerable articles, Borges himself praised him as "the writer of le mot juste." Such a distinction, one should add, is seldom awarded to an immigrant. I can think of only a few others who have achieved it, among them Vladimir Nabokov, Joseph Brodsky, and Joseph Conrad.

I began by speaking of Gerchunoff in relation to Mendele Mokher Sforim because, although the two belong to two different worlds and even different languages, both managed to create a sense of literary tradition and continuity absent before. Mendele was considered by Sholem Aleichem to be the grandfather of Yiddish letters, as Gerchunoff became a cultural mentor and compass for later Jewish writers in Argentina such as Gerardo Mario Goloboff, Mario Szichman, Alicia Steinberg, and Isidoro Blaisten. In fact, the comparison is a clue to the linguistic reality the Argentine had to face: by writing in Spanish, he subscribed to the chain of Spanish and South American letters; Yiddish, the language of most of the immigrants, was left behind after he began publishing and was replaced by Spanish, a cosmopolitan, secular vehicle.

Indeed, one has to consider that very few Jewish writers, even if they had some knowledge of Yiddish, could write anything beyond a crude transliterated version. That's why some, including Gerchunoff himself and his successor Mario Szichman, used transliterated Yiddish in dialogue. Besides, a Yiddish-reading audience today is practically nonexistent. Mendele found Yiddish the appropriate vehicle for communication with his people; for Gerchunoff, it was Spanish, the idiom of "exile," that turned them into "normal" citizens of Argentina. The two were equally celebrated as speakers of the collective soul.

During his youth, Gerchunoff had an acquaintance, Leopoldo Lugones, a representative of the modernistas in Argentina and paternalistically philo-Jewish and proimmigrant, who gained access for him to *La Nación*, a very influential newspaper in Buenos Aires. Yet Lugones's last sour years and his own ideological odyssey are symbolic of the attitude of Argentina as a whole toward the Jews: at first a socialist and a liberal, in his mature years and up until his suicide in 1938 he was a fascist and a nationalist. By then the Jews, "alien" people in his eyes, were unacceptable to him as equals because they represented the unwelcome outsider. This hostility has its counterpart. Take the example of Rubén Darío, the modernista par excellence and famous Nicaraguan poet who in 1888 wrote *Azul . . .* (Blue . . .), a book whose impact on Hispanic letters was equivalent to that of T. S. Eliot's *The Waste Land* on English poetry. Darío saw the Jews as appealing citizens, paradoxically both symbolic of an eternal voyage and deeply rooted in the Argentine soil. In a beautiful poem entitled "Song to Argentina," he celebrated the biblical heritage and bucolic present of the citizens of Entre Ríos and Santa Fe. Here is a rough, free translation of one of its stanzas:

> Sing, Jews of La Pampa!
> Young men of rude appearance,
> sweet Rebeccas with honest eyes,
> Reubens of long locks,
> patriarchs of white,
> dense, horselike hair.
> Sing, sing, old Sarahs
> and adolescent Benjamins
> with the voice of our heart:
> "We have found ZION!"

The very same tone is to be found in the twenty-six stories collected by Gerchunoff in *The Jewish Gauchos*, the book to which he owes his fame, a parade of Spanish-speaking but stereotypical Jewish men and women from eastern Europe adapting to the linguistic and cultural reality of the Southern Hemisphere. The autonomous narratives that make up every chapter, some better than others, re-create life, tradition, and hard labor in this "new shtetl" across the Atlantic. The focus is on relations between Jews and gentiles, the passion to maintain the Jewish religion yet understand and assimilate new customs. What is most striking about the book to today's reader is the political ideology it professes: 1910, one should know, was the centenary of Argentina's independence. Gerchunoff meant his text to be a celebration of the nation's friendly, tolerant, and multiethnic spirit.

He had moved to Buenos Aires in 1895 and, beginning in August 1902, contributed regularly to many newspapers, among them *La Nación*. Even after the tragic loss of his father, he stubbornly went on believing that Argentina was a true paradise. He saw the province of Entre Ríos and the cosmopolitan Buenos Aires as a diasporic "holy land" of sorts, where the contribution of the Jews would always be welcome in shaping the national culture and where all manifestations of anti-Semitism would ultimately vanish. Needless to say, such optimism flourished for only a single generation. It evaporated even faster than the hatred it stood against.

In the short story "Camacho's Wedding Feast," included as the first entry in this volume, Gerchunoff describes the sorrows of a Jewish family when their daughter, about to be married to a rich Jew, is suddenly carried off by her gentile lover, Camacho, on the very day of the wedding. To be sure, the motif of the stolen bride is universal, having been used by Boccaccio, Federico García Lorca, and Charles Dickens. Yet note Gerchunoff's selection of the Argentine character's name: Camacho was also part of the cast of *Don Quixote of La Mancha*. With his literary echoes, the author of *The Jewish Gauchos* is able to create a tale in a style that reminds us of oral storytelling. He does it by having a tête-à-tête with the reader and by shaping an unpretentious, colloquial prose that foreshadows the experimental techniques yet to come in Latin America. Here's the illuminating passage:

> Well, as you can see, my patient readers, there are fierce, arrogant gauchos, wife stealers, and Camachos, as well as the most learned and honorable of rabbinical scholars in the little Jewish colony where I learned to love the Argentine sky and felt a part of its wonderful earth. This story I've told— with more detail than art—is a true one, just as I'm sure the original story of Camacho's feast is true. May I die this instant if I've dared to add the slightest bit of invention to the marvelous story.
>
> I'd like very much to add some verses—as was done to the original Camacho story—but God has denied me that talent. I gave you the tale in its purest truth, and if you want couplets, add them yourself in your most gracious style. Don't forget *my* name, however—just as our gracious Master Don Miguel de Cervantes Saavedra remembered the name

of Cide Hamete Benegeli and gave him all due credit for the original Camacho story.

And if the exact, accurate telling of this tale has pleased you, don't send me any golden doubloons—here, they don't even buy bread and water. Send me some golden drachmas or, if not, I'd appreciate a carafe of Jerusalem wine from the vineyards my ancestors planted as they sang the praises of Jehovah.

Three things are evident from this passage: the author's deep and honest love for his new country, Argentina; his parody of *Don Quixote*; and his sense of tradition, both Jewish and Hispanic. This last is crucial: by referring to Cervantes, Gerchunoff, as a member of a cultural minority, nevertheless placed himself in the grand tradition of Hispanic letters. While on the one hand he wanted to forge a link with the great master of Renaissance Spain, on the other he sought to relate himself to the Jewish past by referring to such biblical symbols as the wine "from the vineyards my ancestors planted as they sang the praises of Jehovah." Thus two paths intersect in *The Jewish Gauchos*, and the encounter is dynamic and reciprocal.

The Jews of Gerchunoff's community of Entre Ríos behave like gauchos, and the gauchos, in turn, inherit from the Jews a set of ethical values. Writing at the moment of Argentina's first centennial, the author sings to a new communion and to a fresh, hopeful love affair. This glorification of assimilation is puzzling. As Naomi Lindstrom claims, "The [novel] assumes that the long-standing Hispanic population of Argentina are the hosts, whereas the new Argentines coming from eastern European Jewry are guests who must take care not to disrupt preexisting national life with their alien ways." The goal for Gerchunoff's patriotism is to dream of a democratic society where Jews share and actually contribute to the new culture. But was that the goal of the Jewish immigrants as a whole?

Within a few years after 1910, things turned sour in Argentina. And Gerchunoff's perception of the country as a new Zion was not left unchallenged. On the contrary, it was opposed and even repudiated by Jewish intellectuals and literati. More than that, his response to a major crisis for the Jews in Argentina was regarded as disappointing for a figure of his stature. Anti-Semitism reached its height in 1919 with the Semana Trágica, the tragic week, an explosion of xenophobic fear that amounted to a full-blown pogrom with numerous injured and dead. (David Viñas, a Jewish novelist born ten years after the tragedy, made use of this sad event, a reminder that the heart of the Americas was not untouched by the same hatred left behind in the old continent, in a novel published in 1966.)

The intensification of negative feelings toward the Jews, generated by a wave of nationalism during the administration of Hipólito Yrigoyen, contributed to profound disappointment and skepticism regarding the future of a pluralistic society in Argentina. Though deeply affected, Gerchunoff did not publicly comment on the event. His silence was taken as a sign of cowardly passivity and perhaps self-criticism; some thought he might have come to the conclusion that assimilation was impossible in a country with such profound anti-Semitic feelings. The public would have to wait for a coherent statement. Of course, Gerchunoff was no politician; yet in Latin America the opinions of intellectuals are often the only channels through which deep political and ethical concerns are expressed.

Leonardo Senkman, in his 1983 study *Jewish Identity in Argentine Literature*, discusses the various essays Gerchunoff wrote to articulate and explain his ideas. In response to Adolf Hitler's ascendancy to power in Germany, Gerchunoff's arguments finally became clear in his brief prologue to a 1937 Argentine edition of Ludwig Lewisohn's *Rebirth: A Book of Modern Jewish Thought*. Speaking out against a restriction imposed on Jewish immigration by the Argentine government, which limited the quota of immigrants to at least a third of the number in previous years, he openly defended the right of the Jews to live anywhere at any time without prohibitions.[*] It is not difficult to feel in his words a fear of the growth of anti-Semitic literature at the time of the invigorated Nationalist Party, which supported Yrigoyen, and its call for the expulsion or even annihilation of all Jews in Argentina. Yet Gerchunoff's general passivity is palpable when placed in relation to the Zionist struggle for an independent Jewish state in Palestine that was taking place in those years. Though angry, he never advocated any kind of Jewish collective self-assertion. I translate:

> What should we do? Jews and Argentines, we can protest, fight, expose the hidden goals of the policy of cowardice and crime. And it would be

---

[*] Leonardo Senkman, *La identidad judía en la literatura argentina* (Buenos Aires: Pardés, 1983).

proper to set a foundation for the right of the Jew to life, the right of the Jew to go on living exactly in the same place he was born or where he was left by fate, in the name of the following evidence:

(1) No effort in history to get rid of the Jewish element has been successful, precisely because the Jew, anywhere, is irreplaceable when he performs on the stage of the human spirit, and ineradicable even when one tries to dissimulate his physical presence by means of alien dicta forced on him. . . .

(2) It is positively useless to persecute the Jew, take away from him his goods, or place him in a ghetto, because he may accept that circumstance and will find a way through it. He will be resurrected when given the chance, because those same ones that are willing to beat him, eventually will protect him. . . .

(3) When persecuted, humiliated, or molested anywhere on the planet, the Jew will expand his solidarity with other Jews, because precisely in that he finds his dignity. . . . And in that sense, the Jewish character and his diasporic pride will be confirmed when his attachment to other Jews is awakened.

Gerchunoff calls at first for intellectual protests against anti-Semitic acts because he thinks he may persuade his enemy by intellectual means. That persuasion remained a hope, of course, not a reality. As time went on, he sank into disillusionment and silence, and eventually he isolated himself from his community. Although he became quite enthusiastic about certain Jewish topics, such as the Talmud, he remained evasive and ambivalent. When Jewish symbols appear in his late fiction, it is always in a remote and distant context, with reference to Heinrich Heine or Baruch Spinoza, never the current scene. His dream of a Promised Land in South America was slowly collapsing, along with other liberal values. At the outbreak of the Second World War in 1939, about 218,000 Jews lived in Argentina. Yet only a decade later, the country turned into a nightmare for all integrationist hopes.

Arguably the most horrific events in that nightmare took place in 1994, when the Asociación Mutual Israelita Argentina (AMIA), the Jewish community center in Buenos Aires, was the target of a terrorist attack that left almost one hundred people dead and many more injured. The event took place more than two years after another anti-Semitic attack in Buenos Aires, this one against the Israeli Embassy, in which twenty-nine people died and more than two hundred were injured.

The investigation into the AMIA attack led to Iran, but President Carlos Menen, who was of Lebanese descent, impeded a thorough investigation. As a result, the wounds remained open. The AMIA attack was the first major terrorist incident against Jews not only in Argentina but also in Latin America. The outcome of that event left the Jewish communities in the region vulnerable, fearful of further aggressions. While Gerchunoff couldn't have foreseen the atrocities, in his disenchantment he produced a litany that augured a time when Jews would become individualized as objects of animosity.

A number of journalistic investigations as well as literary works and movies have dealt with the terrorist attack. A decade later, ten directors, including Daniel Burman and Alberto Lecchi, made a film anthology called *18-j* (2004), after the date of the attack. Also, in 2009 Marcos Carnevale premiered *Anita*, about a young woman with Down syndrome who wanders Buenos Aires after her mother is killed in the AMIA bombing.

Among others, Gustavo Perednik published a fictionalized chronicle called *Matar sin que se nota* (Killing without a Trace, 2009). And Marcelo Brodsky and I created a *fotonovela* about the preparations for the attack called *Once@9:53am* (2012).

ARGENTINE ECHOES

The history of Jewish Argentine literature includes many others considered to be Gerchunoff's successors. Among them is César Tiempo (pseudonym of Israel Zeitlin, 1906–1980), a famous-in-his-time playwright, critic, and poet who had immigrated to Argentina from the Ukraine. He was highly esteemed as a man of letters and a travel writer whose poetry almost uniquely refers to one central metaphor: the Sabbath. This interest is reflected in some of the titles of his works: *Book for the Break of the Sabbath*, published in 1930, or *Joyful Saturday*, which appeared in 1955. He always willingly wrote for a gentile audience and, probably influenced by Israel Zangwill's *Dreamers of the Ghetto*, used the vivid imagery of the Buenos Aires Jewish ghetto to draw an appealing distinction between the Jewish and Christian Sabbaths. As a liberal, Tiempo identified with the oppressed and humiliated and favored a multiethnic society. His two famous theatrical pieces, *I Am the Theater* and *Creole Bread*, staged in the thirties, dealt with the subject of assimilation and Jewish versus gentile justice.

Like Gerchunoff, he was deeply depressed by outbursts of anti-Semitism; yet unlike him, he actively responded with written arguments and oral protests against the racist campaign inspired by the infamous writings of the propagandist Gustavo Martínez Zuviría. The director of the National Library in Buenos Aires, Zuviría, under the pen name Hugo Wast, in 1938 had written both *The Kahal* and *Gold*, inspired by *The Protocols of the Elders of Zion*, the infamous anti-Semitic tract immensely popular, even today, throughout Latin America. Yet despite Tiempo's public complaints, nothing changed. At times even the national press, as if echoing his writing, denied the presence of racial tension in the country. As with Gerchunoff, the political events of course made him skeptical about Argentina's democratic future, and they also frightened his young Jewish followers.

Another important Jewish figure in Argentine literature is Bernardo Verbitsky (1907–1979), a prolific realist writer who published long novels dealing with Jewish identity in contemporary Argentina and the world at large. They include *Hard to Start Living* (1941), an essential text for understanding the cultural situation of Buenos Aires in the thirties. The critic and novelist David Viñas (1929–2011), whom I mentioned in reference to the Semana Trágica, in his 1962 novel *Making a Stand* argues for a nation that is at once multiethnic, democratic, and tolerant.

Jewish writers and intellectuals of later generations suffered the horrors of military dictatorship, persecution, violence, and exile. Among them was Luisa Mercedes Levinson, half-Jewish and a close friend and colleague of Borges's, who wrote "The Cove"; she is the mother of the Argentine-born New York experimentalist Luisa Valenzuela, author of *The Lizard's Tail*. Another crucial name is Germán Rozenmacher (1936–1971), a talented young man who felt that the constant attempt to participate in the country's everyday life created deep psychological scars among the Jews. The protagonists of his stories, collected in one volume in 1970, are lonely creatures, many of them failed artists with identity problems, who aspire to enter gentile society but are unable to do so.

His tenacious belief in assimilation always brings the reader to the conclusion that for him no Jewish existence proud of its accomplishments could flourish in his native Argentina. In "Blues in the Night," perhaps his best short story, Vassily Goloboff, a music professor who once sang in the Moscow Opera and who rejected his Jewish name and identity after immigrating to Buenos Aires, returns to religion in his later years. In the tradition of the encounter between Leopold Bloom and Stephen Dedalus, one day he has a sudden rendezvous with Bernardo, a young Jew, in which they share memories about broken families and talk about their enchantment with *I Pagliacci*. But no happiness comes to them in the end.

In the same generation as Rozenmacher are the storyteller Gerardo Mario Goloboff (b. 1939), the author of a trilogy that includes the 1988 novel *Pigeon Keeper*, about rural life in the mythical town of Algarrobos; Humberto Costantini (1924–1987); Pedro Orgambide (b. 1928); Isidoro Blaisten (1933–2004); Alicia Steinberg (1933–2012); Marcos Aguinis (b. 1935); Ricardo Feierstein (b. 1942); Cecilia Absatz (b. 1943); Aída Bortnik (b. 1943); Nora Glickman (b. 1942); Mario Satz (b. 1944); Marcos Ricardo Barnatán (b. 1946); Mario Szichman (b. 1945); Ana María Shua (b. 1951), Marcelo Birmajer (b. 1966); and Andrés Neuman (b. 1977). Szichman, the author of *At 8:25 Evita Became Immortal*, is particularly interesting. In the late 1960s he tried to create a family saga that would encapsulate the diverse personalities and viewpoints among Argentine Jews and explore relevant issues such as the community's response to Israel, assimilation, the world of business, and religion. It is quite obvious that not only the works of Gabriel García Márquez but also Yiddish novels such as I. J. Singer's *The Family Carnovsky* made a transforming impression on him. He shows some of the stylistic elements of magical realism—a narrative style made popular after the publication of *One Hundred Years of Solitude*, which mixes reality with dreamlike components and uses as its setting the exotic Latin American landscape— but he is more concerned with genealogy and tradition within the family circle.

In *The Jews of Mar Dulce* (1971), *The False Chronicle* (1969; revised in 1972), and *At 8:25 Evita Became Immortal*, the Pechof family is followed through their immigration in 1918, their rejection of gaucho agricultural life, and their transition to the urban life of Buenos Aires during the thirties and forties. Although the narrative moves back and forth in time, Szichman stops around 1952, when his characters discover their unacceptable status as Jews in Argentina and desperately struggle to assimilate by changing their surname to Gutiérrez Anselmi. By means of an ironic, self-hating point of view, mixing Yiddishisms with a convoluted Spanish, the author builds a vision of the impossibility of Diaspora life in Argentina as he re-creates the customs and idiosyncrasies of Jewish life in South America with astonishing detail.

Unlike Gerchunoff, Berele or Bernardo (Szichman's alter ego) is permanently searching for an answer to his father's strange, political death in the city dump. And by deciphering his father's last intentions, Berele discovers the cause of the entire family's dilemma. What is interesting about Szichman's fiction is the way it revises national history. By placing his characters in a variety of periods, from the Semana Trágica to the military coups in the forties and the defeated revolution in 1956 (when Berele's father perishes), Szichman makes an unquestionable statement: no regime, no juncture, in Argentine history is good for the Jews because their historical presence on the River Plate is a mistake. If Gerchunoff at one time believed Argentina to be a heaven, Szichman sees it as hell.

Two of the most engaging writers to emerge in the nineties are Shua and Birmajer. Unlike Szichman, they use humor—often caustic humor—to explore the identity of Argentine Jews. Shua is a master of the short story. She has produced a number of anthologies, among them some on Jewish humor. She also practices what has come to be known as flash fiction, short stories sometimes a paragraph long. Birmajer, a devotee of Isaac Bashevis Singer, is perceived as the chronicler of El Once, the Jewish neighborhood of Buenos Aires. His fiction is an attempt to understand, in subtle ways, the sociological components that shaped Argentine Jewish life.

I have also included stories written in Yiddish by Samuel Rollansky, a man of letters resoponsible for sustaining Yiddish in Argentina, and José Rabinovich, whose writing explored poverty among Jewish immigrants.

JORGE LUIS BORGES

Of the non-Jewish writers in Latin America who have considered Jewish images and themes, such as the Kabbalah, Israel, and the Holocaust, the first and most outstanding figure is Borges, a passionate lover of lo hebreo— things Jewish. Mention his name and you conjure up the ability to reduce everything to metaphysical mystery: toenails, much too insignificant for the poet to write about, suddenly become, in one of his odes, the only organic element that resists death; or the world itself, too large for anyone to understand, becomes, in some of the stories compiled in *Labyrinths*, a voluminous book that embraces all possible and impossible knowledge. At once a keen semiotician, a devotee of medieval philosophy, and an innovative homme de lettres who was able to invent a distinctive fictional universe, Borges had an important influence on the international literary scene. Three of his stories are included here, in the appendix.

During the 1960s it was fashionable among Latin American writers to start every dissertation, essay, or short story with an epigraph taken from this Argentine fabulist. Only a decade later, one could discover remnants of his style between the lines or plot structures of Gabriel García Márquez or Carlos Fuentes. In Europe and the United States, artists and writers such as Umberto Eco, Bernardo Bertolucci, John Updike, and John Barth adored him because of his prodigious knowledge and metaphysical brilliance; others, like Stanislaw Lem, the Polish science fiction writer, complained that he was a monstrous iconoclast, an egotist and pseudoscholar with a dazzling command of erudition and logic but incapable of understanding the dilemmas of the modern world. Since 1961 when he shared the International Publisher's Prize with Samuel Beckett and his oeuvre gained international acclaim, becoming more and more the subject of academic study, both sides of the love-hate controversy have been expressed in a fascinating showcase of opposites: Borges himself would have said that his detractors are substantially the same as his fans.

Borges's Jewish connection is well documented. Starting with the monumental literary biography of Emir Rodríguez Monegal and moving on to the works of Edna Aizenberg, Saul Sosnowski, and Jaime Alazraki, much has been written about his attraction to the golem, "the People of the Book," Isaac Luria and Hebraic mysticism, Kafka, and Spinoza. Borges's mother, Leonor Acevedo Haedo, believed she had some Jewish ancestors, probably conversos who came to the Americas after the 1492 expulsion from Spain. It was this possibility that made Borges the target of anti-Semitic attacks in the thirties. The magazine *Crisol* published an article asserting that he was a Jew, and Borges's response in another periodical, *Megáfono* (April 1934), at once showed admiration and pride toward Judaism. "Statistically speaking," he wrote,

The Jews are very few. What would we think of someone in the year 4,000 who discovered everywhere descendants of the inhabitants of the San Juan province? Our inquisitors are seeking Hebrews, never Phoenicians, Numidians, Scythians, Babylonians, Huns, Vandals, Ostrogoths, Ethiopians, Illyrians, Paphlagonians, Sarmatians, Medes, Ottomans, Berbers, Britons, Libyans, Cyclops, and Lapiths. The nights of Alexandria, Babylon, Carthage, Memphis have never succeeded in engendering one single grandfather: only the tribes of the bituminous Black Sea had that power.

In the same article, he joked about his roots:

Borges Acevedo is my name. In the fifth chapter of his book *Rosas y su tiempo*, Ramos Mejía lists the family names of Buenos Aires of that time to demonstrate that all, or almost all, "descended from a Hebrew-Portuguese branch." Acevedo is part of that catalogue: the only document of my Jewish roots, until the confirmation of *Crisol*. Nevertheless, Captain Honorario Acevedo has made some research I cannot ignore. He indicates that Don Pedro de Azevedo . . . my great-grandfather, was irreproachably Spanish. Two hundred years and I don't find the Israelite, two hundred years and the ancestor eludes me.

Borges's childhood had a duality of languages, English and Spanish (later enriched by Italian and French). He kept saying, even writing, that he first read *Don Quixote* in Shakespeare's tongue, and when a few years later he finally got to the original, he thought it was a lousy translation. His first literary attempts were made in 1914 in Switzerland, where his family had been spending some time. It was there that he enrolled in the College Calvin and developed a friendship with Maurice Abramowicz and Simon Jichlinski, who probably introduced him to Kabbalah. In Switzerland he also studied Latin and German, a language that led him closer to Judaism because it enabled him to read Martin Buber, Gustav Meyrink, and later Kafka in the original. In 1919, on their way back from Europe to Buenos Aires, his family went to Spain.

It was in Madrid that Borges established his friendship with Rafael Cansinos-Assèns, an Andalusian who, according to the Argentine, founded ultraism, the aesthetic movement that tried to introduce into Spanish the innovations of the European avant-garde—Dadaism, cubism, surrealism, and expressionism. No doubt this was a major event in the writer's life. Cansinos-Assèns wrote several books dedicated to Judaism. His cosmopolitanism sought out the universal resonance in every simple thing. While Spain stubbornly upheld its close ties to Catholicism at the time, he expressed himself openly against orthodoxy and dreamed of being ultranational. In fact, he believed the Hebraic legacy of Spanish culture to lie precisely in the juxtaposition of races intending to abolish all differences. Even more, he thought that implicit in Judaism was an eternally antiestablishment posture. He wanted to do away with tradition, with canonical forms of art. Borges inherited from Cansinos-Assèns not only his rebellious attitude but also a desire to see the Jews in the abstract.

On his return to Argentina in 1921, Borges read the long poem *The Gaucho Martín Fierro* (1872–1879) by José Hernández, a book that deeply influenced him. Perhaps only three important Jewish names were known in the Argentine literary arena of the time: Gerchunoff, Tiempo, and Verbitsky. The first two also wrote for *Proa* and *Martín Fierro*, the two periodicals where Borges published his first pieces. During the Second World War, Borges maintained very good relations with the Argentine Jewish community. He was an antifascist and openly expressed his indignation over Nazi ideology. Zuviría, mentioned above, took advantage of Hitler's rise to power with his infamous novels, published under the pseudonym Hugo Wast, in which he practically called upon the country to exterminate the Jews.

Three years later, important Argentine Jews and non-Jews formed the Anti-Defamation Committee against Racism and Anti-Semitism. Borges was one of its strongest supporters. In his fiction, his attitude toward Nazism appears in "The Secret Miracle"; toward anti-Semitism in "Deutsches Requiem." The first is a tribute to Kafka; the second a dissertation on the evils of Nazism. Similarly, in the forties he openly expressed antimilitary views with regard to the Peronist regime. It is said that as a result, while Borges's corpse was waiting to be buried at the Plan Palais cemetery in Geneva in 1986, neo-Peronist groups were actively defaming the author's reputation in his own country.

From 1948 on, Borges showed great sympathy for the state of Israel. He traveled there twice, first in 1969 and again in 1971, to receive the Jerusalem

Prize. He was an outspoken supporter during the Six-Day War and afterward lectured on the theme of Jewish longing for the Promised Land based on readings of the Bible and Talmud. But his attitude is less sentimental than philosophical and moral: he believed that Israel might be the answer to ancient national goals and desires but that it could also transform the Jew into a simply material being. According to Borges, the Jew has been a polyglot through the ages, a self-made rationalist, a persistent fighter for his right to exist as an extraordinary citizen; he has won a place beyond history and therefore has become almost parahistorical. Israel as a nation may damage the esoteric qualities that have long flourished in the individual; this return to history, he once said, may steal the distinctiveness of the Jews and transform them into politicized creatures, with the same trivial habits as everybody else.

One can analyze Borges's oeuvre and argue that, influenced by Cansinos-Assèns, he loved only the ideal image of the Jew: the cosmopolitan, the philosopher, the Kabbalist, the polyglot, but never the simple person. Whenever Borges portrayed Jewish characters in his fiction, they were always heroes of the supernatural, champions on a theological and philosophical scale. He never wrote about ordinary people concerned with mundane problems. Something similar happened to his intellectual interests: in reading Spinoza, Borges never let the argument of the Amsterdam Jewish community get in his way; he wanted to see Spinoza purely as a philosophical hero.

There is another example of how Borges preferred the spiritual to the material. Influenced by Gershom Scholem, the foremost contemporary scholar of Jewish mysticism, Borges in his sixties became interested in the Hasidic movement of the late eighteenth and early nineteenth century. Yet he never quite understood the theological and social reform it achieved; he saw the Baal Shem Tov only as the master in love with his magic and esotericism, never as a rebel who, like Luther, broke with the medieval conception of the rabbi as an untouchable intellectual genius. Here and there Borges mentions Hasidism but never in relation to the way the movement brought ordinary people to the center of the historical arena, replacing the Maimonidean image of the wise man, half prophet and half philosopher. Borges does not mention these features because he was never interested in the actual circumstances of ordinary people. On the contrary, he preferred to look for the metaphysical element, the unseen.

The same thing happens to his view of Israel. After 1971, he never commented publicly on Israeli politics, as he did on other international subjects; neither did he show any interest in literary or intellectual trends emerging from the young state. Yes, he tried to learn Hebrew, but as with Kafka and Walter Benjamin, the attempt proved unsuccessful; the only words that remained in his mind were Kabbalistic concepts from the *Sefer Yetzirah* or the *Zohar*. Nevertheless, one should be careful not to read into this a change of feeling: while Borges idealized the abstract Jew, he never felt uncomfortable among Jews, as his friendships with Abramowicz, Jichlinski, and later Gershom Scholem proved.

In relation to the Kabbalah, there are many instances where symbols or references appear in Borges's work. Several times he pointed to Meyrink's novel *The Golem* (1915) as a book that attracted him to the world of Jewish esotericism. On his second trip to Israel, he learned from Scholem about such archetypes as the Ein-Sof and the Shekhinah. He even refers to the author of *Major Trends in Jewish Mysticism* in one of his poems, "The Golem." On a more down-to-earth level, Borges contradicts Gerchunoff's mystique of the gaucho as an authentic part of the Jewish experience in Argentina in his short story "The Unworthy Friend," included in *Dr. Brodie's Report* of 1970, as well as in "The Forms of Glory," written by Borges and his friend and colleague Adolfo Bioy Casares (published in 1977).

Argentine writers have long worshiped the original gaucho as a national idol, a courageous peasant of the Pampas, everywhere carrying his guitar, his poncho, and his vengeful spirit. Lugones and Ricardo Güiraldes celebrated the gaucho as the quintessential national folk myth, and Borges came close to doing so in "Biography of Tadeo Isidoro Cruz (1829–1874)." Although Borges found in *The Gaucho Martín Fierro* the clearest expression of Argentine identity and a fountain of personal creativity, he viewed the phenomenon of "Jewish gauchos" as a complete anachronism. The term *gaucho judío* achieved prominence with Gerchunoff, yet Borges openly denies that such characters ever existed in real life. Jews were businessmen, merchants, and storekeepers, not cowboys, he argues, and the age of the horseman in the Pampas preceded the Jewish immigration. According to Borges, Gerchunoff portrayed *chacareros*, peddlers descended from the gaucho; thus he confused poor immigrant workers with national heroes like Martín Fierro.

MOACYR SCLIAR

Up until now, I have discussed along somewhat general lines the art of two Argentines, one Jew and the other gentile, both cornerstones in the literary tradition represented in this anthology. There is a third writer, much younger than Gerchunoff and Borges, who is equally important in disseminating and shaping things Jewish in Latin American letters: the Brazilian novelist and fabulist Moacyr Scliar. His fiction owes a lot to his compatriots Jorge Amado, João Guimaraes Rosa, Mario de Andrade, Samuel Rawet, and the Ukrainian-born Clarice Lispector, but it is also a direct descendant of Sholem Aleichem, Isaac Bashevis Singer, Rabbi Nahman of Bratslav, and the traditional Yiddish folktale. His characters and settings are Brazilian, but his concerns are the continuity of Judaism, God's relationship with his creatures, and the universe as a sacred space.

Born in 1937 in Porto Alegre, Rio Grande do Sul, the son of a businessman who emigrated from eastern Europe, Scliar was the author of at least ten novels and seven collections of stories, including *The Carnival of the Animals* (1976). His work earned him major international literary prizes, such as the Casa de las Americas. Although retired since 1987, he worked as a public health physician and, like William Carlos Williams and Anton Chekhov, divided his time between literature and medicine (he died in 2011). His joyful, humorous characters, at times endowed with supernatural powers, are wanderers, soul-searching Marranos, political activists, or half-Jewish, half-animal centaurs. Love, mental disorder, redemption, and the coming of the Messiah are frequent themes. What is Jewish about his writing? His intellectual comedy, his passion for storytelling, his affinity with Yiddish.

In *The Strange Life of Rafael Mendes*, for instance, a converso, discovering that both the prophet Jonah and the philosopher Maimonides are among his ancestors, immediately takes it as his duty to continue the tradition of wisdom, excellence, and ethics. In *The One Man Army*, an anarchist tries to build a large communist colony, New Birobidjan (after the so-called Jewish state created by Joseph Stalin near Siberia in 1932) near Porto Alegre, but his adventure turns into disaster because of Brazil's deep devotion to capitalism. Meyer Guinzberg, the central character, reacts to his defeat by transforming his redemptive fantasy into a frantic love for pigs and horses. Scliar's other creatures indulge in pagan rituals or belong to antinomian sects like that of the pseudo-Messiah Sabbatai Zevi. They are discontented with civilization, unhappy yet looking for answers in philosophies and ideologies that are either outmoded or alien to life in South America.

Published in 1978, *The Gods of Raquel* is one of Scliar's best novels and also the most outstanding work in the literary tradition represented in this anthology. An artfully constructed yet stylistically uncomplicated narrative, it tells the story of Raquel, a Jewish girl with existential and religious doubts. Her parents are Hungarian immigrants who arrived in Brazil thinking it would be the Promised Land. The setting is Parthenon, a district of lunatic asylums in Rio Grande. Raquel's father, an unsuccessful Latinist, opens a hardware store called Vulcão, named after the Roman god of metalwork. In the context of his business and him sending his daughter to a convent school, Raquel's odyssey in search of her own identity takes place.

She is introduced to Christianity by friends and teachers, and so strong is this religious influence on her, so omnipresent the church's rituals and paraphernalia in her daily activities and conscience, that after a few years Raquel is ready to convert. But her leap from one faith to another is not easy: as a Jew, she suffers religious persecution and is often victimized by the nuns in the convent. Besides, eternity frightens Raquel. She believes a choice must be made between Christ and Jehovah, and, unable to make up her mind, she denies herself participation in either religion. In her journey, she befriends Isabel, a gentile, who soon becomes a partner in her quests but later turns into a rival when both girls fall in love with the same boy, Francisco. Christianity and Judaism thus become competitors, enemies. Isabel eventually marries Francisco, and Raquel engages in an extramarital affair with him. To stress his powerful allegorical message, Scliar inspirits every object in the book, turning it into a pagan deity.

His protagonist intelligently concludes that to fully assimilate into Brazil's society, a Jew needs to renounce his or her true beliefs. Raquel refuses to do so, and her voyage takes a rather fascinating turn: Miguel, a worker at Vulcão of Native origin, introduces her to sex, and through it to idolatry. His existential dream, we soon find out, is to build a tropical synagogue—a sacred altar where Judaism, Christianity, and a number of pagan cults coexist. Raquel helps him in his endeavor. In a final scene that is at once haunting and unforgettable, she is seduced by Miguel and persuaded to perform bizarre primitive acts involving a variety of religious symbols and terrifying rituals. To my mind, no other Latin American writer has so far managed to describe as successfully as Moacyr Scliar the religious turmoil and confused identity inhabiting the mind of a Jew living in the Southern Hemisphere.

Perhaps Scliar's most famous work is *The Centaur in the Garden* (1980), a novel in the tradition of Kafka's *Metamorphosis*. Like Gregor Samsa, Guedali Tartakovsky, the protagonist, is a peculiar creature, half-human, half-animal. Yet in his case the grotesque physical appearance, an amalgamation of human and animal features, is meant to create not surprise or terror but laughter. After all, in the tradition of those monsters found in Ovid and Kabbalistic bestiaries, or the compelling demons of Isaac Bashevis Singer, he's a centaur—but a fully circumcised, Yiddish-speaking centaur who is also a devoted reader of Sholem Aleichem and I. L. Peretz. Not knowing whether to kill him or have him disappear into the forest, his family hopes to educate Guedali into "a respectable Jew." But they are ashamed of him. Feeling frustrated and hurt, he flees his home to become independent. Escape is here the key word: divisive internal forces are so strong in Scliar's creation that they ultimately tear him apart.

At first, to support himself, Guedali works in a circus, where he falls in love with a female centaur. They marry and have children. Their dream, of course, is to achieve normality; that is, they hope to lose their distinctiveness. Soon after, they both travel to Morocco, where Guedali undergoes a surgical operation performed by a charlatan. To everyone's astonishment, he becomes human—or almost human; except for his cloven hooves, he's the same as others. But whatever kind of normalcy he achieves, the transformation turns into such a boring and vacuous routine that he struggles to become a centaur once again, and on his return to Brazil he loses all sense of identity. The novel clearly explores the deep and unequivocal desire by the Jewish minority in Brazil and elsewhere in Latin America to assimilate into the milieu, a move that sooner or later destroys its uniqueness and self-esteem. But the story is more than an allegory: the fantastic elements acquire a life of their own as the bizarre is approached in a realistic context.

A satirist, Moacyr Scliar had a marvelous narrative touch that recalls Lewis Carroll as well as Borges. Like the Argentine, he took upon himself the task of reappraising major historical events with an intellectual inquisitiveness, but also with a joie de vivre absent in the author of "Pierre

Menard, Author of the *Quixote*." What is most interesting is that, although Scliar chronicled in historical detail the range of Jewish experience in Brazil, his treatment of the Holocaust is relatively spare. Robert Di Antonio, the author of *Brazilian Fiction*, who has studied the novelist's contribution to Latin American literature, was also puzzled by silence on such a critical event in contemporary Jewish history. Scliar's "novels and short fiction," he claims,

> have incorporated various, and little known, aspects of Judeo-Brazilian historiography: the settling of Baron Hirsch's agricultural communes in Quatro Irmaos; the Jewish gauchos; the aftermath of the Soviet Union's attempt to establish a Jewish state in Birobidjan; the world of the Jewish Mafia, the *Zewi Migdal*; an anachronistic accommodation of the life of Sabbatai Zevi, the charismatic false messiah; the long history of Brazil's Sephardim; and the Jewish white slave trade in Rio Grande do Sui. However, Scliar, one of Brazil's leading writers and one who has a large and devoted international following, wrote little on the subject of the Holocaust. Perhaps in response to the Yiddish admonition *M'ken nisht* (one cannot), he felt the subject too tragic to be dealt with. He deals with it only tangentially and from a very unique perspective.

The best example is "Inside My Dirty Head—The Holocaust," a story by Scliar in *The Enigmatic Eye* (1986) and reprinted here. Told from the point of view of a young boy whose father is a traditional eastern European immigrant, it describes his puzzlement about Mischa, a Holocaust survivor found sleeping in doorways in Porto Alegre. The boy sees Mischa as an alien figure and sees the numbers tattooed on his arm as imbued with a perverse magical potency: he dreams of the Holocaust survivor winning the lottery with the number tattooed on his arm yet losing the prize once the number is surgically removed. According to Di Antonio, "The childlike reasoning is a narrative device to express tangibly the sense of guilt of many Brazilians who were personally unaffected by the events in Europe." Scliar suggests that the Holocaust cannot be written about in a literal or conceptual way, perhaps because it is beyond meaning and comprehension.

Other Brazilian writers, like Rubem Fonseca (*Vastas emocoes e pensamentos imperfeitos*, 1988) and Zevi Ghivelder (*As seis pontas da estrela*, 1969), have written about the Holocaust and its consequences. While in North America the theme has become an attractive and sometimes lucrative topic, a sort of unifying, rallying point in the country's Jewish culture, writers in Latin America seldom deal with it. Although the United States had a fundamental role to play in the Second World War, the countries south of the Rio Grande either remained silent and impartial or their dictatorial governments gave political asylum to ex-lieutenants and ex-soldiers of Adolf Hitler—as well as to Jews. It was often the case that in cities like Asunción, São Paulo, or Montevideo, refugees from Auschwitz or Buchenwald would encounter their German victimizers walking on the street. Yet those horrific encounters never really captivated the national consciousness. The fictional treatment of Holocaust issues in Latin American literature is often apologetic, detached, or sentimental. More often than not, these works explore the aftermath of the massive extermination but not its causes or specific details. Moacyr Scliar's "Inside My Dirty Head—The Holocaust," which focuses its attention on the mental aftershocks in the mind of a Jew in Porto Alegre, differs from the accounts of survivors such as Primo Levi or Elie Wiesel in its preoccupation with post-Holocaust trauma.

The list of writers in this literary tradition in Brazil, with a population of about 160,000 Jews in 1980 and around 150,000 in 2010, most of them in São Paulo and Rio de Janeiro, is not as long as that of Argentina, but it is distinguished. Samuel Rawet (1929–1985), an engineer born in Poland, is one of the most significant early figures. *Tales of the Immigrant*, his collection of stories published at the age of twenty-seven, which includes "Johnny Golem" and "Kalovim," is clearly influenced by Hermann Hesse. Rawet's concern is the Jewish process of assimilation into Brazilian life. By adapting to their new milieu, he suggests, they lose sight of their true identity; using one of his favorite metaphors, they "evaporate."

The Seven Dreams, a more mature work influenced by Edgar Allan Poe and Kafka, again focuses on misanthropic, obsessive characters tormented by their inner selves. Rawet's obsession with the Jews, whom he perceived as highly intellectual and model citizens, continued in *Ahasuerus' Trip* (1970). But unexpected events changed his mind, suddenly causing him to feel ashamed of his religious and ethnic background. The result was a total rejection of his past. This personal transformation is evident in *I-You-He* (1972), a discursive narrative dealing with larger Brazilian social issues. What is absent in this book is actually more interesting than the subject matter: Rawet wanders around metaphysical and philosophical problems but leaves out his most urgent concern: Judaism. This existential detour ended up tragically, with his suicide at the age of fifty-four. He was incapable of finding an answer to his doubts and ambivalence.

Another Brazilian Jewish writer of note is Carlos Heitor Cony (b. 1926), a well-known journalist in Rio de Janeiro who early in life studied in a seminary but became disenchanted with religion and turned to politics. His most famous novel, *Pessach: The Crossing*, published in 1967, deals with a novelist who suffers from personal and political doubts but begins to accept his Jewishness when he turns forty, just as he unexpectedly becomes a member of an urban guerrilla group. Cony is significant because he chronicles the plight of middle-class sophisticates, yet critics vehemently refuse to regard him as Jewish, and Cony himself is ambivalent about his ethnic identity.

The most influential Jewish writer in Brazil, after Moacyr Scliar, is Clarice Lispector (1925–1977). Like Rawet and Cony, she was ambivalent toward Judaism. An engaging prose stylist born into a poor Ashkenazi family in Tchetchelnik, Ukraine, she lived first in the town of Recife, Pernambuco, and at the age of twelve moved to Rio de Janeiro. Her father, a farm laborer, eventually became a sales representative. A voracious reader, she began writing unconventional, unstructured children's stories while still a child; many of them were sent to the *Diario de Pernambuco* but were rejected. In Rio she completed her secondary schooling at Joao Barbalho School and entered the Faculty of Law, from which she graduated in 1944, just one year after marrying a fellow student, who subsequently entered the foreign service. Her husband, Mauri Gurgel Valente, was first posted in Naples, and the couple moved to Italy. All together they spent many years abroad, living in Switzerland and England and spending eight years in the United States (from 1952 to 1960). Not until 1959 did they return to visit Brazil, where Lispector and her husband later divorced.

The author of some twenty volumes of fiction, nonfiction, and literature for children, none of which deal openly with Jewish topics, she gained experience as a journalist, first on the editorial staff of the press service Agencia Nacional, then with the newspaper *A Noite*. Her first novel, *Near to the Wild Heart*, published in 1944, when she was only nineteen years old, was an immediate critical and financial success. As translator Gregory Rabassa notes, Lispector's style, deeply influenced by the European modernists, "is interior and hermetic": the action, always subjective, is seen from the point of view of characters involved in the plot. Although critics believe her to be a better short-story teller than a novelist, Lispector continued to write long narratives, including *The Apple in the Dark* (1961) and *The Passion According to G. H.* (1964).

How do we place her in this tradition of Jewish Latin American literature if only her origin, but not her themes and concerns, is Jewish? Similar questions are often asked about Kafka, a Jew who created a rich and culturally resonant fiction without ever referring to the word *Jew*. Scholars agree that Lispector's distinctly European sensibility and her worldview have Jewish overtones: the sense of family life and the value of individual existence; a glimpse of a small wealthy community, with unique religious customs, isolated from the rest of the country. Clarice Lispector is certainly a pillar, tutor, and promoter of the cultural openness following the Second World War, when women writers in Brazil, Mexico, Argentina, and other parts of the region emerged not as part of a formal movement but, collectively, as a major literary force. Understandably their themes have to do with their long history of silence and the ensuing struggle to regain their bodies, voices, and souls. Now considered a cornerstone of feminism in Latin America, Lispector recalls Virginia Woolf in her insistence on penetrating the inner life and in her views of domestic affairs from a women's perspective. The piece selected here, from her 1960 collection *Family Ties*, explores the disturbing psychological consequences for a woman of her daily routine.

¡VIVA MEXICO!

Although Argentina and Brazil have the most significant and sizable body of Jewish literature and are thus more represented in this anthology, other Latin American nations, such as Mexico, Venezuela, and Peru, deserve at least some attention. In the case of Mexico, although its Jewish community traces its roots to the conversos who accompanied and followed Hernán Cortés and his soldiers in the conquest of Tenochtitlán and the Aztec Empire, most of today's Mexican Jews are Ashkenazim who arrived during the 1880s and went on to build a *kehilah*, the traditional Jewish communal framework, organize a sports and cultural center, and establish Yiddish schools with strong ties to the Bundist and Zionist movements. By 1910, there were some nine thousand Jews in the country, most of them in Oaxaca, Veracruz, Monterrey (a wealthy northern city apparently founded by Kabbalists, or so the legend claims), and the nation's capital. By 1980 that figure had increased to 37,500.

The first Jewish literary figures in Mexico wrote in Russian, Polish, and Yiddish. They were immigrants such as Jacob Glantz, who shared the tastes and style of early Yiddish modernists such as Moyshe-Leyb Halpern, Jacob Glatstein, and Itsik Manger. They published manuscripts, staged the plays of Abraham Goldfaden, and privately engaged a printer to publish and disseminate their work. But it was the second and third generations, already born on native soil, who, from the 1940s onward, emulated Gerchunoff by switching to Spanish, producing novels, essays, and stories that unequivocally belong today to Mexican letters. One of the compelling features of the literature created by Jews in Mexico is its lack of interest in realism. As the reader will soon find out, most of the Mexican writers included in this volume explore esoteric topics in an abstract style rather than their immediate surroundings or experience.

Also of interest is the fact that the most outstanding Mexican men of letters with an interest in Jewish symbols and themes are gentiles, for example, Carlos Fuentes (1928–2012), born in Panama and the country's foremost novelist. The son of a diplomat in Washington, DC, and another true polyglot, he lived all over the world and was completely fluent in English, a talent enabling him to be deeply involved with North American culture. His passionate interest in Judaism is obvious in three of his books. *A Change of Skin* (1967) concerns symmetries of the struggle between Spaniards and Aztecs in Tenochtitlán and that of Nazis and Jews in Europe during the Second World War. In it a group of four young men and women travel in a Volkswagen from Mexico City to Cholula, a town that has 365 churches, one for each day of the year. As they progress on their journey, reminiscences of their pasts intertwine with the reality of the Mexican soul and its complex history. Two of these young people, Franz and Elizabeth (also called Betele), descendants of opposing groups, have links to prewar Europe and tragic reminiscences of the Holocaust.

The Hydra Head (1978), another one of Fuentes's novels involving Jewish themes, is what Graham Greene would have called "an entertainment."

In the literary spy tradition of John Le Carre and Robert Ludlum, it is set against the background of the Israeli-Palestinian conflict and the drama over Mexico's oil. Its protagonist, a James Bond of sorts, is Félix Maldonado, alias Diego Velásquez, a bureaucrat and secret-police agent ready to defend the Mexican oil industry against its enemy, foreign (mainly Arab) invasion. His adventures also allow the author to comment on the insularity of the Jewish community in Mexico City. Finally *Terra Nostra* (1975), a volume celebrated by Milan Kundera as a "masterwork" in the tradition of *Tristram Shandy* and Hermann Bloch's *The Sleepwalkers*, has the Spanish language as its major protagonist, and in a rather ambitious and nonchronological fashion it retells the entire history of Spain and the Americas from before 1492 until 1992. Among the Jewish characters are conversos and Kabbalists like Fernando de Rojas and Samuel ha-Nagid; some incidents of its plot deal with the expulsion of the Jews from the Iberian Peninsula just as Christopher Columbus was sailing out of the port of Palos toward the Bahamas.

Homero Aridjis (b. 1931), a poet, novelist, and prominent environmentalist, in *1492: Life and Times of Juan Cabezon of Castile* (1985), describes in rich detail the persecution of Jews and conversos in seventeenth-century Spain and examines their hope of sailing to new lands. One of the more illustrious poets and writers in Mexico, himself not Jewish, is Jose Emilio Pacheco (b. 1939), the author of *A Distant Death* (1967; revised in 1977), an avant-garde novel in the tradition of the French *nouveau roman*. It has an enigmatic protagonist modeled after Dr. Josef Mengele, the Nazi physician who committed atrocities in Auschwitz and who supposedly died near São Paulo in 1984. Although it is set in a downtown neighborhood of the Mexican capital, the novel's Jewish allusions include Flavius Josephus as well as the Israeli secret intelligence. Pacheco is also the author of a famous novella, *Battles in the Desert* (1981), a re-creation of the metropolitan landscape in Mexico City during the sixties. While the narrative explores the naive love affair between a child and his friend's mother, the larger historical setting intertwines the Six-Day War, Mexico's xenophobia, and its overwhelming nationalism. When compared to other stories of Jewish childhood ("Inside My Dirty Head—The Holocaust," for instance), Pacheco's is interesting for its representation of Jewish childhood and communal life as perceived by a non-Jewish boy.

Among the featured Jewish writers in Mexico are three women: Margo

Glantz (b. 1930), Angelina Muñiz-Huberman (b. 1936), and Esther Seligson (1941–2010). The first, a daughter of Yiddish poet Jacob Glantz and the author of *Genealogies* (1982), is mainly a literary critic and memoirist, whereas the other two are best known as short-story writers. In 1986 Muñiz won the prestigious Xavier Villaurrutia Prize for her collection *Enclosed Garden* (1984), translated into English in 1989, from which "In the Name of His Name" is taken. Her themes are metaphysical: an alchemist's search for God; the inner sexual thoughts of Sor Juana Inés de La Cruz, a nun of the colonial period who wrote poetry and about whom Octavio Paz published a masterful biography in 1982; and the redemptive quest of a man who is challenged to cross a river. Muñiz is a writer highly influenced by Borges but also by Rabbi Nahman of Bratslav. The author's passionate, lifelong readings of the *Zohar* are evident in each of her resonant sentences. Esther Seligson, a theater critic and the translator into Spanish of the Paris-based philosopher Emile Cioran, is the author of *House in Time* (1982), an attempt to rewrite the Bible. Her narratives, an example of which is "The Invisible Hour," are often metaphorical, obscure, perhaps evasive. Like the creatures of Frida Kahlo (a descendant of Hungarian Jews) and the surrealist painters, her characters are not bound by the physical laws of time and space; they perceive fantastic visions of eternity.

I include myself among the Mexican writers in this anthology. My first attempt to define my literary style and expectations in English came in *On Borrowed Words: A Memoir of Language* (2001). Since then Jewish themes recur in my work, from my studies on Yiddish and Hebrew to my explorations of Sephardic literature to my graphic novel *El Iluminando* (2012), about the plight of crypto-Jews in Mexico during colonial times. I have also written a dozen stories, including "Xerox Man," part of *The Disappearance: A Novella and Stories* (2008). Some have been adapted into stage and film. My essays on the topic are collected in two volumes, *The Inveterate Dreamer* (2002) and *Singer's Typewriter and Mine* (2012).

OTHER VIEWS

In 1982 Venezuela, with a population of over 14 million, had a Jewish population of twenty thousand, which under President Hugo Chávez was the target of anti-Semitic attacks. Two writers of excellence that ought to be listed here are Elisa Lerner (1932–2013) and Isaac Chocrón (1929–2011), a playwright and sometime novelist of Sephardic descent. One of the outstanding contemporary Latin American playwrights, Chocrón is the author of several collections of short stories and novels, including *Break in Case of Fire* (1981), about a young man's search for his Jewish past in the Iberian Peninsula and Africa. Lerner, on the other hand, a lawyer and diplomat as well as a playwright, descends from a family of Romanian Jews that settled in the city of Valencia but moved to Caracas in 1936, when she was four years old. A frequent contributor to magazines and newspapers, she is the author of *A Smile behind the Metaphor* (1973), the collection of plays *Life with Mother* (1975), and the book of criticism *I Love Columbo* (1979). The story included here, "Papa's Friends," like the art of Clarice Lispector, describes the inner life of a young woman, in this case the daughter of a wealthy Jewish businessman in Caracas; it also evokes the social life and foibles of the Russian Jewish immigrant community. In 1982 Peru had a population of about five thousand Jews, most of them living in Lima and a minimal fraction of the total national population of 18 million. Nevertheless, Peru has produced a well-known Jewish novelist, Isaac Goldemberg (b. 1945), the author of *The Fragmented Life of Don Jacobo Lerner*, a novel about the conflicts of identity. With its many ups and downs, the career of Goldemberg, who was born in the small town of Chepen, in a way symbolizes that of most of these Jewish storytellers in Latin America.

Having published a collection of poems with the Jewish Cuban writer José Kozer, Goldemberg published his first novel to wide acclaim in 1979, when he was thirty-four years old. Critics such as Jose Miguel Oviedo called it a tour de force, a gem. Yet, like Henry Roth after *Call It Sleep* and Felipe Alfau after *Locos: A Comedy of Gestures*, Goldemberg fell into silence until the nineties, when he regained his voice. Two other works are *Life in Cash*, a collection of poems, and *Play by Play*, an experimental narrative that has as its background a soccer match between the Peruvian and Brazilian national teams. Published in 1984 without much fanfare, it opens with the short story "The Conversion," included here.

In more than one way, Goldemberg's life was re-created by Mario Vargas Llosa (b. 1936), the 1990 presidential candidate, recipient of the Nobel Prize for Literature in 2010, and a novelist of international reputation who wrote classics such as *Conversation in the Cathedral* and *Aunt Julia and the*

Scriptwriter. His novella *The Storyteller*, published in its English translation in 1989, describes the adventures of Saul Zuratas, a middle-class Peruvian Jew, a brilliant yet unhappy anthropology student in Lima during the late fifties. Zuratas falls in love with his object of study, a band of Machiguenga Indians in the Amazon. He becomes intrigued with the role of the storyteller, the keeper of the tribe's collective memory who travels through the deep jungle from one community to another, enchanting everyone with mythological and often iconoclastic tales. As the narrative begins, the starving Indians are declining as quickly as the Amazon forest, and their all-important storyteller has disappeared without leaving an apprentice.

So after considerable soul-searching, Zuratas makes the Indians' cause his own, abandons his graduate studies and his aging father, and marches into the jungle to assume the role of tribal bard. The symbolism is clear: a Jew, a member of a small Peruvian urban minority, is described by the narrator as "the last true redeemer of the Indians in Peru." He takes upon himself the task of saving another minority, and his odyssey is marked by obstacles and defeat. Written in Florence and London between 1985 and 1987, *The Storyteller* contains two parallel stories: of the eight chapters, half are tales told by Zuratas to the Machiguengas, and the remaining attempt a realistic description of his existence prior to his voluntary disappearance in the Amazon—as perceived through the eyes of a mature, accomplished writer living in Italy, Vargas Llosa's alter ego. There is a deceptive device in the book's structure: Zuratas is nicknamed Mascarita, "Maskface," because of a huge birthmark that covers almost half his face, from which grows unsightly hair.

According to Vargas Llosa, the main character was inspired by Goldemberg, who voluntarily exiled himself from his native Peru and went to live first in Israel and then in Manhattan. Like Zuratas, he comes from a small town in Peru and traveled to Lima at an early age (as did Vargas Llosa himself). Both author and protagonist hold similar political views, and their lives must be understood as perhaps desperate attempts to come to terms with their art and identity; the options available to a Jewish storyteller in Peru result in the fictional protagonist's disappearance into the jungle, an exotic fate that exaggerates, through art, the real novelist's need to escape his country.

Guatemala, which in 1982 had one thousand Jews, less than .01 percent of the total population, has three Jewish writers of importance. The civil war and urban violence have pushed most of them out of the country, but fortunately that has not jeopardized their creative productivity. Guatemala is the original home of Victor Perera (1934–2003), a Jew of Sephardic descent who immigrated to the United States early in life. His stories appeared in major New York publications. His was a curious case because having lived most of his life north of the Rio Grande, he switched, as did Gerchunoff, from one language to another—in his case from Spanish to English. A former editor of the *New Yorker*, Perera was the author of *The Conversion*, a 1970 novel about a North American student living in Spain who tries to come to terms with his Sephardic Jewish identity.

The story included here is part of the delightful *Rites: A Guatemalan Boyhood*, published in 1986 and viewed by Alastair Reid, the poet, critic, and translator, as another fine example of how effectively an author can cross from one language into another, bringing all his insights with him. The book, a sum of fictionalized personal recollections of Perera's childhood, is written in a precise, careful language that recalls that of Chekhov and Isaac Babel. The protagonists, their relatives, and their friends living in Guatemala City during the 1950s love, hate, dream about a better future, and engage in business, all in an atmosphere imbued with deeply felt nostalgia. The author's decision to write in English, although perhaps unconscious, is quite meaningful.

In the last twenty years, a handful of well-known Latin American writers, among them Fuentes but also the Cuban novelist Guillermo Cabrera Infante, author of *Three Trapped Tigers*, and Manuel Puig, the Argentine playwright and novelist whose works include *Kiss of the Spider Woman*, have switched, occasionally and at times in a consistent manner, into English. Borges himself became all but an English-language author, using his English "translators" as coauthors and at times secretaries and scribes. A motivation behind this cross-cultural maneuver is the desire of writers to attract a wider audience and a more dynamic marketplace. Indeed, the fact that Perera published *Rites* in English, with a trade publishing house, gave the book the attention few others included in this anthology have had so far—or may ever receive.

Also Guatemalan is Alcina Lubitch Domecq (b. 1953), who now makes her home in Jerusalem. In 1983 she wrote *The Mirror's Mirror: or, The Noble*

Smile of the Dog. A novel clearly influenced by Lewis Carroll and Borges, it described the adventures of an eight-year-old Jewish girl left alone on a battlefield. Her thirty or more stories, including "Bottles," were collected in 1988 in *Intoxicated* and have been published in French, German, and Italian anthologies. Most of her stories—what Irving Howe has called "short shorts"—are hardly longer than a page. Yet like those of Nathaniel Hawthorne, her images are breathtaking insights into the complexities of a genealogical past or a troublesome family life. In one story she describes how a widow is surprised by the sudden appearance on her face of her late husband's mustache. In another, a troubled housewife is trapped in a gigantic bottle, as if metamorphosed into a huge Kafkaesque insect. The message is clear: as with the lucid prose of Lispector, the reader is provided with an idiosyncratic view—at times paranoid, often distorted and disturbing—of the claustrophobic reality of women's lives in Latin America.

THE ISSUE OF CULTURAL IDENTITY

How can Jewish Latin American fiction be compared to the literature created by Jews in the United States or by modern Israeli writers? First and foremost, it is obvious that while writers such as Saul Bellow, Philip Roth, and Cynthia Ozick have acquired a wide international readership, most of the Jewish writers included in this anthology remain unknown, appreciated by a rather small audience, primarily Jewish. The bridge toward internationalization has been crossed by only a few, among them Moacyr Scliar, Isaac Goldemberg, and two or three others not included in this anthology, such as Jacobo Timerman (1923–1999), the Argentine newspaper editor and journalist who wrote *Prisoner without a Name, Cell without a Number*, a personal account of repression by the military junta during the 1970s. But as a literary tradition, Jewish writing south of the Rio Grande still has little echo. Why? The explanation is complex.

Until the 1960s (and perhaps much more recently) European and North American readers knew hardly anything about Latin American letters in general. It was when Borges won the Publisher's Prize and his narratives began to be translated into many languages that others began to pay attention. A narrative boom followed: in 1967 Miguel Angel Asturias, the Guatemalan author of the acclaimed *Men of Maize*, won the Nobel Prize for

Literature, and his contribution was followed by Garcia Márquez's *One Hundred Years of Solitude*, Fuentes's *A Change of Skin*, and Vargas Llosa's *The Green House*. What caused this literary phenomenon? As Emir Rodriguez Monegal forcefully argued, there's little doubt that political, social, and economic factors were involved: the end of the Second World War brought with it the collapse of Western colonialism, and nations in Africa, Asia, and Oceania emerged as new politically independent realities.

It suddenly became clear that high culture was not the property of a handful of European intellectuals but could be found as well on the periphery—in the so-called Third World. In different parts of the globe but with similar goals, V. S. Naipaul, Wole Soyinka, Derek Walcott, and Chinua Achebe, to name only a few, published their works, and their "marginal" voices began to be heard. The list of new literary voices included Latin Americans, yet only a few of them gained the public's attention in Europe and the United States. The less avant-garde themes and styles were regarded as unimportant, and those writers not considered mainstream never entered the international arena. Such became the fate of Jewish writers, along with other minorities, in countries like Mexico, Brazil, and Argentina. World readership was interested in "standard," stereotyped views of the region, not in the sum of its heterogeneous parts. The day will come when Asian, Italian, and black narrative voices emerging from Latin America will also be heard, just as today Maxine Hong Kingston and Toni Morrison are recognized as North American writers of excellence.

Because of the tragedy that befell European Jews during the Second World War, but also as a result of the creation of the state of Israel and the dynamism of Jews in the United States, the political and cultural balance of power in world Jewry shifted its headquarters from Vienna and Berlin to New York City and Tel Aviv. Thus, after 1948, early twentieth-century writers such as Abraham Cahan, Michael Gold, Daniel Fuchs, and Henry Roth in the United States, and Sh. Y. Agnon in Israel, gained recognition as important Jewish literary voices. In setting the scene for successors like Saul Bellow, Philip Roth, Amos Oz, and A. B. Yehoshua, North American fiction is particularly important. Stories and novels such as "Defender of the Faith" and "Eli the Fanatic" by Roth, *Dangling Man* and *Herzog* by Bellow, *The Assistant* and *Idiots First* by Bernard Malamud, and "Envy: or, Yiddish in America," "The Pagan Rabbi," and "The Shawl" by Ozick, together with works by Grace Paley, E. L. Doctorow, and Stanley Elkin, are essential in understanding world Jewish literature today.

Their themes have transcended the particulars of Jewish identity to confront universal human concerns. In 1967 Philip Rahv argued, "The homogenization resulting from speaking of [North American Jewish writers] as if they comprised some kind of literary faction or school is bad critical practice in that it is based on simplistic assumptions concerning the literary process as a whole as well as the nature of [US] Jewry, which, all appearances to the contrary, is very far from constituting a unitary group in its cultural manifestation."

And today one can indeed speak of the long list of Jewish writers in the United States not as specifically Jewish but as mainstream writers who happen to be of Jewish origin. They have managed to jump the gap from the ethnic to the universal through their exploration of issues of selfhood, acculturation, memory, and history. Thus they transcend simply parochial interests, especially as these themes are universalized in an increasingly multicultural North American society. The broad success of Jewish writers from the 1950s through the 1970s (now somewhat eclipsed by the increasing interest in the cultural traditions of black, Hispanic, and Asian minorities) was possible because the North American audience could identify with Jewish artists, as with other ethnic writers, and pursue their development.

Moreover, the translating process their works undergo, to be read in Berlin or Rome or Buenos Aires, itself further diminishes their narrowness of outlook. But they are beyond national borders. In part, their success is due to a voracious secular readership, made up of upwardly mobile, well-educated urban Jews in the United States, always eager to explore their identity as cosmopolitan citizens in a technological age. In fact, the heterogeneity that Philip Rahv talks about, together with the relatively large size and cultural comfort of North American Jewry as members of an open, democratic society, has made it possible for their artists and intellectuals to mature and overcome their parochialism. And the fact that Yiddish, both in daily life as well as in journalism and literature, was quickly replaced by English, fundamental to the absorption of any citizen into the so-called North American melting pot, was also a catalyst.

The Jewish writers in Latin America have to be appreciated from an altogether different perspective. First, against Rahv's argument, they indeed form a literary faction or school. Unlike other North American Jewish writers, many partially trace their aesthetic influences directly to nineteenth-century Yiddish writers such as Mendele Mokher Sforim and Sholem Aleichem. And although their idiom is everybody's Spanish, the public at large, even after the contributions of Borges or Vargas Llosa, remains essentially uninterested in Jewish themes. Besides, there is a long tradition of anti-Semitism in Hispanic countries, largely supported by the church but also, indirectly, by various governments.

Still, in some minds the Jew remains an atavistic witness to and victimizer of Jesus Christ and an unwelcome member of society. Contrary to their counterparts in the United States, the Latin American Jewish communities are monolithic. They refuse to assimilate, and the broader society also rejects their complete integration. Thus either the Jewish writer's cultural manifestation is within the community, in which case there is little space for self-criticism, or he or she sooner or later rejects the community, choosing to live outside the country, or at least far from its circumscribed borders. The processes of secularization and acculturation of the Jews in Brazil, Argentina, Mexico, and elsewhere in the hemisphere, because of the unstable nature of the region, do not result from a democratic, free-spirited dynamic. On the contrary, they have evolved dramatically and in the face of immense obstacles. Whereas Roth and Bellow have a secure if now shrinking following, the number of Latin American readers interested today in the works of Gerchunoff, or even Scliar, is too small to encourage the literary development of those who follow in their tradition.

The case of Israeli writers, of course, is totally dissimilar. Since the founding of the state of Israel, there is a general recognition that the new cultural reality is not a form of Jewish identity but rather a modern national identity. Following the allegorical prose of Agnon, with its Talmudic, biblical, and folkloric resonance, and since independence in 1948, novelists such as A. B. Yehoshua and Amos Oz have taken as their duty to describe, reflect, and comprehend today's Middle Eastern reality, and especially the Israeli one. Thus, in a moment of crisis and seemingly permanent political turmoil, their mimetic inclination has been toward psychological realism. The Israeli public, highly literate and avid to escape the daily routine through the imagination, reads these literary works with enormous interest. Yiddish, once a challenger to become the national tongue, is now the property of an old, dying generation, unknown or ignored by the young and rejected by the intellectuals. Hebrew, with its amazing rebirth, carries pride and denotes courage and renewal.

More than anything, what really is at stake now, when it comes to linguistic battles in Israel, is the question of the Palestinian writers' relationship to Hebrew as their own idiom.* In terms of the selection of realist topics, while some writers, among them Aharon Appelfeld and David Grossman, trace their roots to pre-Holocaust European culture, and indirectly to Yiddish, the majority has buried the names of Sholem Aleichem and his successors, considering them curiosities of the Diaspora past. Their political life, the permanent threat of Arab-Jewish conflict, and the daily contact with Palestinian aspirations draw their full attention. Being Jewish is not the issue anymore; rather the issue is the quality and future of Israeli culture. The collective identity has been reshaped on a concrete, material level. Similar to the personal and cultural transformation of Saul Bellow from Jew into North American, Oz, Yehoshua, and others are now Israeli, not Jewish, writers.

Will the time come when Latin America will be truly democratic and pluralistic, less intolerant of the particular? Perhaps. Meanwhile, the Jews, in Octavio Paz's view "the few" in the universe of "the many," remain the "other voice" that refuses to be devoured by the monstrous whole. Their labyrinthine worldview has been recorded in literature, where they have successfully built, in spite of the climate of revolution and fantasy, a room of their own, a "tropical synagogue" like that of Moacyr Scliar's *The Gods of Raquel*—a hybrid creation intertwining symbols from the Old World and the New.

---

* See my "Cynthia Ozick and Anton Shammas: Duel Over the Hebrew Language," *Jewish Frontier* 56, no. 4 (1989): 7–13. See also my introduction to *The Oxford Book of Jewish Stories*, edited by Ilan Stavans (New York: Oxford University Press, 1997).

ARGENTINA

Camacho's Wedding Feast

▬ ▬

ALBERTO GERCHUNOFF (1884–1950)
Translated from the Spanish by Prudencio de Pereda

Set at the turn of the century in Rajíl, a shtetl-like agricultural town in La Pampa, this lyrical story, first published as part of The Jewish Gauchos (1910) and among the best in the volume, evokes the often explosive relationship between gentiles and Jews in the Southern Hemisphere. It fuses the universal theme of the stolen bride with a narrative voice and incident borrowed from Don Quixote. Through the tale's folkloristic tone, which finds pleasure in describing the details of pastoral life as well as Jewish rituals and tradition, the Russian-born author, considered the grandfather of Jewish Latin American literature, advances his ill-fated view of Argentina as the true Promised Land.

FOR TWO WEEKS now, the people of the entire district had been expectantly waiting for Pascual Liske's wedding day. Pascual was the *rich* Liske's son. The family lived in Espindola and, naturally enough, the respectable people of the colonies were looking forward to the ceremony and feast. To judge by the early signs, the feast was to be exceptional. It was well-known in Rajíl that the groom's family had purchased eight demijohns of wine, a barrel of beer, and numerous bottles of soft drinks. Kelner's wife had discovered this when she happened to come on the Liskes' cart, stopped near the breakwater. The reins had broken, and the Liskes' hired man was working frantically to replace them.

"The soft drinks were *rose* colored," she told the neighbors. "Yes!" she said, looking directly at the doubting *shochet's* wife.* "Yes, they were rose colored, and each bottle had a waxen seal on it."

---

* A shochet is a ritual slaughterer—Ed.

Everyone agreed old man Liske's fortune could stand that kind of spending.

In addition to the original land and oxen that he'd gotten from the administration, Liske had many cows and horses. Last year's harvest alone had brought him thousands of pesos, and he could well afford to marry off his son in style without touching his principal.

Everyone further agreed that the bride deserved this kind of a wedding. Raquel was one of the most beautiful girls in the district, if not in the whole world. She was tall, with straw-blond hair so fine and full it suggested mist; her eyes were so blue they made one's breath catch. She was tall and lithe, but her simple print dresses showed the full curving loveliness of a beautiful body. An air of shyness and a certain peevishness became her because they seemed to protect her loveliness.

Many of the colonists had tried to win her—the haughty young clerk of the administration as well as all the young men in Villaguay and thereabouts, but none had achieved a sympathetic response. Pascual Liske had been the most persistent of these suitors, but certainly not the most favored, at first. In spite of his perseverance and his gifts, Raquel did not like him. She felt depressed and bored because Pascual never spoke of anything but seedlings, livestock, and harvests. The only young man she had seemed to favor was a young admirer from the San Gregorio colony, Gabriel Camacho. She had gone out dancing with him during the many times he used to come to visit.

Her family had insisted she accept Pascual and the marriage had been arranged.

On the day of the feast, the invited families had gathered at the breakwater before Espindola. A long line of carts, crowded with men and women, was pointed toward the colony. It was a spring afternoon, and the flowering country looked beautiful in the lowering rays of the sun. Young men rode up and down the line on their spirited ponies, calling and signaling to the girls when the mothers were looking elsewhere. In their efforts to catch a girl's eye, they set their ponies to capering in true gaucho style. In their eagerness, some even proposed races and other contests.

Russian and Jewish songs were being sung in all parts of the caravan, the voices fresh and happy. At other points, the songs of this, their new country, could be heard being sung in a language that few understood.

At last, the caravan moved into the village. The long line of heavy carts, being gently pulled by the oxen, had the look of a primitive procession. The carts stopped at different houses, and the visitors went inside to finish their preparations. Then, at the appointed time, all the invited guests came out together and began to make their way to the groom's house.

Arriving at Liskes', they found that rumors of the fabulous preparations had not been exaggerated. A wide pavilion stood facing the house with decorative lanterns hanging inside on high poles, masked by flowered branches. Under the canvas roof were long tables covered with white cloths and countless covered dishes and bowls that the flies buzzed about hopelessly. Old Liske wore his black velvet frock coat—a relic of his prosperous years in Bessarabia—as well as a newly added silk scarf of yellow, streaked with blue. With hands in his pockets, he moved from group to group, being consciously pleasant to everyone and speaking quite freely of the ostentation and unusual luxury of the feast. To minimize the importance of it all, he would mention the price, in a lowered voice, and then, as if to explain his part in this madness, would shrug his shoulders, saying, "After all, he's my only son."

The Hebrew words *ben yachid* ("only son") express this sentiment very well, and they were heard frequently as many guests expressed their praises of the fat Pascual. Even his bumpkin qualities were cited as assets in the extraordinary rash of praise.

His mother was dressed in a showy frock with winged sleeves and wore a green kerchief spread over her full shoulders. Moving quickly, in spite of her ample roundness, she went from place to place, talking and nodding to everyone in the growing crowd, which was soon becoming as big and fantastic as the fiesta.

Under the side eave of the house, a huge caldron filled with chickens simmered over a fire, while at the side, in the deeper shadow, hung a row of dripping roasted geese. In front of these were trays with the traditional stuffed fish stacked for cooling. What the guests admired more than the chicken-filled caldron, the roast geese, stuffed fish, and the calf's ribs that the cooks were preparing were the demijohns of wine, the huge cask of beer, and, above all else, the bottles of soft drinks whose roseate color the sun played on. Yes, it was so. Just as they'd heard in Rajíl, there were the bottles of rose-colored soft drinks with red seals on the bottles.

The music was supplied by an accordion and guitar, and the two musicians were already essaying some popular Jewish pieces. Voices in the crowd were tentatively humming along with them.

The bride was preparing for the ceremony in the house next to Liske's. Friends were dressing her, and her crown of sugar was already well smudged from constant rearrangement. Raquel was very sad. No matter how much the other girls reminded her of her wonderful luck—to marry a man like Pascual wasn't something that happened every day—she remained depressed. She was silent most of the time and answered with sighs or short nods. She was a normally shy girl, but today she seemed truly sad. Those eyes that were usually so wide and clear now seemed as clouded as her forehead.

In talking about the guests, someone told Raquel that Gabriel had come with other people from San Gregorio. She grew more depressed at hearing his name and, as she put on the bridal veil, two big tears ran down her cheeks and fell on her satin blouse.

Everyone knew the cause of her weeping. Raquel and Gabriel had come to an understanding months ago, and Jacobo—that wily little know-it-all—had claimed he saw them kissing in the shadow of a paradise tree on the eve of the Day of Atonement.

Pascual's mother finally arrived at the bride's house and, in accordance with custom, congratulated the bride and kissed her noisily. Her voice screeched as she called to let the ceremony begin. Raquel said nothing. She shrugged in despair and stood hopelessly while the group of friends gathered at her back and picked up her lace-bordered train. The future father-in-law arrived with the rabbi and the procession started.

Outside Liske's house, the guests were gathered about the tables, while inside the house Pascual, who was dressed in black, waited with friends and the father of the bride. When they heard the hand clapping outside, they went out to the grounds and the ceremony began.

Pascual walked over to the canopy, held up by couples of young men and women, and stood under it. He was joined immediately by his betrothed, who came escorted by the two sponsors. Rabbi Nisen began the blessings and offered the ritual cup to the bride and groom. Then the bride began her seven turns around the man, accompanied by the sponsors. As she finished, an old lady called out that there had only been six, and another turn was made. The rabbi read the marriage contract, which conformed entirely with the sacred laws of Israel. He sang the nuptial prayers again. The ceremony ended with the symbolic breaking of the cup. An old man placed it on the ground, and Pascual stepped on it with force enough to break a rock.

The crowd pressed in to congratulate the couple. Her friends gathered around the bride, embracing and kissing her, but Raquel was still depressed. She accepted the congratulations and good wishes in silence. Other guests gathered around the long table and began to toast and drink.

Old Liske proposed some dancing before they sat down to supper, and he himself began by moving into the first steps of the characteristic Jewish piece, "the happy dance," to the accompaniment of the accordion and guitar. At the head of the long table, the bride and groom stood together and watched the growing bustle without saying a word to each other. Facing them, standing very erect and pale, was Gabriel.

The guests called for the bride and groom to dance. Pascual frowned anxiously and shook his head. He did not dance. The calls and applause receded, and everyone stood waiting in embarrassment. Gabriel stepped forward suddenly and offered his arm to the bride. The accordion and guitar began a popular Jewish polka.

Gabriel tried to outdo himself, and he was a superb dancer. At one point he said something to Raquel, and she looked at him in surprise and grew still paler. People were beginning to whisper and move away. Israel Kelner had taken the arm of the shochet as they both stepped away from the watching circle.

"Gabriel shouldn't have done this," Kelner said. "Everybody knows that he's in love with Raquel and that she's *not* in love with her husband."

The shochet pulled at his beard and smiled. "I don't want to offend anyone," he said. "I'm a friend of Liske's and he's a religious man—but Pascual is a beast. Did you see how mixed up he got when he was repeating the *hareiad* pledge during the ceremony? Believe me, Rabbi Israel, I feel sorry for the girl. She's so beautiful and fine . . ."

Little Jacobo took Rebecca aside and talked to her in Argentine criollo— he was the most gaucho of the Jews, as demonstrated now by his complete gaucho dress. "Listen, *negrita*," he began. "Something's going to happen here."

"A fight?" Rebecca whispered with interest.

"Just what I'm telling you. I was in San Gregorio this morning. Met Gabriel there. He asked me if I was going to the wedding—this one, of course. I said yes, I was, and he asked me about doing something later . . ."

"A race?" Rebecca interrupted. "You mean to say that you made a bet with Gabriel? Oh, you men! And they said that he was heartbroken!"

"Oh, well," Jacobo said. He shrugged his shoulders. "As they say: Men run to races . . ."

As night began to fall, the paper lanterns were lit, and many guests walked off a distance to see the effect of the lights. It was a special privilege of the rich to have such lights, and the last time they'd been seen here was during the visit of Colonel Goldschmith, a representative of the European Jewish Committee.

The next item was dinner, a banquet that bars description. The guests were seated and the bride and groom served the "golden broth," the consecrative dish of the newlyweds. Then the platters of chicken, duck, and fish began to circulate; and the wine was poured to a complete and unanimous chorus of praise directed to the hostess.

"I've never eaten such tasty stuffed fish."

"Where could you ever get such roast geese as this?" the shochet asked.

Rabbi Moises Ornstein delivered the eulogy and added: "I must say that no one cooks as well as Madam Liske. Whoever tastes her dishes knows that they are a superior person's."

Fritters of meat and rice, wrapped in vine leaves, were served next, while more beer and wine quickened the spirits of the guests. The bride excused herself, saying that she had to change her dress. She left the party accompanied by her friends. Her mother-in-law had started to go with them, but Jacobo stopped her. "Madam Liske!" he said. "Sit down and listen to your praises. Sit down and hear what we think of this wonderful banquet. We'll be mad if you leave," he said, when she seemed reluctant to stop. "We're enjoying ourselves very much and we want to share this with you."

"Let me go, my boy," she said. "I have to help my daughter-in-law."

"Rebecca will help her. Sit down. Sit down. Rebecca!" Jacobo turned to shout. "Go and help the bride!"

The old lady sat down—everyone about had joined in the urging—and Jacobo brought her a glass of wine so that they could drink a toast.

"When one has a son like yours," the shochet said to Madam Liske, "one should be glad."

The toasts were offered and drunk, and this clinking of glasses, lusty singing, and music could be heard over all the grounds. The sky was full of stars, the atmosphere lightly tinged with clover and the scent of hay. In the nearby pasture, the cows mooed and the light wind stirred the leaves. Jacobo got up and excused himself.

"I have to see about my pony," he explained. "I think he might need a blanket."

"I'll look after my mare," Gabriel said, as he stood up to go with him. They moved away from the group, and Jacobo took Gabriel's arm. "Listen, the bay is saddled and waiting by the palisade," he said. "The *boyero*'s kid is watching him and the gate is open. At the first turn there's a sulky all set. The Lame One is watching there. Tell me, have you got a gun?"

Gabriel did not seem to hear this last point. He patted Jacobo's arm and started to walk toward the palisade. After a few steps, he turned to look back. "And how will Raquel get away from the girls in there?"

"Don't worry about that. Rebecca's there."

When the girls who were with the bride did return to the party, Madam Liske asked for her daughter-in-law. "She's coming right away with Rebecca," they told her. Then Rebecca returned alone and gave the old lady still another excuse. Jacobo was doing his best to distract Madam Liske with toasts. Others took it up, and there was a great clinking of glasses and mumblings of toasts.

The musicians continued to play and the guests to eat and drink. The jugs of wine were being refilled continuously, and no one's glass was ever low. Pascual, the groom, looked fat and solemn and said nothing. From time to time, he would dart a quick look at the bride's empty chair. The gallop of a horse was heard at that moment, and then, soon after, the sounds of a sulky starting off.

Jacobo whispered into Rebecca's ear: "That's them, isn't it?"

"Yes," the girl whispered back, "they were leaving when I came away."

The continued absence of the bride was worrying her mother-in-law and, without saying anything, she slipped into the house to see. She came out immediately.

"Rebecca, have you seen Raquel?" she said.

"I left her in the house, Señora. Isn't she there?"

"She's not."

"That's funny . . ."

The old lady spoke to her husband and to her son, Pascual. The guests were beginning to whisper among themselves. They saw that something had gone wrong. The accordion and guitar went silent. The guests began to stand up; some glasses were tipped over, but no one paid any attention. A few of the guests moved toward the house. Others asked: "Is it the bride? Has something happened to the bride?"

The shochet of Rajíl asked his friend and counterpart from Karmel about the point of sacred law, if it was true that the bride had fled.

"Do you think she has?" the shochet of Karmel asked.

"It's possible. Anything is possible in these situations."

"Well, I think that divorce would be the next step. The girl would be free, as would be her husband. It's the common course."

Meanwhile, the excitement was growing all around them. Old Liske grabbed the gaucho's little son. "Did you see anything out there? Out there on the road?" he said.

"Yes. Out there, on the road to San Gregorio. I saw a sulky, with Gabriel—he was driving it—and there was a girl sitting with him."

"He's kidnapped her!" Madam Liske screamed. Her voice was close to hysteria. "Kidnapped her!"

Shouts and quick talking started all over the grounds now. Most of the crowd was genuinely shocked and surprised. When old Liske turned to abuse the father of the gaucho boy, the man stood up to him, and they were soon wrestling and rolling in the center of pushing and shouting guests. The table was overturned, and spilled wine and broken glass added to the excitement.

The shochet of Rajíl mounted a chair and shouted for order. What had happened was a disgrace, he said, a punishment from God, but fighting and shouting would not ease it any.

"She's an adulteress!" shouted the enraged Liske, as he sought to break out of restraining hands. "An infamous adulteress!"

"She is not!" the shochet answered him. "She would be," he said, "if she had left her husband 'after one day, at least, after the marriage,' as our law so clearly says it. This is the law of God, you know, and there is no other way but that they be divorced. Pascual is a fine, honorable young man, but if she doesn't love him, she can't be made to live under his roof."

The shochet went on in his usually eloquent and wise way, and he cited similar cases acknowledged by the most illustrious rabbis and scholars. In

Jerusalem, the sacred capital, there had occurred a similar case, and Rabbi Hillel had declared in favor of the girl. At the end, the shochet turned to Pascual: "In the name of our laws, Pascual, I ask that you grant a divorce to Raquel and that you declare, here and now, that you accept it for yourself." Pascual scratched his head and looked sad. Then, in a tearful voice, he accepted the shochet's proposal.

The crowd grew quiet and the guests soon began to leave, one by one, some murmuring, some hiding a smile.

Well, as you can see, my patient readers, there are fierce, arrogant gauchos, wife stealers, and Camachos, as well as the most learned and honorable of rabbinical scholars, in the little Jewish colony where I learned to love the Argentine sky and felt a part of its wonderful earth. This story I've told— with more detail than art—is a true one, just as I'm sure the original story of Camacho's feast is true. May I die this instant if I've dared to add the slightest bit of invention to the marvelous story.

I'd like very much to add some verses—as was done to the original Camacho story—but God has denied me that talent. I gave you the tale in its purest truth, and if you want couplets, add them yourself in your most gracious style. Don't forget *my* name, however—just as our gracious Master Don Miguel de Cervantes Saavedra remembered the name of Cide Hamete Benegeli and gave him all due credit for the original Camacho story.

And if the exact, accurate telling of this tale has pleased you, don't send me any golden doubloons—here, they don't even buy bread and water. Send me some golden drachmas or, if not, I'd appreciate a carafe of Jerusalem wine from the vineyards my ancestors planted as they sang the praises of Jehovah. May He grant you wealth and health, the gifts I ask for myself.

In Honor of Yom Kippur

SAMUEL ROLLANSKY (1902–1995)
Translated from the Yiddish by Alan Astro

Samuel Rollansky (also known as Shmuel Rozhanski) came to Argentina in 1922. He wrote a daily column for Di Yidishe Tsaytung *of Buenos Aires from 1934 to 1973. His lifelong contribution to Yiddish literature is the one-hundred-volume anthology* Musterverk fun der yidisher literatur. *Rollansky died in Buenos Aires in 1995, the year after the terrorist bombing against the AMIA, the city's Jewish community center. "In Honor of Yom Kippur" is a vignette on life in Buenos Aires on the holy day of Yom Kippur.*

TOGETHER WITH HIS family, Mendl finally made it over to the home of their old friends, Yosl and his wife. For a long time they had been promising to come over but never had gotten around to it. Now sitting with Yosl, Mendl apologized: "You understand, we're so busy, and it's so far away."

Yosl concurred, saying: "I've started to believe that living in different areas of Buenos Aires is like being in two different cities. It's exactly one year since you came over, last Yom Kippur."

"It's great to be together," the friends and their wives agreed. "Today we don't have to work, so we can throw a little party. Fortunately, there's such a thing as Yom Kippur, if you work for Jewish bosses as we do."

Mendl and Yosl, who had already been friends back in the old country, had the same political and antireligious leanings. True, they had had their sons circumcised, but not because they wanted to.

"After all," they said, justifying themselves, "there were family considerations, our fathers . . . We couldn't cause the grandfathers such heartache. What could we do, if those were the circumstances?"

Mendl and Yosl were happy to get together on Yom Kippur and reminisce about holidays in the old country.

"We'd eat chocolate cookies that we'd buy from the Russian! People would rip them right out of his hands! His store was packed! All the young people would sneak out of synagogue and grab a bite."

While they remembered the old days, they watched their wives putting some sponge cake and brandy on the table. Smiling, they pointed out: "It's a holiday, after all! Yom Kippur, to be precise!"

"Do you really think," Yosl confessed, "that if you had come over on some ordinary Sunday, my wife and I would have treated you as honored guests? Well, sure we would, but we wouldn't have served up such delicacies. Sponge cake and brandy on an ordinary Sunday? We offer Sunday visitors a cup of tea, a cookie, a piece of chocolate."

As he spoke, Yosl motioned toward the table, indicated with his eyes that his friend should approach, and extended to him a glass of brandy and a plate of sponge cake. Mendl hesitated, as though he wondered whether he ought to imbibe, but then accepted.

"As you no doubt recall," he apologized, "I am opposed to alcohol, but today I won't refuse. I never take a sip of brandy, but in honor of Yom Kippur . . . How many times a year, after all, does Yom Kippur come around?"

Mendl took the drink, sipped it, and his eyes watered. "Wow," he choked, "that's strong stuff."

Nonetheless, he drank. It burned his palate, but he recovered. Yosl refilled his glass. Though his head felt swollen and stiff as though imprisoned by iron bars, he still couldn't refuse. Yosl smiled at him fixedly. Mendl answered with a hiccup: "Hap-hic . . . py Yom Kip-hic . . . pur! Sor-hic . . . ry!"

And Mendl drank. His feet and head felt leaden, but he drank.

He sat down when the floor started to bend. In order to take the brandy, he himself had to bend. His sleeve brushed a glass, and the contents spilled on the tablecloth. Mendl heard Yosl's laughter blending into his words: "Yom Kippur, ha! Once a year, ha!"

Sitting at the table, Mendl watched Yosl's wife cut him a piece of roast suckling pig. Mendl's eyes felt dry and sticky. He rubbed them and tried to focus. In his blurred vision, he made out the head of a pig, its chin and big broad lips that seemed to slobber.

"Eat!" said Yosl's wife, elbowing him. "What are you waiting for? An engraved invitation?"

"Me?" said Mendl, with a start, as though he had taken fright. "That's for me? Thanks, uh, but I won't eat that. Not because it's pig, but because I don't eat meat."

"C'mon!" exclaimed Yosl, insulted. "I'd expect that from a religious Jew."

"True, but, no . . ." Mendel argued. "I can't. I don't like it."

"C'mon! Cut it out!" said Yosl, unyieldingly. "Any other day of the year you can do as you wish, but not today, not on Yom Kippur."

Mendel bent to his plate, took a knife and fork, and felt as though he were offering a sacrifice in honor of Yom Kippur.

A Man and His Parrot

JOSÉ RABINOVICH (1903–1977)
Translated from the Yiddish by Debbie Nathan

Yoysef Rabinovich was born in Bialystok and immigrated to Argentina in 1924. He wrote for Di Prese *as well as* Nayvelt. *He is the author of the poetry collection* El violinista bajo el tejado *(The Fiddler under the Roof), which appeared in 1970. "A Man and His Parrot" is an Isaac Bashevis Singer–like humorous tale about daily life with a mascot.*

IT IS BARELY six in the morning and the stars are still out, but Manuel has to get up.

It isn't a job that wakes him. That obligation used to get him right to his feet, but now? Now just getting dressed is drudgery. His pants, his shoes—they resist when he puts them on. His hands have become so powerless that they can hardly drag his clothes on. He and his clothes are mutual enemies. His feet, like an old man's, don't want to walk—they balk. He can't stop yawning. What is he yawning about? Maybe he didn't get enough sleep? On the contrary, he slept too much. If only someone would knock on the door and say, "Manuel, time for work!"

He is itching to do something so his hands will turn back into hands. So his body will be hard and strong. So he will stop yawning. So he will be a real man! But since nobody comes to his door or into his heart, Manuel moves like a phantom, with his socks in one hand and a shoe in the other. In his hands, his clothes look like rags. His hands too.

Manuel gets up to make maté for Matilda. He rolls the bitterness inside his mouth and catches it in his throat, unable to swallow but unable to spit it out either. And the harsh taste refuses to stay in his throat. It goes all through his body and is concentrated around his heart. What a life!

Matilda needs a maté brought to her in bed and put in her hand to drink. His wife deserves this: after all, she is supporting them. It would be so good if he didn't have to do this. His excuse is that she is not sustaining only them but also another life inside her. In such a case, a man should take care of his wife. He dotes on her a bit more to make it easier for her to carry the burden he put in her body.

But ever since he became the housewife and she the breadwinner—even though she still seems like the same old Matilda—something has been piercing him like cats' claws, destroying him. It's a good thing to serve one's wife a maté in bed. It's an honor for the wife and no disgrace for the husband. But the terrible thing is that his wife knows that this is only a duty he is forced to carry out because she brings home the rent money. Too, she buys him socks on the street, and she—not he—instructs that money be taken from the box on the table to shop for what they need. That is why it's no good bringing his wife a maté in bed. Still, he knows Matilda isn't that kind of woman. She cares about him. She doesn't mind going to work, or even that he is unemployed. She doesn't think the things he imagines that she thinks. But she could be thinking them. After all, any woman would, and besides, Manuel is forcing her to think that way. It is thus no surprise that his clothes look like rags in his hands when he gets dressed at six o'clock to bring his wife a maté in bed.

The stars are still in the sky, and it is still dark outside. It is winter. If it were summer it would already be light by now, bright and pleasant, and he would not have to turn on the electricity in the kitchen. Matilda can make maté in the dark. Manuel can't, even though he would rather be in the dark. In the dark, the work doesn't seem so distasteful.

There's maté, and sugar too, but no coffee to sprinkle in. What a numb-skull he is—they were out of coffee yesterday too. And she can't drink maté without it. Or maybe she can, but she claims she can't. She usually says that everything he does is fine. But it seems to him that she really feels just the opposite yet doesn't want him to feel bad that he's the housewife. So she says she can't drink maté without coffee so that he will be encouraged to learn how to run the house.

He sneaks into the kitchen on tiptoe so their parrot won't see him.

Damned parrot! They've put up with so much from each other; they've had a long-standing, bitter war. Who will be the victor? Who will survive? Manuel, of course. After all, he has more years left to live than the parrot. Still, the parrot has given Manuel so much heartache, so much real anguish, that he is letting it die of thirst. As long as the parrot screams "Master!" Manuel will not put water in the cage.

The parrot is just another problem. He would let it scream if there were no neighbors in the courtyard—would let the bird yell "Master!" until it exploded, and who would care? If no one else could hear, Manuel would not be taking it to heart.

Of course he would not feel happy about being mocked. After all, how can anyone be happy who peels potatoes, lights the stove, stokes the fire, cracks eggs, washes dishes, and also hears screaming right over his head, "Master! Master!"? It's OK when the parrot screeches once then takes a break.

But as soon as it notices Manuel, it starts up and will not stop. More than once, Manuel has been so enraged that he has felt like throwing a plate at the parrot's head. He is sure that his neighbors are quietly quaking with laughter. And that even Matilda is laughing. Back before he was unemployed, she never laughed when the crazy parrot screeched "Master! Master!" until it got hoarse. That is because Manuel was the breadwinner then. He liked it that the parrot recognized him. Back then, everyone enjoyed the shrieking, even though there really was no reason to laugh. And now, since he has become unemployed, even Matilda has begun to snicker when the parrot starts in with its cheery screech. The more the bird screeches, the more his wife's snicker reveals its teeth. But would she laugh if she knew about the relentless, bitter war being waged so stubbornly and silently by Manuel, so he won't have to listen anymore—and by the parrot, so Manuel will put a drop of water in its bowl? Would Matilda laugh then?

What is more, if Manuel thought it was merely in the bird's nature to scream, the same way a rooster has it in him to crow, maybe he wouldn't care. The neighbors wouldn't laugh either. But everyone sees and hears how hard it is for the bird, who shrieks "Master!" as tragically as if someone were cutting its throat. The parrot's labored cry to Manuel whenever he goes into the kitchen provokes laughter from wives in the other kitchens—so much laughter that the women could explode from it.

When the bird lets out its mocking fury, Manuel would just as well heave the whole thing, parrot and cage, out the window and do it so hard that even the Messiah, were He to come, couldn't revive the bird. But that would be the end of Manuel too, because people would run after him through the streets, as though he were a madman. Better to quietly carry the parrot out and get rid of it. But people would discover that trick too.

The parrot has already been without water for three days. Manuel gives it seeds and little pieces of stale bread, but he wouldn't be feeding the bird either if he weren't scared about being seen starving it. So he merely denies it drink. They can see from outside the cage if the parrot has food or not. But no one can see the tin water bowl.

Matilda drinks her maté and leaves for work. Manuel gives her a hug, just as he should. His situation demands it. He receives instructions on what to cook for lunch. He listens, smiling. His situation demands it.

The parrot notices him and starts choking, screeching. "Master!"

Manuel gives an involuntary glance at the sky, which is gloomy and on the verge of rain. Something about its appearance presses down on that place, the one in both beast and man, where anguish lies hidden. He goes back in the room, starts making the bed, and notices tiny infant's undershirts beneath the pillows. Matilda had been sewing them before she went to sleep and left them there. Tiny shirts. Manuel starts thinking. He cannot see anything in front of his eyes. Later, when he is again able to see, he rushes to give the parrot a drink of water.

Innocent Spirit

– –

ALICIA STEINBERG (1933–2012)
Translated from the Spanish by Andrea G. Labinger

A haunting tale by the author of Musicians and Watchmakers *(1971), who often wrote with an autobiographical trend in satirical, even irreverent ways, "Innocent Spirit" is a coming-of-age story about Jewish-Catholic relations in Argentina. Steinberg was also the author of* Call Me Magdalena *(2001) and* The Rainforest *(2006), among other works.*

HIGH SCHOOL IS over. There are farewells, laughter, and tears. All my lies are still intact. I'm a student of unknown origin, with no religion, no important ancestors. I wear a serious, responsible expression. I shine my shoes regularly. I wash my hair with a shampoo whose fragrance I'll never forget: it's the scent of springtime, which invades me as I bathe under the shower that's warmed by an alcohol burner and sing Bing and Frankie tunes while getting ready to go to a party. I'm a klutzy dancer, but I dance till I drop. I have fleeting romances whose greatest attraction consists of describing them to Rosario on the phone.

But no, that came later, much later: right now I'm one of those girls who wear cotton anklets and low-heeled shoes and stare at Ana Cristina's silk stockings and high heels out of the corner of their eyes. I go back and forth, whirling between lessons, recess bells, and B-plus grade-point averages. My mind is full of holes where knowledge ought to be. I focus on Señorita Granate's tits as she recites Alfonsina Storni's verses for us in literature class. Granate must have her bras made to order at the Venerable House of Porta. Another thing I'll never forget is the day when Señorita Granate, who taught us algebra in senior year, came to class with a black eye. Matilde hid behind the abnormally large head of a student who enrolled in the school on the minister's recommendation.

"God punished her," Matilde whispered, choking on her own laughter. "God punishes . . ."

Catholicism is the only decent religion. Judaism is ridiculous and embarrassing; Protestantism is trivial and foreign. Helen and Mary Brown, the two English Protestant girls in our class, are friendly. They smile at me endlessly, as if begging my pardon for their aberrant faith. When winter comes they start knitting sweaters that they never finish; when the real cold sets in, Mary shows up in a strange green felt scarf with embroidered roses on it. We all watch her with the most uncompromising malice; finally, Matilde strikes the right note (no metaphor intended) and figures it out: the scarf is the Brown family's piano keyboard cover. This incident demolishes my idea that all English people are rich. That, and the humbleness of the Browns' house in Villa Devoto, the shadowy figures of the parents, two British phantoms that cross the decrepit dining room where we have tea.

In our group there are twenty-two more or less devout Catholics, two Protestants, and one Greek Orthodox girl. Isabelle (God knows why they gave her that French name; she's Greek) does what she can to garner some prestige for her religion; to accomplish this, she insists on its great similarity to the Roman Apostolic Church. Isabelle's Spanish is labored, as if all the syllables were accented. She says that in the rituals of her religion, it's not only the priest who drinks the consecrated wine but also the faithful, all from the same chalice.

"And-it's-not-dis-gus-ting," she adds.

In any case, there are very few truly religious girls, and among those I count as Catholics there is at least one freethinker and an agnostic. They're atheists, in fact, but you can't say that word at school. The religion teacher holds out some hope of saving those who belong to other creeds, if one day they come to embrace the True Faith, but for atheists there is no salvation.

Sometimes I'm a fervent Catholic. I believe that after I die, I'll go to heaven or hell, or maybe purgatory, but for sure I'll go someplace. I believe that the Jesus of statues, religious stamps, and picture books exists and that he spends all day watching me to see what I'm doing. And yet I sin. I sin and sin again; I strike my chest and say, "Oh my God I am heartily sorry."

After graduation I land a substitute position in a convent school. I'm fascinated by the corridors of immaculate mosaic tiles, the stained-glass doors leading to the chapel. Sometimes I arrive early and chat with the sister who acts as doorman. The girls at the school claim that she's the soul of goodness: she lets the students escape at night to meet their boyfriends. Only two get pregnant and are returned to their parents. No one can explain this phenomenon because the girls would sooner kill themselves than denounce their Galician angel of mercy. The doorman sister was born in Galicia and has only one desire in life: to go back to her country before she dies. She tells this to me while placing a little package in my hands.

"It's stale *pan dulce*," she says. "But if you add milk and eggs to it, you can make a very tasty bread pudding, exquisite . . ." and she closes her eyes as if in ecstasy. "A very good, pious woman gave it to me . . ."

The students attend Mass in the chapel every morning at seven. I envy the students, the nuns—I envy their habits, the uniforms, the watery soup, the frigid mornings at Mass . . . that's what being Catholic is! The crucified Christ smiles at them when I'm not looking; as soon as I turn my back, he changes his suffering expression to a companionable smile and offers them the Kingdom of Heaven.

I don't know if the doorman sister ever returned to Galicia. But she surely ascended to heaven after she died, and Saint Peter let her in without asking to see her papers, while he opened the package of stale pan dulce that Sister had just deposited into his hands.

Someone's getting married, and we're invited to the reception. It's a Jewish wedding, but that doesn't matter, as long as I don't mention it at school. After the marriage ceremony we find ourselves seated at long tables, waiting for the food. They've put me next to a group of fancily dressed, heavily made-up young ladies. I have my illusions that later on somebody will ask me to dance, which doesn't happen. As it's a spring evening, I've arrived bare legged (without those wretched anklets). My tablemates are talking about guys, whether certain guys have phoned them or not.

"Hey," says a coral-painted mouth to an ear adorned with a costume jewelry hoop. "Hey, guess what! He called me."

"Who?"

"Moishe."

I'm flabbergasted. I don't understand why a girl would get so excited about someone named Moishe. But they pay no attention to me. It seems that Moishe has been playing hard to get and hasn't called that girl for the past few days. She doesn't call him either, so he won't get a swelled head, and the tactic seems to have been successful: at last he calls and asks her out. They keep on discussing similar situations between other girls and other guys. It looks like these people spend half their time sleeping and the other half phoning or not phoning one another.

At first I eavesdrop surreptitiously, looking down at my plate or at some bottle, but without realizing it, I'm gradually inching closer, and as I become more intrigued by the conversation, I tilt more and more in their direction, staring directly at the one who's talking, shifting my eyes back and forth like at a tennis match.

"And then what?" asks the coral-colored lips.

A pair of gray eyes, corresponding to the vermilion mouth that was about to respond, glares at mine. My cheeks are burning; tears spill down my face. I want to disappear or explode like a bomb beneath the table and make all the horrible young ladies go flying through the air.

After a while, I watch them out of the corner of my eye. They keep on chatting brightly; they've forgotten me, just as you forget a fly that you've just shooed away a few seconds before.

When the dinner is over, I get up from the table and don't approach anyone else. I don't sit in the chairs that ring the dance floor either. I just stand there, gazing at some random object as if it fascinates me. After a while I move to another spot and start thinking about another object; for example, the wedding cake, made of cardboard, or the huge Star of David formed by tiny lightbulbs hanging from the ceiling.

The following Monday at school, I mention that I've been to a wedding, and they ask me in what church the religious ceremony was held.

"They didn't get married in church," I reply. "They're agnostics."

★

"It isn't true."

"It's true."

"It can't be. It simply can't be."

"Yes, it's a fact. Matilde leaves her used sanitary napkins under the dresser. The maid complains, and rightfully so."

"But it can't be."

And yet something tells me that it can. I remember how Matilde carries around a cruddy piece of paper in her pocket, and when you ask her what she's got there, she shows you the contents: face powder. And an equally cruddy piece of string, the kind you use for tying packages, sticks out of the collar of her school smock. I try to pull it off, thinking it got caught there by mistake. But it's tied in a knot.

"What's that, Matilde?"

Matilde smiles, pokes her hand around inside the neck of her smock, and shows me a medal of her favorite saint dangling from the string. I remember my visit to her house, the pile of empty bottles on the patio. Anything is possible.

Then I'm not the only one who's miserable?

But we never discuss our respective misery. In our class there are at least two girls who are driven to school by a private chauffeur. It's a sure bet they don't leave used sanitary napkins under their dressers. And they don't carry a thermos with hot coffee and milk into their bedrooms either, in order to be able to get up in the icy mornings, when it's colder inside the house than out.

I never mentioned that business about the thermos, but it was a great invention. I used to place it on a chair beside my bed, and when the damn alarm clock went off, I'd stretch out one arm, trying to wake up as little as possible, and pour some coffee with boiling milk, already sweetened, into a cup I'd left on the chair for that purpose. Once the hot *café con leche* had run down my gullet, I would be alert and brave enough to climb back underneath the covers and remove my nightgown. Then I'd stick out my arm, grabbing and putting on, one by one, the items I'd laid out so carefully the night before, like the thermos and cup: my underpants; the garter belt—a hateful garment that served to hold up stockings and that was always missing some hook or fastener. Petticoat, shirt, skirt, sweater, stockings. Once my stockings were on, I'd poke my legs out from the warmth of the bed, exposing them to the frigid bedroom air, in order to put on my shoes. Overcoat, scarf, cap, and off I'd go to the bathroom. Crossing the patio in that temperature was no less complicated than crossing Avenida Nueve de Julio. I returned to my bedroom for the thermos, carried it into the kitchen, and consumed the rest of the café con leche, this time with bread and butter. I grabbed my book bag and headed for the street. It was as dark and freezing as midnight. Once, because I had set my alarm clock incorrectly, I arrived at school an hour early. I had to wait for them to open the doors, and then I entered the empty vestibule. At least I had a roof over my head, although inside it was even colder than it was outdoors. In the vestibule was a group of reproductions of impressionist paintings. I studied them in detail, one by one. They had a lot of foliage but not a single human figure. Much later another student came along, and then many others. Some arrived without gloves, their hands swollen with chilblains, like Francisca, the one who danced the *muñeira*. Others had pretty, knitted angora gloves. We all chatted until the head monitor arrived, a woman whose mere glare was sufficient to cause chills, even in summer. But it was early and school hadn't officially started yet: she smiled. A bell rang and we filed out to the patio to sing the hymn. Then to our classrooms.

As she calls the roll, our monitor keeps her free hand in her pocket and hops around a little. She's cold too. This year our classroom faces the street. The window's very high, so from our desks we can't manage to see the people passing by. You might say this is a kind of jail, and we can only guess at the faces of the free people walking around out there. But it's not true. This isn't my prison: it's my freedom. In here, I'm not who I am but who I want to be, or rather I'm the most presentable part of myself. I've left at home the Jew, the sinner, the girl who replaces the missing fastener on her garter belt with a safety pin, the one who prepares her thermos of café con leche to face the icy mornings, the one who thinks about penises, vaginas, and coituses. To school I bring the nice, lively girl, the one who knows how to make the others split their sides laughing, the one who says she's Catholic, although nobody believes her, the one who invents lies about her ancestors, but who, on the whole, is acceptable and even envied, because now that the clouds of her earliest years have parted, she understands everything and can even explain it. I'm sixteen years old, seventeen. I'm split in two pieces that are, nonetheless, irreconcilable, and for a long period of my life, I'll go on that way: split in two.

Celeste's Heart

— —

AÍDA BORTNIK (b. 1942)
Translated from the Spanish by Alberto Manguel

The protagonist of this brief tale by the award-winning screenwriter of The Official
Story *(1985), published for the first time in 1989 in Alberto Manguel's translation,
is a rebellious Jewish girl in an authoritarian milieu. Forced to act against her will,
against common sense, she slowly and courageously speaks out, expressing her valor
not in grand-scale historic events but in silent resistance toward the most conventional of daily acts.*

CELESTE WENT TO a school that had two yards. In the front yard they held
official ceremonies. In the back yard the teacher made them stand in line, one
behind the other at arm's distance, keeping the arm stretched out straight in
front, the body's weight on both legs, and in silence. One whole hour. Once
for two whole hours. All right, not hours. But two breaks passed, and the bell
rang four times before they were allowed back into the classroom. And the
girls from the other classes, who played and laughed during the first break as if
nothing had happened, stopped playing during the second break. They stood
with their backs to the wall and watched them. They watched the straight line,
one behind the other at arm's length, in the middle of the school yard. And
no one laughed. And when the teacher clapped her hands to indicate that the
punishment was over, Celeste was the only one who didn't stretch, who didn't
complain, who didn't rub her arm, who didn't march smartly back into the
classroom. When they sat down, she stared quietly at the teacher. She stared
at her in the same way she used to stare at the new words on the blackboard,
the ones whose meaning she didn't know, whose exact purpose she ignored.

That evening, as she was putting her younger brother to bed, he asked once again: "When am I going to go to school?" But that evening she didn't laugh, and she didn't think up an answer. She sat down and hugged him for a while, as she used to do every time she realized how little he was, how little he knew. And she hugged him harder because she suddenly imagined him in the middle of the school yard, with his arm stretched out measuring the distance, the body tense, feeling cold and angry and afraid, in a line in which all the others were as small as he was.

And the next time the teacher got mad at the class, Celeste knew what she had to do.

She didn't lift her arm.

The teacher repeated the order, looking at her somewhat surprised. But Celeste wouldn't lift her arm. The teacher came up to her and asked her, almost with concern, what was the matter. And Celeste told her. She told her that afterward the arm hurt. And that they were all cold and afraid. And that one didn't go to school to be hurt, cold, and afraid.

Celeste couldn't hear herself, but she could see her teacher's face as she spoke. And it seemed like a strange face, a terribly strange face. And her friends told her afterward that she had spoken in a very loud voice, not shouting, just a very loud voice. Like when one recited a poem full of big words, standing on a platform, in the school's front yard. Like when one knows one is taking part in a solemn ceremony and important things are spoken of, things that happened a long time ago, but things one remembers because they made the world a better place to live in than it was before.

And almost every girl in the class put down her arm. And they walked back into the classroom. And the teacher wrote a note in red ink in Celeste's exercise book. And when her father asked her what she had done and she told him, her father stood there staring at her for a long while, but as if he couldn't see her, as if he were staring at something inside her or beyond her. And then he smiled and signed the book without saying anything. And while she blotted his signature with blotting paper, he patted her head, very gently, as if Celeste's head were something very very fragile that a heavy hand could break.

That night Celeste couldn't sleep because of an odd feeling inside her. A feeling that had started when she had refused to lift her arm, standing with the others in the line, a feeling of something growing inside her breast. It burned a bit, but it wasn't painful. And she thought that if one's arms and legs and other parts of one's body grew, the things inside had to grow too. And yet legs and arms grow without one being aware, evenly and bit by bit. But the heart probably grows like this: by jumps. And she thought it seemed like a logical thing: the heart grows when one does something one hasn't done before, when one learns something one didn't know before, when one feels something different and better for the first time. And the odd sensation felt good. And she promised herself that her heart would keep growing. And growing. And growing.

Remembrances of Things Future

——————————————————————————————

MARIO SZICHMAN (b. 1945)
Translated from the Spanish by Iván Zatz

Critics concur in viewing the author of this sardonic tale as the true Latin American inheritor of the tradition of self-denigrating Jewish humor. His famous novel At 8:25 Evita Became Immortal *(1981), which won the Ediciones del Norte Prize, describes the three-decade-long pilgrimage from immigration to assimilation of the Pechoff family in Buenos Aires, complete with their change of name to Gutiérrez-Anselmi to hide their Jewish identity.*

Set in Poland in 1939—according to the Hebrew calendar the year 5700, a time when Argentine Jews, victimized by the Semana Trágica pogrom and other blunt anti-Semitic attacks, were beginning to recognize the nation as incapable of sustaining democratic values and tolerance—this comic story, published here for the first time, deals with the bombing of Jewish schools, both progressive and Orthodox, and the response of government authorities to Jewish resistance. The narrative viewpoint is that of the mother of Shmulik the galley-proof messenger, a poor woman unable to understand the political implications of her son's unexpected disappearance. The implicit themes, of course, are the Holocaust and Jewish self-hatred.

AT THE TIME that the people in Pinye Ostropoler's town began to search for the whereabouts of their family members, the postman got into the habit of calling twice at first, and three times by the end, until there was no one left in any condition to receive the mail.

Every morning of that hazard-filled year of 1939, the postman would show up in his impeccable gray suit, and with a smile he would present the good news. In the afternoon, he would show up rigorously attired in mourning clothes, to deliver the instructions to one of the neighbors. It never failed that someone in town would think, "I am sure that someone in my neighbor's family must have done something to deserve these instructions." And those suspicions were usually confirmed. The instructions would order the neighbor to go to the town's century-old tree and pick up a message left atop the fourth branch from the bottom; thus he would find out that his relative's whereabouts had been lost after his becoming an infiltrator. It was signed, "A friend." Usually, after reading the letter, the neighbor would pack up his bundles and take a chartered ship to other lands—ridden by guilt but never by fear, for Poland was a country endowed by laws of a profound humanist content, a beautiful tradition went hand in hand with its population, and may God grant you peace.

One of the few occasions on which this routine was broken happened with Shmulik's mother. Shmulik was the galley-proof messenger. Until receiving the instructions and finding out that his whereabouts were lost after his having become an infiltrator, the woman had been proud of her Shmulik, because his official whereabouts had been a calendar factory in the mountainous region of N. The woman had thought that such whereabouts were immutable, for she had told her Shmulik the fable of the naughty boy who was kidnapped by the monkey after having taken his hands out of his pockets; and so her son never dared to play around with his own buttons or his salary, thus reaching a position where he earned money by the fistful.

When the poor woman received the instructions, she asked Pinye to come along with her to the tree because she did not know how to climb it. Pinye collected the message and that is how the woman found out that it seemed as if her son's whereabouts had been lost. "If you had shown concern for your little treasure's whereabouts, you would have known by now that he is taking his hands out of his pockets. It takes only one step from that to becoming an infiltrator," said the message, signed by the usual friend.

"How did I go wrong?" wondered the poor woman. Perhaps she had given her Shmulik a secular education? But that had been the only way to keep him out of the fun and games. Other kids of his generation had decided sometime in their puberty to take their hands out of their pockets, and there you have it now: they spend the entire day with their noses stuck in some Talmudic scroll trying to find their whereabouts in an unattainable past splendor, while their women take food out of their own mouths to keep the children fed. But not her Shmulik. Deprived of the use of his hands, Shmulik had to rely on his nose to find the right way to go, and from having used it so many times to steer the sled during the winter, its shape was now aerodynamic. Besides, at the Hebrew calendar-printing shop where Shmulik worked, they were not interested in the past but in the years to come. This was something that, in that year of 1939, the Jews demanded to see in block letters, since they considered it beyond reach. That is why all the members of the community would fight to get calendars; they wanted to lay their hands on a tomorrow riddled with seasons and ceremonies evocative, first, of their martyrs and then of their heroes, sure that the massacre at the hands of Chmielnicki would always be rescinded by the victory of Bar-Kochba.

The calendar-printing shops could not keep up with the demand, and Shmulik's capacity to maintain his hands in his pockets was highly valued, because his long arms allowed him to create huge openings that the typographers would stuff with galley proofs. And, with a slight turn of the head, Shmulik could follow the direction of the wind at twice the speed of other galley messengers.

The owner of the calendar shop rewarded such skill by depositing two hundred zlotys in Shmulik's cap every month. This allowed him to pay for his room and board with a family, whose members were in charge of putting the spoon in and out of his mouth, unbuttoning his clothes, and mending his pockets; even so, he still saved 120 zlotys, which he sent his mother through Nusn, the water carrier.

Shmulik had won eight prizes for best messenger of the month, and the medals clinked proudly on his cap. The owner of the calendar shop had even hinted that there was a possibility of making him a partner. And out of the blue, all this was about to be thrown out the window because the selfish child decided to take his hands out of his pockets—such was the mother's lament to Pinye. Instead of feeling guilty on account of the message in the tree and packing up her bundles, the mother decided to search for her son's whereabouts so she could reproach him for his sudden decision to ruin his own life.

Pinye listened to the woman's grief and counseled patience. Maybe Shmulik had no further need of a whereabouts. The poor woman, however, was not ready to resign herself. Everyone must have a whereabouts, ran her argument. Pinye suggested that perhaps her son had taken his hands out of his pockets to reach for a bottle and, stupefied by the alcohol, had awakened the next day married to a Gypsy. One of those days while the mother was needlessly worrying, the son would be getting ready to give her the great *nakhes* [happiness] of making her a grandma.

The woman reproached Pinye for his insensitivity. It was clear that he had not been the one to give up his life to provide her Shmulik with an education, she told him. Her son was incapable of doing such a thing to his mother.

To placate her, Pinye recommended that she treat her son not only as a youngster who is respectful of tradition but also as an ingrate about to lose his whereabouts. The poor woman, disturbed by such words of consolation, sent a letter in the next morning's mail to the calendar shop where Shmulik worked, demanding to know his whereabouts. She was one of those old-fashioned mothers whose only concern was to devote her whole life to her son, the letter stated.

When the poor woman received a reply by telegram, indicating that the company could not furnish such information and asking her to please not compromise them further, she decided to modify her strategy by sending reproaches written directly on the envelope. She had the habit of addressing her complaints to "The Ingrate Who Is About to Lose His Whereabouts." None of her letters received a reply.

The poor woman came back to Pinye for advice. What did he suggest she do? She did not intend to rest until she found out her son's whereabouts. Wouldn't it be best to go to the police and search in the Missing Persons Bureau? Pinye pleaded with the poor woman not to involve any of the authorities until she knew what to expect. Could she have possibly forgotten about Gitele? She had searched for a half brother who had been accused of becoming an infiltrator. And what happened? When the authorities finally discovered where he was, Gitele remembered that she had had a whole brother before his disappearance. Pinye recommended that the woman wait for a while. The best thing would be to carry out some discreet inquiries. He could take care of the matter.

The woman thanked Pinye for all the trouble he was taking and this time sent her letter in the afternoon mail, addressed to the owner of the calendar-printing shop. In it she worried about the whereabouts of her son, so respectful of tradition but an ingrate about to ruin his own life. In the postscript she implored the heavens to let there be no suspicious contents in the packages her Shmulik carried.

The owner of the calendar-printing shop received the woman's message, went to the town's century-old tree, collected the letter, and read it, fearing that he had sullied his family name because of some infiltrator. He rolled it up into a ball, threw it into some bushes, packed up his bundles (among which were several boxes with brand-new calendars), left his house in the late hours of the night, and took off for other lands in a chartered ship, the *Cracow Baroness*. The ship obtained denials of asylum in Southampton and Reykjavik and wound up stranded in the Sargasso Sea. Some of the calendar packages were jettisoned to sea when the captain decided to lighten the load on the ship, and they ended up washing ashore in Calais. The cryptographers of the French intelligence service analyzed the calendars and determined that they were texts in code from German spies confirming the invulnerability of the Maginot Line.

Meanwhile, the letter sent by the poor woman to the owner of the calendar-printing shop was found by a park ranger, who unfolded it, smoothed out its creases, examined it by flashlight, adjusted his cap, scratched his head, thought that "he must have done something to deserve this message," and immediately notified the authorities.

The following day, the police were ordered to discreetly surround the printing shop in order to capture the poor woman's son. They knew the infiltrator's description very well: he generally walked around with his hands in his pockets and carried around packages suspicious in nature, as attested by the postscript in the letter written by his mother and the hurried departure of the printing-shop owner.

That afternoon, the police investigation met with success. A stranger, his cap covered with medals, crossed a checkpoint on his sled, carrying two suspicious-looking packages under his arms. When asked about what he carried, he replied that they were galley proofs from over there, pointing toward the printing shop with his aerodynamic nose, since he had his hands in his pockets. The policemen exchanged knowing glances and allowed him to infiltrate the place.

Not ten minutes had gone by when the bomb squad arrived and placed an explosive charge among the suspicious packages, blowing them up. A

hole the shape of the foundation was left where the printing shop had previously stood. And exactly in the center of that hole were the remains of a
sled, a cap covered with medals, and two suspicious-looking packages, somewhat tattered but able to be collated. They contained galley proofs full of
foreign-language characters.

The chief of police, fearing a conspiracy, called an expert in ancient languages, who confirmed his worst suspicions. Someone, in 1939 in Poland,
was sparing no effort to fire up the minds of the Jews, filling them with nonsense about the future. And what a future! In a few months they expected to
reach the year 5700. The chief of police ordered barricades built on the main
access roads to the printing shops to prevent the presence of new infiltrators.

The next day, the poor woman was informed of her son's death in a confrontation with the forces of law and order. Inside the medals on his cap
they had found microfilm strips detailing a conspiracy on the part of some
Hebrew calendar makers, whose intentions were to sow dissent.

That night, fearing that they had inadvertently sown dissent, the three
most important Hebrew calendar makers packed up their bundles, among
which were some boxes of brand-new calendars, left their homes in the
late hours of the night, and took off to other lands in a chartered ship,
the *Countess Petrovia*—ridden by guilt but never by fear. The passengers
obtained refusals of asylum in Hamburg and Oslo, and their ship finally
ran aground in Antwerp, where they were interned in a concentration camp
as prisoners of war.

Some of the packages were analyzed by cryptographers of the Belgian
intelligence service, who determined them to be messages in code from German spies recommending respect for the neutrality of that country.

Meanwhile, in Pinye's town, the police were able to quell dissent by blowing up suspicious-looking packages, which Shmulik had dropped off at the
doorways of various printing shops before his confrontation with the forces
of law and order.

When there wasn't a printing press left untouched, the Hebrew calendar makers met in the barn they were allowed to use as a synagogue to
undertake the analysis of their current historical juncture. Might it be that
anti-Semitism was happening in their region, they inquired. But a delegate
from the Jewish Congress asked them to pipe down, because it wasn't as if
they lived (a) in Germany, where the official policy was to stick a yellow star

on every Jew; or (b) in the Ukraine, where the official policy was to drag out the Jews into the main street, chained by the neck, and make them fight the bear while the stationmaster refused to sell them tickets to travel, not even on the roof of the train; or (c) by all means not in Russia, where the czar's official policy was to deny any participation of the Black Cossacks in the pogroms, while Rasputin went around curing all his children, turned into hemophiliacs by the Jewish conspiracy. Given that anti-Semitism was not an official policy, the best thing was to turn to the local authorities, recommended the delegate from the Jewish Congress while pulling up his lapels, since the heat radiated by the gathering of malnourished bodies could not sufficiently counter the cold that entered through the hole where once the roof had been.

Pinye then told the delegate about the disgrace heaped upon the poor woman. One of her messages had fallen into the hands of the local authorities, with results known to everybody. Her ignorance of her son's whereabouts had begun to get every printing shop blown up.

"Couldn't it be that her darling little treasure had been mixed up in some mess?" asked the delegate. "'Cause there are printing shops, and then there are printing shops. It isn't the same to have an Orthodox printing shop as a *progressiver* one. Take the Jews of Tarov, for instance. Their schools started to get blown up. But there are schools, and then there are schools. It is not the same to have an Orthodox school as a progressiver one." They could ask Lubcek, right there in the flesh, how the Jews of Tarov confronted their situation.

Lubcek, the Hungarian, explained to the gathering that the blowing up of Orthodox schools caused the children to go back home, while the blowing up of progressiver schools caused the children to be twice lost. "When they blow up one of our schools," said Lubcek, the Hungarian, "our children stay home and play all day. They don't get tired of playing, the little blessings from God: Oh, how they play! Then we feel remorse, we go to the synagogue, the rabbi reads some chapters of the Talmud where the prophets have foreseen that this would come to pass by reason of the sins we have committed, and we rebuild the school in double shifts so that our children are not deprived of their education. The government sends a communiqué, addressed to the noble and suffering Hebrew community, promising a deserved punishment to whoever is held responsible, and Father Zozim, chaplain of the local chapter of the Black Cossacks, comes to the reopening of the facility. On the other hand when the progressiver schools are blown up, all the students go underground, the government uncovers a conspiracy to have the throats of its most distinguished citizens brought to the guillotine, and one of the subversives always ends up murdered at the hands of one of his own comrades so that they can pin the blame on the police."

The people attending the meeting decided to send a petition to the authorities begging for their case to be considered. After all, they were Orthodox calendar makers, not progressiver.

The calendar makers were met with open arms by the mayor; the blowing up of their printing shops had deprived him of the 20 percent levy on alien activities. The mayor offered them tea with lemon and they all celebrated when he drank it in the Russian manner, clenching a lump of sugar between his teeth. After praising the noble and long-suffering Hebrew community and announcing a new luxury tax to be collected by his son on the first and fifteenth days of every month, the mayor ordered the chief of police to extend any and all necessary protection to the calendar makers. And more.

Regrettably, the overzealousness of the police was detrimental to the activities of commerce; with their eyes ruined by the profusion of searchlights looking for clues in their facilities and their behinds injured by poorly trained guard dogs, the majority of the calendar makers decided to leave in a chartered ship, the *Monrovia Duchess*. The travelers were able to obtain denials of asylum in Havana and Barranquilla, they crossed the Strait of Magellan, and from there the ship went straight to the Sargasso Sea, where it ended up stranded next to the *Cracow Baroness*.

Meanwhile, six Hebrew calendar makers who had been unable to take the ship on time with the rest of their colleagues were summoned by the chief of police to his office. On the functionary's desk was a cookie jar that read "Citizens for Responsibility Fund." The chief of police said that he had called on them to exhort them to renew their labor. He reminded them that their country was endowed by laws of a profound humanist content, a beautiful tradition went hand in hand with its population, and may God grant them peace. No one was forced to embroider a yellow star on their clothes; nor were they forced to go out on the street to fight the bear, and, moreover, stationmasters allowed Jews to travel on the roof of the train. They were living in the year 1939, this was Poland, and, moreover, the noble and long-suffering Hebrew community expected to reach in a few months the year 5700. The indigenous population thought this difference to be an unfair privilege. Why not try to make the Hebrew calendar gradually come to match the Gregorian one? If they could find a way to bridge that gap, he would be very grateful to them. He appealed exclusively to their sense of duty. Indeed, he considered them to be responsible citizens. Or at least responsible. Discussions about their citizenship would come later. By the way, any contribution of two hundred, five hundred, or a thousand zlotys was entirely left up to the donors.

The calendar makers, mindful of the appeals from the chief of police, decided at that moment to begin producing calendars with increasingly lapsed dates in order to bridge that gap. The victory of Bar-Kochba continued to be marked, but the massacre of Chmielnicki was abruptly deleted, eliminating in one blow four hundred years of *tsuris* (misfortune). One of the makers even proposed to follow the suggestion of an expert on Delaporte calendars to limit each month to twenty-eight days. He figured out that this way, in a thousand years the Jews would be able to accomplish a history almost as wretched as that of the Polish people. But the proposal was discarded, since it meant that every year would begin exactly on the same day, obviating the need to make new calendars.

Afterward, the calendar makers began competing with each other to see who could avoid the most years of calamity. For instance, when one of them decided to cancel 1321 because that was the year of the Chinon Massacre, another responded by eliminating with one pen stroke the years 640 and 1096, thus wiping out the campaign of forced conversions in Byzantium and the Crusaders' massacre in Ratisbon. Each time they were able to eliminate a few years from their calendars, the makers would appear before the chief of police, proudly demonstrating how the gap between the Hebrew and Gregorian calendars was decreasing. "We have already reached 4383, but that won't be all, that won't be all," the spokesman for the calendar makers would inform the chief of police. "It is my belief that, within a short time, we will be able to achieve even less history than the Swiss."

Clearly, the zeal that went into excising their past would sometimes limit the horizon of the calendar makers, like the time they discarded 1492 to eliminate the expulsion of the Jews from Spain and were left with the Americas yet to be discovered. But the dwindling Jewish community did not complain about such potholes. The calendars had returned happiness to them, and they did not wish to lose it by clinging to historical rigor, for life itself already is full of sorrow.

Meanwhile, the poor woman who had lost her son's whereabouts in the confrontation, with the force of law and order received 120 zlotys from Nusn, the water carrier, accompanied by a newspaper clipping reporting the strange presence of a man with his hands stuck in his pockets ten minutes before the printing shops were blown up in places as remote as Radom, Kielce, and Pwtrkow. The latest conflagration, said the reporter, had propelled the stranger toward the *Monrovia Duchess*, a ship scheduled to make stops in Havana and Barranquilla.

Mad with joy, the mother ran to show the clipping to the chief of police, who, upon seeing the reappearance of the likeness of someone who had died in a confrontation with the forces of law and order, searched in the Missing Persons Bureau, removed one name from the list, inserted it in the list of people who had died in a confrontation with the forces of law and order, placed the poor woman's son in the list where that recently found person had just been, and decided to apprehend the infiltrator dead or alive.

Initially, the chief of police had thought of continuing to quell the pockets of dissent with the help of the bomb squad. But immediately afterward, torn between the need to deal with the purveyors of social schism and the problems of the Internal Revenue Service, he decided to convene the calendar makers and ordered them to immediately report to him the presence of any infiltrator with his hands in his pockets. Furthermore, he informed them that as of that moment, they were to mark the national holidays in their Hebrew calendars, which carried a 10 percent tax on indigenous activities. And until the new collecting office could be set up, they would be able to deposit their tax payment in his personal account.

The Hebrew calendar makers gladly accepted those demands. They had no problem in reporting the presence of infiltrators, since they had been informed that the latest whereabouts of Shmulik's likeness was reportedly aboard the *Monrovia Duchess*, near the Sargasso Sea. As for the other part, they were enthusiastic about sharing their calendars with the Polish people, since that could only increase their sales.

However, upon inspection of the indigenous Polish calendars, the makers stumbled upon an unexpected difficulty. It might have been that those calendars were made in poor-quality printing shops, or perhaps it was due to negligence on the part of the historians, but the fact was that the majority of the national holidays coincided with the celebration of some pogrom.

The Hebrew calendar makers were in a real quandary. If they entered the national holidays they would lose all their Jewish clients; if they left them out, the protection offered by the local authorities would cease. Perplexed and undecided, they opted to ask for an appointment to see their protector.

The chief of police received them in his office and told them he was at their disposal. When the calendar makers presented him with their dilemma, the chief of police responded that they lived in a free country. There was no prior restraint, mail was not opened, and there were no laws or suspension of constitutional guarantees, a beautiful tradition went hand in hand with the population, and may God grant them peace. If they wished to continue making calendars without mentioning those dates on which the precious blood of the Polish people had been spilled, well, that was up to them.

That night, five of the six calendar makers tossed their few belongings into their trunks and took off aboard the *Moscovia Princess*, intending to join their old colleagues. The travelers were denied asylum in Valparaiso and El Callao. Even the Bolivian authorities offered to reject them, despite the fact that their nation lacked any access to the sea. Finally, the ship stumbled upon the *Cracow Baroness* and the *Monrovia Duchess* in the Sargasso Sea. The emaciated passengers of the *Cracow Baroness* and the *Monrovia Duchess* were transferred to the *Moscovia Princess*.

After meeting with denials of asylum in some minor ports, the *Moscovia Princess* ran aground in Antwerp, near the *Petrovia Countess*. While the combined passengers of all four ships were being interned in a prison camp, the Second World War broke out and they were liberated by the Nazis, who mistook them for Croatians. The calendar makers gathered their dwindling belongings and fled on to France. The war caught them by surprise over there, and they were forced to hide in caves and survive on wild truffles and strawberries. When the liberation took place, they were put in front of the firing squad, first because they spent the years of hardship living like Persian kings, and second because the code messages in their calendars had proclaimed the invulnerability of the Maginot Line, allowing their French patriots to rest on their laurels.

With respect to Shmulik's mother, every month she continued to receive

120 zlotys through Nusn, the water carrier, during the first two years of the war, and 200 zlotys from the last calendar maker left in town. The only thing that the calendar maker asked for in return was confirmation of Shmulik's definite absence from the town.

Armed with the newspaper clipping provided by the poor woman, and hoping to stay in business, the calendar maker decided to make use of the infallible recourse of currying official favor by plastering his calendars with previously forgotten national holidays safely distant from the dates of the pogroms. Everyone was happy, especially the Polish people, who for the likes of them had never imagined the existence of so many victories. Nonetheless, even with the greatest of effort, it was impossible to find a full supply of national holidays. Some months had to be fixed by including the Miraculous Apparition of the Virgin. For other months, the calendar maker would add mottos such as "Do not forget that next month we have a bounty of national holidays" or "There are only fifteen days left, how much can two weeks matter when we already have an important national holiday coming up?" But then came a recalcitrant month. There wasn't a single national holiday that could bring about any popular enthusiasm; nor was there a single Miraculous Apparition of the Virgin, and the next month marked a patriotic victory that had left the nation with 62,500 square miles of unredeemed territory provisionally occupied by Germany and Russia.

The calendar maker thought and thought about it and finally arrived at what he supposed to be a good way to solve this. "Fortunately, as soon as next month's victory goes by, we will have something to celebrate," he wrote. But he would not be in any condition to do so.

Conversely, Shmulik's mother was able to celebrate her reunion with her son. One day she received a letter from Shmulik that announced his return and detailed his odyssey, starting with his escape from the explosions and ending with his arrival in Spain. The first detonation, he explained to his mother, had blasted him a distance from the shop, making it impossible for him to collect his cap filled with medals. After getting away from that place, he had been very busy dropping off Hebrew calendar galley proofs in the doorways of other printing shops, but the explosions kept throwing him farther and farther away, until he ended up without a job. At that moment, he discovered that there was no further purpose in going about with his hands in his pockets. He tried other fields of endeavor, but word had been getting around that his nose was like a magnet for the bomb squad, so he chose to get away, for a while, from everyone he knew. That was the reason he went aboard the *Monrovia Duchess*. Until things cleared up, the poor woman's son said the best course of action was to travel, to be at one with nature, to spend each night under a different sky. In order to avoid new temptations, he had decided to begin proofreading captain's logbooks written in unknown languages. He was particularly interested in ignoring the language used in the logbook of the *Flying Dutchman*. But the log was sewn together with a grammar of the Bru language, the tongue of an Austro-Asiatic people, and Shmulik had become so fascinated by its complexity that he gave up all suspicion and studied it until he became an expert. Did his mother know that the Bru language had forty-one vowels? Thanks to that newly acquired knowledge, he was able to find out in the captain's logbook the way to free the ship that had run aground and pilot it over to Amsterdam, where a mine sent them flying through the air. Holding onto a piece of wood, Shmulik had floated all the way to Copenhagen and was able to seek refuge inside a windmill. He now figured that it would take him two more days to reach his hometown. Perhaps, he told his mother, they could get together under the century-old tree.

This time, the poor woman decided to seek Pinye's advice before taking action. Pinye suggested to her that there were sons, and then there were sons. It wasn't the same to have an Orthodox son as a progressiver one. The problem was that Orthodox children would return home in difficult times. On the other hand, progressiver children died twice. Why didn't she consider her son to be progressiver and thus lose him a second time?

The next morning, the poor woman went in tears to the *Free Tribune* news office and announced that she no longer had to know her son's whereabouts, since she had found out that he was dead. That very night the poor woman put her meager belongings in a trunk and left to meet with her son. The reunion was a tearful one.

The next day, the mayor read in the *Free Tribune* that the poor woman's son had been assassinated by one of his own comrades anxious to pin the blame on the constitutional authorities, and the mayor demanded the resignation of the chief of police for falsely attributing his death to a confrontation with the forces of law and order. Furthermore, as a Draconian measure, he decided to increase the postman's rounds to three a day, seeking to make up for losses of tax revenue by confiscating the property of absentee landlords.

A Nice Boy from a Good Family

ANA MARÍA SHUA (b. 1951)
Translated from the Spanish by Andrea G. Labinger

Ana María Shua was born in Buenos Aires. She has published books in various genres and is the recipient of many literary awards. Three of her novels and three of her books of microfiction have been translated into English and published in the United States. Among her many international recognitions, she was awarded a Guggenheim Fellowship for her novel The Book of Memories *(1998). Shua's novel* Los amores de Laurita *(Laurita's Loves [1984]), from which this excerpt is taken, was made into a motion picture. Shua is recognized as one of the principal Latin American cultivators of the* microrrelato, *a genre of extremely short fiction. Her fiction for adults and children has been widely anthologized and translated into many languages.*

LAURITA'S HEAD THROBS as she stands there for a moment, pausing but about to leave, with her hand on the doorknob, as she tries to understand the force of that surprising gust of wind that's lifted her so high, all the way to the seventeenth floor of the Santos Dumont Building on Avenida Gorlero, Punta del Este, to this empty apartment, beside Kalnicky Kamiansky, who, sitting on the floor in his underwear, sobs in anguish, invoking his grandpa León while the radio blares "Hey Jude" by the Beatles.

Her guilt is so evident that it's pointless to try either to justify or refute it. Laurita isn't looking for absolution, just a slightly reduced sentence. At this point she's not even attempting to reconstruct the facts or figure out where her culpability began: when she accepted the invitation to go upstairs and into the apartment or much earlier, when her own grandmother offered to introduce her to a nice boy from a good family and she'd said yes, of course, she'd love to, all too eager to demonstrate that she had nothing against the good Jewish families that were prepared to offer their coveted male offspring on the open market.

The fact is, Laurita was growing bored during that terribly hot summer in Punta del Este, where (as her mother had reminded her once more before they left, as they loaded the car with jars of jam and blocks of cheese because everything was so expensive in Uruguay) such a nice atmosphere prevailed.

A few days earlier, wordlessly rejecting the comfortable, casual old clothes that Laurita usually wore, her mother had taken her to the finest boutiques on Callao, Quintana, and Avenida Alvear, where she'd bought her three new outfits consisting of bell-bottom pants and short-sleeved jackets, a light summer coat, several blouses and shirts, and even a long, golden cocktail gown, an item her mother had declared essential for places like the San Rafael Casino. Feeling humiliated, Laurita had protested and argued with her mother as well as with the blameless saleswomen, but now she was quite happy with her new wardrobe, which her mother had insisted on packing into the suitcase herself, carefully folding the garments to avoid wrinkles, like an experienced hunter who examines, oils, and carefully lays out the weapons that his son must learn to use on their next expedition: Punta del Este, elite game preserve.

The atmosphere, however, was indeed fabulous, and Laurita wasn't about to object to going out with one of those luminous, tanned young men whom she saw and ogled (but never directly) on the beach, those boys who took their parents' cars out at night, speeding along the ocean drive toward unknown destinations, accompanied by slender blondes.

But Laurita had no friends in Punta del Este. She had never been there before and so wasn't familiar with the local rituals of flirtation. Every afternoon she strolled fruitlessly down Avenida Gorlero, bedecked in her best finery, and even though by a week after arriving there she was resigned to the general lack of knowledge of Hinduism, the lack of sensitivity toward the Latin American political situation, the total ignorance of Borges's work, and even the confusion of the subjunctive mood with the conditional tense, not a single gentleman had invited her to join him for a spin in his turbocharged vehicle along that ocean-side speedway.

Hey, where are you from? a smartly coiffed young man had shouted at her from his car after Laurita had endured ten days and ten long evenings of playing knock rummy with her grandma, who, equally devoid of friends and nearly as bored as Laurita, missed the unruly crowds at the Bristol, where everyone or practically everyone spoke Yiddish and drank tea with pastries.

Japan, Laurita shouted back, but as she would later learn, the question made sense because Miguel was from Uruguay, was formally engaged, and in three months would be married forever. And so naturally he was concerned about the nationality of his casual dates and was careful to avoid Uruguayan girls, especially if they were from Montevideo. He tried not to be seen with Laurita in places where he knew he might run into his compatriots. And even though she had liked his opening moves, the way he showed his hand from the start, she couldn't help wanting to take a bit of revenge by refusing to remove her kerchief when he showed up the following afternoon to invite her out for tea and cake at an inn on the road to San Rafael.

Two enormous rollers with their respective clips crowned Laurita's head, which was adorned with seven additional bobby pins that poked their own tiny, curious heads out from beneath the green scarf that covered the masterpiece; a thick, gooey fragrance of Pantene completed the ensemble that any bride, a real bride just three months before her wedding, would never have allowed herself to wear.

On the way to the inn, Miguel stopped his little Fiat and attempted the difficult maneuver of embracing her with one hand while with the other trying to activate the mechanism that would lower Laurita's seat, converting it into a kind of bed. It was obvious from the careful coordination of his movements that Miguel had practiced this complicated operation many times before, and Laurita wondered if there had been an actual woman present during those rehearsals, because Miguel seemed much more interested in completing the maneuver with his left hand as planned than in securing her cooperation with his right.

But the seat-lowering lever was stuck, and Miguel returned to his own place to consider the situation with both hands on the wheel, so demoralized and furious, so absent from Laurita, that he seemed to have forgotten about her completely. Damn lever, Miguel repeated, punctuated by harsh invectives hurled against cars in general, those manufactured in Turin by Fiat in particular, and all the inhabitants of the Italian peninsula and its territories, without even stopping to consider the possibility that Laurita might be willing to move ahead despite the mechanical breakdown. One minute later he let her out of the car and concentrated on dismantling the damaged mechanism, dirtying his hands with grease, huffing and protesting while Laurita stood, bored, by the side of the road.

One hour later they arrived at the inn, both of them in a foul mood. Laurita ordered a waffle with honey and Miguel a lemon pie. They gazed at each other as they ate, revived a little by the sugar. Miguel was a chemist. His father owned an important laboratory. His friends called him Tenfingers—You'll soon find out why, he said with wicked pride, rubbing his legs against Laurita's under the table.

But Laurita never found out why because that very night Miguel came back and announced that his fiancée had unexpectedly arrived in Montevideo, but that he'd try to see Laurita at all costs, would see her, in fact, in very short visits for the rest of that month, never at night, and never for long enough to allow Miguel to develop his seduction technique, that incremental series of advances which, considering the embarrassing failure of his initial attempt, he now considered indispensable to her conquest.

Why not be grateful, then, for the unforeseen arrival on the scene of Kalnicky Kamiansky, deus ex machina, summoned by her grandmother to rescue Laurita from long afternoons devoted to Lautréamont and filled churros, an act of simultaneous consumption that in her mind would forever link Maldoror, terrifying as an eagle, with the taste of sugar on the crispy, golden, slightly greasy crust of the churros. Laurita had always enjoyed reading, but especially in winter: the cold beckoned her to armchairs, solitude, and woolen socks. In the summer it was nearly impossible: the heat gently, acidly called out to her, forcing her to lose herself, eyes heavenward, in the color and texture of the sand.

I'm a doctor, Kalnicky Kamiansky had told her as they walked along the shore, avoiding the jellyfish that evaporated sadly amid the seaweed and oil stains, unfortunate details that it was best to ignore if one was to justify the high price of ice cream and rentals. And, pausing to emphasize what he was about to announce, Kalnicky completed the utterance: not just a doctor but practically a cardiologist. He was specializing, working at his uncle's practice. Kalnicky Kamiansky, pride of his parents, he of the very close-set eyes and ample hips, said that his only regret was that his Grandpa León hadn't lived to see him receive his medical degree.

"Do you know," he asked Laurita, "do you know who León Kamiansky was in the Jewish community?"

But Laurita, alas, had no idea who León Kamiansky had been, let alone in the Jewish community, an entity that had always struck her as a little vague and always intimidating, one with which she'd never maintained a relationship, one to which she so inevitably belonged that it seemed unnecessary to participate in it, its institutions, or its groups.

I am a Kamiansky, Kalnicky Kamiansky, he assured her with enviable pride. Do you know who the Kamianskys were in Russia under the czar? Laurita tried to collect her scattered knowledge of Russia under the czar, but her readings of Tolstoy or Pushkin had nothing to say about the Kamiansky family's activity in the court of the Emperor of All the Russias.

Laurita liked Kalnicky Kamiansky's fierce attachment to his Grandpa León; in fact it was the only thing about him she *did* like, and while he insisted on pointing out the wonders of the apartment that his parents had given him on the seventeenth floor of the Santos Dumont Building, living room and bedroom with an ocean view, she would have preferred to steer the conversation toward the subject of León Kamiansky, deceased leader, philanthropist, temple founder, businessman.

Her parents were happy to see her finally dating a nice boy from a good family: the investment was beginning to pay off, and Laurita wanted to demonstrate her goodwill to the utmost, although she secretly felt it was unfair because, like her, they wouldn't have been able to tolerate the joyous itemization of possessions in which Kalnicky Kamiansky obviously delighted and wallowed: his resonant surname, his university degree, his Peugeot 404, his apartment in the ghastly bulk of the Santos Dumont Building. Kalnicky Kamiansky grossly exceeded the virtues that her parents had expected in a nice boy from a good family.

However, Kalnicky Kamiansky had invited her to dinner. To a restaurant. For seafood. Never before had a man invited Laurita to have seafood with him at a restaurant. Sometimes men had asked her out for coffee and it was perfect: Jungian archetypes with a latte; cultural malaise and spaghetti al pesto at Pippo's. Laurita had even wangled a memorable barbecue at Pichín along with Hegelian dialectics; the mythical horizon and croissants; Engels and Gramsci with a crepe at La Martona, and everything was comme il faut except for the fact that sometimes Laurita had to pick up the check. But never, never before had a man been prepared to make such an investment in her by inviting her to a restaurant in Punta del Este for seafood.

Laurita was touched, shaken, and, above all, astonished to discover this unexpected, whorish vocation of hers: a man was going to spend money for the pleasure of her company, and that pleased her. It pleased her enormously. Women, she had once read—randomly opening one of the volumes of Freud's *Complete Works*, so nicely bound in real leather, so expensive, so official looking—women, because they are polymorphous perverse, are especially suited for prostitution. What nonsense, but it wasn't that sort of polymorphous perverse pleasure that she expected from Kalnicky Kamiansky, but rather to be paid for, evaluated, the as-yet-unknown pleasure of watching a man take money, genuine money, out of his wallet in order to pay a lofty amount for the pleasure of being, of having been, with her. How lovely, Laurita, her mother had said, at last you're going out with a well-dressed, decent boy who takes you to dinner, a nice boy from a good family.

And so Laurita chose moderately expensive dishes, and Kalnicky Kamiansky didn't even wait for the shrimp cocktails, overflowing with Russian dressing and too much lettuce, before explaining that he also owned an apartment of his own in Buenos Aires, Barrio Norte, living room, two bedrooms, two baths, even though for now he still lived with his parents. Ever downward, unaware of the steep precipice over which his words were pushing him, he went on enumerating, taking inventory: my family has a chalet in Los Troncos, a huge chalet, in the neighborhood of Los Troncos de Mar del Plata. It used to belong to my grandfather. You should see the garden, what an incredible garden, said Kalnicky Kamiansky, gazing at her tenderly over the fried calamari.

But Laurita wasn't inclined to go on with the real estate survey; she wanted to enjoy her dessert. Laurita had discovered that all men and women in this world have at least one story, a good story worth listening to; even Kalnicky Kamiansky, doctor-and-practically-a-cardiologist, one-bedroom apartment in Punta, bachelor pad in Buenos Aires, shared chalet in Los Troncos, had one, and it wasn't hard for her to find it, extract it from him. Kalnicky Kamiansky's story was a love story, and it both pained and delighted him to tell it.

It also pained Laurita to listen to it; his boring, meaningless words hurt her ears; it was painful to hear him express an affection that was probably real with the conventional vocabulary and monotonous, hackneyed expressions of a soap opera.

She wasn't Jewish, this true love of Kalnicky (now more than ever) Kamiansky's. She was a neighborhood girl who studied at the Pitman Academy. He loved her dearly, she loved him dearly, but she wasn't Jewish, and he suffered to think of the name Kamiansky, that surname so distinguished by his Grandpa León in the Jewish community, linked with a miserable Sánchez, a common Sánchez, dragged through the mud. Kalnicky Kamiansky had suffered terribly, deliberating over the problem, and when his Grandpa León fell ill he knew he had to leave her. She herself asked me to, you see how much she loved me, she herself asked me to break it off so that she wouldn't see me suffer so much. Don't think my grandpa León said anything to me; he wasn't that kind of person; he never pried into my life; he knew everything, and he just looked at me, nothing else, with those sad eyes of his, and I understood. It was worse when he died. I felt like crap whenever I was with her; it always seemed like my grandpa León was right next to me, looking at me with his sad eyes.

When I have a son (at this point Kalnicky Kamiansky had regained his composure; after a brief pause he remembered the charlotte and was pouring the warm chocolate sauce over the nearly melted ice cream, which overflowed the dish), he said calmly, looking right at Laurita, I want to give him my grandpa's name, but a little more up to date; León is sort of old-fashioned, don't you think? When I have a son, I'm going to call him Lionel.

Later, on the way home, they kissed in Kalnicky Kamiansky's comfortable Peugeot, and Laurita once again had the opportunity to be surprised at herself, at her body, always ready to desire, even a man as radically undesirable as Kalnicky Kamiansky, practically-a-cardiologist, nestled against her chest. Only abstinence, Laurita told herself, could justify this urge, this general, mechanical urge, which chance had at that moment centered on that disagreeable man who was kissing her enthusiastically and ineptly. If you're willing to make me happy, Kalnicky Kamiansky ickily murmured as they said good night, I'll treat you like a queen.

It was hard, then, very hard, to explain why Laurita agreed to see him again the next afternoon, one more date that she'd decided would be their last. Hard to explain why she had allowed herself to be embraced so tightly on that lonely little beach where it was cold, seagulls squawked unpleasantly, and reality dully overcame imagination.

You've made me happy, Kalnicky Kamiansky unexpectedly announced to her, and not even then did Laurita quite understand the exquisite metaphor he used to refer to his orgasms; so summarily had poor Kalnicky Kamiansky come, so abruptly, not even against her body, so drily that she didn't even notice; but many years later it came back to her when an enormously fat taxi driver, after staring at her intently in the rearview mirror, had gushed: I'll give you everything, baby, if you make me happy I'll give you everything, even my Ford Falcon, baby, everything.

You've got to see my ocean-view apartment, Kalnicky Kamiansky had proclaimed on the little beach. You've got to see it: it's wonderful, amazing, a gift from my parents when I graduated from medical school; you've got to see the ocean from the seventeenth floor of the Santos Dumont Building, what a sight, you can't miss it, you'll have to see it.

I don't want to go to bed with you, Laurita told him. No, silly, you've got a dirty mind; you can only think of one thing. I want to show you the ocean, the ocean view, you'll see what an apartment it is; besides, it's empty, there's no bed; it's all mine, a gift from my parents. I'm not going to bed with you, Laurita had repeated in the elevator, as he carefully abstained from touching her in order to demonstrate the purity of his intentions; it was merely a question of showing off his property, his horizontal wealth.

I'm not going to bed with him, Laurita said to herself. So then why are you here, you stupid fool, when you know perfectly well what comes next? And it was true: it had an ocean view, Kalnicky Kamiansky's one-bedroom apartment did, just as he'd claimed, and he insisted on leaving the door open *so you'll see what a dirty mind you have*, and it was empty, I'm going to furnish it next season, we'll see if the exchange rate improves, completely empty, just a portable radio on the wooden floor, it's so hot in here, he said, aren't you hot, it's awfully hot, why don't you take off your shirt? Wanna dance? I said *dance*, that's all, don't think I meant something else, said Kalnicky Kamiansky, that heartbreaker, with incredible subtlety, I can't stand the heat, what a miserable climate, as he stepped out of his pants, a nice boy from a good family in underpants moving to the beat of "Hey Jude" sung loudly over the radio by the Beatles, one of them anyway, whom Laurita's terrible auditory memory was unable to identify.

Laurita's head throbs as she stands there for a moment, pausing but about to leave, with her hand on the knob of the half-opened door, halted by the sobs of Kalnicky Kamiansky, who sits on the floor, crying, invoking his Grandpa León. Why? asks Kalnicky Kamiansky between hiccups and tears, Why does this have to happen to me, Grandpa León, why did you die, Grandpa, why did I have to break up with that nice girl who really loved me, Grandpa, and now I have to get involved with one of those psychoanalyzed Jewish chicks who thinks she's so smart because she's read Mahatma Gandhi's latest best seller, when any woman of mine would live like a queen, Grandpa?

The Closed Coffin

MARCELO BIRMAJER (b. 1966)
Translated from the Spanish by Sharon Wood

In literary terms, Marcelo Birmajer sees himself as a descendant of Isaac Bashevis Singer. His work re-creates life in El Once, the Jewish neighborhood in Buenos Aires. He is the author of Three Musketeers, *among other novels. He also wrote the screenplay to Daniel Burman's movie* Lost Embrace, *released in 2004. "The Closed Coffin" is a vivid tale of friendship and intrigue.*

I'D SPENT THE whole day trying to do this review. I intended to read the book early in the morning and write my comments in the afternoon. But I'd only managed to finish reading just as the evening light was fading, and that was only by skipping numerous pages.

I pride myself on being a reviewer who actually reads the whole of the books he is writing about: if the book is such hard going that I have to deviate from this principle, I don't review it and that's that.

I couldn't entirely blame the author for the fact that the book couldn't be read in one shot. Over the last few months I'd been developing a sort of symbolic affliction: it was harder to read when I was being paid for it.

This book in particular wasn't bad, but you could see the author had let a short story run away with him and it had turned into something else. The publishers had seen fit to publish it as a short novel. Actually the story wasn't so much a long short story as a long drawn-out one, and you could see the difference between those two things in the last part of the tale. It was called *The Lady of Osmany*, and it was about a widow who went to the police because, over a period of several days, she had heard the sound of violent hammering coming again and again from the apartment below in the middle of the night. The incident was part of a police drama of murder, mystery, and maybe ghosts.

Recently I had only been able to sit myself down to read a book with a critical and productive mind when my son had gone to sleep, around twelve o'clock at night. And I still had to wait another half an hour for my wife to take off her makeup and go to bed before I could type the first letters with no fear of any sudden noises interrupting me.

But, as if we were living in a fantasy story, shortly before one o'clock, someone, somewhere in the building, presumably just below me, started shifting furniture around. You could hear the sound of it being dragged, of chairs falling over, even a few blows with a hammer. Maybe someone was moving, or cleaning up at an odd time (when we are awake we always forget that other people are sleeping). Or maybe a neighbor was being robbed and murdered. Whatever it was, I couldn't write with that racket going on. The benign influence bestowed by the early hours of the morning on anybody who was prepared to forgo hours of sleep in order to finish off his labors was being eroded by this unplanned cacophony of sound.

I switched off the computer, picked up a notebook and pen, and whispered to my sleeping wife that I was going to a bar to finish my work. She answered with an alarmed murmur, as if she were replying to one of the creatures that populated her dreams.

Just in case, I tore off a sheet from my notebook, wrote down the same message, and left it next to the door.

Since I got married, I don't usually go out at that time of night, and certainly not to go to a bar. But I had no choice: my deadline for the review was the following afternoon, I had lots of things to do the next morning, and with all that noise I couldn't write.

Before my marriage I would sometimes go out during the early hours of the morning. I suffered anxiety attacks that I could only control by getting out of my house and finding a place where I could watch other faces, cars, or any movement that was more or less normal. Thanks to God, marriage and fatherhood had turned me into a tranquil man once again.

I crossed through the streets of the part of town where we lived and headed for a bar open 24/7 on Agüero and Rivadia. Strangely enough, I didn't feel the heavy melancholy that might have gone hand in hand with the recollection of a habit from a previous age in which I had been a lonely and sometimes tormented man. I felt only the sweet euphoria of the married man, happy to recall the vestiges of freedom that he no longer imagined possible. I chose a large can of beer, a bag of salty snacks, and sat down behind a trio of teenage girls. Their chatting didn't distract me: on the contrary, I began to work eagerly, and looking at them filled the necessary pauses before correcting a paragraph or starting another one. I was so pleased that I treated the book better than it deserved. The beer helped.

Then a man came up to my table, smiling.

He stretched out his hand.

For a moment I thought, "He's the author."

Along with the bangs coming from the apartment below mine, this coincidence could have changed the natural course of my life. But a moment later I realized that the book had lain for the whole time with its front cover facing down on the table and that, from where this man had been sitting, it would have been impossible for him to see what book I was reading.

The man said my name and asked if it was me.

I looked at him, astonished, and finally I exclaimed: "Pancho!"

It was Pancho Perlman.

He was still smiling. I don't know exactly how fat he was, but his face looked as though it was about to burst. It was blown up so much it made his eyes look slanted. He must have been about three or four years older than I was. (I worked it out as if it were his face, and not our actual dates of birth, that marked the distance of time between us.)

The name itself was hardly a difficult one to remember. After all, there aren't many Jews nicknamed Pancho or called Francisco, and he was the only one in the Jewish club where we had met.

But there are details that erase all other traces. Pancho Perlman's father had killed himself when he was a child. And when I was a child too.

I don't know why, but I had gone to the vigil. The Jewish vigil, with the coffin closed. I remembered a cream-colored cloth with the Star of David embroidered in the center of it covering the coffin. I also remembered that the cloth had a cigarette burn on one of the corners, and this had seemed to me to signal the fact that the man had taken his own life.

I didn't ask my parents about this, but for years I remained silently convinced that, when a Jew commits suicide, besides burying him against the cemetery wall they would make a cigarette burn on one of the corners of the cloth with the Star of David on it covering the coffin.

I think I only freed myself of this heretical way of thinking—if I really freed myself of it—when I had to go to the dreadful vigil of a friend who had killed himself in the flower of youth, in the flower of his success, and in the flower of his life in general. I never knew why he killed himself.

I wasn't sure why Pancho Perlman's father had killed himself, either.

I invited Pancho to sit down at my table and began the task of working out how to tell him that I had to hand in a piece of work the following day. Yes, we hadn't seen each other for twenty years; yes, I had been at his dead father's vigil (or *suicided* father, which sounds weird); yes, we had a whole life to tell each other about, and fate had brought us together like an old married couple. But, I had to explain to him, my family needed me to earn money and I had to finish my work.

"Those of us who don't commit suicide, Pancho," I thought with a cruelty that frightened me, "have to get on with things."

"I read everything you write," he said. "You are one of the few journalists I find interesting."

"Thank you," I said. "I do what I can."

"I'm going to get a coffee," he said.

"Look . . ." I began.

But Pancho was already on his way to the counter. He came back with a coffee in his hand.

"They don't let you write everything you want, right?"

"Not at all," I said. "But I have to finish a review now."

"Right now?" he said, disbelieving.

"Right now," I confirmed. "And what about you, what are you doing here?"

Pancho took his time answering.

Finally, unsure as to whether he should open himself up to me or not, he replied: "There are some nights when I can't stand being on my own in the house."

This confession defeated me. I could insist that I had to work, but I no longer had the will to seriously suggest to Pancho that we put off our meeting for another day.

"Did you get married?" he asked.

"I have a son," I said.

Pancho had left the coffee on my table but still hadn't felt sufficiently invited.

"Sit down," I capitulated. "What about you?"

Pancho squeezed his body in between the bench and the Formica table as best he could. A blue shirt, thrust into his pants, pressed against his belly. He wore blue jeans that were frayed at various strange points and suede shoes with no shoelaces.

He hesitated too before answering my question.

"Mine's quite a story," he said. "I married twice and I had two children with the worse one."

"How old are they?"

"Seven and nine," he said. "But my ex-wife doesn't let me see them."

In the silence that followed his dramatic revelation, I decided I would listen to Pancho for however long he wanted and only afterward, whatever time it was, would I finish my piece. I'd get back home just in time to put it on the computer and sleep a few hours before going to my first appointment tomorrow morning. I needed strong coffee.

"I'm going to get a coffee," I told him.

Pancho nodded. A smile of extraordinary happiness spread over his face. It was the serenity of the lone, tormented man who, in the early hours of the morning, had found someone to talk to.

I walked over to the counter thinking about Pancho's simplicity. Sancho Perlman, he should be called. All his life he had been a transparent man. His feelings, his desires, were written all over him even before he could express them himself. With his slightly twisted face, his gestures were even clearer.

Passions and pains did not come to the surface so easily in my family. Each member of my family possessed a fixed expression that bore little relationship to real experience and ran the gamut from sadness to joy, depending on who was standing in front of them. Words came later. And beneath them, without ever being made public either for ourselves or for others, our tragedies and joys. Nobody is sufficiently intelligent to know his own feelings, and my family would never have permitted itself to say something that was not intelligent or about which it didn't know at least 75 percent.

The Perlmans were not necessarily poorer than we were, but they were certainly more vulgar and less educated. The dish they most aspired to was steak and fries, and their classic dessert was crème caramel. They thought we were strange because we liked fish that wasn't simply cod fillet. Betty Perlman dressed very badly, but she tried to swap clothes with my mother. This meant that my mother lent clothes to Betty and, just once in a blue moon, accepted something from her that was always left hanging in the closet and deliberately wrinkled, so Betty wouldn't realize that my mother hadn't actually put it on. Natalio Perlman was more of a practicing Jew than my father, but he knew much less about Jewish culture in general.

My family wasn't especially sophisticated, and we easily fit into the middle class. The Perlmans, however, were squeezed in with the barely definable segment of people whose basic needs have been met but who have no interest in any other kind of need. The Italian grotesque and the Jewish sense of overwhelming bewilderment came to mind with their open mouths when they ate, their clichés and commonplaces when they spoke, and their general lack of interest in the world.

And yet . . . and yet . . . the Perlmans laughed. Not the maniacal laugh of my father or the polite laugh of my mother. They laughed unselfconsciously. They laughed at silly jokes or something that had happened to any one of them. Natalio and Betty Perlman kissed each other. They would go on trips and leave the two children with their grandparents. At times the Perlmans, Betty and Natalio, would scream bloody murder at each other in front of us, and my mother would say to me: "You see, they're all lovey-dovey but really they hate each other."

I never dared to answer her: "No, they don't hate each other. Human couples also yell at each other and get angry at each other. Hatred is what's between you and my father, who never kiss and never yell."

But I had no right; nor did I know enough about couples, whether my father and my mother or Betty and Natalio.

And today I still don't know much about my relationship with my wife; nor did I think Pancho knew why, exactly, he had separated from his wife or why she didn't let him see his children.

"Why did you split up?" I asked him, coming back with my coffee.

"Do you know about the Lubavitch?" he asked.

"Yes," I said. "They even get mentioned in one of my stories."

The Lubavitch were a sort of Jewish "order," with their Orthodox ideas and reformist methods: they used vans with loudspeakers, they organized activities, and they tried to spot who was Jewish in order to offer them a prayer.

"Now you can put them in another story too," said Pancho. "My wife became a Lubavitch. I was always strongly Jewish; in my house we observed all the holidays. But my wife really overdid it. She cut her hair, she wore the skirt, she threatened to let the boys' side-locks grow. Can you believe it? I couldn't stand her. I'm a Jew to my bones, but I also have my traditions and my way of doing things. Now the Lubavitch are telling my wife not to let me see my children."

I was about to say, "What do your parents say to all this?" when I remembered that Natalio Perlman could no longer be counted among the living.

"What about your mother?" I asked.

"She's a wreck," he told me. "She says she doesn't want to live anymore. I'm trying to reach some kind of agreement with my ex-wife, to let my mother see them once a week."

"How often do you see them?"

"Whenever I can," said Pancho.

And he drained the cold coffee still left at the bottom of the plastic cup.

Pancho Perlman, the simple man, wasn't that simple after all. And yet despite it all, he still was. All families, everybody, suffered tragedies throughout their lives: accidents, terrible quarrels, or, as in this case, divorce. What differentiated the simple from the sophisticated was their attitude in the face of each cataclysmic event. Pancho Perlman hadn't taken his neo-Lubavitch wife to marriage counseling. Nor had his wife tried to overcome her frustration with macrobiotic food and yoga. At the first hurdle within her psyche, or her marriage, or whatever it was that was coming apart, Pancho Perlman's wife had cut straight to the chase, gone back to the shtetl, to the pious customs of her forefathers.

And divorce—no dialogue, no calm exchange. Passion and hatred: I never want to see you again, and don't even think about seeing your children ever again.

It was no way to resolve things, and yet it's true that there is, indeed, no way to resolve things. Pancho Perlman and his wife simply knew this before many others did. I just implored my wife not to walk out on me, to be able to stay in my home until my son reached his thirtieth birthday. This was all I needed to keep within the limits of what I thought of as normality.

The only suggestion I could think of for Pancho was to become more observant and, in that way, try to win back his ex-wife. But I didn't dare say it. Anyway, he had gotten married again, while I was beginning to feel a bit hungry and a ham-and-cheese sandwich on wheat bread was clamoring to jump into the microwave. This wasn't the best moment to urge anybody to go back along the path of our ancestors.

I got up to get the sandwich as Pancho was telling me about his new wife, a mulatto from Ecuador.

The book about Señora Osmany seemed like a splendid novella to me now, discreet, appealing, and I could find no fault in its plot development or its length. The beeping of the microwave seemed to be counting the years of my life: I thought about how many good books had missed the chance for a good review just because the critic hadn't taken a few hours more in the early morning and hadn't bumped into Pancho Perlman.

"That would be all right," I thought to myself, "steak and fries, crème caramel, a mulatto from Ecuador."

In his own way, Pancho Perlman had followed the family pattern. And I continued to admire his simplicity. But . . . why had Don Natalio Perlman committed suicide? I've already said—I don't know. Nobody knows why people commit suicide. Neither do we know why we want to live. But committing suicide is strange, while wanting to live is normal.

Natalio Perlman was a normal man. His food was normal, his behavior was normal, his love for his wife and children was normal. It was even normal for him to go to bed with the cleaning lady, the so-called shiksa.

Mary was from Paraguay, and hardly exuberant. She had a decent pair of breasts, and in the club we talked about her along with all the other shiksas. But her breasts weren't much bigger than Betty's, and she wasn't that young anymore either.

Why had this wholly predictable event derailed into tragedy?

Many husbands like Perlman had affairs with either their own servants, a friend's servant, or a Madame X. The most that usually happened was that the servant was sacked, or sent packing, or maybe there was a proper separation. But a suicide?

According to some people, Mary was pregnant. How would I know? It was also rumored that Natalio lost his head over this woman and that she had a husband in Paraguay. My parents didn't believe either of these versions. In my house indulging in gossip or spreading it around was looked down upon. How relieved my parents must have felt when they witnessed the utter failure of simple people!

That's what happens, I could hear my mother say, to those who sneak a kiss at the door, to those who laugh inadvertently, to those who spread gossip, to those who exhaust themselves amid shouts and crazily make up again. That's what happens.

A whole life of constraint, of repressed passions, of measured-out sex was at last rewarded with an indisputable prize: we, darling, do not kill ourselves.

And yet . . . and yet . . . In my family there was a suicide. My mother's brother, no less. At the age of nineteen, my uncle Israel had committed suicide. It was in 1967, and I had just turned one.

The difference between simple families and sophisticated ones in the face of tragedy! I first learned of the existence of my uncle Israel when I was fifteen years old. I mean, in the same moment I learned that he had existed, that he was nineteen years old, and that he had killed himself. As if it were an adoption, my grandmother had guarded the secret of her son's suicide. But her son wasn't adopted; he was dead.

My cousins were told he had died in the Six-Day War. When I was an adult, some ten years after learning of the existence and death of my uncle, the memory of his name sent a shudder down my spine. He had the same name as the Jews' own country, which had been about to disappear at the time my uncle killed himself. The Jews succeeded in defending themselves and their country, but my uncle failed to defeat his inner demons. Just as my young friend failed, and Natalio Perlman too.

And why had my uncle committed suicide? I don't know. Nobody knows.

When my mother ran out of other options she told me some story about psychosis. But this was all very obscure: he'd been a normal boy until he killed himself.

My uncle had been present at my birth and at my circumcision. He had held me in his arms, yet I knew nothing of him until I was fifteen. That's how sophisticated families dealt with tragedy.

The simple Perlman family had wept over Natalio's coffin, they had invited friends and acquaintances to the ritual of tragedy, they had buried him in the Tablada Cemetery—an intimate ceremony with just Betty, the boys, and the grandparents. Jewish tradition exacts a penalty for suicide, and those who die by their own hand are buried against a distant wall and visited only by close family. But everyone around knew he had killed himself.

Gunshot? Poison? I couldn't remember. And I wasn't going to ask Pancho at two o'clock in the morning. My uncle, I knew, had put a shotgun in his mouth, sitting out on a terrace, after being a normal boy for nineteen years.

The sandwich had made me sleepy and I had to go and get another coffee.

When I came back I wanted Pancho to go so I could get back to work. Instead, I heard myself ask, "How was it your father killed himself?"

How could I have asked that? Had I gone crazy? Was this how the scions of sophisticated families behaved? Was this how I followed the family path of rigor and restraint? What happened to the man I was, the man who knew that telling the truth resolved nothing and so the best thing was to talk about trivia and not bother anybody?

Pancho seemed to be looking at me, I thought, as if a dozen questions were going through his head. Is this guy crazy? Is he asking how my father killed himself, or why? And *the way* he asked: Is that coldness in the face of tragedy or compulsion to question an enigma that weighed down on his whole childhood?

I could have answered yes to all of them.

Could there still be a tiny drop of coffee left in his cup? Why was he raising the shapeless white plastic to his lips?

Whatever was still in the cup—damp sugar granules or just emptiness—Pancho drank it.

He looked at the clock hanging on the wall—ten past two—he looked at the three adolescent girls—one of them had fallen asleep—and he said: "My father didn't kill himself."

There followed a dialogue in which all my retentive capacities were overwhelmed. I didn't know if I was asking what I wanted to ask. I didn't know what I wanted to keep quiet about or what to say. I didn't know what I wanted to know. I was sure, and I think from that moment onward I will always be sure that, whatever I knew, it would not be the truth.

"Was he killed?" I asked.

"No. He's still alive."

The closed coffin, the cloth with a burn in one corner, the tears of a simple family—all a fraud.

Natalio Perlman had run away with the shiksa. Betty Perlman couldn't accept this and told everyone he was dead. She had held a vigil for him in her house. She had made the whole town believe he'd killed himself.

Her father, mother, and in-laws had permitted her to say Natalio was dead. They had driven in the vigil cars, I don't know where to, and then come back again. The children had been told the truth: that he had run away with Mary. But for the rest of the world, Natalio, his father, had killed himself.

I saw Pancho for a few years after the death of his father. If I remember rightly, the last time was just after my bar mitzvah.

I don't know if, after that, he managed to keep the secret the way he did with me. And I didn't ask him then, at two-thirty in the morning.

I imagine he told his wife and children the truth. And I imagine that telling them the truth made no difference at all. There are few affections of the soul that can be communicated. Would he really have told his wife and children the truth? What for?

Wasn't it better to let them believe that their grandfather and father-in-law was dead rather than recounting the unrecountable tale of a woman who falsely grieved for her runaway husband?

In my mind's eye I saw the mark on the edge of the cloth, and I felt a wave of nausea. I got up and ran to the restroom. But as I looked at myself in the mirror, instead of vomiting, I understood: the mark in the corner of the cloth wasn't a mark of suicide—it was there to tip off the insiders that the coffin was empty.

"Don't worry, boys, the coffin's empty. This is all a farce."

I went back to my table, mentally talking to my mother. "You see, Mother? People who sneak a kiss at the door, who laugh and yell, not only do they not commit suicide, they don't die at all."

"That shocked you, didn't it?" asked Pancho.

I nodded.

"How could you keep that a secret?" I asked him.

He shrugged.

"But I suppose my grandmother managed to wipe out the existence of her son, as far as I was concerned at least, for fifteen years."

"He's in Argentina now," he told me.

"Who?" I asked.

"My father. Natalio."

I looked to see if there was anything else to eat or drink, but nothing appealed to me.

"The Paraguayan woman left him, probably about ten years ago now. They didn't even get to Paraguay; he found out she was married. Or that she had a man at least. My father ended up subsidizing their marriage. The other one was the lover, and my father was the cuckolded husband."

"Did he come back recently?"

"It was to try and make things up to my mother. He let her go on saying he was dead. Besides, my grandparents never forgave him for running off with a non-Jewish woman."

"Why did they let me go to the vigil?" I asked.

"We never knew how you ended up there."

"I think I came to see you," I said, "and suddenly I found . . . found . . ."

"No," said Pancho, "that can't be right."

"Who knows," I said. "We were very young."

Like a hologram hovering in the air, the image of Pancho standing next to me popped into my head, both of us with short pants, trying to work out how to be children, Jewish children, in the Once district in a gentile country. Now we were trying to work out how to be adults.

I looked all around me.

"Have you seen him?" I asked.

"I haven't seen him for two months," he told me. "He's not too good." And he added, with a hidden coherence: "Now that my mom can't see her grandchildren, she needs company too."

"Have they seen each other?"

"I don't think so. He lives in a bed-and-breakfast place."

"What does he do for work?"

"Nothing. He lives off what he made smuggling in Paraguay. Maybe he still has some of his ill-gotten gains."

The words *ill-gotten gains* sounded like a bugle at a wake. A real wake, this time.

"I'm not going to be able to sleep tonight," said Pancho, the simple man.

"I have to work."

"I'll leave you to it," he said.

I was going to say there was no need, but he left. They were, after all, a simple family. Simple people do not commit suicide. At most, they fake them.

The Lady of Osmany was a great book. "It achieves the requirement of any fiction," I wrote, as one of the teenage girls flaunted her enormous and very pretty rear end in search of a bowl of fruit salad, "which is to evade reality in a logical and realistic manner."

COLOMBIA

Temptation

SALOMÓN BRIANSKY (1902–1955)
Translated from the Yiddish by Moisés Mermelstein

Salomón (Shloym) Briansky was a Zionist from a Hasidic family in Poland. In 1934 he immigrated to Bogotá, where he published three volumes of fiction, all written in Yiddish. "Temptation" is a wonderful psychological tale with a Hasidic sensibility.

NATHAN, THE SHOEMAKER from Porisov, a small Jewish village in Poland, came home one evening shortly before his departure for Colombia with a Torah scroll under his arm. With a slight shiver, he lay the holy object down on the table. His wife, Tzipporah, who at that moment stood skimming the broth, froze with the spoon in midair. "What can this mean?" her staring eyes asked in silence. What was a Torah scroll doing in her house? But Nathan—tall and broad shouldered, with a dense, pitch-black beard that framed his full, fleshy cheeks—hardly paid attention to his wife's wide-open eyes. He took off his frock coat, wiped the sweat from his brow with his sleeve, and asked if supper was ready.

"I was about to set the table," Tzipporah said, coming out of her stupor. "But where are we going to eat if a Torah scroll is on the table?"

Nathan quickly picked up the scroll and placed it in the cupboard. Only when husband and wife sat at the table, eating their kasha and broth, did Tzipporah ask whence the holy scroll had come. At first Nathan did not answer, but when his wife repeated the question, he said that an opportunity had arisen to buy it at a reasonable price.

"What is a reasonable price?" asked Tzipporah with amazement. "Since when have you, my husband, become a dealer in Torah scrolls?"

"You've gotten quite good at picking on me!" snapped Nathan. "What a plague of a Jewess you are! You were already told I got it for a reasonable price; now stop pestering me."

From the way the words were uttered, it was clear he could not explain why he had suddenly spent a whole hundred zlotys on a Torah scroll, especially on the eve of such a long trip.

Such were the circumstances that had led to the unexpected purchase: a notification from the post office had arrived that afternoon announcing a certified letter. It occurred to Nathan that this must surely be related to his departure, because the mail he received—such as it was—always had to do with some momentous occasion. He took off his apron, put on his frock coat, and went to claim the letter. It consisted of a thick stack of papers regarding his trip. But they were written in gentile letters, which he was unable to read. He did not trust his daughters to decipher them, even though they had some understanding of the language, so he decided to go to Mordechai Mezritsher, whose son was versed in gentile matters and spoke many tongues.

Mordechai Mezritsher was a small Jew about fifty years old with a pair of lively black eyes that darted around like birds in a cage. He was pleased that Nathan had come by.

"Ah, a visitor. Have a seat, Nathan. What's new?"

"To be frank with you, Mordechai, I have not come to see you but your son. I would like to have him read some papers I have just picked up at the post office. People say he is quite the expert in such matters."

"I wish he devoted his mind to the Talmud instead of immersing all his senses in those heretical books. Then I would have a learned son," sighed Mordechai. "Come in, you are needed to do a favor," he called.

Mordechai's son was a comely, dark-skinned lad with sparkling eyes who sewed bootlegs on a machine all day long and studied during the night. Everything became clear to Nathan after the boy deciphered the papers and explained the details to him.

In the midst of their conversation, Israel-León, the tailor, stopped by. All three of them prayed at the same synagogue, where many craftsmen gathered. The arrival of yet another guest pleased Mordechai, a joyous and animated fellow who did not frown at a drink with close friends. He asked them to sit down and wiped the sweat from his face. "It's terribly hot outside," he remarked. "A cold glass of beer would be a delight." So they sent the apprentice to fetch some bottles of beer.

"What do you think of that, Israel-León?" Mordechai said. "Nathan is fleeing from us. He just got all the papers." He asked Nathan when he planned on leaving, but instead of waiting for an answer he went on.

"Tell me, dear Nathan, what kind of place is that Colombia you are off to? Do Jews live there? Do they have a rabbi, a kosher slaughterer, a synagogue to pray in? And, finally, dear Nathan—may you ever be healthy—how does a Jew like you, close to fifty years old, decide to escape to the devil knows where?"

"Well, what can one do, Mordechai? It's hard to make a living here. And besides, I have daughters to marry off," Nathan said with a sigh.

They remained seated for a while in deep and heavy silence. Nathan's simple words went right to their hearts. The bitter present and uncertain future of all the Jews in Poland were clear to them. Suddenly, Israel-León's voice cut through the silence: "Why should we add more weight to the heart of a Jew who has decided to throw himself into such an adventure? Anyone who wishes to remain a Jew and follow Jewish law can do so, even in the desert. A Jew like Nathan would not undertake such trip lightly. Do you know, Nathan, what has just occurred to me? It would be a wonderful thing if you could take along a Torah scroll. You're setting off for a land where there will be few Jews, if any. Even if a congregation could be gathered there, who knows if they have a scroll? And perhaps God has appointed you to be the first Jew in that faraway land to assemble a quorum for prayer."

"It certainly would be a wonderful thing," agreed Nathan. "But a Torah scroll could cost several hundred zlotys, and where am I to get the money?" For a long moment the wrinkles on Israel-León's brow deepened. Then his face lit up.

"You know what, Nathan? In our small synagogue we have several Torah scrolls. We could give one of them to you, and with God's help you will someday send us money to pay us back," he said.

That very day, between afternoon and evening services in the tailor's synagogue, some ten men gathered. At first, these simple Jews could not grasp what Israel-León was asking of them. Just think, to take a Torah scroll out of the Holy Ark and send it off to a remote place! Israel-León explained that this would be a good deed of which each of them would partake, and they owed no less to one of their members who was about to set off on such a long journey. At that moment, Berl Israel, the main trustee, intervened: "Listen to me. Nathan is one of us. He has worshiped among us for over twenty years. Many of his hard-earned zlotys lie in these walls and in the holy books we have here. I propose that we ask him for a down payment of a hundred zlotys, and with God's help he will mail the remainder to us later."

Hirsh Odeser, who had been Berl's rival for years, grumbled that a general assembly should be convened to decide the matter, but Berl objected that this was not the time for politicking. They resolved to give a Torah scroll to Nathan and celebrated with a few drinks. The blessings and well-wishing lifted Nathan's spirit; true joy, the finest wine of all, warmed his heart. He, Nathan the shoemaker from Porisov, might well have the honor of being the first Jew to bring a Torah scroll to a distant, foreign land.

Half an hour after taking leave of his friends and starting home, his merriment began to wane. The three digits making up the number one hundred appeared suddenly before him in the dark. They danced before his eyes and mocked him with questions: "When did God name you his envoy in charge of supplying Jews with Torah scrolls? It's just a foolish notion that some religious Jew—and an idle one at that—has put into your head. Go back right away, return the scroll, and get back your hard-earned zlotys. It would be a far greater mitzvah to leave that money to your wife and children."

He stood there for a while but suddenly panicked. "Nathan the shoemaker," a hidden voice warned him. "Who are you to play with such a holy object? Do you believe you are purchasing mere leather and thread?"

A shiver of dread ran through Nathan's body. "It is wrong to regard such holy objects lightly," he muttered to himself, trying to apologize. He pressed the Torah scroll to his chest and strode home.

So that is how—along with Nathan's shoe lasts, rulers, hammers, pliers, and files—the first Torah scroll, wrapped in clothes and bedding, sailed over the stormy waters of the Atlantic to that distant, foreign land, Colombia.

The glowing sky hanging over the suburbs on the Atlantic shore poured fire overhead. The burning sun shone on the half-naked black and bronze bodies of porters carrying huge loads. Shopkeepers kept wiping sweat off their faces. Crowds beset kiosks that sold cold drinks. The sound of car horns blended with the loud cries of people hawking lottery tickets and newspapers. Amid this multicolored mass—black faces, curly woolen hair, white pupils of the eyes, and thick hanging lips—one could discern the occasional tourist. Tall, blond, clad in a white suit, with a colonial hat on his head, dark glasses, and a camera hanging from his shoulder, around he walked, contemplating the scene from above, like a wealthy relative attending the wedding of poor kinsfolk.

Under the radiant sky, on the hot steamy asphalt, into the midst of this multicolored cluster, the Master of the Universe had also thrown some fifteen of His chosen people: Jews from towns and villages in Poland, Lithuania, and Bessarabia. Instead of discovering the legendary El Dorado, where gold is raked off the streets, they found fiery climes that fry the brains and a frosty cold that ices the heart. The longing for their homeland gnawed and devoured them, but the way back was cut off. So they trod the burning sand in the streets of the poor neighborhoods. They knocked on doors, and with the aid of a few words of broken Spanish peddled merchandise on the installment plan. Slowly, very slowly, they adjusted to the new surroundings.

The narrow and sandy street was crammed with single-story houses, small shops, and workplaces. Shoemakers sat on low benches by open doors. The sound of sewing machines, sanding planes, and wood saws could be heard throughout. The hoarse, drunken voice of a man trying to drown his bitter fate in alcohol issued forth from a liquor store. White, black, and bronze women trudged about, disheveled and shabby, and bought from odorous groceries and butcher shops. Naked children played in the hot sand, their dirty faces covered with flies. Dogs, tired from the heat, lay about with outstretched paws and hanging tongues, not even caring to chase the clouds of flies away from their bodies.

In this little street, in one of the workshops, bent over an old shoe, sat Nathan the shoemaker. His shirt, damp and open, showed a mighty, hairy chest. True, only a vestige of his once dense beard remained, a tuft barely covering the point of his chin. Still, it was the same old Nathan, the same full, ruddy cheeks, only tanned a little darker. Hardly a year earlier, shortly after treading for the first time the earth of his new home, Nathan had met the few Jews there. He was shocked to discover how they procured their livelihoods.

Two of them, who befriended Nathan, advised him to become a peddler. Among the wares they sold on credit were not only ladies' underpants and slips but also crucifixes and holy images. When Nathan saw such merchandise, he fell speechless. Upon recovering, he stammered: "How can a Hasid like you, Meyer-Ber, ordained as a rabbi, and a pious Jew and a Torah scholar like you, Simon, even come close to such an impurity?" In the old country, Nathan, a typical shtetl Jew, would actually shut his windows to avoid hearing the impure chants of Christian processionals passing by. He could not grasp how others like him could bring themselves to make a living by selling such things.

"Well," said Meyer-Ber, smiling, "making a living may be compared to saving a life, and that is permitted even on Yom Kippur." Nathan still could not fathom this. An infinite distance separated him from such objects; generations had carved out an abyss between him and them. A voice at once within him and from far away in time commanded him, "No, no, never shall you draw livelihood from *their* holy objects."

After some sleepless nights, Nathan reminded himself that he had brought along his shoemaker's tools, stacked away somewhere at the inn where he was staying. He counted the dollars that he had sewn into the shoulder pad of his coat and decided to return to his old trade. It was not hard to find a workshop, and a year passed by as he set on his bench, mending the worn-out shoes of his poor neighbors in the barrio.

One cannot say that the beginning went smoothly. No, it was not easy for him to adapt. First there was the problem of the language. And the craft itself was different here. But Nathan stubbornly overcame all difficulties. Most of all, God's Holy Name stood by him, helping him to succeed. The poor folks of the neighborhood took a liking to the foreigner with the athletic build, who sat on his low bench from dawn to sunset, smiling good-naturedly with his shining black eyes. The quality of his work was good, and he was willing to lend a few cents with a smile. True, he would not become rich this way. But he made a living, praised be God's Holy Name, and always had a few dollars to mail back home. Nathan had even managed to send some zlotys toward the debt on the Torah scroll. He also deposited several hundred pesos in the bank. Some time later, he would return home and live as God had ordained. "Because," thought Nathan occasionally, "what kind of a life is this in this strange land, far from wife and children, bereft of Sabbaths and holidays, without a synagogue, a rabbi, or a kosher slaughterer?"

At other moments, Nathan thanked the Eternal One for bringing him to this new land. Mostly he did so in the evening hours, as he was about to close his shop. The burning sun would start to shrink, becoming a blood-red disk sinking quickly into the pleasant waters of the sea. At such times, Nathan would sit at his bench, unable to avert his glance from the fiery disk that had already reached the horizon. Slowly, the disk would sink into the water. Minute by minute it descended; soon it had dived halfway into the sea. Only a small part could still be seen, resembling a human head trying to peer over the horizon. Then, suddenly, the entire disk had vanished. Only a faint gleam, like a dying flame, remained to color the sky dark blue. Alone, the edges of the horizon reflected the fiery disk, as night arrived in this part of God's earth.

Nathan stayed seated, unable to take his eyes off the Creator's wonders. Serenity enveloped him, especially when he had had a good day. How much would that day's income amount to, converted to zlotys? Nathan reckoned some thirty zlotys. Wait a minute, he thought, as he recalculated. He had never had a head for figures. Why thirty? More than forty. Back in the shtetl he would have been satisfied to earn that much in a week. He thanked the Eternal One for the favor shown him, and his heart swelled with joy and hope. In one more year, he would be able to marry off his two eldest daughters properly, and with God's help, all would turn out fine.

Sometimes, however, he was seized with remorse. It started some two months after he had set up his small shop. One evening, a darkskinned woman about thirty years of age came into the shop. She looked around as if searching for something. When Nathan asked what he could do for her, she asked in Spanish if the maestro could make her a new pair of shoes. He stammered in his broken Spanish that here he only resoled shoes, but in the town he came from he had been the best craftsman, and his shoes were sheer adornments.

"*Muy bien,*" said the woman. Nathan asked her to take a seat. She sat down and Nathan prepared to take her measurements. Not a believer in the new fashion of measuring with a tape, he looked around for a piece of paper. The preliminaries lasted all the longer as his glance began to slide along the stranger's fleshy body. It took him a while to find the right piece of paper, and when he did, it ripped. One could not say that happened intentionally, but everything simply slipped from his hands. His glance fell upon her high and firm breasts, delineated by her tight dress; upon her partially bare back, her round shoulders, and naked arms. When he was finally ready, he asked her to remove her shoe and began to trace her foot on the paper. He felt the warmth of her slight foot on his wide, bearish paws, and a flame rushed through him. His hand started to slide up her leg, higher and higher. Strangely, the woman did not discourage him. Her full body just twitched nervously.

In the course of the few days required to finish her shoes, she came in often. She stayed a bit longer each time, asking innocuous questions. At first, Nathan could not understand why she ordered a pair of shoes from him rather than from one of the big stores. The more he pondered this riddle, the more his imagination presented him the succulent silhouette that ignited his blood with passion. One night, around ten o'clock, as Nathan sat half-dozing in front of his shop, she strolled by. The street was deserted. He greeted her, and she stopped in her tracks. He took her by the hand. She looked around, entered the shop, and stayed until dawn.

As it is written in the Talmud, one sin leads to another. Nathan's blood streamed with turbulence, like a violent river that has destroyed the dam that restrained it, leaving the waters unchecked. After all, no hindrances stood in his way. The women of the neighborhood were drawn to him like flies to honey. Especially the dark-skinned women, who invented all kinds of excuses to come to his shop. The radiance of his pitch-black eyes and his steely arms inflamed their blood.

And Nathan? He drank from this well like a desert wanderer who cannot quench his thirst. He felt as if he had cast away half his age. His sins, which lay like a load on his back, would frighten him from time to time. But that fear was no more than a shadow that vanished as swiftly as it had appeared. Back home, a Jew was held in check by a wife and children. There, he had been a craftsman who worshiped in a synagogue and fretted about livelihood. But here, where there were no obstacles, a man could do whatever he liked. At such times, Nathan would gladly have welcomed a miracle that would cause his strong body to shrink suddenly and become small and thin.

Days, weeks, and months passed. The Hebrew month of Elul approached. True, in the new land, no signs reminded him of the impending Days of Awe. No one blew the ram's horn or knocked on his shutters at dawn, calling him to worship. But looking at his calendar one afternoon, he realized with a start that in a few days it would be time to attend the first services. He panicked. "Master of the Universe," he sighed, "the Days of Awe are upon us, but no preparations have been made." Indeed, it was no surprise that the few Jews involved in prostitution rings should not care about the Days of Awe. But what of Meyer-Ber the Hasid and Simon the rabbi? Had they also forgotten the High Holy Days?

Nathan removed his apron, in preparation to go downtown, seek out Simon and Meyer-Ber, and discuss the matter with them. Just as he was about to leave the shop, a customer came in with some work that had to be done immediately. Soon night had fallen. The store where Simon and Meyer-Ber were likely to be found had already shut. Nathan, dead tired from the day's work, decided to leave the matter for the morrow, when God willing he would attend to it. At that moment, accursed Satan—who will stick his rotten snout in the way whenever a Jew is about to perform a mitzvah—stole into Nathan's heart and gnawed on it like a worm.

Satan demanded an explanation: "In what holy book is it written that you of all people—Nathan the shoemaker—have been appointed by God to organize a Jewish congregation? You brought along a Torah scroll that you had purchased with blood money. If you approach them meekly, you will never recover a single peso. When will you get back the hard-earned money you poured in? How do you plan to repay the debt? If pious Jews like them can trade in images of Jesus and crucifixes, surely you can exploit the situation to recover your money. Don't rush. Take it easy. If they can do without High Holy Day services, so can you."

And because the lust for money is so strong, Nathan heeded Satan's counsel and failed to seek out his coreligionists. Two days passed very slowly, two days that seemed as interminable as the very wanderings of the Jewish people. Nathan's unrest, mixed with helpless anger, grew with each hour that Simon and Meyer-Ber did not appear.

On the evening of the third day, they entered his shop, along with a huge man with a thick, red neck. Nathan recognized the man. Everyone in town knew of his shady dealings, but nobody dared say a word. He was a bully and an informer. On the other hand, he performed favors for his fellow Jews, such as intervening with the authorities on their behalf. He would go down to the port and greet immigrants as they arrived, helping them get the official papers they needed. He also lent them their first pesos. Behind his back, he was called Reuben the Rat, but to his face he was called Don Roberto. Nathan stared at the man with curiosity and surprise. He reckoned that

Meyer-Ber and Simon had come about regarding the matter that weighed so heavily on his heart, but what had this character to do with it?

The three of them sat down. Meyer-Ber spoke first. "As you well know, Reb Nathan, the Days of Awe are approaching. Two years ago there was no possibility of organizing services. Last year, we had the requisite number but no Torah scroll. Today, however, we have a quorum of Jews—may they multiply—and you have a Torah scroll. Therefore it would be a sin not to conduct proper services. So we have come to borrow the Torah scroll from you."

At that, Don Roberto took out one hundred pesos and rasped, "I contribute one hundred pesos from my own pocket."

Nathan listened but did not answer. For a while there was deep silence, during which Israel-León's tightly drawn face appeared before Nathan. His sad and cloudy eyes spoke mutely to him: "Nathan, God forbid! Do not dare profane the great honor the Lord of the Universe has bestowed upon you. He has charged you with bringing the first Torah scroll to a distant, foreign land, so that Jews there might properly worship during the Days of Awe." Nathan harkened to Israel-León's sad voice, and said: "Thank you very much, my fellow Jews. I appreciate your gesture, Don Roberto. You may take the Torah scroll. There is no need to pay." And the first time the melodious call to the Torah was heard in the distant, foreign land of Colombia, Nathan's heart swelled with joy. Silently, he thanked the Eternal One for the privilege granted him: to bring the first holy scroll. And a silent happiness warmed his soul, for God had helped him withstand the temptation to trade for money this very great mitzvah.

CHILE

Solomon Licht

- -

YOYNE OBODOVSKI (b. ?)
Translated from the Yiddish by Moisés Mermelstein

Yoyne Obodovski first settled in Argentina and then lived for twenty-five years in Chile, finally moving to Israel. "Solomon Licht" (licht in Yiddish means "light") is a haunting pogrom story.

THE NIGHT HAD already fallen. The starry sky gazed down, forlorn, on the infinite skyscrapers and the electric signs dazzling with fiery colors, teasing the helpless night, challenging its dominion.

The city was already half-asleep. The wheels of an electric streetcar could be heard from time to time, and the hiss of a late train cut into the nocturnal silence.

Solomon Licht was still awake. He leafed nervously through one book after another. A strange indifference kept him from concentrating. A burden lay upon him, filling the void of his small, square room. Each movement, the slightest shrug, cast a mute shadow on the bare walls. His small figure suddenly grew into a huge silhouette. Solomon enjoyed feeling small, even smaller than he actually was. Uncomfortable within the four gray, bare walls, he switched off the light and climbed up to the roof, where he often secluded himself. Solomon deeply inhaled the air of the approaching spring, his eyes fixed on the clear starry sky. The night and he, it seemed, were both homeless in the neon metropolis.

As he started to pace the wide roof, memories came to him. He saw himself as a child in the small Ukrainian village, where nature bewitched the spirit, urging it higher and higher. He shuddered anxiously and stopped. He closed his eyes, as if deciding no longer to view the events of every day with them. Then he freed his memory to roam the paths and byways of his ever near past.

Almost forgotten episodes, covered in mist, became clear, awakening bittersweet longing within him. The entire village—the inhabitants, surroundings, even the water mill, the croak of frogs, and the dreamy sounds of night—wove into his soul. In his spare time, when he could escape the din of the city, he ceased to be Solomon Licht and became the village itself, spreading the luminous bliss and the fragrant freshness of orchards and meadows.

He shuddered with pain. He opened his eyes and resumed pacing, as if warding off an ominous vision that barred his way back to the past. He heard the melancholy chiming of the church bells, which resounded with sinister boding in the stillness of the village. A peasant mob formed hastily, armed with knives, axes, and scythes. Rifles cracked, as Jews were being chased. A few feet away from him, a fallen friend lay moaning, life draining from his prayerful stare.

Solomon sensed a foggy film over his eyes, and his pace tottered.

Leaning on the railing, he forcefully pressed the palms of his hands against his temples, which twitched as though gnawed by worms. He was tormented by the thought that he was no more than a living gravestone to a murdered village. He was still young and full of lust for life, but his shattered soul hovered between past and present. All his impressions intertwined with that past. There, he had left his roots as well as the sun that warmed and nourished them. He could not accustom himself to the present. The big city, with its din, was alien to him. It seemed to be a gigantic larva feeding on the life juices of its inhabitants, rendering them consumptive. Everything here was artificial: the people were like moving mannequins with hollow souls. They lacked the impulse of nature, inner joy, the melody of divine creation.

Solomon wondered whether he was exaggerating. Perhaps he was the moving mannequin that staggered at the edge of life, then stood like a weed, transfixed. The theaters and coffeehouses were, after all, always crowded. Laughter resounded everywhere. A good show or movie excited people. For Solomon, however, all this was painful. It seemed to him they strove to fill the emptiness of their souls with noise and to drive tedium out of their lives.

That is why they flocked to the theaters and coffeehouses and delighted in petty conversation.

Solomon pondered: By what means could he reconcile himself? The past was cut off, and the present was a gray routine. Where could he take refuge? Solitude gnawed corrosively at his soul, which howled a bitter lament.

Solomon recalled how the same melancholy seized him in his village. A sad tune would issue forth from him and return to the depths of his soul; or rather, his soul and the tune itself would sing to him until his soul emerged renewed and cleansed. Here, however, the tune was nowhere to be found. Or, perhaps, it was roaming in the amusement halls among the tables in the coffeehouses, but no one could perceive it. It was too still, too whispering. Souls that had been hollowed out like barrels could only respond to deafening noise.

The stars started, slowly, to vanish, and the sky became a black stain that frolicked uncannily with the glimmer of the city's tower of light. A cool dawn breeze loitered about the electric cables. The shine of swinging streetlamps danced on the sidewalks and walls. Fatigue afflicted Solomon in all his limbs. Slowly, he climbed down from the roof. As he stood at the threshold of his room, a force pulled him away. In a short while, he was roaming the streets like a stray shadow.

By the time the sun shone as a red disk on the horizon, Solomon was already far from the city. Two rows of gold-shimmering grassland stretched downhill before him. Birds, chirping as they left their nests, greeted the newborn day. Solomon thirstily breathed in the country air and gazed in wonderment. He had found himself anew. All the fibers of his body sang with youthful happiness, and his lips murmured a prayer for the unredeemed souls.

Asylum

— —

ARIEL DORFMAN (b. 1942)

Ariel Dorfman, born in Buenos Aires, wrote about his upbringing in the memoir Heading South, Looking North *(1998). He teaches at Duke University and is the author of plays, poems, stories, and novels, all—like "Asylum"—with a political bent. His play* Death and the Maiden *(1991) was staged on Broadway and made into a movie directed by Roman Polanski. His other works include* Blake's Therapy *(2001),* Other Septembers *(2004), and* Feeding on Dreams *(2011).*

BARRERA LIKED TO tell everyone that he hardly slept at night. No more than a few hours, a few winks, that's what he liked to report to his son each morning, with a smile on his face, almost triumphantly, as if the persistence over the years of that alleged insomnia were a bizarre medal of honor, proof of some strange superiority over other mortals. That's how he'd gotten to where he was in the world, that's how he'd crawled out of poverty and *abandono*, by working more, by sleeping less, not at all, hardly a wink.

But now it had come true with a vengeance.

Si quieres que esto se termine, ya sabes lo que tienes que hacer.

Ever since that initial message in Spanish had appeared on Ricky's screen, ever since then, Barrera wasn't sleeping at night. Not a minute, not an hour. Nothing, nada.

"What does it mean, Dad?"

He had stared at the words on his son's computer, automatically translating them in his head, not quite ready to articulate them out loud, something warning him to beware, but beware of what?

If you want this to end, you know what you need to do.

Ricky looked at him quizzically. "If I want what to end? And what is it they want me to do, these people from this—this Comando Anesthesia who are sending me this—this—? Who are they?"

Barrera shrugged his shoulders. "How should I know?"

"C'mon, Dad. Look at what it says. ASK YOUR DAD. In the subject of the e-mail, see, ASK YOUR DAD."

"Yes, Ricky, I read the subject of your e-mail, thanks, that's why I'm here, that's why you dragged me away from my work, I can read it, I have read it, I still don't know what it means, probably it's just spam, or maybe one of your friends at school thought it would be fun to play a joke on me, a prank . . ."

"You think it's a prank?"

"Spam or a prank. What else could it be?"

And then Barrera had reached down violently over his son's right shoulder and then past Ricky's hand hovering on top of the keyboard; Barrera jabbed down and pressed the delete button, watched the message disappear from the screen, erased, gone, gone forever.

"Hey, I wanted to answer that!"

"No, you wanted *me* to answer, you wanted me to—what?—what were you going to suggest that I translate? *Dear Comando Anesthesia, exactly who the fuck are you? And exactly what the fuck do you need me to do?* and then they respond, *Te dijimos que le preguntaras a tu papá,* and if you studied Spanish like I've been asking you to for—but that's not the point, the point is they'll insist again that I have some sort of answer, and then you'll respond that—though no, in fact, it'll be me doing the work, responding for you, I'm supposed to be the go-between here, right? *Mi papá no tiene la menor idea, my dad hasn't the foggiest idea,* and so on and so forth, back and forth, *mensajes estúpidos* come and go, somebody laughing their heads off at us, at me, wasting my time, wasting your time, even wasting their time, whoever the hell they are, the bastards."

"OK, OK. I don't see why you're so upset. If it's only a joke, like you said . . ."

Ricky was right, of course: Barrera had overreacted. Later on, in his room, unable to close his eyes even for those few winks he always bragged about, Barrera had berated himself. Hadn't he been feeling for months that he was being locked out of his son's existence? Hadn't he been lamenting to the mirror just this morning that the boy no longer seemed to need him, rarely came seeking advice, seemed to be growing more distant as his seventeenth birthday approached?

If you want this to end, you know what you need to do.

Maybe he should follow the advice offered in that silly message. If he wanted *this* to end, this discomfort between father and son, then he did know what he *needed to do*: apologize to Ricky, offer his help, open wide the door he had just so rudely and imprudently slammed shut. He'd take care of it in the morning, at breakfast, after having made the kid his favorite, the buckwheat pancakes *tan norteamericanos* that Cynthia had taught him how to griddle to perfection, a subtle gift from the boy's dead mother, one more remnant of her aroma in their town house; yes, Barrera would execute that plan, he'd—no, better still, he'd retrieve the message on his own, rescue it from the deleted items, and reply to it himself, explain that he would love to know what this was all about, even if it was a hoax or some such *tontería*, perhaps even confide in this Comando Anesthesia that he wanted to surprise his son with a detailed account, maybe the anonymous sender would commiserate with this father trying to impress a wayward son.

It was four in the morning, Ricky was asleep, now was the time.

Barrera logged into his son's e-mail, slipped in the purloined password, waited for the in-box to fill up.

Another message from Comando Anesthesia was waiting.

IF YOUR DAD PRETENDS HE DOESN'T KNOW WHAT TO DO, THEN SHOW HIM THIS.

Barrera hesitated.

Erase this message.

That was the first thing that flared up in his mind—to be replaced quickly by—*no, I can't, I can't do that. One thing is to read his mail to keep tabs on the boy, keep him out of trouble, but this, I've never done anything like . . . not like this,* and immediately: *Even if I did, if I could, who's to stop this madman? Who's to stop them from sending the message over and over again, sending it when I'm not there to delete, when I can't eliminate the damn thing?*

He was saved from a further flood of panicked thoughts by the shadow of Ricky behind him. And then Ricky's voice.

"Open it, Dad."

Not even reproaching him for sneaking into that oh-so-private e-mail account, not even angered by his father's refusal to cooperate before, by this betrayal of trust now. Merely matter of fact, merely *Open it, Dad*, only that.

Barrera double-clicked obediently, almost sheepishly, and there it was, there it was.

Te vamos a matar como a un perro. No, como a un perro no, porque los perros merecen mejor suerte. Te vamos a matar como se matan a los seres humanos: lentamente, para que sepas lo que te está pasando.

"Tell me what it says."

"No."

"*Perro* means dog. Is it about the dog you keep saying you'll buy me."

"No."

". . . the dog you promised to buy me if . . . ?"

"If you studied Spanish. Which would have been helpful, right? You could be reading this nonsense on your own, right?"

"You want to know what I think, Dad?"

"I'd love to know what you think."

"I think this Comando fellow—whoever is behind these messages—I think they want you to read it to me, that's why they sent it in Spanish, even if the subject is in English. I think it's meant for both of us, that's what. So—don't force me to show it to somebody else, Dad. It said to ask you."

"We are going to kill you like a dog."

Barrera heard his voice translating—*isn't that how I make my living?*—what he had spent his *puta existencia* doing, the one thing he did well since he was a child, well enough so that he wouldn't have to do it forever in some godforsaken consulate near the stinking coconut oil–infested docks of Buenaventura, or close to the dangerous streets of Medellín, or even in air-conditioned quarters in Bogotá. Adroit and exact and rapid enough so he could graduate to an office in Washington and then to another more spacious one and ultimately a large room like the one he now occupied. Head of translators from and into Spanish at the department, head honcho, his job now and then, pressing and crushing and cornering each word in Spanish until it exposed the nakedness of its meaning, squeezing all peril and murk and ambivalence out of the language of his mother as he transferred every sentence into the quiet, clean certainties of his father's gringo tongue. That was Barrera's job as a kid, building a daily channel between the dark woman from that port city who had given him birth and the tall blond foreigner who left them when Barrera was eight, making that man who was his father, had been his gringo *papá* for eight years, making him understand what the alien mass of sounds and syllables really meant, just like now he was going to make sure his gringo son understood, and just as he had helped her understand, the *hembra espléndida* who was to be his gringa wife, who had once been his wife. Barrera had been doing this all his life, and now here he was again, one more time, automatically translating those words that he should not be uttering, that he had not heard for almost eighteen years, that he did not want his son to take to someone else, that Barrera wanted to keep under wraps, domesticate, make those words safe, anodyne, and under control, yes, anesthetize them.

"We are going to kill you like a dog." Barrera's voice was neutral, almost remote. "No, not like a dog, because dogs deserve something better. We are going to kill you like a human being should be killed: slowly, so you know what is happening to you."

Ricky didn't react. Just like his mother, just like Cynthia to not give away her hand, tip anyone off to what she was thinking.

All they could hear in the silence of the night was the sullen whir of the computer, stirring codes or clicks or memories inside its spotless metal frame, deep inside its metal frame or maybe not that deep, maybe on the surface, all shiny and gleaming spotless.

Barrera knew that he was supposed to explode at the suggestion of this threat to the family, swear that he would call the police, call security at the department, hunt down the perpetrator of this madness, of this—that's what Ricky expected of him, that's what any father would do, that's what he couldn't bring himself to—not a sound, he who was so good at words and with words and at ease in two languages, abruptly transformed from head honcho into resident deaf-mute. That's what he was.

"What's going on, Dad? What in hell is this? Who would want to hurt us?"

And before Barrera could answer, another message flashed into the in-box, another letter from Comando Anesthesia, another subject heading:
THIS IS NOT A THREAT. YOUR DAD KNOWS THIS IS NOT A THREAT.

Now it was Ricky's arm that reached over his father's shoulder, stretched a hand out and down to click twice on that message, revealing new words in Spanish:

Que tu papá te diga lo que sucedió en Colombia justo antes de que nacieras.

Ask your father to tell you what happened in Colombia just before you were born.

Barrera didn't translate it right away. This was crazy. Lots of things happened in Colombia, everything had happened in Colombia: his own birth, his bifurcated childhood, his fatherless adolescence, his tentative employment at the consulate in Buenaventura, his work ethic, his genius for interpreting, his hours at the US-Colombian Friendship Institute reading every book on every shelf, his—that's how he'd answer the inevitable question Ricky was about to unleash, his whole life before his son had been born. That's what—though not what—Barrera was thinking, not what he'd been thinking ever since the word *perro* had come up, *no, not like a dog, because dogs deserve something better.*

"What happened in Colombia, Dad? Before I was born?"

As if Ricky no longer needed a translator, as if that word, *Colombia*, that country where Barrera's parents had miraculously met and fallen in love and conceived him, as if that one word were enough for the boy to suddenly read and comprehend Spanish, as if he had not refused to learn it, to speak it, to acknowledge its existence.

"Nothing," Barrera said quickly, too quickly. A mistake. It was a mistake to deny anything that soon, when you're in a hurry all sorts of blunders have a chance to surface. What Cynthia had told him as she sorted out those who sought asylum legitimately from those who were faking it: *Always be suspicious of the ones who answer right away, who don't take their time.* But Cynthia was not around to counsel him about what to do now, not around at all, in fact, and Barrera couldn't help himself. He needed to slip out that one word, *Nothing*, before *la mujer* who was sending these e-mails interfered yet again, continued her harassment and—but it couldn't be that woman, *esa mujer*. She didn't know English, she wasn't even—maybe the computer, something inside the computer itself? Had the computer itself found a way to—? *Wait, wait, that's even crazier, this makes no sense, stop it, I've got to end this.*

End this. If you want this to end. Si quieres que esto se termine.

They waited, both of them, father and son, like twins caught in a mother's twisted womb. They waited for guidance or a revelation or something else, anything else, a truce, maybe a truce.

It was dawning outside.

It was dawning outside and there were five days left before Ricky turned seventeen.

"I have to get to work and you—"

"Yeah, school."

"I'll drop you off."

"No need to."

"I'll drop you off."

The first thing Barrera did at work, before he had even stripped off his coat glistening with snow, before he tasted the coffee his secretary had poured for him, piping-hot Colombian Juan Valdés java always there when he arrived at precisely 8:45 each morning, before he even said hello to her, to anybody, the first thing was to log on and scuttle into Ricky's e-mail and—

There it was.

On his screen, floating like an eye in the sky of his screen, on his screen like an eye opening and closing.

Antes de que cumpla los diecisiete, lo tienes que hacer antes.

Before his seventeenth birthday, you have to do it before then.

He logged into Ricky's e-mail account. *Was it also there, had she found a way to—?*

It was there, also there in the subject: SOON HE'LL BE OF AGE. And the same words in the message itself in Spanish, which the automatic translator inside Barrera kept repeating: *Before his seventeenth birthday, you have to do it before then.*

He clicked savagely on the reply button. *Quién eres?* he wrote, and then he deleted the words in a rush. He knew who it was, who it had to be on the other end of the e-mail, the one person it couldn't be, that woman was—.

Barrera drank down the coffee in one gulp, burning his throat, happy to feel his mouth and tongue and throat scalded, throbbing, proof that he was alive, that Ricky was alive somewhere in the same city and the same galaxy, even if he was probably looking at the same words right now, *Antes de que cumpla los diecisiete, lo tienes que hacer antes.* And Ricky wouldn't show it to any of his classmates who spoke Spanish or any of his teachers, and he wouldn't mention it to Barrera when they met that night for dinner, not then, not ever. Ricky would make believe, just like his father, that nobody was sending these messages, nobody was erasing them.

Because Barrera did erase the next message, over and over.

The number 2,516.

When it appeared, at three in the morning, with Ricky slumbering in the next room and Barrera watching his son's in-box, as if it were a wild animal about to leap out of the machine. One second after that number flickered inside the new message from Comando Anesthesia, his finger was there, stabbing it: obliterated, gone, gone forever. Though no, it came back, it returned from who knows where, the e-mail reappeared on the screen each time he erased it, and now, now, now the number was reemerging directly on the screen. It did not come in a message, it did not tumble into the in-box, did not have a subject, not from anyone, not with a reply even feasible, just flashing on and off the screen, invading his screen and Ricky's screen, *not a wink*, he responded to his son's unasked question the next morning, *I never sleep, you know that.*

Except this time it was true.

And this time Ricky was the one who pretended that everything was normal, everything was fine. This time it was the boy's turn not to say anything.

Not a word.

Not even to remind his father that his birthday was coming up, three days from now.

Barrera called in sick.

He heard Ricky puttering around the house, sitting at his computer and then getting up noisily and then sitting down quietly again. And Barrera didn't tell his son he should be going to school, didn't tell him anything, both of them secluded in the house as if a blizzard had descended in the garden, right there outside the door, a plague seething just beyond the threshold if either one of them dared to open the door.

Barrera looked at the empty screen, waited, tried not to close his eyes, closed them and instantaneously opened them again, because that woman was inside the in-box of his eyes, in there and out there and in here somewhere, *esa mujer.* He wasn't going to fall asleep, he couldn't afford to fall asleep.

His eyes strayed to the picture of Cynthia. Her last photo before she became too ill to go out, not a sign of what was gnawing away at her bones, a smile like heaven on her lips, and underneath, the words she wanted him to remember when things got rough, the words she had written in her flawless, tight script, *Don't ever look back.*

"Easy for you to say that," he said to her. And then shook his head. No, no, he wasn't going to start speaking to Cynthia's photo as if it were a person of flesh and blood and limbs and ears. What came next? Talking to the screen as if it were—asking what would happen if these messages started to appear in every screen, everywhere, for everyone, if—*A todos, no*, came the answer on the screen. *Sólo a tu hijo.*

Not everyone. Just your son.

Barrera tried to rub that one out as soon as it materialized, get rid of the son of a bitch. It didn't go away, it wouldn't go away until it was good and ready. Those words came and went of their own accord now, regardless of what he did, regardless of the fact that now only two days remained until Ricky's birthday, neither of them mentioning this, calling in sick, father and then son—*yes, a bug is going around*—eating up the supplies in the fridge and the pantry, not venturing out even to retrieve the *Washington Post*, watching the papers accumulate outside like a dead dog in the snow, hardly acknowledging each other's existence, except at breakfast, except to say *thanks for the pancakes, Dad*, except to answer *just like your mother used to make them, hijo*, not mentioning that one day from now, tomorrow, it was going to be Ricky's birthday. The only difference between them: that the son slept at night and that Barrera had not slept for five days, for five nights. Not a wink, not for a minute, not for an hour. Now truly *nothing, nada.*

Staring at the night, staring at the night as if it were a screen, staring at his wife's photo as if it were a window into day.

Antes de que cumpla los diecisiete.

Four hours to go before his son turned seventeen.

Si quieres que esto se termine, ya sabes lo que tienes que hacer.

But he didn't, he didn't know what he needed to do.

Dime qué tengo que hacer?

What if he did ask the photo what to do, what was needed?

Don't ever look back, his wife's only answer, then and now.

Dime qué tengo que hacer, qué quieres de mí?

He didn't know anymore if he was thinking those words or saying them out loud, *What do you want from me?* The glimmer of a whisper that nobody present or faraway could ever have registered. Not even Barrera could have heard those words, so faint, so quiet, not with a tape recorder, not with a secret camera. Ricky couldn't eavesdrop on those words—that's how hidden Barrera's thoughts had become.

What do you want from me?

The screen said nothing.

Do you want to take my boy, is that what you want?

No answer, not a shimmer on the screen, before his mind foundered for lack of sleep, faltered into a sea of confusion, unable to distinguish anything anymore, having to comfort himself with those words written so many days ago they seemed a mirage, *This is not a threat, your dad knows this is not a threat.*

What do you want from me?

"What happened in Colombia, Dad? Before I was born?"

It couldn't be Ricky who was asking that again. He went to his son's room, and Ricky was blessedly asleep, smiling; the kid was smiling into the softness of the pillow, smiling as if hell did not exist, as if he would not have to awaken to his seventeenth birthday a few hours from now and find out that hell did exist.

"Nothing," he whispered to Ricky. "Nothing happened."

He left the room and went straight to his own computer and opened an e-mail addressed to his son. He typed in what he had just murmured to Ricky, spilled the black and quiet milk of denial onto the screen, a last desperate attempt to keep at bay the other words, the other words that had been simmering inside him since the message about the dog, the *perro* on the screen—*we are going to kill you like a human being should be killed: slowly, so you know what is happening to you*—since then.

"Nothing," Barrera wrote. "Nothing happened." And he heard his voice say, "That's God's truth," and he began to write those words as well and then found his fingers erasing them, all of it. He discovered the blank screen once again there, the cursor blinking on and off and once again asking him to— asking him to . . . what, what did that woman want from him?

"Ricardo," he said those syllables out loud and then wrote his son's name down on the screen. "Querido Ricardo, Ricky mío," my Ricky, my Ricardo. And then he was about to write: "We all do things in our lives that"—but no, it wasn't that. And then: "There was a woman many years ago who"— and it wasn't that either.

It was, it was . . .

It happened before Ricky was born.

"This happened before you were born, Ricardo. I like to tell myself that it happened so you could be born, so I could marry your mother. So I could come to this country and live a decent life without violence, escape from the fate of the father who abandoned me, the mother who made her living by selling what women sell. I knew that I would never leave you alone. I knew that I would stay by the side of the gringa I loved.

"I met her at the consulate at Bogotá, your mother. You know that much."

Barrera read over what he had written.

Yes, what he needed to do.

Si quieres que esto se termine.

His hands were commanding themselves, were flying solo, were flowing word after word onto the keyboard and through the screen and into this letter to his son.

"She liked me. I realized that she liked me because—well, there are things that men know, that women know, that don't need to be expressed with words. But she made her case, so to speak, by always asking that this new mulatto interpreter from Buenaventura by way of Medellín, that this man Barrera be the one to translate for her whenever there was a particularly complicated situation, a complicated person, someone whose visa we would have to deny, some pain that was being inflicted and which she couldn't avoid and wanted to share and I was the employee she chose for that sharing. I was the one . . . An ally, someone who would understand, even approve, perhaps forgive her hard choices.

"That morning, we . . ."

Barrera stopped. He erased the last three words.

"That morning when that woman came in, she . . ."

And again he stopped and again he removed the phrase.

"It started—what happened, I mean—it really started the night before. Your mother and I, we'd been out for drinks and intended to go dancing after dinner. She was trying a *sancocho de pescado*—but not me, no fish stew for me. Buenaventura had cured me of the sea—I was a steak man—and I can remember the precise moment when everything changed, when what was to happen the next day was set in motion.

"We were at a table on the sidewalk and two gamins—you know, street kids—they were watching us from behind a parked car. They'd been shooed away by the waiter and then the maître d' and then some burly security guards, but the boys—waifs, really—kept on popping up, peering at us. One of them, well, he even winked at me and sort of smirked, a leer perhaps I'd call it, but his teeth were perfectly white, straight and perfect, as if he had been well nourished at home, as if nobody had ever beat him or punched him or raped him or forced him to roam the avenues of Bogotá. I knew that kid. I could have been that kid when my father left us in Buenaventura. I think that if I hadn't been blessed with English, with the certainty that I belonged elsewhere, I'd have taken to the streets myself, and I'm sure that my mother wouldn't have come after me to bring her son home. My mother was too busy sniffing for a substitute for her vanished gringo, my vanished gringo dad. So when the gamin winked at me, I knew what his lewd gesture meant. It was a wink of encouragement, that said, yes, I should ask the gorgeous redhead home with me, I should show her a good time, promised me that she would say yes—and how strange that I should need his approval, from that lost child not older than eight, because I turned to her and said: *You know, I never sleep, but I think tonight will be different. Tonight I won't sleep due to another reason.* And she answered, as the street urchin had anticipated she would, she answered: *We'll see if you're right.*

"My response to that acknowledgment had been unexpected—not what she or I had been planning, I think, but maybe not unexpected for the two gamins. Because I stood up with my plate—half the steak was still on it and all the potatoes and remnants of a lovely béarnaise sauce—and I carried it with me to the kids and just gave it to them, plate and all, a reward for their witnessing of my triumph, what I had not dared to do or ask or dream of up till that moment, and somehow also a way of telling them, *You can also make it this far, like I have. I educated myself, I read every book in every library, I found a way. I'm going to make love to this wondrous gringa and then we're going to leave this stink hole of a country, and I did it all on my own. You don't have to stay behind. You can come along too. You can also change your life.*

"And I waited a bit, while they tasted the steak, munched at it in a much too leisurely way for two famished scamps so I asked them how the meat was, if it was good, and the kid who had winked at me, he repeated his perfect smile with his perfect teeth, so out of place in that grimy, bedrugged face, he said, in Spanish of course, he said: 'The steak up the street, at El Barranco, it's better, free-ranging cattle, more tender, juicier, you know.' And he deciphered the surprise in my eyes and added: '*Sobras.*' Leftovers. He and his pal had been scrounging in the garbage. They knew where the best meat could be found, and now he was acting as my culinary guide to Bogotá, my gourmet gamin.

"When I returned to the woman who was going to be your mother, she listened to my story and nodded in that birdlike, wonderway of hers, just like you. From the moment I met her I was so taken with her ability to stop what she was doing, like a *chachalaca*, a bird you'll only see if you were to finally come back one day to Colombia with me. Think of a bird that can dance the cha-cha and then cease suddenly, Ricardo, well, that's how she looked at me, entirely still, as if she were wary of some assault from nearby. The very first time I laid eyes on her I realized how vulnerable she was underneath that show of toughness. And it wasn't just that we had to be cautious—in fact, as employees of the US government in a country torn apart by civil war and narcos and the FARC and bombs, we'd make a nice morsel for anyone intent on kidnapping, her especially. I wasn't worth anything, not then, later yes, when I became a citizen, took on the country of my dad. Now yes, if someone were to kill me now . . . But I was telling you about that look of hers, which came, I said, from somewhere other than fear of the immediate violence that could be done to us. No, it came from some older tremor, something else we shared. She looked at me when I came back from giving away my steak and said: 'You're too good to be true.' And then: 'Mañana.' One of the few words in Spanish she ever learned, knew before she was sent to Colombia, the word everyone associates with Latin America and siestas, everyone assumes I represent when I tell them I was born way down south. Your mother repeated it in English: 'Tomorrow. I'll come home with you tomorrow night. Because, first, in the morning, there's something I need you to do, first you have to do something.'

"A test. That's what she had in store for me.

"It was a woman. Maybe you won't believe me, but I can't remember her name. Someday we can look it up, there must be files on her somewhere. Her husband was called Esteban, Esteban something. And he had been killed, headed a trade union, a coffee worker I think, maybe textiles, food workers?

And his wife was seeking asylum, or a visa if asylum couldn't be granted. One for her, one for her son. Her seventeen-year-old son. Yes, seventeen."

Barrera stopped. He reread the last paragraph. He erased the *Yes, seventeen*. Then he erased *Her seventeen-year-old son*. Ricky didn't need to know the age of that boy.

"That boy, that young man—name of Luis? maybe Lalo, yes, Lalo I think it was, from Eduardo—Lalo had received a death threat. I had read it in her file. They were going to kill him like a dog. No, not like a dog. Yes, that's how they were threatening to kill him. Slowly.

"Before the woman came in for the interview, your mother left the room. Left me alone with her. On purpose. 'I want to see how you handle this, by yourself,' Cynthia said, stepping out the back door, adding, there on the threshold, almost as an afterthought, that I'd been selected for a training program back in the States. She'd recommended me, the sky was the limit. I remember those words, the sky being the limit, everything open for me, her and the country and the future and someone like you, the sky. She'd recommended me, your mother reiterated, but she wanted first to observe me, in action, she said, *one last crack*. I also remember those words, just as I can still remember, have been repeating to myself all these years the word for word of the death threat.

"That's what I was examining attentively when that woman entered the room and sat down without my invitation, just sat down and pierced me with the black coil of her eyes as I read the message written on that crude piece of paper scrawled by someone who did not mind if an expert analyzed the handwriting, if the criminal's fingerprints were smudged all over that scrap of paper, a person who was an expert himself, an expert at creating fear in others, not concerned about his own fear, that's what I understood as I read.

"'Have you denounced this to the police?' I asked in Spanish.

"'2,516.'

"'Perdone? Qué dijo?'

"'2,516,' she said. 'The number of trade union members who have been murdered in the last ten years, 2,515 plus one, my husband.' And she pronounced his family name, the one I can't remember now, she said Esteban, Esteban and that surname. And before I could comment, offer my condolences, say something, anything, she added: 'Do you know how many arrests there have been, how many culprits have been arrested?' And she answered her own question: 'One,' she said. 'One man has been arrested, a policeman, a policeman who should have been protecting people like my husband and instead was killing them. One person, that's all, and he'll be out on bail soon and then he'll be up in the mountains with the *paras* and never be seen again.'

"Inside your mother's big broad desk, I knew a tape recorder was turning, registering every word of hers and mine, I knew that in your mother's office a security camera always recorded everything, every whisper.

"I answered: 'You can't expect us to take in every person who's threatened, who says she's threatened, who offers no more proof than a piece of paper whose origin we can't substantiate. Surely you can see that, ma'am. *No podemos aceptar a todos.*'

"'A todos, no,' she said. 'Sólo a mi hijo.'

"*Not everyone. Just my son.*

"And then she winked at me.

"It wasn't really a wink, more like the flutter of an eyelid, a shuttering, the rapid deployment of a butterfly in her eyes, closing them just enough so I wouldn't catch even a glimpse of the promise of tears, because she was not going to give me or anybody else the satisfaction of seeing her cry. *She's cried so much there's nothing left*, and then the opposite thought, *She hasn't cried for years, is scared to start because she may never stop, like my mother never dared to let herself go, not ever.* And then that woman stood up, refused to sit down again, though I insisted.

"She didn't explain why, just stood there, brusquely said one word. 'God,' that's the word she said and added: 'God often comes to us from behind, remember that. He comes when we least expect him, from behind.' And again her eyes that opened and shut rapidly.

"And I don't know why—yes, I know why, of course I know why—I confused that fluttering again with a wink. It joined me and her to the gamins of last night, that night before the night you were conceived, and it wasn't me answering her, I forgot where I was, who I was, what I wanted to become, forgot who was listening to me from the other side of the back door. I forgot how often in the past I had taken the files and folders and papers that your mother would pass to me, how often I had closed them with a snap. And now it was open, that file, the death threat was lying in there, calling to me, asking me to read it again. And when I picked it up because I could not say no to it, deny it one last appraisal, what revealed itself, what had been hidden below that death threat, was the faded photo of her dead husband and also the prettified visa photo of her living son, one next to the other, her two men, and then, if only for a minute, it was just me and my sad beating heart, if only for a minute, and I said:

"'*Naturalmente*, of course, we'll give you asylum, a visa, ma'am. *No le quepa duda.* Don't doubt it.'

"'That's a promise?'

"And I said yes.

"And she said: 'Swear it on your son.'

"'I don't have a son,'

"'Swear it on the life of your unborn child.'

"And that's what I did, Ricardo. I swore I was telling her the truth, swore it on your life.

"I never saw her again.

"Because your mother came into the room as soon as that woman had gone.

"She looked at me. 'You really are too good to be true.'

"She did not say anything else. Just waited. Like you do, so often, let the silence grow until somebody like me, somebody who feels uncomfortable with stillness and has survived by filling the universe with words—since I can recall I would jump into the space yawning between my father and my mother. I would leap in, vault in, rush in to see if I could bring them closer, because I could tell they were going to separate, that I was the one who had kept them together. My existence had done that, my birth had made my father stay, and I spent the first eight years of my childhood going back and forth between them, saying in English to my dad what my mother meant in her Buenaventura Spanish, extricating from my dad's Ohio accent what he wanted from my mother, back and forth, *ida y vuelta*, giving them refuge in the common territory of my tongue, holding them to each other as I felt them drift apart. Their home, I had to become their home if they were to stay by each other's side, and your own mother knew this, merely by instinct and cunning and command, that she didn't need to do anything other than let me dangle in the silence of her puzzlement, her challenge that I explain myself.

"And I did.

"It took me less than a minute, not even a minute to close that file, snap it tightly shut.

"'Asylum denied,' I said. 'No visa for either of them. Not clear if they have terrorist connections.'"

"She didn't say anything, again she just let me swing awhile in the dark sun of her gaze.

"'I just didn't have the heart to tell the woman,' I said. 'To her face, I mean, I just didn't have the heart.'

"And now Cynthia answered. 'Yes,' she said. Just that one word. She said yes to me.

"So that night . . . I like to think that was the night when you were conceived, Ricardo, I like to think that something good came of this, not just our marriage and my training and my promotion and my future citizenship and my new country—you, I like to tell myself that you were born because I did what I did, because of what happened in Colombia, what the messages demanded of me, that I tell you. That's what I have to say, what I need to tell you before you are seventeen."

Barrera stopped.

Behind him he sensed his son, told himself that the boy had been there for who knows how long, reading over his shoulder for who knew how long. And somehow this time Barrera found the strength not to turn around and address Ricky. He found the patience to swallow any word of welcome or of dismissal, was given the strength by someone, perhaps his wife, perhaps his mother, both of them dead. He discovered the strength to wait and let his son say something first.

"So who is it?" Ricky asked, finally. "Who is sending us, you and me, these messages?"

Almost as if he were a child asking a magician to explain how the rabbit could disappear, be cut to shreds and then reappear, one last moment of innocence before he outgrew it, one last chance.

"It can't be the husband," Barrera said, taking his time, "because he's dead, that man called Esteban."

"And the woman? The woman whose name you can't recall?"

"Not her," said Barrera. "And not her son, Luis or Lalo." And then he added: "They were executed. The night before your mother and I left Bogotá."

"How did they die?"

"Not that," he said. And then, still without turning around to look at his son: "There are things you really don't need to know. Not yet."

"I don't need to know what was done to their bodies?" Ricky asked. "How slow it must have been?"

"You don't need to know."

Ricky didn't speak for a while. Barrera could barely imagine him there at all, thinking all this over. Then: "Alright. So who else knew what happened in that room, what you promised? A colleague, someone, anyone?"

"Only me," said Barrera, "I'm the only one who knows. From time to time, I ask your mother, ask her picture—not with words but with my eyes, you know, I suggest that maybe there could have been another way, that maybe we could have found a different . . . Even if I know that she was also acting under orders, only following protocol. This Esteban had been fingered as sympathetic to the guerrillas, was a subversive. The son had been videotaped chanting slogans against the US, was a rabble-rouser at the local high school. And above your mother in the pyramid of power there was someone else, and then the head of that department and the man above them, and somebody upstairs would have eventually seen the asylum granted and would have reprimanded her, maybe demoted her, maybe denied me my transfer or my residency or my citizenship one day. It was me or that woman, our son or her son, that's how things are—" and by now Barrera was speaking to the computer, straight to the screen or what was inside the screen or beyond it. "All of us, just doing our job, just securing the border, just keeping our children safe, better to be safe than sorry. That's what I say silently to your mother, have said to her since she died."

"And what does she answer?"

"Nothing. Not a word. What could she tell us? What could she answer?"

"Unless . . ."

"Unless . . ." Barrera said.

But neither of them dared to add another word, tell each other what they were thinking, what they were both . . .

This was as far as he could go. This was the end.

Barrera sensed a sudden absence, was certain that his son was no longer behind him, that Ricky had decided to return to his room before dawn arrived, that's where he wanted to greet this day when he would be seventeen, when he would be of age.

Barrera waited. He gave the boy time to cross the corridor, open the door to his room, sit down in front of his own computer. He waited until he was sure Ricky was ready, and then, without looking one last time at the letter he had written, without correcting one word of it, he pressed the send button.

It was on its way, his response, what he needed to do.

He prayed it would be enough.

And he wondered, Barrera also managed to wonder, as the sun began to rise into that foreign sky, if he would sleep well that night, if he would sleep at all in the nights to come.

PERU

The Conversion

‑ ‑

ISAAC GOLDEMBERG (b. 1945)
Translated from the Spanish by Hardie St. Martin

Used as the opening door to Play by Play *(1984), the writer's second novel, this story narrates the physical and spiritual plight of Marquitos Karushansky, like the author half-Jew, half-native Peruvian and "injured existentially" by the discovery, during adolescence, of his ambiguous ethnic identity. The protagonist's identity and history—narrated with verve, irony, and playfulness—are symbolized, most painfully, by his ritual circumcision. Goldemberg is also the author of* The Fragmented Life of Don Jacabo Lerner *(1976), among other works.*

FIVE THOUSAND SEVEN hundred and thirteen years of Judaism hit Marquitos Karushansky like a ton of bricks. At the age of eight, shortly after coming to Lima, classes in Hebrew and the history of the Jews at León Pinelo School; bris at the age of twelve; bar mitzvah at thirteen, when he was a brand-new cadet at Leoncio Prado Military Academy. *Bris* was the little word taken from the Hebrew and used by the Jews in Lima to avoid saying *circumcision*, which left a bad taste in the mouth and made them bite the tip of their tongues, as if to spit it out. "Never you say *circumcision*, correct word is *bris*; *circumcision* is from Latin *circumcidere*, 'to cut around,' and has no historical weight. But *bris* means 'covenant' and is in Bible from time our father Abruhem sealed pact with Adonai." That's how Rabbi Goldstein, with his weeping willow beard, explained it to him. *Adonai*, of course, was also a word Marcos had recently picked up. Saying *God*, which seemed to have a cholo, half-Indian ring to it, was absolutely out of the question. And it was really something to watch him swearing, *Chai Adonai* here and *Chai Adonai* there! Whip 'em in the front and whip 'em in the rear! Chahuee!

Chahuaa! Pinelo, Pinelo, rah, rah, rah! First you've got to promise not to tell. I swear to God, who is my shining light! What? To God! No, that doesn't count. C'mon, do it right. Chai Adonai! You're a liar. Let's see if you can swear it's true. Chai Adonai! Swear you didn't steal the ballpoint. Chai Adonai! Marcos gradually became used to the word, it was like not swearing at all, and he got a big kick out of it.

Marquitos Karushansky's circumcision, or rather his bris, took place on the same day as the opening of *The Ten Commandments* at the Tacna movie theater. What's more, Dr. Berkowitz's office, where the operation was done, was only half a block from the theater. Marcos was operated on in the afternoon, sometime between five and seven, and the show was to start at eight. But he and his father missed the opening. The saddest part of it, old Karushansky said, was not being able to see the film together with the rest of the Jewish community of Lima. They had to see it four or five days later, sitting among Peruvians, and it wasn't the same, it wasn't the right atmosphere. What did those cholos know about the Bible anyway?

It had all started when his father announced, like a patriarch in the Old Testament: "Next year you be ready for bar mitzvah but first is necessary you have bris." Marcos remembered his eyes wandering to the smudgy windowpane and then his voice, mocking and at the same time trying to reassure him, he shouldn't worry; they had also snipped off the foreskin of Jesus the Jew.

They showed up one day in Dr. Berkowitz's office, where the physician, very professional, very freckled, explained: "Bris is an extremely simple operation. All it amounts to is cutting off the prepuce, the end of the skin that folds over the head of the penis and covers it. Then it's much easier to keep the glans clean. No sebaceous matter collects around it, and this reduces the risk of catching dangerous infections." Marcos didn't know what he was talking about and went back with his father to the doctor's office the next day. The nurse had already left, and they were greeted by a silence like the Sabbath's in the homes of Orthodox Jews. Before he knew it, Marcos was stretched out on his back on the operating table. Dr. Berkowitz was standing beside it, scalpel in hand, arm poised, and his father, sweat running down features drawn tight in pain and disgust, his father was lying across his chest, pinning his arms, papa's chunky body on top of his. Would he ask him for a camphor ointment rubdown later? Every night at bedtime the ritual of the rubdown would begin, and Marcos would massage him furiously, as if he wanted to tear off his skin, as if he were trying to draw blood from the heavy body with an oval head. He would pass the palm of his hand down the slope of the thick short neck, up the incline of the shoulders with their overgrowth of hair, matted like the fur on a battered old grizzly, his body stripped of every shred of nobility, letting out low grunts, soft moans of pleasure.

His penis had been put to sleep but not enough to kill the pain from the clamp holding on to his skin as if it would never let go. Then the doctor, warning him not to exaggerate, because too much anesthetic could leave him paralyzed for life, raised the needle to eye level to make sure he had the right amount in the syringe. His whole body shuddered when the needle entered his glans. His father pressed all his weight down on his chest, and on his lips and chin Marcos could feel the rough beard, soaked with sweat and tears. Now his penis was a soft mass, a spongy mushroom, an organism with a life of its own, capable of tearing free with one jerk and slipping all over his skin, looking for a way into his body, or capable of dissolving and leaving a smelly, viscous fluid on his groin. He knew his penis was already in the open, and he tried to imagine its new, hoodless look. In his mind, he compared it to the image he had of his father's member, its extreme whiteness, the perfect distribution of its parts, the scarlet crest topping the head of the sleepy iguana, with its vertical blind eye. He wanted to examine his phallus, to hold it above his eyes like a flower, to fall under the spell of the rosy calyx snug around its neck, to weigh it in his hand and stroke it warmly back to the familiarity it had lost. He was conscious of the small pincers clutching his foreskin tight: they were fierce little animals with fangs, beady eyes, and metallic scales on their backs. At the same time, he felt the pressure of his father's dead weight on him as a reproach, the embodiment of all the insults he had ever had to take. He thought about how, when he went back to school, he wouldn't have to hide from his friends in the bathroom. He would be able to piss casually now, to pull out his prick, take his time shaking it out, boldly pressing hard to squeeze the last drops out, and then turn around defiantly and show it to the others, to all his schoolmates at León Pinelo, proudly. Now let's see who is man enough to say I'm not a Jew.

The doctor left them alone in the back office: he told them he'd return in half an hour, they'd have to wait for the anesthetic to wear off, and Marcos watched his father nodding yes. Then the old man started to pace with his hands clasped behind him. He marched up and down next to the operating table, eyes straight ahead, without bending his knees, swinging each leg sideways slowly in a semicircle, before setting his foot down on the tiles. The controlled stiffness of his body, the deliberate halt after each about-face, before he started pacing again, reflected all the misery and resignation stored up in him. But Marcos knew every detail of this tactic his father had used, over the past two years, to put a certain amount of distance between them, to make him understand that behind this temporary withdrawal, all the things he had ever silenced were crying out, louder than words, against his bad luck and his unhappiness. If he had had any hope of crossing into his father's world, he would have asked him to come over to the table, dry the sweat on his forehead, take his hand in his, and help him clear away the skein of solitude unraveling endlessly in his chest. But he was sure the old man would avoid his eyes, as he did whenever he pounded on him with his fists, only to feel sorry afterward and break down like a vulnerable Mary Magdalene.

His senses had become dulled. His father looked older now: his beard had taken on a grayish tint, and a hundred wrinkles had formed around his eyes. He tried to think of his mother, but he couldn't retain a solid image of her behind his eyes. He had closed them and felt himself rushing down a toboggan run, rolling over and over without being able to stop. Only his father was solid; all the objects in the room had melted into ribbons of vapor swirling around him, and only his father's presence kept him from turning into a gaseous substance too.

He didn't move a muscle when the doctor's voice burst into the room like a garble of voices and sounds, and asked him if he was feeling better. He nodded without unlocking his eyelids, and the doctor and his father helped him off the table. His eyes were still closed, he staggered as if whipped by a blizzard, and the weight of his nakedness embarrassed him. The mere brush of the doctor's gloved hands on his member, the slight pull of the threads sticking out from the skin under the glans, made him feel wretched and he had the urge to piss. He guessed the pain this rash move would bring on and stopped himself just in time; the doctor was fitting a jockstrap stuffed with wads of gauze on him, and he had the sensation that he was pissing inward. His bladder was tightening up and his inward-flowing urine plunged through his ureters, was picked up by the renal tubes, flooded his kidneys like a winding current, and was pumped, bubbling and humming, into the bloodstream. He felt that he was burning up inside, explored by the fine probe of an intense blue flame. The doctor's voice jolted him back to reality. A sudden smile lit up the doctor's face as he put out his hand in an outlandishly formal way and made a big show of shaking Marcos's father's hand, saying, "Mazel tov, Señor Karushansky, congratulations, mazel tov . . ."

The lights on Tacna Avenue woke him all the way. Walking to the corner, they passed the Tacna movie theater, its front covered with giant posters showing scenes from the movie: a beardless Charlton Heston, dressed as an Egyptian warrior, was giving a wasp-waisted princess a he-man's hug; over to the right, Charlton Heston again, beard and wig, tunic and sandals, on a promontory, arms extended like a magician's: abracadabra, let the waters divide.

As they stood on the corner trying to get a cab, Marcos thought of the late afternoon when he had arrived in Lima, four years before. Through the smoke rising steadily from a charcoal pit, where some shish kebab on tiny skewers was roasting and giving off a tempting aroma, he saw his father with his hands in his pockets, coming toward the El Chasqui travel agency, where he and his mother were waiting. Then, like now, they had stopped on a corner, loaded down with bundles and suitcases, to get a cab. He looked out the side of his eye at his father, sitting cross-legged next to him; his arms were folded stiffly across his chest. Through the window on the other side of his father's aquiline profile, he watched the streetcars stretching, lumbering over the flashing tracks. Tall buildings loomed up unexpectedly, swaying like the carob trees back home, and then, with the speed of a fist coming straight at his eyes out of nowhere, the slender pyramid of the Jorge Chavez monument, like an airplane full of lights—manned by a crew of graceful winged granite figures taking off into the night.

He had seen pictures of the Plaza San Martín and the Plaza de Armas in his schoolbook and had thought of Lima as a ghost town where time had stopped without warning, freezing cars as they moved along and pedestrians as they walked. He liked to invent all kinds of stories about those unknown people suspended in midair like grotesque puppets. He had even tried to see if he could make out his father among those men in dark suits and hats. Sometimes he felt sure he had found him sitting on a bench reading a newspaper, or spotted his profile coming around a corner, and he would run to the kitchen and point him out to his mother. Without hiding her amazement at her son's fancies, she would stroke his head nervously and always tell him no, with an understanding smile. But now, sitting on his father's right, he didn't have to imagine him anymore. The city itself seemed to have come out of its sleep, happy to open the night and show him his father's world. And with all his senses set on the course of this moment so new to him, fluttering around him like a playful butterfly, he accepted that world unquestioning, wholeheartedly, as if it had always been his by right.

The taxi plunged into the warm shadows of a Salaverry Avenue studded with lights. His father was still just sitting there, his face outlined by the pale flash of the car's window, oblivious of the clusters of trees reflected in his eyes as they shot past. On the right, the Campo de Marte spread out; deserted, bleak, it disappeared for stretches at a time behind groups of houses and reappeared, somnolent and hazy. Marcos was quiet too, afraid to shift a leg that had fallen asleep and trying with his imagination to lop it off from his body and stop the swirl of bubbles climbing to his groin slowly, noisily. He let the stale air out of his lungs and sank a little into the seat, thinking that old guy is my father, I can tell by the musty odor of his clothes. He smells like dirty synagogue draperies, old velvet, damp wool, like the moth-eaten cashmere and poplin remnants he keeps in back of the store. He's probably taking the annual inventory right now, setting bolts of cloth on the counter, running his hand over them like a shepherd fondly stroking the backs of his sheep; or maybe he's repeating over and over the words he spit out at me this morning, "In a few hours you be at last one of us, at last one of us, at last one . . ."

As the cab made a sharp turn, coming out into Mariátegui Avenue, its chassis seemed to bristle up like a cat; it went down the street, chugging along unsteadily, entered Pumacahua Street, and pulled up at the corner of the second block, where the houses came to a dead end, cut off by the Club Hípico's garden wall, a solid line of trees and wire. His father helped him out of the car. They walked the short distance to the project entrance and silently headed for the apartment at the rear.

In the bedroom his father helped him undress; he knelt to take off his shoes and then took them to the foot of the valet clothes stand, dressed up in the rest of his clothes and looking like a silly scarecrow. He knelt down again to help him on with his pajama pants and then stood up with a heavy sigh, seeming to come from somewhere far away; he turned down the covers, settled the boy in the center of the bed, and covered him with a rough sweep of his hand. "So if you want something, you'll call," he told him abruptly, going to the door. Marcos heard his father's footsteps fading down the hallway toward the living room, and now, as he lay submerged in the warmth of the covers, the silence started winding its way through the shell of his ears, humming like the sea, and he could feel the solitude he had been longing for begin to take root in his spirit. He swept the room with his eyes, pausing carefully at each object, trying to figure out what hidden common bond there was between so many disparate things. He sensed that the suffocating mishmash of furniture, spread through the rest of the house like heavy underbrush, summed up his father's horror of empty rooms. Landscapes and scenes of Israel, torn from calendars, lined all the walls: the Sea of Galilee (or Kineret, as his father knowingly called it), hemmed by a tight ring of hills; a street in Yerushalaim crammed with shops and pedestrians, exactly like Jirón de la Unión Street, right, Marcos? This is the capital of Israel; you wouldn't believe everyone in streets are Jewish, right? Blond-dark-redhead and even real black children in a tiny school in Tel Aviv; also the vast wilderness of the Negev with red red sand and where are located the mines of King Shlomo, who was very wise; do you know story of two women are fighting for same son and going to King Shlomo . . . ? And also many pictures of Kibbutz Givat Brenner, founded in year '28. I was one of founders, Marcos, see how beautiful, all people glad working in fields, look how happy everybody, and in fact his father had also worked in the kibbutz, intoning "Erets zavat chalav, chalav, erets zavat chalav," humming into the wind, land of milk and honey, "Erets zavat chalav, chalav ud'vash," and in other prints there were young patriarchs, hands twirling the udders of the goats, sinking into the labyrinthine nurseries of the bees . . .

Marcos remembered the first time he had set foot in the house. Startled by the jungle of furniture as he stepped through the door, he stood rooted to the spot; he felt as if all his bones were giving way under a sudden deafening avalanche of rocks. Then his father took his arm and almost dragged him inside toward his room, saying, "Come, don't be afraid." Left standing alone in his bedroom with his suitcase beside him, he could hardly stay on his feet, a weary taste of rancid almonds in his mouth. From the back of the house his father's voice, as studied as a concierge's, reached him: "This is your room, here you will sleep. Bathroom is a few steps to your left; in front of bathroom is kitchen. You find everything there, unpack your bag, then fix yourself something to eat."

That night, as soon as his mother had gone to her room, the ritual of the bath got under way. "Am going get off all dirt from your body," his father said, rolling up his sleeves with an air of nostalgia for his ancestral past, like an old Orthodox Jew ready to wind the leather maze of phylacteries around his arm. He made Marcos climb into the tub and he let the stream of water out: it came on by fits and starts with a choking sound, then broke out in spurts till it picked up the steady murmur of an easy flow. Steam filled the bathroom with drowsiness, blurred the solid walls, and turned his father into a shadowy figure kneeling next to the tub and already beginning to soap his body with rhythmic skill, as if he were holding a newborn baby or a body not yet born, molding its form with the nimble fingers of a Florentine goldsmith. The scene was taking on the importance of a ceremony. The image of baptism in the son's mind corresponded closely to the rites of the biblical patriarch being officiated by his father: an initiation that would take the boy, cleansed of impurities, into his own world. Transformed now into an exterminating angel, his father seemed about to rend his flesh with the pumice stone, a primitive porous knife, without a grip, buried in the depths of his massive fist. The frenzied whirling of his father's hand had all the appearance of an act of martyrdom, and Marquitos saw himself being subjected to an ordeal but felt so sure he would come through unharmed that he endured the stabbing stone, held back his tears, and smothered his pain by biting his teeth down hard. Everything else afterward—scrambling out of the tub, scampering to his room, the comforting fetal position under the covers—took place in suspended time, on the hazy verge of sleep.

MEXICO

Genealogies (excerpt)

MARGO GLANTZ (b. 1930)
Translated from the Spanish by Susan Bassnett

Two favorite immigrant genres, memoir and autobiography, allow for an intimate exploration of the triumphs and obstacles of the new milieu. Genealogies (1981), among Glantz's best-known works, is precisely that: a family album complete with photos and vignettes of the writer's family past and present, a narrative of how Mexico has at once welcomed and rejected the Jewish population that emigrated from Russia and eastern Europe and of how the immigrants responded to their exotic new environment. This excerpt, ambitiously framed between 1920 and 1982, views the experience of Glantz's father during the Bolshevik revolution and his journey across the Atlantic as part of the communal history of the Jews of Mexico. The straightforward prose incorporates techniques from journalism and storytelling. Glantz is also the author of The Wake (2005).

"A TALL COSSACK and a short one passed by our house, with their hands covered in blood, and my mother, crying her eyes out, washed their hands in a bowl." My father's mother wore those broad skirts that we all know now, after reading or seeing *The Tin Drum*: she hid my two aunts, Jane and Myra, girls of sixteen and seventeen, under them.

"I was almost out of my mind. I walked (I was only a boy), I ran from one place to another and crossed the town over the little bridge that led to the baths, and I tried to find shelter in my uncle Kalmen's house. He was my father's brother. It was 1917. I went into my uncle's house, and I almost went mad. My uncle had a long curly red beard, all crimson with blood, and he was sitting with the blood pouring down and his eyes open. The fear of death still hadn't left him. Perhaps he was still even breathing!

Beside him, wrapped in a sheet, were all the household utensils, everything made of silver or copper, the Sabbath candlesticks, the samovar. I was scared stiff. I had no idea what to do. I just ran out of the village like a madman. The pogrom lasted several days. I went out into the country and I found an abandoned well, deep, but with no water in it, and I clung to the rungs and spent several days down there. When I heard that everything had calmed down, I came out. Before that, I could hear the terrible cries of the girls and children."

It all happened so fast that one pogrom piled up on top of another.

"In those troubled times different groups were chasing one another, and as they went through towns and villages they sacked everything in their path."

It all sounds so familiar. It's like those revolts that our nineteenth-century novelists wrote about and like what you read in novels about the Mexican Revolution, the revolts and the levies, the confusion, the sacking of towns and villages, the deaths.

"The Bolsheviks came back, and we had some of the short rifles left by the bandits and some of the horses too; only the reservists who'd been in the world war knew how to defend themselves. The rest of us were saved by a miracle. Many of the bandits were peasants who knew us, and as they were stealing they preferred to kill so that they couldn't be denounced."

Yasha hid in the house of a muzhik, a friend of his grandfather's, Sasha Ribak, "with an enormous moustache, like the poet Sevshenko" (the great popular poet of the Ukraine). My father stayed hiding in a corncrib, breathing through a hole, even when bandits stuck their bayonets into it. Ribak took him food and water and let him out when things calmed down a little. As soon as things started up again, back my father went to his hideout.

"General Budiony's Bolshevik Cossacks arrived. When things were a bit calmer, I came out. When it was dangerous I went back into hiding again. I remember Sasha well; he was very good. I wrote a poem about all that, in 1920, in Russia."

"And what about your mother and your sisters, how were they saved?"

"We survived by chance, by luck. My mother and my sisters hid in the top of the house, where there was a loft used as a storeroom, in the space under the rafter. As the groups were all chasing each other, they hardly had time to look, and they sacked and killed everything they found in their way. My mother was saved that first time because she washed the Cossacks' hands."

My grandmother and two aunts were given permission to leave Russia around 1923 to rejoin their family in *America, America* (the title of the famous film by Elia Kazan). My father was doing his military service and had to stay in the Soviet Union.

"Your mother was afraid that I'd get lost in the revolution. I was very impulsive. It was a dangerous situation, and the revolution didn't tolerate people who were impulsive. What the revolution demanded was total commitment from each individual, and those who tried to see things their own way were put on the list of counterrevolutionaries. Well, I was pretty well done for, as you can imagine, being a gabby Jew. And later on they arrested me."

"Why did they arrest you?"

"They arrested me for . . . you see, I was marked down in the revolution as a man with nationalist deviationist tendencies."

My grandmother and my aunts stayed on in Russia for another year after being granted permission to leave, because my grandmother was afraid she might never see her son again. But in the end they traveled to Turkey, and then they couldn't go any further because the North Americans had restricted their immigration quotas and only the mother was eligible to enter the United States. However, my father was also granted permission to leave, though afterward he went to a protest meeting about unfair practices that prevented people from obtaining work. One of the men who had been refused work threw himself out of a fourth-floor window as a protest. Then the police arrived and put most of the protesters in jail, including my father.

At this point in the story, a friend of the family turns up, a pro-Soviet Jew who left Russia round 1924 and immigrated to Cuba in 1928, from where he had been chased out by Machado's henchmen because of his militancy. He has brought some Soviet journals sent him from New York, worth 123.50 pesos.

"They used to reach me quickly direct from Moscow. They only cost 17.50 pesos then, but you have to pay a full year's subscription."

"When did you leave Russia?"

"My family left first. My father went to the United States in 1912. He left my mother in Russia with the children. In 1914 he sent us tickets, and we were due to leave on the nineteenth of August and the First World War broke out on the twenty-ninth. My father went back to Russia in 1922, but he couldn't settle because he was a businessman and they accused him of being a bourgeois, so in 1923 he went to New York with his other two brothers. I went to Cuba in 1924, but then they brought in new regulations about immigration quotas so I couldn't go on to the United States."

"That's what happened to us too," says Yankl.

"I went on to Mexico later, because otherwise I'd have ended up drowned in the bay at Havana sooner or later."

His friend leaves, and my father comments: "He stayed you know. He's one of the very few who stayed on the Left."

He insists on recalling that meeting where a worker threw himself down from the fourth floor. I remember something similar in one of Wajda's films.

"Then the riot started," interrupts Mother. "The police were there and they started taking workers away. They took your father along with a friend of his, a journalist who was about forty. Your father didn't turn up, and I was worried and I started looking for him around the police stations. I asked different policemen about him, and nobody knew anything. I said to one of them, 'You've got your people all over the place. Don't you know or can't you tell me?' He told me he couldn't say anything. It was a Thursday. On Saturday a lady came to see me. I was playing the piano, and she asked me if I was Glantz's fiancée. I was surprised, but I said yes. 'I've brought you a message from your fiancé that my husband gave me, because both of them have been arrested.'"

"I traveled third class, that is, your father and I did. And I couldn't eat anything, because the food was so awful, even though there were times when we went hungry. There was a very bright woman who got on well with the *zeil meister*, and she used to give us herring with vinegar and onions, and that was a real treat. I sold everything in Moscow because I was going to Cuba and Russian clothes wouldn't be any use over there. I had some very smart gray suede shoes, which were open down the front, and a pair of stockings that I had to darn every day. In Holland we got some money from Uncle Ellis and I bought two dresses, a black crepe one, which was very smart, and one in lovely soft green wool."

It's raining. San Miguel Regla is really beautiful, with its gentle countryside

and all the trees, the house with its slender columns, that huge, friendly hacienda that I almost like better than Marienbad, a place I've only ever seen on
film, except that I'm a bit of a snob and it seems rather more exotic to me,
as the mother of my Colombian friend said, when we were in Paris and she
was talking about American clothes: "They're so nice. They look so foreign!"

Mother goes on talking: "Your father wasn't worried. In the daytime we
stayed under cover and at night we slept in our cabin." (And to think that so
much love can actually wear itself out!)

"There was a very interesting man traveling with us, a very strange man, he
spoke Russian but I think he was born in Poland. We called him Miloshka,
which means 'favorite.' He disappeared when we got here," she sighs, then
continues: "You know, when we came to Mexico I didn't know how to use
earthenware pots, so at first I boiled milk in a pan a lot, and now I can't stand
blenders. I prefer to mash things in an old Mexican earthenware bowl. You
can get used to anything, that's for sure. Though I still don't know where I
really am."

"What do you mean?"

"I still don't know if I'm on my own or what. I don't want to send your
father's books because it'll make the place seem so empty."

"You should send his books and his papers so they can be put in order
and cataloged. I think it's the right thing to do; they'll be very useful for people who are trying to write the history of the Mexican Jewish community."

The ground is wet. We have been sitting in a little garden, surrounded
by cloistered arches, on antique-style leather chairs, like the rest of the
hacienda, like the bedrooms. Later we sit around the fireplace. The cleaning woman says softly, "There's a bit of watery sunshine." Everything is so
peaceful, so lovely, so melancholy. I've eaten so much I can hardly move. I
go out for a long walk, through the trees, past the pools, the remains of
the old metal smelting furnace, and memories flood back with every step,
memories of the former owner, the Marquis of Guadalupe, Count of Regla,
my mother's memories.

"That's how I learned to make strudel."

"When did you learn that? Did you learn it at home? Did your mother
teach you?"

"Yes, I learned quite a lot from her in Russia. In Tacuba Street, number 15,
there was a restaurant and there was a Russian man who had immigrated

there recently and he was chief cook, and I don't know how it came about, but I think I said to him that you could make strudel in the little coal-burning ovens, the portable ones, with two chimney vents and two openings, and they were making strudels and I made one and he liked it a lot . . ."

We go in because it is starting to rain.

"He said to me: 'Such a lovely young woman, with all sorts of talents, and she's interested in strudel.' And I just got on and made it, and I don't even remember how much he paid me. We used to go to the club in the evenings . . ."

"You and strudel man?"

"No, me and your father. We used to see Mr. Perkis there, and Dr. King and Katzenelson. Everybody changed their names. First they were living in the United States, and then when the First World War broke out they went to Mexico to start again, and they founded the Young Men's Hebrew Association."

"With an English name?"

"Yes, English, because they'd just come from the United States, you see, they looked after us, in a way. Dr. King used to give your father dental products. I've told you that already. And your father used to teach Hebrew at first to some of the children, our friends' children when they were preparing for their bar mitzvahs. Some people were very kind, and we were very grateful to people too. Horacio Minich's father, for example, taught natural sciences in the Yiddish school, but since I didn't know any Yiddish I couldn't even teach things I knew about."

"So what did you know about?"

"Lots of things. I was always learning. I never seemed to stop. Playing the piano, science, art, even singing. But I ended up having to make strudel. That's the way it is. We brought lots of books instead of clothing. We had a basket of books that weighed sixty kilos. They were very important books and important people used to ask to borrow them and most of them we never set eyes on again. That's the way it is."

"Do you still have any of those books?"

"Oh yes, there are a few left but I'm going to send them to Israel. There was a group of non-Jewish Russians here too, some very nice people. They were quite old. Well, at least they seemed quite old to me."

"How old were they?"

"I don't know, but they were a lot older than we were. They lived in Xochimilco, which was a big place in those days, very beautiful with a lot of flowers everywhere and boats covered with greenery. They had an herb garden, they were typical Russians, very refined, honest, special people. There were some others who were former nobility. What were their names? How could I forget? Oh, yes, they were called Sokolov."

"Who were? The ones with the herb garden or the others?"

"No, the other ones, the nobility, were much younger. I don't remember what the others were called, but they had a little house in Xochimilco. It wasn't much more than a hut. They made us a typical Russian meal. They were so pleased to be able to speak Russian with someone."

"Anything else, Mother?"

"Oh, Margo, it all happened fifty years ago. Every night we used to go to the club. It didn't matter if you were on the right or the left. Nobody bothered. Then Abrams came, and he was an anarchist, a real leftist. It didn't matter what we did during the daytime to earn a living, because in the evenings we all went to the club."

"Why didn't it matter what you did in the daytime?"

"Well, we sold bread, or I don't know, some people were peddlers, street traders during the daytime, but in the evening we all came together for something better. There were all sorts of people, some as young as fourteen or fifteen. You never knew them. Maybe you did or maybe you didn't, but we all had to use Yiddish because we couldn't manage any other way. Some of them had come from Poland and some from Russia and some came from tiny little villages where they spoke a sort of Yiddish, and some even came from the United States and goodness knows what sort of English they could speak. So we all had to learn Yiddish, and when I started I couldn't understand anything because there were so many dialects, from Warsaw and Lithuania and Romania and Estonia and little Polish villages. I couldn't understand a word and then I started to learn gradually. Your father used to read to me. He was in bed a lot because he had trouble with his lungs and sometimes he used to cough up blood, and then he had to lie down because that frightened him. Your father used to read me Yiddish books. He used to translate them into Russian and that's how I learned. I knew the alphabet because when I was a little girl I'd been taught that before I went on to high school."

"Didn't your mother speak Yiddish?"

"Of course she did, but she spoke a Ukrainian dialect, which was completely different. Later on all sorts of very well-educated young people used to come to our house . . ."

"Later on when?"

"In Russia. Before I went to high school. They used to come to Odessa from their little villages to study and take important exams. I remember before the First World War there was one of those students living in our house, a Zionist, who knew Hebrew perfectly. We put him up and fed him and he used to give us Hebrew lessons. He gave lessons to Uncle Volodya, but I don't remember if Ilusha and I did any. That's how I learned the alphabet. He went to Israel later. Your Uncle Volodya told me he went on to become minister of finance."

"In Israel?"

"Yes, in Israel. Uncle Volodya could remember his name, but I can't. I learned the alphabet and when I learned some Yiddish I wrote a letter to my parents once, just a few words. My mother wrote back in a terrible state because I'd suddenly written to her in Yiddish and she didn't think it could be me. She thought I must be dead. So then I wrote back again to her in Russian and calmed things down. That's what it's like when your children leave home . . ."

I come back to where I once was. I go through the park, past the pools, and everything is damp, mildewed. It is slippery underfoot. There are flowers everywhere. I go over to a prickly-pear tree and try to pluck some fruit. The pear defends itself and sticks its spikes in me. I go back to my room to try and pull out the prickles with a pair of tweezers from my arms, my cheeks, and the side of my mouth, my hands, and my fingers. My father died, early in the morning of January 2, 1982.

Living with someone probably means losing part of your own identity. Living with someone contaminates; my father alters my mother's childhood and she loses her patience listening to some accounts of my father's childhood. Once we had all gone to the cemetery on the first anniversary of my uncle's death and Lucia recalled the attempted pogrom that my father had experienced. So I asked him to tell me what had happened to him:

"I was working in the Jewish Charity Association at 21 Gante Street, on the corner of Venustiano Carranza, which used to be called Capuchinas, and your mother had her shop called Lisette on Sixteenth September Street, number 29, selling ladies' bags and gloves. I came out of the charity place and there was a big meeting under way (it was in January 1939). I was on my way to the shop when I met a young man called Salas. He knew who I was. He'd been a student in Germany and spoke very good German. He came toward me with two other lads and he yelled 'Death to the Jews. Jews out of Mexico!' and I had a willow stick with me, and I broke it over his head and it split into three. He grabbed it out of my hand and tried to push me in front of a tram, but I held onto a lamppost and wouldn't let go. I don't know how I managed to break free and run to the shop, which was shut, though the steel door still wasn't down.

"The police came right away. I don't remember how many there were. There could have been fifty or a hundred, and Siqueiros's brother; if he hadn't been there I'd have been killed. He said to me: 'They'll have to get me before they get you, Jacobo,' and he stretched both arms out wide. He was a giant of a man. They had a truck outside full of stones and they were throwing them at the shop and they smashed the shop window and took everything they could get. I don't know how I got out of there."

"Where was Mother?"

"She'd gotten out with the assistant. There were stones flying all over the place. I didn't know where to hide, because everywhere I went there were more stones. I thought I'd never get out of there. I thought I was done for. There was nothing I could do. There were so many people outside and so many stones and I was covered in blood. There was a man called Osorio outside, a Cuban whom I knew quite well, and he stood up on a platform and made a Hitler-type speech, and even though he knew me, he spoke against me and against Jews in general. When they ran out of stones, they went to San Juan de Letran, where your Uncle Mendel had his drinks stand, and they came back with great chunks of ice, which they started throwing at me, and a massive lump of ice hit me on the head and that was a sign from God, because the ice saved me. I was bleeding heavily, because I'd been hit on the head, but that ice was a sign from God. I wouldn't have survived without the ice."

"Where were we?"

"You were all very little. I don't think you ever saw any of that. General Montes appeared later and he put his cloak around me and said, 'Don't cry, Jew. I'm here to save you.'"

In the Name of His Name

ANGELINA MUÑIZ-HUBERMAN (b. 1936)
Translated from the Spanish by Lois Parkinson Zamora

An audacious interpreter of mystical texts, this Mexican critic and novelist of Sephardic ancestry has made a career of telling allegorical tales. This one, from her award-winning collection Enclosed Garden *(1985), is a tribute to Sephardic culture, especially Kabbalistic imagery, but also to Mendele Mokher Sforim, particularly his novel* The Travels of Benjamin the Third, *and to Rabbi Nahman of Bratslav's story "The Rabbi's Son." The river the protagonist dreams of crossing, which supposedly ceases its flow on the Sabbath, is taken from Jewish folklore. Compared to Seligson's "The Invisible Hour," this tale has a clear-cut symbolic code. Muniz-Huberman is also the author of* The Confidantes *(2009) and* A Mystical Journey *(2011), among other works.*

ABRAHAM OF TALAMANCA pondered long upon the word of God before making his decision. He had studied the signs and portents of the world. He had read and reread the Great Book and sought its revelation. Somewhere he would find the divine word. He felt a profound anxiety, though he did not know why; he knew only that the answer was there somewhere and he could not find it. Not that the world was mute but that he could not understand its language. Not that God was silent but that he could not hear Him. He continued to search and time continued to pass. To be possessed by a certainty that cannot be explained, a truth that cannot be proven. A sound that has no time. A color that cannot be painted. A word that cannot be deciphered. A thought that cannot be expressed. What then does he possess? How can one live by doubt, divination, foreshadowing?

162

Abraham of Talamanca senses his ideas spinning round and round in the confined and infinite chaos of his mind. Arrows fly in his head and at times he supports his head in his hands, so heavy it seems to him. And then comes the pain. It begins with his eyes, which, as a source of enlightenment, embrace much and suffer much. He who does not see does not weep. He who does not weep does not ache. A sword stroke at the center of his skull. Pain that makes a fiefdom of his arteries, a whip of his nerves, and a torment of his muscles. Abraham, who loves light, flees into darkness; he searches for the word and flees into silence. Pain imprisons half of his head, while the other half struggles for lucidity. But the battle is never won; pain triumphs, and with his hands Abraham covers his eyes: no light, no word. Thus he loses days, which turn to nights, nights of the soul, which become darker and darker.

But the answer does not appear. After thirty days of constant pain, in which the unafflicted side of his head rested no more than the afflicted, he made his decision. He would go in search of the Sambatio, the distant river of the Promised Land, the river that flows six days a week and ceases on the Sabbath, or perhaps instead flows on the day of the Sabbath and ceases on the other six. The frightful roar of the rushing river, which carries rocks, not water, and sand, and which on the seventh day, shrouded in clouds, keeps total silence. The river protects, for him who crosses it, the paradise inhabited by the Ten Lost Tribes. If he should manage to reach it, Abraham the Talamantine, and if he should manage to cross it.

He would leave behind his books, his studies, his prayers, his meditation. He would try the paths and byways of pilgrims and wanderers, soldiers and vagabonds, merchants and adventurers. Tranquility and wisdom would be lost along the way. He would go unrecognized and lose himself among the rest. To be lost and alone and so to find himself more deeply. And with the cool of the dawns and the dust of distant places, he would forget that search for the unknowable. He would breathe deeply the air of mountain and sea. He would belong to nothing, to no one. The absolute freedom of one who has only himself. He would try for once to be God. Impossible to be integral; always dual; always the divine presence. I speak to myself and He answers me, spark of eternity. Can't one be alone? Absolute solitude? No, no, no. He always appears, God, the One without a name, the One sought after, desired, never found, He who requires perfection. So we wander, with Abraham of Talamanca, in search of the unsearchable.

Abraham prepares his departure, taking few possessions, fulfilled in himself. The pain has disappeared. Now he knows what he seeks; he seeks the name of God and he knows that it will appear when he crosses the final river at the end of the long journey. He seeks the meaning of the word, that which is beyond asking. He cannot accept the imperfection of the sign. The difficult connection between things and their names. The attempt to enclose in the space of a word the idea of perfection, of unity, of infinity, of creation, of plenitude, of supreme good. God is a conventional sign. How can one find its true essence? *Baruch ha-shem.* Blessed be His Name.

To approach immensity little by little. Slowly twining the links of the chain. More slowly still ascending the steps toward illumination. Losing ourselves in the partial and fragmented reflection of a thousand facing mirrors. And still aspiring to rise higher and higher. That longing to fly that is only achieved in dreams. To climb the mountain. To arrive at the summit of pure air and blue sky. Below, seas and rivers and lakes.

Through open fields and enclosed gardens, along paths and byways, up and down, the road unwinds before Abraham the wanderer. And when the land runs out and sand borders the water, he furrows the water and creates light foam and soft waves, which, uncreating, erase his vain steps. The sun is ensconced in an immense blue cradle, and the four phases of the moon as well. When at length the sea loses its freedom and the high rocks force it to recede and close upon itself, the foot of the wanderer again falls upon the worn sand, so often trod, so often shifted and displaced.

The Holy Land he touched not only with his feet but also with his hands, raising the fine dust to his lips, kissing it. Only then did he begin the pilgrimage. Eyes, feet, hands, lips, eager. Whether the ancient tomb, the golden rock, the stones of the desert. And then, northward, in search of the Sambatio. In search of the revealed word. But the river is a mirage. It appears and disappears. It recedes and overflows. It sings and is silent. It approaches and withdraws forever. For years, hope detains Abraham. Then certitude detains him. Meanwhile, the Word has sounded. He knows that it is there, that it circulates within him: like the blood that flows through his body, it fills him to overflowing. It encourages him, nourishes him, gives him life. It has no form but that given to it by the vessel that contains it. It moves freely, flawlessly, smoothly. It has no equal.

Abraham no longer speaks. He no longer writes. The Word has eliminated words. The Name is. The Revelation cannot be communicated. Silence fills everything, finding its proper form.

Abraham has stopped searching for the Sambatio. The name of His Name flows in his veins.

Like a Bride (excerpt)

ROSA NISSÁN (b. 1939)
Translated from the Spanish by Dick Gerdes

The author of two semiautobiographical novels, Like a Bride *(1992) and* Like a Mother *(1996), Rosa Nissán writes about Sephardim in a predominantly Ashkenazi Mexican Jewish community. Her work has been adapted into film. The following is the first part of* Like a Bride.

EVERY NIGHT I kneel down by the window and look at a bright star that just might be my guardian angel. Then I recite "Our Father" to God and say a "Hail Mary" for the Virgin. I hope that one of them will protect me like they do my classmates, even though my parents are Jewish. Today I prayed that I wouldn't have to change schools. They want to put me in one only for Jews. Where do Jews come from, anyway? Dear God, please help me stay at the Guadalupe Tepeyac School, and please make sure that I'll never leave this place, and especially now that I'm going to start the last and most difficult year of elementary school. Only here, and with your help, can I make it. I promise to do whatever you want—follow the Ten Commandments, go to catechism on Saturdays, and whenever I die, I'll be a guardian angel for anyone you want. In the name of the Father, the Son, and the Holy Ghost. Amen.

At eight o'clock in the morning, just before beginning our studies, we pray. We put the palms of our hands next to our mouths, close our eyes, and recite the prayers together. I like the way it sounds. We make the sign of the cross with our right hand, and then we sit down to study. The school desks are neat—the part we write on lifts up, and we put all our stuff inside. I have a little Santa Teresa picture glued on the top, in the middle, and other little flowered virgins are in each corner. I spend a lot of time giving them little kisses with my finger so they'll protect me.

After we do our lessons and finish our assignments, the nuns reward us with one more picture. Since I'm one of the best behaved, I have the most pictures. I have to hide them, because my mother doesn't approve of them. But she does see me make the sign of the cross every morning.

"I would rather you leave the room when they pray," she said the other day. But I don't want to. Then someone would ask me why I'm leaving the room, and besides, I like praying.

Yesterday at recess we were making sand castles, and when I moved to make mine bigger, I stepped on another girl's castle. She got so mad that she threw sand in my eyes and then yelled, "Jew! Jew!" at me. Her yelling frightened me, because most of the girls don't know. Then some other kids formed a group, and in a flash a bunch of them were screaming, "You killed Jesus," and then they made the sign of the cross right in my face as if I were the devil. And I yelled back at them, "That's a lie. I'm not a Jew. I pray and go to confession just like you do."

It's almost one o'clock in the morning and I can't sleep—I just keep remembering how they threw sand in my eyes.

Dreams of hell. I dreamed the same thing last week, over and over, my bed's on fire. Even though it's dark, everything's lit up with yellow, orange, and red flames. Tombs pop open like jack-in-the-boxes, and people rise up and start walking toward God. He's the one who's going to reward or punish us. I only see the lids pop off the coffins, and then the dead people start to walk.

"The Last Judgment . . . we'll all be there someday," said Sister Maria. "Then we'll know if we've won a spot in heaven, or if we'll grow tails and sprout horns."

I know that those who have gone to hell play tricks on children so they'll be bad.

Last night the neighbors on the second floor came over and we played "Chance." I got the devil and lost, because no one got the wicked card. That little red devil with the wicked eyes danced around in my dreams way into the night—grasping an iron fork, he stirs the ashes around, then he comes and goes, does whatever he wants, casts a glance at me, shows me his horns and the red-hot edges of his pincers. I freak out when I imagine that this day could actually arrive. I hope it never does. Why would all of us who come back from the dead have to walk around nude? I don't like to be seen nude, and I wouldn't like to have to get up that day and have everyone see me like that. What a horrible punishment! I'll meet all those people from a thousand years ago—Benito Juárez, Napoleon, Miguel Hidalgo, and Costilla (my other grandmother), Cinderella, Cuauhtemoc. And how is he going to walk? They burned his feet. I'll bet he's going to rise up as good as new, everyone knows that with God nothing is impossible and . . . you know, it just might be fun, if I get to know so many people, but . . . nude? Oh, no! How embarrassing! And nothing to cover myself up with?

1. Thou shalt love God over everything else (I love him and I pray to him).
2. Thou shalt not take the name of God in vain (I'm not going to swear anymore, but when I do and I tell a lie, I'm going to cross myself, but not properly, so it won't be any good).
3. Thou shalt honor your father and mother.
4. Thou shalt honor the Sabbath and holy days.
5. Thou shalt not kill.
6. Thou shalt not fornicate (I'll skip this one, I don't even know what it means).
7. Thou shalt not steal.
8. Thou shalt not commit false testimony (I only tell a few lies, besides they're the worst thing that I can say to Mommy).
9. Thou shalt not covet thy neighbor's wife (I don't understand. Whose wife?).
10. Thou shalt not covet that which is not yours (that's easy, I never want anything that isn't mine).

If I can just manage to follow those rules, I'll go to heaven for sure, and I'm really happy that the Ten Commandments are the same for Jews as they are for Catholics. Whew! They share something in common! At least I can repeat them in school just the same as at home. It's easy to obey them, because the thought of going to hell is terrifying. I want to go to heaven. I'll be an angel like the ones in the pictures, and I'd like to be the one in the middle, invisible. Wouldn't it be great to be invisible! To be everywhere at the same time, flying from one place to another, without anyone seeing me? Then I could get close to those children and whisper in their ears, "Don't be afraid of the devil! Spend your time on Sundays helping an old person, loan your crayons even if some kids are mean to you and break off the tips."

They say the devil speaks to children through their left ears, telling them to play nasty tricks. And their guardian angel speaks to them through their right ears, advising them to be good. Those little blond angels, who are dressed in light blue and have transparent wings, live in heaven. They can see God, the Virgin, and all the saints. They talk to them.

"Cross, cross, make the devil go away and Jesus stay." Don't get near me, you ugly devil. Get away! Leave me alone! I know that these little devils are very insistent and they're always at your ear, saying, "Steal that pen, hit your brother, pull her braids, make fun of her." Sometimes they are so convincing, because the devil shows you how to be cunning. And they can be really mean.

My clothing will be pure white, I'll fly around from place to place, I'll teach children to be good no matter which country they're from . . . although I'm not sure I'd like to be an angel for a Jewish kid; maybe I'll adopt a Roman Catholic. Then one day I'll go to heaven. Wings made of a delicate material like a bird's skin will sprout from me, and I'll dump buckets of water from the clouds on everyone below so they can feel the rain.

The girls in my classroom receive gifts and have parties twice a year—on their birthdays and their saint's days, but the Jews don't celebrate saint's day. The teacher asked me when mine was. The only thing I could think of was to tell her that I would ask my mother. I don't think there's a Saint Oshinica, but I'm going to look at a calendar and, if there's a Saint Eugenia, I'll be in luck.

Since we live right on Guadalupe Avenue, we can see the people streaming by on their pilgrimage to the basilica. They're always singing, dancing, laughing, drinking, hugging each other, carrying their children and sick ones, food, and blankets. Each congregation has its leader who protects them so that the following group doesn't overtake them in the unending procession.

As soon as we hear them coming, we run to the balcony. We never get tired of watching them, and sometimes the groups are as long as three city blocks. As they amble down the street, it makes us feel sad. Now that we're approaching the saint's day of the Virgin of Guadalupe, there are so many different groups passing by with their banners, all of which have the image of the Virgin—the mother of the Mexican people and their country—embroidered with golden thread.

They must enjoy it. They come from Toluca, Queretaro, Pachuca, everywhere. When they're right in front of our house they begin singing the traditional Mañanitas. They're happy because they're about to arrive at the place where the Virgin first appeared. Tears fill their eyes out of emotion, and they feel so close to each other. Some crawled on their knees . . . and they still have fifteen blocks to go!

The smell of hot tortillas invades the entire neighborhood surrounding the basilica. On just about any step you can find women heating up corn tortillas, the small ones that they sell five or ten at a time, wrapped in cheap colored paper. I wonder why all those candles are for sale everywhere around the basilica? They're slender and beautiful, and they're decorated with pink flowers.

Sometimes we would go into the church and listen to Mass. We'd walk through the street with all the vendors' stalls and then climb the little hill, which we can see from our window. There's a small white house on top with a cross on the roof. That's where the miracle happened to Juan Diego, an Indian. Wasn't he lucky! I hope that happens to me someday. If it really was a miracle, then it can happen to me too. Afterward, we'd go back down the hill, and in order to get home, we'd take the trolley that runs up and down Guadalupe Avenue. That way we wouldn't be late and my mother wouldn't find out that we had gone to the villa again.

I believed them, I truly believed my parents when they told me that the Jews didn't kill Christ.

"If they bother you again, just tell them that Christ was a Jew and had had his bar mitzvah."

"Oh, Daddy, do you think I would say that? They'd just get mad at me."

When my mommy went to Monterrey to see my other grandfather, Micaela quickly finished her chores and took us to the villa again; we ran into some of her friends, and we walked together. Then I heard one of them say, "Listen, Mica, don't work there; the amount the Jews pay isn't much; they never pay much." I acted like I didn't hear anything, because I don't know what to think or do when I hear those things. And what if later on they start on this thing about the Jews killing Christ? Everyone already knows about it. Then we went inside the church on the hill for a while, and I just stood there staring at Christ crucified on the cross. Look what they did to him! A woman who was kneeling next to us just sobbed as she stared at the blood flowing everywhere. Poor thing. Well, who wouldn't hate the people who did this? They're bad! And it was so long ago, and she still feels horrible about it. If that woman who is weeping finds out that I'm Jewish, she might even kill me. The good thing is that Micaela likes me a lot, and she doesn't really buy all that stuff, and you really don't notice that I'm Jewish at first. Honestly, I'd rather be Jewish than a black person. But even I get upset and sad! Look how they nailed him to a cross! Can you believe it? What monsters they were!

There's a fabric store at the corner where I live; Bertita and Bicha live in the back part of the store, and they're Mommy's friends. They make pastries and decorate them beautifully. I spend hours just watching them put layer on top of layer, and then there's always just one more. They make little doll-like figures, and using wire and icing they create the sweet little blue, yellow, and red flowers. Sometimes, when they finish a wedding cake, I say it's the most beautiful one they've ever made, but when they put the finishing touches on a birthday cake with the little figure in the middle standing on a pedestal, it always seems to be the nicest. I spend a lot of time with them, surrounded by vats of yellow, red, and blue icing.

The little figures don't look all that great until we make their clothes with little pieces of cloth and then stick them around the waist with some icing. We cover some of the folds with more icing, making it look like a waist-band—then they look really elegant. Using some coloring, we decide if they are going to be dark-looking or fair-skinned, and they're just like we want them to be—poor things!—but they always turn out fabulous.

Bichita and Bertita are friends of a priest who teaches catechism at a church near our house on Saturdays. He teaches us to pray. A lot of kids go there. Ever since I've learned to cross myself, I can use my right hand faster, because it's the one you use to make the sign of the cross. Afterward, they give us anise-flavored candies. I just love them. I never miss classes; the pastry ladies just tell my mother that I'm with them, helping to decorate cakes. So I go to catechism secretly, because I want to have first communion, and they're the only ones who can help save me at the Last Judgment; maybe, just maybe, by saving me, God will forgive my whole family too.

Several families from the old country live in this neighborhood called Industrial. They are my parents' best friends. They were already good friends before they got married. My mommy introduced Max to Fortunita, his wife. Now they have children too, and we're all very close. I'm the oldest. Today Mommy and some of her friends decided to go to a Hebrew school in the Valle district and see if the school could send a bus to pick us up where we live. When we got home from school, we found out they had enrolled us in that school.

Did all of these kids also kill Christ? They all seemed so gentle. I thought: it doesn't seem like they would do it. How could they even remember? They play marbles, ring around the roses, and everything we did at the other school. Are they the same though? It's hard to tell if they're really Jewish. I don't know why, but I'm not interested in making friends with any of them.

Wow! Third year is really different. I'm learning the multiplication tables. And we're beginning to write in ink, which has been hard for me. It was easier with a pencil. Now we get everything stained—our notebooks, our backpacks, our fingers, and our checkered school uniforms. We bring ink bottles and blotters to make our lessons look better. With pencil, everything gets erased. Ink is better. This has been a big change for us. They treat us like we're older—we use ink bottles.

Our teacher, Mr. Gomez, is the most demanding teacher in the school, and he's the meanest too. I'm in his room. For an hour, starting at eight o'clock in the morning, he makes us draw our circles perfectly. He imitates the action and then draws them all linked together on the board, telling us all the while that these are calligraphy exercises, and that he doesn't understand our scribbling. This is exactly the part I like best, and when we're working hard in class, that's when I'm not so afraid of the teacher.

My mother is really happy that he's my teacher. She says he's very demanding, and that's why he's a good teacher. Even if he is, he has an ugly face. That's why I sit near the back, half-hidden, so he won't see me when he asks questions. The other day he asked me three times, but I didn't respond, because I didn't even hear him. I remember that the nuns were great. Then he calls out our names with a gruff voice, as if we were soldiers. I'll bet he doesn't even laugh at home.

The bus going to the Condesa and Roma neighborhoods continues on to Indus trial. I've got a friend whose name is Dori. She's in my class and rides the same bus. We return to school in the afternoon to learn Hebrew, which is a strange language. You write it from right to left, exactly the opposite from Spanish. Now, whenever my grandfather scolds my father or my grandmother, I'll be able to understand him. Ah, I just remembered that at my grandfather's house they only speak Farsi. They use Hebrew for parties. Oh well, whatever!

Max and Fortuna moved to the Hipódromo neighborhood because they wanted to be closer to the Sephardic school and live nearer to their friends from the old country. The other families are looking for places to live around there too.

"What are you waiting for, Shamuel, don't pass this up! What are you going to do here by yourselves, wasting away alone? You and your wife who are still so young! Don't pass this up; let's move together, we'll take you there. There's an apartment on the corner near our house, it's not rented, it's on the fifth floor, and it's cheap! Come and see it on Sunday! It's great!"

I told Dori to check out the corner of Cholula and Campeche Streets because we were probably going to move there. She got excited, because it's only a block from her house and the apartment building was beautiful. I can't believe it: I'll be living close to my best friend. Now I can't wait for the day when I'll finally be her neighbor.

Now that they're building a movie theater near our house, we're going to move. It took them so long to do it that we didn't even get to go to the opening. The only time I've ever gone to a movie was when Max invited us one

Sunday morning. He took us to the Alameda. What a place! When it went dark inside, it seemed like we were in a dark street, and there were pretty little houses lit up on either side. I don't know if anyone lived inside them, I'm not sure, but maybe they were really stars on the walls. And what a movie! Max's children are so lucky to get to go all the time. My dad has never taken us to the movies. He's always working on Sundays, and then my mother shuts the blinds at six o'clock in the evening and puts us to bed, saying it's already nighttime and that no one goes out at night. I don't think I'll ever get to go again. If I could just see that movie over again . . .

This is the first night in our new house, and I'm excited. I want it to be morning already, because Dori is coming to take me to see her house. She wants to show me how close it is to mine. We're so lucky!

The building is nice. It's pink, which is my favorite color—after all, I'm a girl. That's the only thing I like about being a girl, we get everything in pink; it's prettier than blue. We have the whole floor to ourselves, because there are only five apartments in the building, one on each floor. We live right on the corner, so we have balconies that look down onto both streets. On the Cholula Street side, we get the sun when it comes up. That's where the living room and kitchen are, and you can see the Popo store from that side. The bedrooms are on the other side: one for my parents, one for my three brothers, and one for my two sisters and me. Now we won't have boys and girls sleeping in the same room. Too bad! It was more fun that way. If only Moshón could stay with me. He's going to be bored with the two little ones. There are two bathrooms. One is small, and the other has a tub. The kitchen is so big there's room for a breakfast nook and the washing machine. And my mother put the banana tree on one of the balconies. The sitting room has a long balcony with flowers. When I look out the window of my brothers' bedroom, I can see the neon sign for a movie theater. It is divine (no one says divine, that's only for God, Our Father); I mean it's neat to have a movie theater so close. It's called the Lido, and it's already open. This is a fancy neighborhood!

I've got a bunch of school friends who live around here; well, they're everywhere. Maybe there aren't any Catholics here, I'm not sure. Now all of us who used to live in Indus trial live here, next to each other. Even my granddaddy moved from his house on Calzada de los Misterios and bought one in the Roma neighborhood, on Chihuahua Street, near a park that has a huge water fountain in the middle. What a house! It's really something else. It has an indoor patio, and the floor and walls are decorated with smooth tiles, and there must be over one hundred flowerpots on the floor and hanging on the walls. The flowerpots that I like the most are the ones decorated all over with pieces of broken dishes. They're like the ones we have at our house—they even have the same designs. And, by the way, the dishes that my mommy bought in La Merced Market are a thousand times better than the old ones, because while you're eating your soup, all of sudden little animals—a bear, a dog, a duck—start to appear inside the bowl. It's fun discovering them while I eat! I hope these don't get broken very soon.

I don't know why my mommy's friends feel sorry for her because we live on the fifth floor. It's not too tiring to climb the stairs, and besides, we do little things to make life easier—if the mailman or the milkman or anyone comes with something, we just drop a little basket with a string tied to it over the balcony. That way we don't have to go up and down the stairs. When we get home from school, and before we climb the stairs, we yell up to the apartment to see if we need to buy bread or tortillas. On the days Mommy goes to market, she pays a little boy to help her because no one in the family can carry all those bags up five floors.

After having gone to the Sephardic school many times and eaten in a hurry while the bus waited downstairs where we used to live, it's been a relief to live in this neighborhood because when the bus drops us off, there are still a lot of kids on it. While they're taking them and then returning to pick us up again, we have time to play on the sidewalk with Dori and her two brothers, who come to wait also.

Mommy didn't set aside her usual routine even when Dori came to eat. She sits the six of us around the table together and she lets us know that the belt is just over there; we don't talk; we eat quickly; we don't even argue; then she sends us down to the street to play; and she doesn't want us to throw anything. Fortunately, we can play ball or skate outside; there are always a bunch of kids playing in the street. I don't understand how all these things can make that silly Dori laugh. She said my mother is very nice and it's nice to have a bunch of brothers and sisters. Nice? It's horrible! And it's even worse when you're the oldest one and you have to stop them from fighting and they hit you really hard because you're the oldest. Look . . . she doesn't even have a mother. But my mother is nice? Well, she's even less than nice when she gets mad and digs her four nails into my arm, making it bleed. Now there are little scabs like fingernail scratches that were really visible last week, and when I said something to my dad that I shouldn't have, she did it again. How was I supposed to know that I shouldn't have said anything to him?

Acapulco is really beautiful! And I never believed that the ocean could be so big! It never ends! I was lucky to be invited. I'm the only one of my brothers and sisters to go to the ocean. My aunt Chela and I slept in one room and my grandparents in another. And my aunt took so long to get ready! She puts on one lipstick, then another, looks at herself in the mirror, makes a face, touches up her eye makeup, looks at herself again—this time from another angle—smiles, looks again, makes another face, then looks at herself out of the corner of her eye. After this ritual, she remembers that someone else is in the room with her—that's me—and says, "Oshinica, I'm ready, let's eat breakfast. If we don't, your grandfather will disown us, he'll think something has happened to us, or that I spend too long getting ready. Actually, I've spent less time here than back at home, mainly because I didn't spend so much time styling my hair."

I had already put on my long, flowered beach robe, the one my daddy bought from Chucho in the store across from ours in Lagunilla Market. It covers my bathing suit. Finally, we're all decked out for our entrance into the dining room where my grandparents are waiting.

"Good morning, Daddy," she says as she kisses his hand, and then greets my grandmother in the same way.

"Oshinica, aren't you going to kiss your grandfather's hand?"

The hotel is on top of a mountain and you can see the huge, beautiful ocean from the dining room. And right now I'm thinking about my aunt, who looks so pretty this morning, knowing that she has an elegant bathing suit on underneath her robe, and another one that she hasn't worn yet in the closet. It has a picture on it, with a woman diving into the ocean and a bright sun in the background. I've never seen a more beautiful bathing suit! They buy her whatever she wants. My mother doesn't find it very amusing. She says they spoil her so much that she's useless. But, with me, she's great! She likes me as if I were her little sister. My daddy, her only brother, is fifteen years older than she is.

Shabbat always begins at six o'clock on Friday evening, just as the first star appears in the heavens, and it ends the next day with the first star. I sing in the choir at school because the teacher said I had a good voice; Moshón doesn't. That's why I go on Fridays, and if we don't, we won't be able to sing at weddings. They pay us to sing too. That's the only way I can earn some money, but I also like to go to the synagogue because we always have fun there. Since the bus picks us up before prayer time, we've got half an hour to fool around. At the corner of Monterrey and Bajio, where the synagogue is located, between the bakery and the store, a woman is usually selling hot tortillas, but she's not always there. Our big thrill is to eat. First we buy some bread rolls and strips of cooked chile wrapped in paper. Then we put them together and have a feast. We continue walking with fire coming out of our mouths, and then a little later we buy tortillas (if we have any money left).

At 7:15 we take our places in the choir. The prayer begins with our singing, well, our shouting. I don't know why the people like our toneless voices—it's so silly to say that we sing nicely, and that our temple is the best one around because of the choir.

I don't like taking baths with my brothers and sisters anymore, because Dori laughed at me. My mother gets the four of us older ones into the tub, sits on the edge near the hot and cold faucets, soaps my head, scratches me with her nails, goes to the next one, Moshón, and at the end Zelda and Clarita, then back to me. Every eight days each one of us gets scrubbed down three times. I asked if we could bathe separately, but she says it's too much work. The next step is even worse: brushing our hair and making long braids for all of us girls. We begin crying from the very moment she begins brushing out the tangles. It's frightening to have to take a bath, but the good thing is that once our hair is braided, it doesn't get tangled again. During the rest of the week she just undoes the braids and sprinkles lemon juice on them so they won't get tangled.

Every day my daddy gets up early and goes to Chapultepec Park to do his rowing. But he doesn't leave until he sees us safely on the bus, and the only thing I don't like is that he makes me eat two soft-boiled eggs, which is the only thing in life that makes me sick to my stomach. Just looking at them makes me want to vomit, but I swallow them quickly, after which I always start running toward the bathroom as if I were going to throw up.

Daddy has a lot of friends at the park, like Don Gume, who has a clothing store in the Escandon Market, or another, the milkman, who lends my dad his bike. They're almost always together in the park because they take the same bus line: Chorrito, in Juanacatlán. First they walk together for a while, and then each one rents a rowboat. We go there on Saturdays, Sundays, and every day during summer vacation. We always have fun with him; Mommy doesn't like to have fun. Mothers only like to clean house. I like going there because we get to row the boat, first me and then Moshón, and afterward he buys us fruit drinks and pieces of papaya at a stand on the edge of the lake. While we're eating, he rows us around the lake really fast. I can row fast too, and when we pass through the tunnel underneath the street—the long one that goes to the other side of the lake—I don't even hit the oars against the sides. Since Moshón can't beat me, he gets all bent out of shape. I can even do more pull-ups.

"Hey, Dad, why don't we rent two rowboats tomorrow and we can race to see who wins?"

I want to marry my dad because he's really handsome. Or even Moshón will do.

"Like I was telling you, Ernesto, that's the way life is, my twentysomethingth child, first it was a girl, impossible; you know Oshinica, my granddaughter, I adore her, she has my mother's name, may she rest in peace. I didn't say a solitary word, you know I've got good manners, I don't stick my nose into things; in fact, I had called the hospital several times to see if the girl had opened her eyes yet. Two years later, thank God, a boy. I was his godparent, and it was my right. He was named after my grandfather because in our religion, as you know, it's required that the grandson carry the name of the grandfather. My daughter-in-law didn't go to the circumcision ceremony; if the baby needed her, she was there, but she couldn't even give much milk; she has boys, takes care of them, raises them, and that's it. Anyway, to make a long story short, her third child was a girl. Only God knows what he's doing. And, eleven months later, lo and behold: another girl. She gave us a total of three of them. For the last two, the mother chose names from her people. Can you imagine? Three dowries! My son is going to have to work like a dog in order to get them married. Would you like some coffee? 'Hey! A cup of coffee for this man.' As I was saying, right now I would like for my daughter Chelita to get married, and I can vouch for the fact that she's a doll with a creamy-white face, a real sweetie pie, and obedient. We've had some real pests come around, because those Arabs are asking for hundreds of pesos— and if the boy is from a good family, even as high as several thousand pesos. Between you and me, that's the way it is. I tell you these things because you are my friend; I've known you ever since I arrived in Mexico . . . Ernesto, why are you getting up? It's still early; it's barely ten o'clock . . . wait a little longer!"

My granddaddy got sick, and I think Dr. Ernesto did too, because as much as my granddaddy wanted him to stay, he left there quickly. What horrible things he said!

What a neat green rocker! It's cool the way it rocks back and forth. But I don't think they'll let me try it because last Friday, after Moshón had gotten all comfortable in it, they said, "Get out of that rocker! Your grandfather is about to come home, and he'll get upset."

I know they'll never let me sit in it. So my five brothers and sisters and I sat all squished together on a couch and, once we got absorbed in a TV program, we forgot about fighting for the rocker. Grandfather makes his appearance. We all jump up at once, just like when the school director comes into the classroom. Tall, standing erect, one hand in his pocket and the other ready to tweak our little chins, we take turns giving him kisses. Chelita, my aunt, is also standing, hunched over a bit, and speaking like a mouse to show him how insignificant she is compared to the superiority of her father. She kisses his hand and puts it on her forehead as if to receive his blessing. He puts his hand forward, and while we kiss it, he looks the other way. That's his way of doing things. Next, he takes his hand out of his pocket and changes channels on the TV. Once he has decided which program we'll watch, he sits down in his rocking chair.

Sometimes I just stare at the photographs on the living room walls. They all look so old. There's one I especially like of my granddaddy sitting at a table. I don't know how they took them, but there are other grandparents from different angles, some laughing and others very serious. What a funny picture! Next to the window there's a picture of us sitting together arranged by age: first me, I was laughing with my braids and a huge topknot, my mother really knew how to make those curls in my hair too. I was smiling and giving Moshón, who was always handsome, a big hug; then Zelda and Clarita. We all look great together! Next to our picture, there's a map of Israel, and a blue-and-white flag with a Zion symbol in the middle, and it reads below, "Israel, nation of Hebrews." In the next picture, Aunt Chela is wearing a green dress and a protruding hairdo; then comes my father when he was still single, and above the chimney, which has never been used, there's a Mason diploma with silver-and-gold edging that my grandfather is really proud of. He says it's a secret group and some of his best friends are Masons. No doubt about it, my grandfather is really pompous.

Today I went upstairs to his room and on top of the chest of drawers there were a million oddly shaped and different colored bottles of cologne; one of them has a little black ball on top, and when you squeeze it, a wet, strong smell comes out. I adore going up to his room because it's as elegant as a king's chamber, and so is my aunt's bedroom: it's all hers, and it has a dressing table and stool. I've never seen myself from the front and the back at the same time before. Is that the way they see me when they see me from the side? I didn't really recognize this new Oshinica, and I think my nose is too big if you look at me from the side, but . . . what a luxurious bedroom . . . and it has a terrace with cane furniture. She has her own bathroom. It's violet with turquoise and white. Then I begin poking around in her chest of drawers. Wow! Is that neat or what? It's like getting inside my aunt's world. She has hose, invitations, spools of thread, little boxes; everything's a secret, but I just go about opening and closing doors and drawers.

Here there's plenty of room to store things; at our house all I have is the bottom drawer of the chiffonier. That's where my mom puts my folded underwear, so I can't really hide anything there. Oh, how I'd like to be able to lock it and have my own private space! Even if I just had a place to hide this diary, so I wouldn't have to live in fear that someone is going to read it. It's no one's business but mine.

A lot of times I hear the adults say they'd give anything just to be kids again. Being a kid is marvelous, we're supposed to be happy, not be in need of anything, and laugh at anything . . . and also, they begin gazing nostalgically. I don't understand it. What do they see that's so great about it? This is being happy? My mother yells at me, she spanks me, and at school they punish me. I still haven't finished writing "I must obey my parents and my teachers" five hundred times. For more than a month now, I've had to fill up page after page of the same thing. And they won't let me talk in class either. The only homework I have time for is to repeat this writing, and I like it, especially when all the lines are connected. I can do it fast and they look great. I think that those adults who believe those things about childhood probably couldn't draw those lines, or their parents didn't scold them. And if that's true, will it be worse when I grow up?

Do I want to look like my mom, my grandmother, or my aunt? No, I'd rather look like my grandfather, my dad, or even my brother. Those women are so boring, and they're dumb as well! Well, I guess my mom isn't so dumb, but she's not all fun and games either. My grandmother can't even go to Sears by herself, and it's only two blocks away. But she goes secretly with Uba. Women are supposed to stay at home; it doesn't even occur to them to go rowing. My dad is really nice; the men go out to work and the women take care of the children or the brothers and sisters, like me. At least I don't get bored, because I can go outside and always beat the guys at soccer or baseball.

"That man dressed in blue, is he the groom?"

"I don't know, honey, but I think so. The other one looks too old, but let's go to the park, because your grandfather doesn't want anyone to disturb him."

"Is it really possible? That ugly guy wants to marry my aunt?"

"I don't know. I'll ask your grandma later. All I know is that your aunt has been jumpy lately, and who knows what they're going to talk about?

"When I brought the coffee, I heard them talking about the property in Polanco as a part of her dowry. But I shouldn't say anything; your grandfather would kill me. Let's take your little boat to the park, and we'll put it in the water; all the kids will be taking theirs. Didn't you bring yours with you?"

"Yes I did, Uba, and I like to come over here because then you always take us to the park."

When we got back, they were saying good-bye.

"That guy dressed in blue, the one with the straight hair," said my dad, "he's not going to marry your aunt."

I felt faint. Oh my God! What a shame! Everyone was mad.

And my poor aunt, she's so pretty and he's really ugly. She was so embarrassed that she locked herself in her room. My father doesn't have any land or even a car, so how is he going to get me married? When we were leaving, I heard my grandfather say, "They're crazy! Is that all they think of her? They can go straight to hell! They don't know what they want. Well, I dare them ever to find any girl as beautiful as my daughter."

I don't want anyone to know that I cried all night long, or that I bit my blankets out of rage. But what difference would it make if just one of us got mad? What did my aunt feel? What a shame, him rejecting her like that! How embarrassing! She had already gone out a few times with this guy, who had a beard and wore a black hat, and now, when they finally come to formalize the engagement, the deal is off. This isn't going to happen to Moshón. Maybe I'll just stay like a little girl. I don't want this to ever happen to me. It's horrible being a woman. If I'm stronger than Moshón and I can do anything he can, what's the difference? I don't want to even get close to an Arab. Yesterday, when those men arrived, my granddaddy, smiling with his gold teeth, said that I was his little granddaughter, and they said what everybody says: "Like a bride! A true bride!" That means good luck!

Why would I ever want to get married?

"Auntie, you're so pretty. Why would they want to do that to you?"

"Well," my mommy answers, "they're backward and stupid. They never let your aunt go out alone; they always hired a teacher to come to the house. They always made her seem like she was hard to get, and that's why she talks like that. Ugh! They didn't even let her have any friends. And those from Persia? They're all the same. What's the difference? Your grandfather has made a slave out of your father. See what I'm saying? Yesterday he told him to get the car out of the garage just as we were getting ready to go to the movies. That ended that idea. Heaven help him who doesn't do what he's supposed to. Everything will get ruined. And don't you see? If you're not high class, you don't have good clothes, and we're even without a car. In Istanbul, I used to go to the best schools, and our classes were taught in French. My mother's family, of course, was upper class."

✦

Two kids who ride the school bus to the Roma neighborhood began fighting; they had said a lot of bad words in Arabic to each other on the bus.

"I hope you swallow an umbrella and it opens up inside your stomach," said one of them.

"I hope you live 120 years in a hospital," said the other.

"A curse on the ship that brought your father here!" replied the first one.

I get scared when my daddy speaks Arabic to someone. He learned it in the Lagunilla Market and he speaks it from time to time, but not at home, of course—well, whom would he speak it with? Fortunately, no one at school has ever heard him speak it.

"Because of Queen Esther, we Jews were saved," said my mommy. It just so happens that the king of the Philistines, who wasn't Jewish, fell in love with Esther. As the king, he had all the young girls of the kingdom brought to him, and he chose her. Even though his prime minister did everything he could to prevent him from marrying her, it was her beauty that saved the people of Israel. And now we honor that marriage with the Purim celebration in March; at school we have a kermis charity bazaar with costumes; the mothers distribute bread and marmalade called hamantaschen, and they give us wooden rattles to liven things up.

They pick two candidates from each room to play the role of Queen Esther. On the day of the kermis, when they crown the queen, everyone really gets excited. Even the parents get drawn in to it—they buy lots of votes so that their daughter will be elected the queen. How fortunate the chosen one must feel! They've never even considered me; besides, my dad wouldn't ever buy any votes. But still, when they come around to choose the candidates from each room, I always get a little nervous because they just might say my name. But it's never happened. I guess I'm not that pretty. And it's always same girls. Last year, Dori lost by one hundred votes to the daughter of the school president. After the coronation, I like to go to the charity raffle, because the parents who own stores or factories always donate neat gifts. Then they reenact the moment when the king chooses Esther. Out on the patio, we dance horas in a circle around a bonfire. Then we eat. My mommy usually makes a huge bag of popcorn because she was assigned to a food table.

I wet the bed again, and my mommy had taken me half-asleep one last time to the bathroom. I still do it, and I don't even feel it. I guess she has gotten used to it, because she doesn't scold Clara or me; she just leaves the sheets on the bed all week and the stain begins to look really horrible. Whenever we get a new maid, I'm always embarrassed, but then I shake it off—there's no way I can hide in my own house, so I just act like nothing's happened.

My sister and I sleep in either of the two beds and when we realize that we're wet, we just change our pajamas and get into the one that's dry. Zelda just frowns at us and complains that our beds stink; she thinks she's unlucky because she has to sleep with us. We don't do it because we want to, and I'd never be able to invite anyone to spend the night, and I'd never dream of going to someone else's house. Just think what would happen if everyone at school found out! My mommy's right in loving Moshón more than us. He's really clean. These kids that don't wet their beds—how do they do it?

Freddy wets his bed too. We could try putting those of us who wet our beds together in one room, and those who are normal in the other. We can do it, if my mommy wants to; if not, Zelda will have to make sure she doesn't get her bedding mixed up with ours; then she'll have to stop bothering us.

I was going to say that out of the three closest aunts I have, the one I like the best is Chela, although my mommy's sister who lives in Monterrey is nice too. I was sent to stay with them during vacation. I even went to my cousins' school, which I really liked, because everyone wanted to know who I was, and my cousins would act like they were important, saying I was from Mexico City. Just outside the school gate they sell jicama, oranges, cucumber slices with chile, crisp pork rinds, yo-yos, *baleros*, *paletas*, chocolates, pinole, well, you know, all the things my dad says are no good for you—ah, and some caramel-covered apples that you suck on until you reach the apple part. Sundays are the same for me as for anyone else: I love to buy, buy, buy. But it's not the same in Mexico City. There's nothing to buy because when we get out of class, the buses are waiting inside the school yard, and even if they *are* selling things outside the gates, we don't ever see them.

Alegre is five years older than I am. She has a bedroom all to herself, and I like being her cousin. And she has so many friends! She does things the way she wants to, she wears checked shirts that have the necks and sleeves like a man's shirt, and she has a wallet for her money just like my dad's—ah, and she wears pants too. On Saturdays, she invites three or four friends over to spend the night; we haul mattresses, pillows, and blankets down to the living room, turn up the record player, and stay up as late as we want. What a great life! At home, if we make any noise after my mom turns out the light, she yells at us, "Enough! Be quiet. Or I'll give you all a good whipping."

Aarón asked me if I wanted to swim; I thought he meant in a swimming pool, but no, he meant on the terraced roof behind the kitchen. We put a board in front of the kitchen door to keep the water from leaking inside. We started filling up the patio at eight o'clock in the morning, and by eleven it was up to our knees. Even though it was freezing cold, we swam in our underwear. I can't believe I even opened my eyes underneath the water and I could see the bottom. It was a fantastic day! When my aunt came home, I got scared, but she didn't get mad. She just laughed, put a towel around me, and said, "Girl, you're so crazy. Just look at you! Really, you do some of the silliest things."

Before I went to sleep, she said to me, "Tell me, have you heard the stories about crazy Ishodotro of Yojá? They used to tell them to us when we were little kids in Istanbul." I adore the way my aunt laughs. And she has that mischievous look in her eyes. It seems a little strange to me because grown-ups don't do pranks. I wanted her to tell me the stories, even though they're the same ones my mom tells us.

What a strange aunt! If she lived in Mexico City she might get along with my mom, and then maybe my mom would be easier on us.

This year, I'll finish sixth grade. It's the year when they start taking most of the girls out of school—this is the year they begin to live at home with their mothers. They take sewing lessons, they learn how to cook, make desserts, and who knows what else; but all of a sudden they become pretty and get married. The boys are allowed to continue their studies. Oh, heaven forbid! What if they do that to me? What am I going to do at home all day long?

There are two bakeries near our house, but we always go to the one on Nuevo Leon, even though it's farther away. My mom likes their bread better. The only bad thing about it is that to get there we have to walk past Rosi's house, and every time her mom's standing at the window, and when she sees us walking by, she yells out, "Are you going for bread, honey? For the love of your mommy, get me a couple of loaves too."

And there's no way you can say no to her, right? So she's always taking advantage of my brothers, or me, and as a result, she always gets fresh bread brought to her door. And yesterday, when I brought her the bread, she had even more nerve: "Honey, dear, could you please help me move this table, and that plant, and this pot?"

And she asked Moshón to bring her some soft drinks from the store across the street. We're definitely not going to walk by that old bat's house anymore. No wonder they call Rashelica the brazen old . . . I mean, well, she has some nerve! Even though it takes longer, let's walk all the way around the block, and besides, why doesn't she send Rosi dear, as she calls her, to do those things?

Sitting at the window that looks down to Piedad Street, Aunt Cler helps while away the hours. She is accompanied by the sounds corning from a large oval-shaped radio. This afternoon we listened to the comedy programs on Radio XEW and XEQ. Between programs they play songs by singers such as Avelina Landin and Amparo Montes—"I'm walking down that tropical path / my eyes are full of passion and my soul feels like crying"—or something like that. And at six o'clock, *Doctor Heart*. It's a neat program that helps people solve their problems. I love hearing about things that I never knew existed. I'd like to write her an anonymous letter with a fake signature so that my mom wouldn't find out, but I bet they'd never pay any attention to an elevenyear-old.

"So long as you've got your health, the rest is unimportant; you should be thankful to God that you're not an invalid, blind, or an orphan," says my father. "The people who write to her have nothing else to do; they're just vain."

And do they have problems! I'd like to ask her what I need to do to quit wetting my bed or to stop my mom from yelling at me.

"Dear Friend . . ." she'd probably answer. But what a lovely lady! How I wish someone would say that to me sometime! My father says people who talk like that are hypocrites and he doesn't trust them.

Is that really true? Maybe so.

While we listen to the programs, I watch Aunt Cler sew and sew, and I see that she's concerned about what's going on in the soap opera—if they had caught Esmeralda or if the daughter had deceived her father. Silently she changes the color of the thread, finishes the last stitch, and happily admires the juicy purple grapes that grew from her hands on the throw pillows that will adorn her couch in the living room.

My mom goes into the kitchen to fix that tasty dessert that old Aunt Cler makes from rolled orange rinds. Her maid is off on Mondays, that's why we go to see her on those days.

"She can't be left alone; what would she do if someone comes to the door or she needs to go to the bathroom? If no one is around, what would she do? Heaven help me if something were to happen to her. And, to top it off, she's in a wheelchair. Poor thing! She can wheel around a bit. Uncle David, thank God, will come this evening."

And that's the way it's been for two years, and ever since her daughter died, she's been paralyzed.

This Monday my mother couldn't visit Aunt Cler, so she sent me with the keys instead.

"That's very nice of you, child. Stay for a while! Let's talk, take your mind off things, you poor dear."

As soon as the train starts along Piedad Street, I try to spot her window from my seat. In that building, there's a window curtain with that starched pride and the elegant hand-stitched lace, behind which I spot aunt's little face with straight hair. I climb the stairs, taking a short rest on each floor; the stairwells and hallways are so wide that you could dance a hora in each one. I think: once she walked up those stairs for the first time, and she'll go down them on the last day of her life. I get the keys out and I'm in the living room. I look around everywhere, there are embroidered doilies all over the place, and you can see the work of her hand in every throw pillow, in every corner. I cross through the sitting room and reach the door of the little room where the sound of the dark wood radio fills the house and my aunt's life. I know that she'll be surprised to see me because she never knows which niece has been designated to visit her that day.

"Ah! Is that you?" she says without cracking a smile.

Those big, deep eyes that I thought would light up just stare at me, giving me the shivers. I don't appreciate her not saying something nice about me coming—not willingly, but here I am. I sit down in this small armless chair, directly in front of her, and I look toward the street. The sun is strong, but it's partly hidden, so we put the blinds down. I like to leaf through her embroidery magazines while we listen to the radio programs. In one of the old magazines, *Family Magazine*, I run across a beautiful cross-stitch and she says she'll show me how to do it. When she sends me to get the orange-rind dessert, I stop and linger in the living room without bothering her. My mom told me that Auntie cleans all of her decorations on the glass shelves herself. She doesn't trust the maids, everything has to be carefully dusted, right down to the last little corner and crack; that's why she gets them out. I take a peek into the bedrooms: I see a picture of her daughter, then a girl younger than me, and I get sad for my aunt who lost her daughter and for the girl who, had she lived, would have inherited the responsibility to take care of her sick mother. That daughter is with her when she's embroidering, watching other lives from the window, listening to the radio, and watching the trains coming and going up and down Piedad Street.

The Invisible Hour

ESTHER SELIGSON (1941–2010)
Translated from the Spanish by Iván Zatz

First published in Indicios y quimeras *(1988), this story can be read as a study of Bergsonian time or as a surrealist vision of eternity. Seligson manages to deal with several layers of time: clock time, calendar time, psychological time, and metaphysical time, thus the quote "Time is either an invention or nothing at all." The anonymous narrator, the owner of a broken quartz watch, takes it to be fixed at a store unlike any other. What follows is an examination of life in and beyond time—a journey through a metaphysical universe in which the experience of time itself is abstracted.*

Blindness is a weapon against time and space. Our existence is nothing more than an immense and unique blindness, with the exception of those tiny bits transmitted to us by our miserly senses. The dominant principle within the cosmos is blindness. . . . Time, which is a continuum, can only be escaped by a single means: to avoid observing it from time to time. Thus can we reduce it to those fragments we can recognize.

—ELIAS CANETTI, *Auto-da-Fé*

"WELL, YES, SIR, we'll have to keep it for observation."

"But how come? The only problem was that the glass fell off."

"We are a serious company, sir. We are specialists. Our obligation is to return it to you in perfect condition."

"There's nothing wrong with it."

"The hands appear to be a little loose, and the face is somewhat dusty. It's only logical, since it had been exposed for a while."

"And how long will you keep it for observation?"

"Come back in ten days, please. Here you have your receipt. You can claim it with this piece of paper. You mustn't lose it, under any circumstances."

And that is how he saw it disappear, in a dainty red velvet case, withdrawn by a pair of mysterious gloved hands coming from behind a narrow window with thin bars in front of it. Then, one of those so-called grave-like silences befell the place. Where could his watch have wound up?

"This crystal is not for measuring time but rather for awakening in one's everyday memory the flash of other instants that need to be urgently freed from their temporary prison." That is what she said while giving it to him, that singular afternoon: a flat sphere, extremely white, the numbers barely marked by silver droplets. There was no need to wind it up, nor to touch or move it: it would tirelessly mark the time, without the slightest slowing down, with the merriment of mercury sliding through the fingers to reach the palm of the hand, lightweight, twinkling, and absolutely silent. The thin hands, silvery too, together with the second hand, would progress in little jumps that looked to him like the back of his Siamese cat when she was petted and the hair on her back would rise and then settle again, trembling slightly. Where could it be now, below the vaults of that old building with brown-grained marble staircases and high walls with straw-colored ornaments on the architraves and bondstone arches? Yes, an old edifice with enormous windows curling around metal volutes, through which the opaline daylight filtered with a milky luminousness. The receptionist would reply with the same chant to any client who approached the counter, "We are a serious company, sir. Our obligation is to return it to you in perfect condition."

She was stiff, without moving a single facial muscle, as if she were a perfect piece of clockwork. And the clients would exit through the revolving doors with the feeling that they had been dispossessed, defeated by an unknown force that could not be at all opposed: in there, one's hours, minutes, and seconds would be sifted through until they were denuded of time. But, doubtlessly, there would be clients who would stay there to wait; otherwise, what were those soft, tawny leather couches with ocher-colored buttons for? Long brownish counters flanked the walls of the room, and at the back wall there was a wide staircase, morosely carpeted in the same red color of the cases in which the watches would leave for an unknown destination.

And it occurred to him that upstairs, behind the finely sanded mahogany doors, in the upper corridor, which could be seen through the convoluted metalwork of the bannister, one found the death chambers, the conservatories, the incubators, the urns, the capsules where the time-catching quartzes would be buried, embalmed, or simply allowed their recovering sleep; and, in the midst of all of that, his own would be there, that marvelous box into which he had deposited his consciousness of the fleeting, the days, weeks, and months that had slowly oozed along. What would he do in the meantime? How could he follow the pulse of his thoughts, that pendular sway that he had tied to the bursts of light given by those sparkles, which it was his task to rescue from the unlimited dullness of the everyday grind? Memories in the shape of an Argand lamp without oil or wick lay languishing in the empty recesses of his mind, left between one oscillation and the other. His work had been interrupted, an unavoidable setback in his mindful task; and only now had he begun to decipher the path along the labyrinth of gears through which he had to enter, a network of minute pins, of small wheels and pivots, crowns, springs, and anchors!

His body shook with a shiver. He covered the whole room with his gaze. A doorman bid the clients farewell with a slight bowing of the head. Two sales clerks behind the counters stood erect as mannequins. A janitor cleaned with an enormous white feather duster the pier glasses on the walls and the large pendulum clocks attached to them. Full of resolve, he straightened his back. Taking his portfolio under his arm, he walked directly to the staircase, like a person with an inevitable appointment upstairs. Nobody stopped him or paid attention. "Trespassing Prohibited," "Personnel Only" read the signs on door after door. Not a single sound outside. Perhaps only the slight shuffle of his shoes on the thick carpet and a creaking of the wood here and there, as if it were breathing behind the doorways. Some bell was ringing, muffled, solitary. Inside, on the contrary, everything was beating: a multiplicity of living organisms, coming apart and fertilizing each other, a multitude of time-giving terms, little seeds of endurance, which a giant gloved hand pretended to remove and return to the dust of the uncreated, to the chaos that came before temporality, to exile, to alienation. With extreme care, he turned the shiny knob on one of the doors. He was greeted by a thick darkness that began to dissipate as his eyes got accustomed to it. He could distinguish the streaks of neon light from the streetlights, filtering through the windows, due to the wrinkled curtains, without fully shining. An endless gallery opened up before him, with an incessant ticking, an interminable collection of bell jars casting their shadows on the mirrored tables where they rested; and inside these, the watches, mechanisms of uniform movement and completely regular cadence, wind-up barrel, main wheel, second wheel, instant wheel, flywheel, compensating balance, hand shaft, rhomboid wheel, hour wheel, crown wheel and rod-quartz crystals, chime clocks, cuckoo clocks, repeating watches, watch chains, stopwatches, water clocks, vibrations, oscillations, pulses, synchronizations; all subject to change, nonetheless having a before and an after, a beginning and an end, all subject to error, it being impossible to eliminate the imperfection between that beginning and that end, not the eternal returning but the cycle, what is advent because it is awaited, and it is awaited even if it is not announced, a wait that suddenly erupts even if expected, the succession of discernible units in a continuum prolonged toward infinity, an infinity that can be measured, however, regularly, rhythmically, one-two, one-two, the abolition of what is discontinuous no matter how much the sense of each day is dependent on the possibility of reducing that to its everyday context subject to office hours and a job that devalues it by turning it monotonous, ticktock. But sometimes he manages to capture some white butterflies and rescue them from the smoke in the garden where he plants roses and forget-me-nots. For he is a scrupulous gardener, and there is not a corner left without a lovingly watered and trimmed plant, supervised from its most tender sprouting, growing, thickening, blooming, feeding on the future, on successions of light and air, chlorophyll and oxygen; slow tropisms, those that search for the sun and those that withdraw from the sun, those that open up during the day and close up at night, the ever thirsty, the ones with adventitious roots, the creepers, the ones with straight stems, those that bloom and those that only have leaves, those with tendrils and those with verticillate leaves. He too, like other children, had arranged them, album plate after plate, to acquaint himself with their shape, knife-shaped, palmate, lanceolate, arrowhead, penninervate . . .

He closed the door cautiously behind him. A slight smell of alcohol and rusted metal tickled the inside of the nose. Where could he begin? And what if his wondrous crystal had not even arrived there yet? How could he make it out, so small among such gigantic secret keepers? He stepped on the fossilized roots of a carboniferous forest as he entered. Breath transpiring; was it his or that of those bodies and assembly joints? As he descended, he was immersed in a subtle gas vapor: a liquid could be felt circulating through his veins, something thinner and lighter than blood. His ears were buzzing. He perspired. An avalanche came down, and in the nursery, the hours began to burst out inside their vials: everything was transformed into an onslaught of thousands of seconds flying around the gallery, crazed fireflies. Everything: time and memory, memory and remembrance, remembrance and continuity, continuity and atemporality. Everything: what he had always postponed, the moments that had not been lived, the distracted hours, the grayish days, the truncated weeks, the severed months like dried-up branches, and some of the years, purulent years molding away in neglect. Neglect? Not entirely. There were also the gems, rubies, sapphires and spinels, garnets, beryl crystals, and of course quartz—that crystal of shiny crystals, margarites, citrines, amethyst, with its iridescent transparency and its contents of moss, speckled agates forming their arborization with the remembrance of their body, fingers of singular afternoons plucking their deepest strings, those whose sound escaped, precisely, the ticktock and the calendar, those that palpitated awake—a name, a face, its laughter—in the marl of his daily perambulations: the invisible hour. He descended. Minute fish scales, slight flakes of endurance would hit upon the membranes that stretched out in his mind like a wide spiderweb: strung in there, innumerable superimposed images would pivot, swirling and stumbling, a vertigo of cells filled up with a mellifluous vapor where the ticktock seemed to suckle, avid bumblebee, on his most distant memories, far away, very far away, spore, sperm, atom, nebula, light particle, energy flow, wave, 186,000 miles per second, ion. He ascended, blowing, helix, spiral, shedding its leaves backward, enveloping itself, forging itself, suturing itself, pod opened to the wind thus recovering its tightly circular coherence, tenderly follicled berry, still a promise, not yet fruit, present, only a present being created in a progressive manner, genesis, continuous elaboration of the totally new, growth of the unforeseen—"time is either an invention or nothing at all." In his throat, then, the shout exploded like a beam, the frightful abyss. And the crystals began to shatter, but toward the inside, as if being soldered to their own interior revolving around that point, that voice that was his, not the everyday voice, however, but another one, a first one, pristine ticktock, dust storm of recovered instants in the clay of the original man, in the simultaneity of the grain and the flower, the sowing and the reaping: unequivocal signs of time, its language of signs, its language of doors opened toward infinity. He ascended in successive commotions, in successive vibrations, slashing the foliage at right and left, inventing his own path, liberating it from silence to turn it into word, articulation of names to give the objects and rescue them from their movable lime, white dew that burst out spraying a multitude of letters, intermittent points like lanterns banging the mouth in their fight to spring out vowels, consonants, syllables, onomatopoeias, rivers of voices in swelling elasticity, rapid and burning vibration that opens its way to his eyes and lips from a depth growing upward to the alike and contiguous in successive stages. Voices and visions of the instruments and artifacts accumulated there danced their shadows before him and inside him without his being able to distinguish, in that simultaneity, where the outer and the inner were. He felt the tired sickle of time reaping the center of the circles that coincided with the center of other circles, and something escaped the measurable and visible to get lost in the transfinite. A chamber clock gave the signal: the space turned over, coextensive and concomitant, the gears came off their flying axles and pivots. His human presence and curiosity had awakened them from their rhythmic and cadence-like sleep to the chaos of the unspoken, of the potentially lived; and, like in nightmares, they spun in place, full of rancor, and with the evident intention of taking on a body and transforming themselves from mere desires, from simple movement, into concrete facts and acts. The arms linked to the clock hands, the legs of the pendulums, the cavity of the faces, the tongues of the springs and flexors, the molars of the crowns and disks came apart in a merry and threatening clamor. Fire spurted from a solar quadrant that he carelessly approached, fascinated by that dance of stellar incandescences—something told him that, this mirage of proximity notwithstanding, Alpha Centauri was over four light-years away—inside that circumference resembling an empty water clock, whose border formed a flaming fringe. He wanted to look inside. But time is also a reflection of shadows. Therefore, the daring man who attempts to decipher it, spell it out, look at it in the light, can be blinded by its brightness. For time is also blindness, a fragment of life wrapped inside a blind layer until occluded. His eardrums and pupils overwhelmed, he began to crash against the mirrors and crystals, attempting to defend himself with a metal rod from the phantasmagoric round assaulting him, cordless marionettes that pulled him by the hair and skin with parsimonious animosity, ticktock ticktock, fine-edged rubies stabbing his retina and shredding his ear, sectioning his vocal cords into the thinnest slices. Thirsting for sharp luminous corpuscles, ticktock ticktock, time turned out its irreversible drunkenness, like a ritual flaying, until touching, blood, and chlorophyll, the yod of all births . . .

Promptly, ten days later, at the invisible hour before the sunset, he picked up his quartz watch, returned in perfect condition. Months later, however, he lost it . . .

Xerox Man

- -

ILAN STAVANS (b. 1961)

Based on a famous incident of the 1990s, this story deals with a Jewish book thief from Buenos Aires in New York whose mission is to steal rare books. It first aired on BBC Radio in England.

Not spoken in language, but in looks
More legible than printed books.

—HENRY WADSWORTH LONGFELLOW, *The Hanging of the Crane*, 1874

MY SHARE IN the explosive case of the so-called Xerox Man, as the New York tabloids delighted in describing Reuben Staflovitch shortly after his well-publicized arrest and as the *Harper's* profile reiterated, is too small: It amounts to only fifteen minutes of conversation, of which, unfortunately, I have an all-too-loose recollection.

I first heard of him at Foxy Copies, a small photocopy shop right next to the prewar apartment building where I spent some of my best Manhattan years. The shop's owner was a generous man in his midfifties by the name of Morris. Morris attended his customers with a kind of courtesy and unpretentiousness out of fashion in the city at the time.

I used to visit Foxy Copies almost daily, as my duties required material to be xeroxed and faxed on a regular basis. I refused to have my home invaded by technological equipment, so Morris, for a nonastronomical fee, did the job for me.

He always received me with open arms. If time permitted, he would invite me to schmooze for a little while at his desk behind one of the big photocopy machines. We would discuss the latest Yankee game or that week's Washington scandal. He would then process my documents as if they were his own. He had read one of my pieces once in a trade magazine and prided himself on having what he called "a distinguished list of clients," among which he included me. "You will make me famous one day," he often said.

In one of our conversations I asked Morris, just to be a nuisance, if he ever felt curiosity about his customers and the stuff they photocopied.

"Why should I?" he answered quickly, but then lowered his defenses. "You want me to really answer your question? Then come with me," and we walked together toward a back room with a huge closet, which Morris opened right away. In front of me I saw a stack of disorganized paper.

"In Brooklyn," he said, "an old teacher of mine used to like strange words. When I bought Foxy Copies, one of these words came back to me: *paralipomena*. It means remnants that still have some value. What you see here are piles of xeroxes clients leave behind or throw away."

The sight reminded me of a *genizah*, the annex in every synagogue, usually behind the Ark, where old prayer books accumulate. Disposable Jewish books cannot be thrown away because they might contain the name of God, which can fall into the wrong hands and be desecrated. So these books are stored until the genizah gets too crowded, at which point someone, usually an elder, buries the books in the backyard.

"A genizah of sorts, isn't it?" I said.

"Yes," Morris answered, "except that a special company comes once every three months or so to pick this stuff up. I hate not to see it properly recycled."

I browsed through the xeroxes.

"Trash, really," Morris said. "Most of it is in plain English. Except for the remains left behind by Mr. Staflovitch," and as he uttered the name, he pointed to a lower pile. I looked at it closely, and its pages appeared to me to be in ancient Semitic languages.

Morris didn't like to talk about his clients, but deep inside, all New Yorkers are indiscreet and he was too. So he told me that Reuben Staflovitch—yes, as I recall, he used the complete name for the first time at that point—was by far the most taciturn. He described him as well built, of average height, always dressed in a black suit, white shirt, and unpolished moccasins, with an unruly beard and his trademark sky blue Humphrey Bogart hat. "He comes in with a black doctor's bag about once every two to three weeks," Morris added, "usually at closing time, around 6:30 p.m. He asks to have a Xerox machine all for himself. With extreme meticulousness, he proceeds to take out from the doctor's bag an antiquarian volume, which takes him between thirty and forty minutes to photocopy. Then he restores it to the doctor's bag, wraps the xeroxed material in plastic, pays at the register, and leaves. Few words are uttered, no human contact is made. He leaves in the exact same way as he arrives: in absolute silence."

I remember talking with Morris about other topics that day, but Staflovitch was the only one who truly captured my imagination. "You know," Morris continued, "it is amazing to watch him do his job. His photocopying is flawless; not a single page is wasted. But just after he finishes, he puts his fingers into the pile and takes out a single copy—only one—and throws it away. Why he does this I have no idea. I never dared to ask. But I save the excluded page out of pity."

I extracted the top page in Staflovitch's pile from the closet. "Can I take it with me?"

"You bet," Morris replied.

That night, in my solitude, I deciphered it: it came from a Latin translation of Maimonides's *Guide for the Perplexed*.

Not long afterward, while on Broadway, I saw Staflovitch himself. Morris's description was impeccable. Except for the Humphrey Bogart hat, he looked as unemblematic as I had imagined him: a nondescript Orthodox Jew just like the ones on Delancey Street. He walked quickly and nervously, with his doctor's bag on his right side. A hunch made me follow him. He headed uptown toward the 96th Street subway station but continued for many more blocks—almost thirty—until he reached the doorsteps of the Jewish Theological Seminary, where, crossing through the iron gate, he disappeared from sight. I waited for a few minutes and saw him reappear, walk uptown again, this time to Columbus Avenue, and disappear once and for all into an apartment building. "This must be his home," I told myself. I felt anguished, though, wishing that I had come face to face with him. I was puzzled by his mysterious identity: Was he married? Did he live alone? How did he support himself? And why did he copy old books so religiously?

When I next saw Morris, I mentioned my pursuit. "I'm feeling guilty now," he confessed. "You might be after a man with no soul."

My fifteen-minute conversation with Staflovitch occurred about a month later, as I was leaving Columbia University after a day of heavy teaching. He was entering the subway station at 116th Street. By chance the two of us descended the staircase together. I turned around, pretending to be dumbstruck by the coincidence and said, "I've seen you before, haven't I? Aren't you a Foxy Copies customer?"

His reply was evasive. "Well, not really. I don't like the neighborhood ... I mean, why? Have you seen me at the shop?"

I instantaneously noticed his heavy Hispanic accent, which the media, especially the TV, later picked on. "Are you from Argentina?"

"Why do you care?"

"Well, I am a Mexican Jew myself."

"Really? I didn't know there were any. Or else ..."

Wanting clearly to avoid me, Staflovitch took out a token and went through the turnstile. I didn't have one myself, so I had to stand in line, which delayed me. But I caught up with him after I descended to the train tracks. He was as close to the end of the platform as possible. The train was slow in coming, and I wasn't intimidated by his reluctance to speak, so I approached him again. "I see you're in the business of xeroxing old documents ..."

"How do you know?"

I don't remember the exact exchange that followed, but in the next few minutes Staflovitch explained to me the sum total of his theological views, the same ones expounded to various reporters after he got caught. What I do remember is feeling a sudden, absolute torrent of ideas descending on me without mercy. Something along the lines that the world in which we live—or, better, in which we've been forced to live—is a xerox of a lost original. Nothing in it is authentic; everything is a copy of a copy. He also said that we're governed by sheer randomness and that God is a madman with no interest in authenticity.

I think I asked him what had brought him to Manhattan, to which he replied: "This is the capital of the twentieth century. Jewish memory is stored in this city. But the way it has been stored is offensive and inhuman and needs to be corrected right away ..." The word *inhuman* stuck in my mind. Staflovitch had clearly emphasized it, as if wanting me to savor its meaning for a long time.

"I have a mission," he concluded. "To serve as a conduit in the production of a masterpiece that shall truly reflect the inextricable ways of God's mind."

"You're an Upper West Sider, aren't you?" I asked him.

"The other day I saw you on the premises of the Jewish Theological Seminary."

But by that point he had no more patience left and began to shriek: "I don't want to talk to you . . . Leave me alone. Nothing to say, I've nothing to say."

I took a step back and just then, by a bizarre synchronicity, the local train arrived. As I boarded it, I saw Staflovitch turn around and move in the opposite direction, toward the station's exit.

A week later the tabloid headlines read "Copycat Nightmare" and "Xerox Man: An Authentic Thief," and the *New York Times* carried the scandalous news about Staflovitch on its front page. He had been put under arrest on charges of robbery and destruction of a large array of invaluable Jewish rare books.

Apparently he had managed to steal, by means of extremely clever devices, some three hundred precious volumes—among them editions of Bahya ibn Paquda's *Sefer Hobot ha-Lebabot* and a generous portion of the Babylonian Talmud, an inscribed version of Spinoza's *Tractatus Theologico-Politicus* published in Amsterdam, and an illuminated Haggadah printed in Egypt— all from private collections at renowned universities such as Yale, Yeshiva, Columbia, and Princeton. His sole objective, so the reporters claimed at first, was to possess the rarest of Judaica, only to destroy the items in the most dramatic of ways: by burning them at dawn inside tin garbage cans along Riverside Park. But he destroyed the literature only after photocopying it in full. "Mr. Staflovitch is a xerox freak," an officer was quoted as saying. "Replicas are his sole objects of adoration."

His personal odyssey slowly emerged. He had been raised in Buenos Aires in a strict Orthodox environment. At the time of his arrest, his father was a famous Hasidic rabbi in Jerusalem, with whom he had had frequent clashes, mainly dealing with the nature of God and the role of the Jews in the secular world. In his adolescence Staflovitch had become convinced that the ownership of antique Jewish books by non-Orthodox institutions was a wrong in desperate need of correction. But his obsession had less to do with a transfer of ownership than with a sophisticated theory of chaos, which he picked up while at Berkeley in a brief stint of rebellion in the early 1980s. "Disorder for him is the true order," the prison psychologist said, and added, "Ironically, he ceased to move among Orthodox Jews long ago. He is convinced God doesn't actually rule the universe. He simply lets it move in a free-for-all cadence. And humans, in emulation of the divinity, ought to replicate that cadence."

When the police inspected his Columbus Avenue apartment, they found large boxes containing photocopies. These boxes had not been cataloged either by title or by number; they were simply dumped haphazardly, although the photocopies themselves were never actually mixed.

Staflovitch's case prompted a heated debate on issues of copyright and library borrowing systems. It also generated animosity against Orthodox Jews unwilling to be part of modernity.

"Remarkable as it is," Morris told me when I saw him at Foxy Copies after the hoopla quieted down somewhat, "the police never came to me. I assume Staflovitch, in order to avoid suspicion, must have enlisted the services of various photocopy shops. I surely never saw him xerox more than a dozen books out of the three hundred hidden in his apartment."

Morris and I continued to talk about his most famous client, but the more I reflected on the entire affair, the less I felt close to its essence. I regularly visualized Staflovitch in his prison cell, alone but not lonely, wondering to himself what had been done to his copy collection.

It wasn't until the *Harper's* profile appeared, a couple of months later, that a more complete picture emerged—in my eyes, at least. Its author was the only one allowed to interview Staflovitch in person on a couple of occasions, and he unearthed bits of information about his past that no one else had reckoned with. For instance, his Argentine roots and his New York connection. "I hated my Orthodox Jewish education in Buenos Aires," Staflovitch told him. "Everything in it was derivative. The Spanish-speaking Americas are pure imitation. They strive to be like Europe, like the United States, but never will be . . ." And about New York he said,

I supported myself with the bequest I got after my mother's death.
I always thought this city to be the one closest to God, not because
it is more authentic— which it isn't, obviously—but because no
other metropolis on the globe comes even close in the amount of

photocopying done regularly. Millions and millions of copies are made daily in Manhattan. But everything else—architecture, the arts, litera- ture—is an imitation too, albeit a concealed one. Unlike the Americas, New York doesn't strive to be like any other place. It simply mimics itself. Therein lies its true originality.

Toward the end of the profile, the author allows Staflovitch a candid moment as he asks him about "his mission," and reading this portion, I sud- denly remembered that it was about his mission that he talked to me most eloquently at the subway station.

"Did the police ever notice that the xerox boxes in my apartment are all incomplete?" he wondered. "Have they checked each package to see that they are all missing a single page . . . ?"

"Did you eliminate that single page?" he is asked.

"Yes, of course. I did it to leave behind a clearer, more convincing picture of our universe, always striving toward completion but never actually attain- ing it."

"And what did you do with those missing pages?"

"Ah, therein lies the secret . . . My dream was to serve as a conduit in the production of a masterpiece that would truly reflect the inextricable ways of God's mind—a random book, arbitrarily made of pages of other books. But this is a doomed, unattainable task, of course, and thus I left these extricated pages in the trash bins of the photocopy shops I frequented."

When I read this line, I immediately thought of Morris's genizah and about how Staflovitch's mission was not about replicating but about creat- ing. I quickly ran downstairs to Foxy Copies. Morris surely must have been the only savvy shop owner to rescue the removed copies. I still had the Mai- monides page with me, but I desperately wanted to put my hands on the remaining pile of documents, to study them, to grasp the chaos about which Staflovitch spoke so highly. "Paralipomena: This is the legacy the Xerox Man has left me with," I told myself.

Morris wasn't around, but one of his employees told me, as I explained my purpose, that the recycling company had come to clear the back-room closet just a couple of days before.

URUGUAY

The Bar Mitzvah Speech

SALOMON ZYTNER (1904–1986)
Translated from the Yiddish by Debbie Nathan

Born into a Hasidic family in Bialystok, Salomon (Shloyme) Zytner arrived in Uruguay in 1925. He participated in Labor Zionist organizations and wrote for Folksblat *and* Haynt *in Montevideo,* Di Prese *in Buenos Aires, and* Naye Tsaytung *in Israel, where he moved later in life. He is the author of three collections of stories,* Der gerangl *(The Struggle),* Di mishpokhe *(The Family), and "Tsvishn vent" und andere dertseylungen ("Within Four Walls" and Other Stories), all published between 1955 and 1974. "The Bar Mitzvah Speech" is a study of social mores.*

IN BERNARDO TZALKIN'S impressive glassware shop, one can purchase as well all manner of religious images, plaster figures of various dimensions, each of which shows the mission and rank assigned to the particular guardian of humankind on this sinful earth. One can also acquire the finest gold and silver picture frames, variously decorated. The shop is as silent and tranquil as a church. The holy statues are placed on shelves at the very front, in diverse poses. Some stretch their arms out in prayer. Others have worried countenances, full of pain, which remind those who enter that earthly existence is meaningless and that true rewards and punishments will be dealt out only in the world to come.

The decorative frames, sparkling in gold and silver on the walls, can hardly bear to see the sorrowful faces and stooped, bowed, shrunken bodies of the saintly figures, who attract the glances of the passersby. When a customer shows up, a silent, bitter struggle breaks out among them. Each icon wants all the newcomer's attention and spreads about a godlike serenity, meant to calm the soul in travail. Simultaneously, the brilliant picture frames use their ornaments—flowers of the most diverse shapes, etched in relief—to charm the new arrival. When the shop is empty, the frames look shimmeringly at the oil paintings and reproductions displayed in the great show window and await impatiently the acquirer who will deliver them from the suffocating atmosphere.

The oil paintings do not perceive the tumult of the street, the deafening shrieks and roars of motors. They yearn to be covered with glass, surrounded with decorative frames, and hung in dark, commodious rooms with draped windows, around which hovers an air of hospitable tranquility.

Bernardo Tzalkin's shop, his present social position, is the product of a dream come true. Years before, he had gone around with a crate of glass. From door to door he went, asking with a timid voice, blushing all the while, "Maybe you need a windowpane?" He trod the streets entire days, hardly managing to cover his expenses, mechanically repeating those few words at every home, every doorway. His thin, drawn-out cheeks, his subdued gaze, his entire demeanor clearly belonged to a man beaten down, who labored hard for each bit of bread, and who lived from one day to the next.

After several years of peddling in the streets, he saw his efforts were fruitless. He sought out a location in a downtown street and set up a glass shop. In addition to glass, he brought in some religious pictures, plaster figures, and frames of various sizes. At first, he himself was shocked by his dealing in icons; as a child, he would carefully avert his glance whenever he saw one. As time wore on, he became accustomed to them. They seemed to him even quite ordinary.

The business grew day by day. The religious items were the quickest-moving of all, especially before the holidays. He soon amassed a small fortune and had an appearance to go along with it. His thin, drawn cheeks filled out, his cautious gaze became audacious and even arrogant. Standing long days behind the counter, he acquired a round, well-fed belly, proudly projected outward, as if exclaiming impudently: "Show respect to Bernardo Tzalkin, the big glass dealer! He's no longer the poor glazier who would pace the length and breadth of the city, begging with a meek voice for a little livelihood. Nowadays, people come to him. In the business world his name is uttered with honor and dignity!"

Bernardo Tzalkin was consumed by his shop. Nothing existed for him except glass, frames, and holy images bought by Christian neighbors in honor of their *shmolidays* . . . He wanted people to know just how comfortable he was, how lavish he could afford to be. He had been too involved in business to notice, slowly creeping up, special birthdays of his two children, born before his good fortune. His son was about to turn thirteen, and his daughter fifteen. The time was right to display his largess.

Bernardo Tzalkin had originally wanted to throw two parties: a bar mitzvah for his son, and a *quinceañera* for his daughter. But his wife so upbraided him that he saw stars. She warned him against letting so much money slip through his fingers and accused him of not knowing the value of a peso. After several evenings of strife and recriminations, they came to an agreement. They would celebrate their son's bar mitzvah and their daughter's quinceañera simultaneously, thereby guarding against useless expenses while attracting twice as many gifts.

Preparing their daughter would not require great effort. They would simply have a white silk gown custom sewn for her, her hair done up in nice curls, and deck her out for the party. With their son it was a different matter. They would have to drum a bar mitzvah speech into his head, which was not about to enter easily. And as though that were not enough, Bernardo Tzalkin demanded that his only son go up to the Torah, pronounce the blessings, and chant the haftorah portion taught to him by a teacher.

Bernardo Tzalkin also wanted a picture of his only son, in his little prayer shawl and skullcap, to appear in the newspaper for one and all to see. That seemed to him a compensation for all the years he had dealt in holy images.

His only son—a hefty boy, with full, round cheeks—was completely taken with soccer. He would come home ruddy and perspiring after playing outside with his friends and would burn with anger at his parents and teacher who demanded he learn the bar mitzvah speech. Most of all, he was annoyed by the haftorah, of which he understood nothing. The strange words frightened him. He would mechanically repeat them after his teacher, all the while thinking that he could be outside having fun, playing ball with his friends. He would break into a cold sweat as he recited word after word. His teacher gazed at him sympathetically, blaming him less than his father. Upon leaving the house, he would remind the boy to practice his speech on his own, lest he shame himself in front of everyone. The boy would breathe more easily when the teacher was gone, as though he had been freed from a heavy burden, and would escape quickly to his friends outdoors.

Bernardo Tzalkin now kept close watch on his only son. Whenever the boy disappeared from the house, he would go find him in the street, pulling him away from the soccer match just as he was about to score a goal. The boy was angry at having to stop playing and with bowed head would listen morosely to his father's scolding remarks, the eternal litany: "Did you forget that you have to rehearse your bar mitzvah speech and the haftorah? There isn't much time left."

The big day was drawing near, and Bernardo Tzalkin had gone all out. He rented the fanciest, most luxurious hall. He arranged with the caterer for a lavish banquet, lest the guests feel cheated. It was, as he whispered to the caterer, a double party, for both his children, and each and every guest should feel satisfied with what was being offered.

He hired a band to entertain the guests, to warm their hearts with the melodies they knew from home. He had invitations engraved in golden letters, which clearly announced that Mr. and Mrs. Bernardo Tzalkin had the honor to invite their friends to a double celebration: the bar mitzvah of their son and the quinceaiiera of their daughter. On each side of the invitation stood a picture of one of the honorees. The boy, with the prayer shawl on his shoulders and a holy tome in his hand, stared dull and discontented; the girl, in her white silk gown, had a smile that suggested that her childhood had come to an end and a new period of life was about to begin.

A day before the celebration, with all the invitations out and everything in the offing, the boy fell ill. Bernardo Tzalkin paced desperately, anxiously, not knowing what to do. He glanced at his son, who lay in bed with a high fever, shivering. His sunken red cheeks, his glassy eyes, his dry lips made it clear that he had a bad cold and would have to stay in bed. Bernardo Tzalkin walked to and fro, wringing his hands in irritation and chagrin, stiffening them as he went over to his son, who lay breathing heavily, almost choking. He threw terrible glances at the boy and hissed into his face, "It's all because of that accursed ball-playing of yours!" Then he added, beside himself, "What are we supposed to do now? What will become of your speech? The guests we've invited? The food that's been prepared?"

His wife sat on the edge of the bed. She glanced anxiously at her son, from whose side she did not stir, as she placed cold compresses on his forehead.

She hazarded an idea: "Perhaps we could put off the party until a later date? You see how bad off the boy is. He's burning like fire."

"What do you mean, put it off?" exclaimed Bernardo Tzalkin. "What do you think this is—a game? How can you stay calm when so many guests are coming! We won't be able to show our faces in public." His voice cracked into a sob.

She made another attempt: "Maybe we could just celebrate the girl's occasion? And put off the bar mitzvah until the boy is better . . ." He dismissed her suggestion with a wave of the hand, as though no response were necessary. He ran over to the telephone and spoke into the receiver with a broken, nervous voice. Have the doctor come immediately! One of his children has a high fever, and he is very worried! Having gotten a reassuring answer, he hung up the phone and began pacing the room again, looking at the door repeatedly, starting at the slightest noise, anxiously awaiting the doctor's arrival.

At the first ring of the bell, Bernardo Tzalkin ran into the entryway, opened wide the door, and welcomed the doctor in. The doctor sat down calmly by the bed and began a lengthy examination of the patient, checking his throat, feeling his pulse, tapping the boy's back with his fingers, listening to his lungs. The parents stood near the bed, following nervously with their eyes the doctor's movements, waiting impatiently for him to utter some word, offer a diagnosis. The doctor shrugged his shoulders, as though to allay their unfounded fears, and said in sparse terms, "There's no danger. The boy has a bad cold and will have to stay in bed a few days to sweat it out."

Bernardo Tzalkin stood there as though he had just been drenched with a bucket of cold water. Perplexed, at a loss for words, he tried to ask the doctor whether the boy could possibly get out of bed the next day for just an hour. It was his thirteenth birthday . . . He attempted to explain that there was to be a big party. All the guests had been invited. Everything was ready. The boy would have to make a speech or otherwise the whole celebration would be ruined.

The doctor refused, shaking his head. He could not understand how it could matter so that the boy give a speech and thereby risk his health. Bernardo Tzalkin interrupted the doctor with a small voice, begging his authorization, trying to make him understand: "For us Jews, it's a big occasion. He's been practicing the speech for a long time." Maybe the doctor could prescribe some penicillin shots, for example, a high dose, so that the next day the boy would feel well enough to be taken to the hall, just to recite the speech before the guests. Then they would bring him back home to bed.

The doctor, a good-hearted man of Spanish ancestry, smiled and patted Bernardo Tzalkin on the back, showing he now understood. He uttered a quick "Está bien" and left the room.

The next day Bernardo Tzalkin stood outside his house, waiting nervously as his wife helped their daughter arrange her hair and gown before a mirror. The white silk drew tightly at the waist, before falling into slight pleats. With each movement the gown rustled, as though expressing the dreams and longings of the girl, about to take leave of her fifteen childhood years.

Bernardo Tzalkin kept looking at his watch, fearful it was getting late. He saw all the guests sitting at their tables and straining their eyes in anticipation of the hosts' arrival. And here they were still lingering. The injections prescribed by the doctor the day before had wrought the desired effect. The boy felt better, thereby vindicating Bernardo Tzalkin. After all, what would the entire party have been like without the bar mitzvah speech?

All of a sudden he noticed the door opening. Out stepped his daughter, bedecked, shining brilliantly. His wife followed, leading by the hand their son, swaddled in warm clothing. He opened up the car door quickly and took his son by the other arm. Together, they helped the boy into the car.

Bernardo Tzalkin was overtaken by cheer. Here he was, taking his son to recite the long-awaited bar mitzvah speech. The celebration was to go forward exactly as planned.

Upon entering the catering hall, he remarked how his son began hesitating, tottering, and seemed about to fall over. The boy's usually ruddy face went pale and gaunt. His eyes were sunken in and surrounded by bluish spots. Bernardo Tzalkin gave a shiver, taking fright lest his son's health worsen and keep him from delivering the bar mitzvah speech.

The band intoned a joyous melody. Merriment and laughter poured over the hall. The honorees were welcomed with great festivity; applause broke out on all sides. Hands stretched out to wish the family happiness. Bernardo Tzalkin was entranced by the music, the jolly faces that shone at him from all directions. The ceremonious music swept over him like a warm wave, embracing and caressing him, making him forget all his cares. The fears regarding his son dissolved. He remembered only that today was a celebration in honor of both his children, a double celebration he had made as sumptuous as possible, renting out the most luxurious hall, arranging for the finest foods—an occasion people were not likely to forget. They would all comment on his unrestrained generosity, his brilliant social standing. And soon his son would recite the bar mitzvah speech.

VENEZUELA

Papa's Friends

- -

ELISA LERNER (b. 1932)
Translated from the Spanish by Amy Prince

Evoking the world of Russian Jewish immigrants in Caracas, this story takes place during the late 1930s and 1940, when Leon Trotsky was assassinated in Mexico City. Told from the viewpoint of a teenage girl confronting the underside of bourgeois family life, it first appeared—ironically enough—in the slick Venezuelan magazine Exceso *in 1991.*

IN APRIL OF 1953, Lydia was locked up in the remote land of a psychiatric clinic, and the gentle white dawns of her uniform were never seen again in Samuel's grocery store. Berta found prosperity after years of cheerful hard work managing the restaurant she had with her husband, Bernardo. Like a versatile sofa bed that never declines to show its hospitality, the restaurant also functioned as an inn. Freed from work, Berta began moving from one dismal house to another: you can all imagine her last home. She entertained herself buying ostentatious display cabinets for the different houses, in which she would place small, well-polished silver spoons. Now that she had money she could offer better service. But the spoons went unused, like cloistered nuns.

Señora Olinda, almost seventy years old, was obliged to close Odessa, the shoe store she had presided over for close to half a century. There were no longer customers looking for shoes with toes like pointed noses, or thin rose-stem heels. Left without the shoe store, she discovered in herself a belated religious vocation and found herself more and more at ease in the synagogue and at the jumble sales they held. Her lips (as in the younger days at the Odessa) were, as always, covered with a throbbing scrap of a vibrant velvet red that at times obscured her smile.

As for Amelia, I heard she was stricken by an incurable disease that drove through her body like a sword watching its knight die on the battlefield. Susana got fat, as big as an ever-growing metropolis. She now lives with only her fatness for company in an apartment building in Miami, where most of the tenants are rich sentimental old women—widows exiled from New York or from some town in Central or South America.

In Miami she has become addicted to vitamins. Yet she often still finds herself returning from Florida on the occasion of the weddings and bar mitzvahs of her numerous relatives. These efforts, at times tiresome, to arrive on time for the family festivities have made her whine in the pharmacy for a renewed supply of her much-appreciated vitamins. "I am always on an airplane. The day before yesterday it was Raquel's wedding in New York. In June, it's on to Caracas for Leah and Isaac's golden anniversary. Next fall I'm invited to Tel Aviv to spend the New Year with Ana Landau. She's a widow now. What a production! I don't know anyone who functions more like a well-organized minister of foreign affairs than a member of a Jewish family. I'm about ready to ask for the ambassadorship. I'm just waiting for the Kafka twins' bar mitzvah in Rio de Janeiro."

Lydia, Amelia, Berta, Olinda, and Susana were my papa's friends. It wasn't a conscious flirtation on their part, nor on Papa's. There never was a more tender, loving, and conciliatory husband than he. Mama was a small anxious despot, a protector. Thanks to her methodical, stubborn, and proud nostalgia—above all, to the crazy collection of things she took with her on the boat—we lived in a far-off town of fiction, one that moved erratically in dark seas, ships of gigantic dimensions like massive caskets transporting entire populations.

The city that my mother founded with such care inside our house never had a real and established spot on the map. This was such an injustice when there was so much beautiful real geography that I began to suspect she was a capricious woman, of a spirit subject to sudden change. The passing of time assured me of my conviction that she is a silly woman, a scatterbrain who changes borders as if they were one-night stands.

Papa, possessor of an educated cynicism, faced reality with distracted compassion. That was why he could not remain forever inside the rigorous region invented by Mama's mournful longings. Some Saturday mornings (if the teacher gave me good marks on the report I brought home from high school), he took me with him on the short but unconventional walks down the narrow streets in the center of town. I suspect Papa's own walk began much earlier. More than one Friday at 7:00 p.m., after greeting God and drinking a small glass of muscatel (his body wore the striped suit like a tablecloth ready to receive its wine glasses), nimble and content (with the jug of his heart half-full of wine), he would run to see his lovely Lydia and his needy Amelia before eight o'clock (the most melancholy time in the universe) when the stores closed.

Mama planned things like an actress in a repertory company of three-act comedies. The celebration of Hanukkah represented the first act. On the pretext of collaborating with the Israel Club, she would make a cake of honey, nuts, and raisins. The club now and then served as a house of charity, a somewhat bohemian, cordial hospice.

On Fridays, protected by the merciful music of prayer, men who looked as though they didn't even have a place of their own to die would appear at the door.

In order to do the honors to the second act, Mama put on her skirt and jacket of silk *imprime* (that's what the pretentious employees of El Gallo de Oro called the printed material) with the firm determination of appearing, hanging on Papa's arm, at the Israel Club, to drop off the delicious cake, decorated with the skill of an English assassin. She also used the argument of wanting to stretch her housewife legs (those crippled spousal extremities, sacrificed like mermaids' limbs in an ocean that prohibits voyages to worldly lands of enjoyment and pleasure) in order to arrive with dignity at the pretenses of the third act. Accompanying Papa on the short trip to his friends' shops (while he made some insignificant purchase), Mama perhaps wanted to assure herself that the visits were not just a useful excuse for a gaze or a verbal caress, performed with the enigmatic touch of love that has no homeland in bed, toward Lydia or Amelia, who, behind their safe sales counters, in the sweetness of dusk, were remote women hidden in the towers of their chaste castles.

Mama admired and at the same time despised Lydia. The variations of her indifference came in all sizes, big and small. Mama, the small domestic despot, envied Lydia her disquieting ability to sell black olives, nuts, almonds, and Maracay cheese, as she did her white uniform, which, free of marital stains, emancipated her, gave her independence.

Lydia was of short stature, a bit heavy. Her ass was the least animated part of her body, but she seemed to keep singing birds in her somewhat meddle-some belly. The hapless uniform nevertheless tried to silence the indiscreet sparrows of a troublesome digestion. Her face, the green eyes, were those of an artist of the time. A shorter and plumper Kay Francis (the bargains she found in expensive department stores gave authority to her warm greetings), she was happy to be able to seize to her waist the liberating banner of stable and certain work.

A Kay, happy to watch life through lenses spread with foggy yellow Kup-perschmidt butter. But Papa would have had to make the sacrifice of buying the necessary (as well as the unnecessary) theater seats in order for Lydia to have really been the haughty Kay Francis, to whom silver-screen husbands presented divine jewels, hidden in the lustrous silver domes of breakfast platters, in humble homage to the night before, when at the elegant party, fox skins drifted from one shoulder to the other like snowflakes swirled by the wind around the gargoyles of a palace roof.

Impassioned stars winked in Papa's eyes when he saw this domestic ver-sion of Kay Francis. Lydia, like the other Saturday morning women, didn't pay much attention to me, a pale skinny girl with braids tightly knotted like the shoelaces of shabby winter shoes, a red dress of Scotch plaid wool, and frail bones like toothpaste that called for immense bottles of calcium brim-ming over like a full water tank. Life was passing by. To find love, one had to rush around like the race walkers in the stadium. Papa and the women counted on those few hours a week to ignite the fires of opportunity, to try to light the logs of burning tenderness from fragile, fast-burning twigs.

I felt sorry for Lydia, something of a respectful pity. Mama cautiously mentioned (with tremendous scorn) that she was "separated." What the hell did that mean? I saw chubby Lydia flapping around in her uniform amid the comings and goings to Samuel's store, like an ocean teeming with life and topped with the whitest waves. Could it be that separation was an adult dis-ease, different from my discouraging lack of calcium? Or is that the way she labeled it because in her house she had a Chinese folding screen that she hid behind to leisurely put in place some linen contraption supposed to reduce the vast habitation of her stomach?

This desolate operation, to tighten or to meticulously loosen the waists of a weary corset, was like that of a ship captain at the moment in which he hoists or lowers the sails that have been entrusted to him.

Papa, loaded down by his Mediterranean riches, black olives glittering like the buttons on a widow's bodice, grapes like fairies' teeth, and the skinny girl at his side like some unattractive trophy of his matrimony, twenty or twenty-five minutes later would enter Amelia's store for gentlemen.

She received him with little claps of happiness and with the melodramatic gymnastics of open arms. Papa's smile was a cordial cliff of luminous teeth. I don't remember if Amelia was married then or if she did it later. It doesn't matter. In any case, her heart sheltered an extraordinary comprehension of and access to the masculine world. The sale of men's shirts and ties gave her these powers.

Sometimes it surprised me that the anxiousness of the greetings, the intimate hubbub of the encounters between Amelia and Papa, depended on a commonplace casual Saturday visit to the haberdashery. It seemed unfair that the affectionate saleswoman wasn't included at our family dinners and that the evident happiness that Papa's arrival brought her had such a limited time frame. My girl's eyes perceived that their mutual delight was reduced to a cautious passion that could have been set in the cold snow of far-off mountains.

Amelia eagerly dressed herself up for the hours she spent in the shop. But the pale mauve or blue blouses, the gray wool skirts, seemed to age rapidly on her body. She looked lovely, however, when she wore her Romanian white silk camisole, covered with pleats and done up in a profusion of multicolored sashes. How beautiful it would have been, her entrance into the house for an innocent domestic meal, dressed in the Romanian camisole and with the fire of her eyes burning in golden affection. Then perhaps Amelia's love wouldn't have been limited to the embrace that stung by its similarity to farewells from a train en route to distant lands. In the ecstasy of being in such close proximity to Papa (different from the stolen and wounding hour that, on his quick visits to the store, he offered her every Saturday), perhaps Amelia would have let him pull up the multicolored sashes of her adornment, as if they were the backdrop or house curtain of a small and illicit theater.

Berta had set up her restaurant in a long thin building a block up from Amelia's store. The tables were at the back, in a raised area that meant climbing three or four bare steps, unprotected by the decorations of the rest of the scene. But for me, to arrive at this upper section of the house was like being installed on the gently sloping hill of a theater house.

There was always something frustrating about these visits to Berta. Papa and I would arrive just as the preparations for the noonday meal were taking place. At the table they would have already placed large platters overflowing with salads of potato, beet, onion, and tomato. The chunks of lettuce were veritable gardens.

When Papa said good-bye to Berta, I knew we were going to miss the show, the real entertainment: the predictable actions of the actors, the customers' unexpected moments. "It's time to go." Papa watched life through the jealous mirrors of haste. Mama's tyranny awaited us in the dining room at 12:30 precisely, with the venetian blind up, the sun shining on a fountain of chopped egg, potato, and onion salad. That's why I was never able to see any of Berta's customers. Not once did I eat at her place of business. A restaurant was a prohibited adventure, a swelling of high waves. In order to get near such proud waters, it was necessary to make a crossing that would take an entire childhood.

The lower part of the house held the bedrooms where taciturn guests took their lodging. Berta had a slender, good-natured husband with the body of a dancer, who used it only to call the actors to their places: light taps on the doors to offer aspirins, front-door keys, correspondence from remote areas, vague messages. He spent the rest of the time in a corner, the chair balanced awkwardly against the wall behind the stairs that led to the tables, watchfully idle (carrying on the shoulders of his thin body the insomnia that flourishes in boardinghouses and also in theaters).

Sometimes he would let the newspaper drop from his hands onto the stairs as he murmured in a faltering voice: "Ay, Leybele! Leybele! Good God, the only one of us who got this far, and they wouldn't rest until they tracked him down in the last corner of the world to kill him."

Papa would hold me tight, tenderly taking my hand, trying to soothe with his smile the misfortune of the world. But a sad haze clouded the proud granite of his teeth.

I remember that Bernardo, Berta's husband, would take a napkin from one of the tables, and it wasn't sweat he wiped off his face. They were small and fragile tears. His Adam's apple would swell up disjointedly, as if he had already served himself salad without waiting for the customers. As if the spine of an evil accursed fish had lodged itself in his throat.

In this restaurant, suspended as in a dream of some high tower, the tables were covered by a type of cheap oilcloth generally reserved for the kitchen. I was enchanted by the innocent little animals and the rough-drawn dahlias printed on the cloth.

The petty maternal despot had never seen such crude material on a table. Now I understand: for her, to omit the white starched tablecloths would have been like renouncing the snow of her native city.

On the occasions that they laid out white tablecloths in Berta's restaurant, criminal fingerprints and blood (Del Monte ketchup spilled by negligent diners) ended up staining them. Anyway, the owner of the establishment would never have had the patience to thumb through fashion magazines for ideas about interior decorating.

And it was Berta who triumphed. She jumped over the tables like a thoroughbred horse going over a fence. She didn't bother herself with haughty refinement. A malady such as that would have shrouded Mama early in her pure white tablecloths of nostalgia.

Berta tended toward stockiness, and the gestures of a sharp and fierce worldliness peeked out from her face. Her eyes were spirited and vivacious. It was impossible for those pupils to fall victim to myopia or any other visual ailment. The abundance in her ebony gaze would have smashed to smithereens the glass of any lens. Those imperial violets! Her hair was all boisterous curls, like that of "Imperio Argentina" or some other torch singer, a joyful celebration of black ringlets.

A peaceful garbanzo bean of a mole, cooked over a slow fire on her skin and placed between the nose and the upper lip, gave belligerent notice of a large and brutal mouth, one that let loose virile laughs and cheerful curses in the way of greetings.

Sometimes the musical laughs, the insolent sarcasm, seemed to abandon her body, which was so occupied with changes in the menu and conversations with unattractive guests whose smiles revealed teeth like rusted grilles. And, indeed, the fighting and the celebrating in her grandiloquent voice migrated to a freer part of the body: straight to her arms. Berta's mischievousness traversed her upper arms until it arrived at her hands, folded in a gesture of prayer (of embrace) toward Papa. But on a moment's notice she would have to go back to the kitchen for more platters of food, for soon the diners would arrive and the oil and vinegar would be scattered around the tables like incense at a church. And Papa had the officious tyranny of home waiting for him.

Perhaps because I was visiting a restaurant without being interested in any of the men who came for the platters of food, I began to dream about a customer who, in the middle of noon's torrential heat, would make his majestic entrance, suited in a black tuxedo and wearing soft patent leather shoes. A man with massive shoulders and gallant manners, with a mustache and graying temples like the actor Arturo de Cordoba.

He would snap his fingers in command and say to Berta and her husband, "Do you see my beautiful suit? Take my order. What dish do you recommend today? I want wine for everyone. But, for the love of God, no more potato salad with beets. I have triumphed. From sunrise on it's a constant party. For Leybele, our unfortunate brother, as well. In his memory. After all, Berta, what are we, anyway? Commerce and memory. One last favor: bring me some shoeshine boys from the corner to shine my shoes. That way they'll realize I don't crawl in the gutters and the streets anymore. I would like everyone to notice that my shoes are made of patent leather, fit for a ballroom."

Berta and Bernardo would appear, surrounded by waiters in starched uniforms like members of an army. In homage to the courteous diner, my fantasy transplanted itself to the great hall of the Paris restaurant, with its vast cemetery of a dining room. The elegant diner chose a filet mignon.

Olinda, in the shoe store Odessa, was always on her feet, a party hostess with no parties, attending to the door and maneuvering the cash register. Her hair was a fuzzy, fat gold cloud. She reigned over the store with a petulant and virtuous grace, dressed in a silk blouse adorned with exquisite designs of delicate lace and pleated Scotch plaid skirts. But in her white complexion, in her mouth painted a surprisingly shameless red, she was a woman of daring. Capable of taking on the whole night as if it were a big house, something unknown, with thick curtains of velvet surrounded by gilded railings. A mansion where it was necessary to break down all resistance, something that had to be possessed in full youth and vigor, when strength for the attack and the decision still remained.

The rotund housebound despot would snivel with spite when she saw her little one arrive with a bag containing shoes bought at Odessa. She also sobbed bitterly on seeing Papa enter with packages of olives and mortadella, purchased in the shop where Lydia worked, or with socks bought in haste at Amelia's bazaar. But for Mama the visits to Odessa were the most mortifying.

Olinda, the manager of the store, was a woman sufficiently audacious to have embarked alone for America. Customers at the store (especially on the days when prices were raised) would whisper: in Havana she stood up her boyfriend, who, it was said, had purchased the ticket for her long voyage. While she was there she had spent all her time dancing the rumba, and between dances she had met the Russian shoemaker who now crafted his wares at Odessa.

But to go to Olinda's shop was like becoming attached to an expensive lover. That was why some Saturdays Papa took me to Susana's shoe store, a less pretentious one next to the market.

Susana was voluminous and large. But the emphasis of her nose offered certain inroads into her character. She herself, without calling for one of the employees (all of melancholy faces and dressed in dark clothes, as if celebrating a burial), sat on a small stool to try the shoes on me. She was generous, complacent, and clever. Her knees, like juicy oranges recently brought in from the field, brushed up innocently against Papa's legs while concealing the arduous struggle with my shoe.

But I think he preferred Olinda, high-priced Olinda, along with the doves who found treasures beneath the bow of a silk blouse. Those doves that the Havana night sent off to hover over the body of the Russian artisan.

Over the years, it seems I have become Lydia, Berta, Olinda, and Susana.

In moments of vain coquetry, I am Amelia. The fugitive illusions of the Saturdays of their youth are my longings today.

An affable and timid man runs in brief and affectionate spells from his frigid marriage to my house; he pops up by chance, like the playing card that a blind man chooses. And then from my comfortable home back to the cold and imposing marble of his conjugal domicile, where, at the cocktail hour, they feed on shriveled peanuts.

The comings and goings of my lover are so rapid and so forced, so that he can return exactly on time to the gloomy castle of his marriage, that last spring he tripped and for months wore his right arm in a sling. Another time, in the winter, he tore his Achilles tendon. The plaster cast, enemy of action and adventure (mountains of snow in the garden, the neighboring park, illicit paths), has him waylaid in the failed throne of a wheelchair.

I adore in my lover the exquisiteness of his manners, the sublime freshness of his body sprinkled with Loewe cologne. As for the rest of it, these fractures have become part of the custom of our passionate love.

He will return next spring on crutches (his suitcases of disability), ready to lose one leg or another as if in some ancient war. Because he will never stop running between his matrimony of solitary eiderdown and the love that we—Lydia, Amelia, Berta, Olinda, Susana, and I—offer him.

Cláper (excerpt)

- -

ALICIA FREILICH (b. 1939)
Translated from the Spanish by Joan E. Friedman

Alicia Freilich's novel Cláper *(1987), from which the following segment is taken, deals with the entrepreneurial spirit of Jewish immigrants to Venezuela. A prominent journalist, she moved to the United States during the Hugo Chávez regime, which targeted the Jewish community. She is also the author of* Colombina Descubierta *(1991) and* Viaje Verde *(2000).*

I'M HAPPY. THROUGH the clean mirror, as through pure crystal, I see that at last, yes, at last the sun is setting and the first evening star has come out. Shabbat ends but my night begins. All I want to do is walk and walk . . .

I'm leaving you, my dear village, and you're seeing me off without knowing it. There is such excitement in your shabby narrow streets. This time Isaac and Pesha are the ones being led to the house of prayers. She will have to dance around him seven times before they shatter the glass in remembrance of the destruction of the temple in the Holy Land by the evilness of Titus the Roman. Cursed be his name! After hearing the noise and seeing the shards of glass, then and only then will they be man and wife according to the laws of our Arbiter, Creator of the Universe.

You know something? It's unusual for a month to go by without a wedding in my village. *Nu?* I guess even in paradise it's not good to be alone. Why did I decide to leave at the end of this Shabbat and not another? I've waited long enough, and the moment of destiny we forge for ourselves has arrived for me . . .

But I have to pretend and hurry without rushing. Thank God nobody notices as long as my mouth laughs and my legs dance by themselves, which is of course what happens to everyone in my village when there is a wedding. If I let myself be dragged into the merriment and forget my trip, I'll have to wait until next fall, and that's too far away; after all I'm no longer a boy.

Is it true what they say, that a person's nature changes every seven years? If it is, then I've already shed my skin three times and I have reached the perfect age to break out of the shell forever. Forever? Do any of us ever really abandon forever the place where we're born and play as children?

A little while ago, on Yom Kippur, as I circled my head three times with the sacrificial rooster—and yelled out the exorcism louder than a crazy man would—I offered God this animal as a substitute for my sins. The bird will go to its death, that's what *kapparot* is, after all, while I shall live a long and peaceful life in America. Amen!

Oy yoy yoy! Here comes Meilaj the mute. Whew! He just passed. Thank you, my sweet little God, for your help. That good simpleton has very sharp eyes and with this full moon . . . Luckily he didn't see me. He was so absorbed with his whistling, announcing the wedding and inviting all Christians to come and see the beautiful bride. Have you ever seen an ugly bride? Everyone praises such beautiful happiness! So, while performing his assignment with virtuosity, the whistler didn't notice me, leaving with a knapsack over my shoulders.

As I pass the temple, I've got to walk more slowly. Awaiting the predestined couple, the wide open main door allows me to see the Ark, which holds its treasure, the Holy Scrolls, on the very same dais where—oy yoy yoy!—so often I've accompanied my Pappinyu at sunrise and sunset prayers.

God sits above and arranges it so that here, below, male and female may be joined at a chosen time. I know that all weddings are parties, but today the room looks more glittering than ever before. A couple of weeks ago, from nobody knew where, came a strange painter who decorated these blessed walls. And he never even charged us a cent! And, what's even more unbelievable, the drawings are intact!

I would look at him in silence because he was a man of few words. But one afternoon I took him some cider and sweet dough with raisins, and he spoke! He was fleeing France. He just wanted to breathe once again the air of Liozno, in Russia, where his family lives. But when he realized how far away it was, he chose to remain in Lendov with us—"almost the same," he said, smiling, never once taking his eyes off the enormous rooster he was coloring blue.

Magical! That's what it was. Magical! Without any books, he knew exactly how to draw the feathers of all kinds of different creatures! From his brushes emanated a violin with wings, and green priests suspended in midair above roofs, and a seven-branched candelabra flying like a burning bramble, and a yellow lion and red cows, and gigantic moons, without a single word. Colored shapes with soul!

The entire town was shaken. So? Nu? Who was this stranger? Marcus Chagalovich or Sagalij he called himself; I no longer remember. Of course, the village divided into two irreconcilable camps. One accused him of being a profligate and a sinner because of the irreverence with which he depicted the sacred commentaries. "Downright pagan!" The other said he had given a false name. They pointed him out as one of the anonymous Just Men, who in every era come to redeem the world. Of course, that would explain why he knew more about the laws than our own venerable teacher, Aaron.

Anyway, the artist was scared off by the whispers and all the gossip. After three days, probably to avoid being cursed by them—God forbid!—without even saying good-bye, or even leaving a single footprint, he disappeared into the night, just as I am doing now, along the very same long road . . .

Luminous was the morning of her inauguration into the world! Without crossing checkpoints or oceans, and while living under the same familial roof, she took the road that divided neighborhood from Milky Way.

She was not moved by her parent's objections; nor, for that matter, did she share their mourning over the distant yet to them ever-present news about the Suez Canal situation. Goodness, the way they moaned and carried on! You'd think these were their very own personal problems or something . . .

The tree-lined path that leads to the main building, with its high oval clock, is both border and path to her liberation. There is a lot to see and many to be seen by. In order to accomplish this, she'll have to sway her hips and get rid of that skinny slouching profile, that "good girl walk," Mom would say. A brave heroine, she had dared to break out of the family padlock, the collegiate gates, and the community fences in order to go beyond this door and enter the foremost university. God, does that sounds great! Now she must walk proudly and provocatively in keeping with the mood of her deed.

At last! Left behind are those gaudy reproductions of Marc Chagall that hang all over the living and dining room walls. Where does Father get this obsession for buying any trinket that imitates the painter? Must be his small-town taste; like all hicks, he mistakes junk for real art. Real art is these stained-glass windows, which, on this particular morning, shed a special light, bringing them into harmony with the modern architecture all around it. What beauty! A splendid open gallery offers her famous muralists, painters, and sculptors in quantities that go far beyond her artistic appreciation, yet it is a most fitting place in which to experience this radical moment dividing her existence.

And the school building? Is it really this two-storied gray box? It looks more like a convent. What cold and penumbral classrooms! Ah, but behind the building, what a glorious field of furry green grass! Why are the walls so bare? No color, not even a line. In fact, nothing hints at the presence of young bright students everywhere.

"They put us up here in this dorm run by nuns, but it's only temporary," explains Cristina Doglio.

The animated voices of the freshmen break the still silence:

"Hey, what's up?"

"Schedule's out . . ."

"Who's teaching philosophy?"

"We get to choose from English, Italian, French, and German!"

"Wow! Look at the syllabus for Intro to Literature. That's a lot of work."

Yes, it's a new and exciting pleasure. Left behind is the daily, cloistered existence of her home in San Leopoldina. Here is an open universe without walls, so varied, it offers itself unconditionally to her every wish. No wonder the school motto is "This lighthouse is here to conquer darkness."

Oy gottenyu! When will I finally be able to leave Lendov? From afar I see Pinchas Gros, the only one of us who lives among the gentiles and in the very center of town. He's a common man, who doesn't even know how to write his name and celebrates the Sabbath alone. I must admit he sure has a great talent for fixing watches and glasses. So why does he live alone? And with a big goat in his backyard? They even use him to threaten children and sinners; after all, who could bear being locked up with that enormous beast and all the noise he makes?

I still have to cross the worn-out wooden bridge, where young lovers walk arm in arm, until around midnight, when Don Josú lets loose his dogs and the lovers rush back to the drugstore. From the street, the lovers look through the open window and enjoy the concert. Oh, I forgot to tell you, the drugstore houses the only piano in town, a treasure that none of us ever really saw but guessed was there. We all managed, at some point, to hear its notes. Standing in front of the colored containers of the drugstore, each heard a different melody. Know what I mean? Only the town priest could enter that house of enchantment. Dressed in priestly garb, he used to go very often to the house with the piano. What did the priest do there? Was he by any chance a privileged cherub? Tell you the truth, I always thought that what interested him was the pharmacist's wife . . . And now where do I hide? Out of Guitzer Street comes Batcha and her crude husband, that chicken guzzler. *Oy vey iz mir!* That's all I need! Bitter as bile that woman is. Why, she'd cut off my hand with her kitchen knife if she so much as suspected that I had said they're not among the best of families. Save me, sweet God! And please don't let the lovers of the mill see me either . . . Ay, ay! One night, I too, dreamed of love while caressing Janala's blond braid, inhaling her clean dress, her knotted kerchief, and her bare lips! From that intimacy at the mill, thank God, not one was ever left pregnant, God forgive! . . .

Farewell, Pappinyu and Mommala! May no evil ever befall you. Without saying good-bye, without hugs or kisses, your son goes away but does not leave you . . .

She got rid of them. She never felt they were real men anyway. Little Jacobs, Moisheles, young Reubens. Always together since primary school. No comparison to these university hunks! Those others were sexless siblings. Angels and seraphs. Soul mates. Was any of them ever like these guys here? Machos with their meaningful glances and provocative gestures? That one over there, for instance, he could be in a Hollywood movie. He's got a Gregory Peck air about him! Ah! And the one next to him! Wow! He's the spitting image of Victor Mature! And what about that hunk of a professor? Exactly like Jorge Negrete! Slim, dark, elegant mustache, reminds me of my Charro singing:

Allá en el Rancho Grande
allá donde vi-vií-a.

Había una ranch-er-iita
que alegre me decí-aa,
que alegre me decí-aaaaaaa

Back there in the big raa-anch,
back there where I once liiii-i-ved.
There was a rancherita
who joyfully would saaaaaa-ay,
who joyfully would saaaaa-ay . . .

All this guy needs is a pistol and a big sombrero! My Mexican charm's got nothing on him . . .

Ahhh, those matinee movies at the Rex and the afternoon ones at the Anuaco! Great, but lasted barely ninety minutes, whereas university life will be four years of handsome men parading deliciously before her. Farewell, my old-fashioned parents! At last I'm a free little bird!

Some hours earlier, during the pause between afternoon and evening prayers, as I counted the minutes, anguished by my upcoming departure, our humble house of god was a boiling caldron. The faithful were gathering in small circles, as if they were still at their market stalls. They were busy arguing: How many had actually died in the Great War? How many had we lost when General Pilsudski repelled the Russian army at the battle of Vistula?

"We should not have participated. That was a big imperialist war, and some of our people sympathized with the Bolsheviks."

"That's nonsense! Didn't we give the Polish legions a Henry Barwinski?"

"Yes, we did, so what? They paid us well for that one, didn't they, idiot?"

"Did you already forget that we were accused shortly after, and still to this very day, of spying for the Russians? Have they quit calling us rightists and anti-Polish?"

"You're the one who's an idiot. You don't even know that the Polish parliament protested that falsehood."

"Nu, so it protested, so? Did anything change? Why? Why do we have to serve in an army where we are always watched and never trusted?"

"Friends, friends. Don't insult each other, please, it's Shabbos!"

"I believe that nothing about this country should be far from our concerns."

"C'mon, we've been here for centuries and we're now citizens of the Polish Republic."

"Any alternatives, stupid? There is maybe somewhere else for us to go to?"

"Maybe."

"Yeah, sure."

"Nu, you stay here then. You'd rather put up with the slaughter of your brothers, the burning of your miserable little houses, and the fact that your sons will never be able to study in a Polish school than suffer a little hunger in the Holy Land or even over there in America. Yes, gentlemen, and in exchange for all the advantages you enjoy here, you have to give your blood to their wars! We're citizens, right? That's what you're saying, right? Sure . . . You poor misguided souls."

"Can you suggest a better place? Can you? Then let's leave right away!"

"There must be someplace on the face of this earth where there are no swords or Cossacks or savage thieves . . ."

Their yarmulkes seem about to explode with all the shouting and shoving and even hitting at times, believe me! But the cantor's deep and tender voice calls them back to prayer, marking the end of the Sabbath, and once again they turn meek before the splendor of the supplication. I, on the other hand, without arguing, am leaving: Momma, Poppa, I really don't want to be either hero or martyr on the Polish battlefield, or anybody else's for that matter. I want to live and die my life for me . . .

One afternoon, two months later, the students crowded together in the corridors to surround a bald young man with deep green eyes. At the same time, another one, thin, but with a noble expression on his face, is taken upstairs.

The group drowns them in hugs and tears. Even Professor Miguel Rosbaum, always isolated in his cubicle and covered in book dust, runs to embrace them. And Father Hernando, one of the most reserved students, talks on and on as never before.

"Who are they, Father Cornejo?"

"Famous people."

"From TV? Movies?"

"The resistance. They're survivors . . ."

"And what are they doing here?"

"Jesus, girl, are you Venezuelan?"

"Yes, by birth, and you?"

"Well, I was born in Spain, but I, for one, know that the UN protested the exile of these young people. Also that General Tarugo—what am I saying?—Marcos Pérez Jiménez, the president himself, was forced to grant them visas, even though one is an active member of the Communist Party and the other of the Democratic Action Party. But I've already said too much, my child. Around here, by God, even the walls have ears."

For seventeen years, she had been insulated from her surroundings. Who among her people took part in those passionate struggles for freedom, liberty, the sorrow of exile and jail, the excitement of a hastily called meeting against the dictator? Being a real citizen meant finding refuge for the democratic activists: distributing food and books to the opposition, whatever sublime task she might be entrusted with. Such a noble cause justified the total giving of oneself, and she would eagerly sacrifice herself for this Venezuela of hers.

Dad and Mom didn't have to find out. Why should they? What good would it do? Voluntarily isolated, they would die of worry if they knew. It was too late for them to accept the demands of a new life. How could these ignorant Polish peasants ever understand, these peasants whose workweek is a universe limited to a taxi route—from Plaza La Rueda to the corner of Carmelitas—from shop to home and vice versa? How could they possibly understand?

Dear Poppa and Momma,

I ask you: If the Polish gentiles win all the wars they start and will start, what do I ever gain? Quite the opposite. I'm neither Catholic, Ukrainian, communist, or even Lithuanian. I'll always be the loser because I am who I am. That's why I'm saying good-bye. So long, really. I'm leaving but am not abandoning you. And, anyway, I remain a fervent Pole in one thing: I worry a lot about the Germans . . .

Only yesterday Pappinyu brought home from shul a guest. This one was even poorer than we are! But to share Shabbat even with only a piece of onion and herring, water instead of wine, bringing a beggar to the table, is the opportunity God grants us to praise him. No one should go hungry on his day of rest.

The paternal words proclaim the arrival of my very last Shabbat at home.

"My friend, have you ever studied?"

"Mr. David, he whose name I'm not worthy of mentioning, gave me life to go to school when I was very little, even though my clothes were patched and torn."

"How lucky, my friend! Everyone: Wash your hands and let's begin the blessings!"

I envy Poppa's voice, which becomes even more beautiful during the prayer:

And there was afternoon and there was morning. Sixth day. And heaven and earth were created and all that they contain. And having concluded His creation on the seventh, He rested and sanctified it because on that day He concluded his work. Blessed art thou, oh Eternal God, King of the Universe, who doth create the fruit of the vine. Blessed art thou, Our Lord God, King of the world, who sanctified us and graced us with Your precepts and granted us the Sabbath to sanctify the memory of Your labor of creation . . .

As the prayer concludes we raise our glasses: "Let us drink to life and for peace! L'chaim! Dear guest, make yourself at home. Tell me, if you know how to study, you're already rich, don't you agree?"

"Thank you. Yes, but dear family, you also should know that poverty sticks to your skin and is hard to get rid of. It clouds wisdom . . . I did study some, but one has to live . . ."

"Excuse me, but poverty is no dishonor . . ."

"Maybe not, Rebbe David, but it can make you do bad things . . ."

"Yes, but I believe those bad deeds can be erased with the mortar of good deeds."

"You really think so? I think that wherever you go, wherever you stop, poverty is always in the middle of everything. That's what I think."

"Will you do me the honor of eating this gefilte fish? And tell me, my friend, did you ever try to overcome it by working with a paintbrush or with a needle and thread?"

"One has to learn many things, sir, and no cloak is big enough to hide poverty."

"Nu, so how do you manage?"

"I manage ..."

A candelabra with two candles barely sheds enough light upon us, but the vast darkness is illuminated by Poppa's every sentence and the amusing answers of Haim Lisrak, our guest, who is poorer than we are. Meanwhile, Momma and my siblings doze off, exhausted. Since sunrise they've been throwing sawdust on the floor, trying to get it to shine, rubbing out ashes, fetching water at the well, grinding and seasoning fish, getting dressed, blessing the candles ... Yes, Shabbos relaxes the spirit but sure tires the body!

"Have another drink, dear guest. It's cherry brandy. A little wine lightens the heart. May you never be poor of soul. May your children grow to study Torah, to marry, and to do good deeds! L'chaim! As long as there is health ..."

"You know, Rebbe David, poverty is worse than fifty plagues combined."

"But God hates only the ignorant ..."

"That may be so, but there is no crueler joke of divine affection that an empty pocket!"

"Listen, Haim, even the poorest beggar with pants full of holes, with seven different coats and seven masks to go begging alms from the same rich man, can enjoy the honor of Shabbat."

"Tsk, tsk, tsk! I certainly won't argue with that, Rebbe. That's why I keep praying: Help me, God, send me the cure. I already have the ailment!"

Outside, my whole village is a single chant to God. Aromas of hot cabbage soup seeping into every corner. I don't remember when I decide to put an end to the dialogue. Anyway, if people who have read Scripture and have eaten at the same table don't exchange words on holy laws, they might as well kneel before an idol. Besides, these two have already argued enough. Before the prayer of thanksgiving for the food we had just received, I interrupt with a not very sacred matter: I ask Poppa to use his formidable influence to have the district bureaucrats fix the public baths. "Oy yoy yoy, my poor nose, Pappinyu! Phew! I've got to cover it tightly before I can even go in to empty out the waste containers. And you know what all the gossips say? That right next to the women's ritual baths, young ladies become pregnant! Seems that the very learned, who sing sublime harmonies and sway as they extol the glories of our Lord, every night of the week are actually reading passionate love letters that *pretty* young girls hand them, while emptying the leftovers into that smelly hovel . . . deep below this mystical village . . . Poppa . . ."

Was there ever a Sunday without guests at home? First in the house in San José and then the one in San Leopoldina. Any writer, speaker, delegate, or visitor who passed through Caracas was compelled to be a dinner guest in the small and modest apartment in the Edificio de Nuestra Señora del Carmen. A pretty incongruous name for a building that housed people with unusual traditions like ours, which many a guest had ironically pointed out to their hosts. We lived there since the time Father almost went bankrupt. It was a place full of books, magazines, and phony Chagalls. Its only luxury was an Erard piano reflected in the glass cabinet full of crystal objects. These had been gifts from the Landaus, the Sponkas, the Erders, and others, when they moved into the lovely house on the same street eight years later, the house that had to be sold in a hurry to avoid foreclosure.

Today's luncheon is one of many. This one is given for the writer Isaiah Rainfeld. As usual, Don Máximo had already taken and brought him back from the business area of town: "Because one must try to distribute the books of this known intellectual however one can. Whether those buyers read the hardbound volumes or just use them to decorate their libraries is irrelevant. It's a fundamental act of charity to help a wise man. Besides, we'll need real dollars to pay for the American edition of poems of resistance in the ghettoes."

During the week, the business on Pasaje Benzo between Madrices and Marron Streets was in the capable hands of the missus. After all, isn't she the expert in buying and selling bras, half slips, and panties? Her husband? Oh he's something else! Culture on agile legs and convincing lips. Yeah, a regular walking encyclopedia. No denying that.

"We sold thirty-six books, Mr. Rainfeld."

"That's great, my friend."

"In three more days, we'll sell all seventy. We'll go to the big tycoons, secluded in their enormous mansions."

"It seems to be easier to write books than to sell them, don't you think?"

"Nonsense. Relax. Nobody ever turns me down. No matter where

I knock, you saw that yourself. They know that I have never traded with someone else's gold. I am not a smuggler. I don't charge a cent of commission for the sacred labor of helping the learned. Just as I learned from my father, David, may he have found peace . . ."

The exquisite banquet the lady of the house prepared, almost at daybreak, overflows on platters. Gefilte fish, chicken soup and matzo balls, nuts, cakes, grapes. The best of the best. "One must always honor the intellect!"

And now, the moment of truth has arrived. Could there be a better setting to bring up the issue of her great leap?

"Father, tomorrow I'm beginning my studies at the university . . ."

"This isn't the moment to discuss . . ."

"I'm not discussing, I'm notifying."

"Tonight when there are no guests, we'll talk . . ."

"Why wait? I already registered, and in fact I'm also going to be teaching at the Colegio Canada."

"I'm embarrassed in front of Mr. Rainfeld. He understands Spanish . . . you're so obstinate . . ."

"That's a fact."

"A daughter of mine? Practically engaged? Should get involved in that dangerous place where Reds hide and the National Security guards go looking for them with guns? That's sacrilege! Please, Mr. Rainfeld, honored guest, excuse us and help yourself to more fish."

Nothing better to dissolve her anger at Father than the Louis Armstrong open-air concert at the Concha Acustica de Bello Monte, brought from heaven itself just for her! Instead of screams, the sensual poetry of Gershwin's "Summerti-i-me and the living is e-ea-sy . . ."

Over there in Lendov, how many strangers had Friday and Saturday meals at my parents' humble table? Impossible to count. Occasionally, the guest might even be a modern freethinker from the city.

"But, Mr. David, Charles Darwin already proved that man is just another animal . . ."

"What are you saying, young man? If that's so, then how come not a single animal ever produced a Darwinich, or whatever his name is?"

"Rebbe, he's an English naturalist, who, after observing the animal species, determined their degree of evolution . . . No, sorry, nothing to do with our God."

"If a horse had something to say he would speak . . ."

"That's not what we're discussing, Mr. David. Beasts have their own way of expressing themselves."

"Yes, yes, they have tongues, that's true, but they cannot say a single blessing!"

"They express themselves in sounds and gestures."

"Young man, the ignorant is not the one who does not know but the one who scorns divine knowledge. And don't you forget that! A goat has a beard, but that doesn't make it a priest. Does it?"

"Ah! Finally we agree on something. Sir, you do admit then that we are the higher ranked in the animal kingdom?"

"You said that, I didn't. Anyway, before you become too big for your own breeches, young man, remember that butterflies precede *you* in the kingdom of divine creation!"

And so they might continue until the moon descended and the sun dazzled us . . .

Ahhhh! Her intoxication continues with the music of Jelly Roll Morton . . . The mixture of sweet wine and wrathful words at the end of Mr. Isaiah Rainfeld's reception fueled her tenacious will to face her opponent and pursue the confrontation: "Father, I beg you! Please try to understand my wish to have a career."

"I understand and cannot tie you to the house or prohibit you from having an honorable profession. Quite the opposite, I want you to amount to something, not be like me, who never got a diploma, who could not study and so had to earn a living knocking on doors, peddling, selling *schmates*. What do you want from me, *kindele*? I'm afraid for you! In that political environment of atheists!"

"But, Dad, you're not even religious!"

"Yes, I most certainly am, in my own way. It's true I no longer pray every day and I don't do a full fast on Yom Kippur, and no doubt because of that my poppa is turning in his grave. But I practice my tradition every moment of my life. And, as you well know, I've made a sacred cult of my mother tongue, Yiddish. Have you ever known me to sleep away from home, even one night? Do I have children on the streets? Do I get drunk? Gamble? Other women? That's what you're going to be exposed to out there. I'm afraid for you and for your sisters ..."

"Please, please, try to understand. We can't stay locked up forever. Each of us has to forge her own life! You did it, or have you already forgotten? You broke with your family and crossed oceans!"

"That was very different, young lady! Don't confuse the issues! I stayed back in Lendov; just my feet left! Can you understand that?"

"No, not at all. Anyway, why not just pretend that I'm not leaving San Leopoldina either; just my beautiful legs are running in search of other roads?"

A seemingly never-ending dialogue was being repeated, but she decided that as of this night it was ending. Max's moist eyes and Rifka's long sad face, marked with silent resentment her leave-taking at breakfast.

Would it have been wiser to go to another country? With what money? Maybe she just lacked the courage to cut, really cut that heavy cord ...

As I was telling you, at the end of Shabbat, I'm leaving, without a word. I have a foreboding that I'm saying good-bye forever to Nune the carpenter, Toiba the cripple, and Leib the hunchback. Oy gottenyu, how deeply my heart aches for Momma, the blanket that covers all my weaknesses.

And when at last, Lendov is behind me, I jump, practically fly to Magelnitze, without spending even a minute in that ugly little town where I used to come so often to buy yarmulkes. Its very smell upsets me. You see, when someone from my village closes his eyes forever, he is wrapped in his tallis, covered in straw, and then sent in a carriage to this overcrowded cemetery. Its stench freezes my bones!

"Magelnitze is sacred because it's where the eternal house is," my father used to say. "It's the good place," my mother usually added. You know what I think? I think it's the only place in the entire world where someone from our village has a right to his own little piece of land! That's what I think. And anyway, this business of putting the dead in facedown, boy, that really buries a person! Even if they swear to me that it's the real Garden of Eden and it's where all the dead will be resurrected, I still prefer gardens that are above and not below ground. Above, always above. You know what I mean? Even with all the hunger, plagues, pogroms. Nu, what can I tell you?

I don't stop at Vialorovsker either, because I know for sure that one-eyed Zina lurks right behind that window. Poor girl, she's been waiting for me to become engaged to her for four or five years now . . . I point my face to heaven and cross the main road like a thunderbolt. I couldn't bear to feel her rancorous gaze.

"Get married? But Poppa, I'm just fifteen years old!"

"So what? I got married at the same age, and I'm just fine, no?"

"But that's not good enough for me. From a cat a scratch; from a child bride nothing but damnation."

"What are you saying, my boychick? To get up early and marry early never hurt anyone. You'll have a good dowry and time to study Scripture."

"Pappinyu, you know why the bear dances? Because he has no wife. Give him one and he'll stop dancing. They sing that one at the market, Poppa."

"But it's a lie, because a husband is like a king and all couples are fine after a year or so."

"No, no, and no. It's never too late to marry or to die, Pappinyu."

"Oy vey iz mir! May the one whose name is blessed forgive your affront, my son! You're very stubborn, and I worry night and day about how you'll end up."

And while he wails, pulling hairs out of his long black beard, I run away to help Momma with the town fair, where she buys us used clothes . . .

That whole week was full of tension and whispers. Finally, on Friday night, when the rest of the family sleeps, he speaks. He looks worried.

"Where does one begin such unpleasant business? My dear sweet daughter, I want to consult you on a very delicate matter." In a low voice: "Please don't get upset. But ah . . . Manuel Rabinovich, the engineer, destined to be your husband, and from such a good family too, grandson of wise people! Well, anyway, he asked for a dowry, a house, car, office, and if possible, some cash . . ."

The father, knowing full well his daughter's wickedly complicated personality, has to tell her the whole truth . . . Should he get a bank loan? What does she think?

"Well, I'm not surprised. It is customary, after all. The problem is I still like him even after six months. Elegant, handsome, first kiss and out together, in a group, of course, to places like that fabulous Montmartre in Baruta with its European music and the naughty Pasapoga with its mambos and *guarachas.*"

"Thanks for the warning, Dad. If I were you, I wouldn't do anything." Of course, in historical terms, a dowry was after all a justifiable institution even under a Marxist focus . . . but it had nothing to do with love. "Tell me, Dad, how much did you make when you married?"

"Your mother with three cotton dresses. . . ."

"Well, that's just about what I think you should fork over . . ." At times, Max could seem primitive and abrupt in his reactions, but he had never been a good peddler. He was unable to sell his daughter. His smile, overflowing with impishness, signed a pact of complicity. On that point at least, there was never any argument.

It was a long way to Warsaw. And to be honest, it was none too sweet. But then again, I guess it could have been worse. On the way to Prztyk and Gora Kalwaria, I befriended a couple of coachmen. I've heard it said that God should protect us from forced exile and from coachmen, but even though these were pretty rough guys, I could tell they weren't totally stupid. Look, these unfortunate men travel for so long facing their horses that after a while they themselves become like animals.

Anyway, I really liked Nisale, the frisky one. After listening to all my *Oy yoy yoy*-ings over my calf pains, one afternoon he asked me: "Tell me, young sir, you seem quite learned. What do we really need our legs for? After all, to Hebrew school we are taken, to our wedding we are driven, to our grave we are carried, to the temple we never go, and in front of all pretty gentile girls we prostrate ourselves . . . So, what do you think, do we need them for anything?"

"Yes, Nisale. We need them to take us to America the Golden!"

He remained pensive. Probably not half as old as he looked with those smooth toothless gums. I took great care to keep to myself my ideas about the feet being the very center of a penitent's soul. Like Joel, the bearded one dressed in rags, who showed up one day at my village. "May his body be feverish for nine years!" "A pox on him!" "He should only grow like an onion, with his head buried in the ground!" they all cursed him. Only a few of the women gave him some stale bread and water, moved by his misfortune.

To make a long story short, Momma, teary eyed, tells me about the great Joel, born in the big city of Vilna, whose voice, at thirteen, was already legendary throughout the country. He sang the prayers with the virtuosity of the chosen. One day a famous gentile composer hears him at an event and, overwhelmed, begs the parents to allow him to be the child's teacher. Years later, while in the capital singing profane tunes, Joel meets Katiuska, a Polish princess. They fall madly in love. So at the age of twenty-two, Joel abandons his singing career, and rejected by his people, he who had been so pious and devout decides to atone for his sins. He goes from village to village, dragging himself to each and every little broken-down house until he gets to ours. What grief his broken-down body bears! And even you two, my very own parents, watch him suspiciously between the slits of the window shutters.

Dear parents, in this letter I can finally tell you that as I felt his childlike face and white hair wandering feverishly around the alleys of my childhood, I was more frightened than I had ever been in my life. A leper without sores.

I was reminded of the story of the king and the two men who guarded his orchard: one blind and one cripple:

"I see some delicious ripe fruit, but I can't reach it with only one leg," says the cripple.

"So what do you need two legs for? If you stand on my shoulders, we'll both eat juicy apples. I don't need eyes to taste them. Why should you need two legs?" And that's exactly what they did. When the king found out, he questioned his guards.

"Your Highness, how could it have been me? I can't climb or walk."

"Do you believe, your Worship, that I could have picked them without seeing?"

The king ordered the cripple to get on the shoulders of the blind man and then sentenced both to die.

Body and soul must always go together, Poppa. I have finally realized that if succumbing to pleasure sickens one's head, then one ends up with pain like Joel's and in an asylum in Warsaw. I will never be a cantor like my brother, nor a mohel like you, Pappinyu, much less one of those chosen to study God's words fifteen hours a day. Now and with this letter, I can finally tell you one of the reasons I left home without kissing you good-bye. Please try to understand. Just like you can't dance at two weddings at the same time, I don't want to separate my heart from my head. Poppa, Momma, dear little brothers and sisters, please don't cry when you think of me . . .

"That's what we need our feet for, Nisale, to save ourselves in America . . ."

CUBA

Jesus

-- -- -- -- -- -- -- -- -- -- -- -- -- -- -- -- -- -- --

PINKHES BERNIKER (1908–1956)
Translated from the Yiddish by Alan Astro

Pinkhes Berniker immigrated to Cuba to join his older brother, Chaim, who had started Dos Fraye Vort, *the first Yiddish newspaper in Cuba. In 1931 he moved to the United States, where he worked as director of a Hebrew school in Rochester, New York. In 1935, a collection of his stories,* Shtile Lebns (Quiet Lives), *was published in Vilna. "Jesus" is a striking piece on Jewish-gentile relations.*

HE DIDN'T TAKE it seriously the first few times his roommates suggested that he start peddling images of Jesus, or Yoshke, as he preferred to call him. He thought they were kidding. How could they be serious? Were they fools? What could they mean? How could they possibly think that he should schlep the goyish icons through the streets of Havana? What was he, a boy, a young lad who knew nothing of the world? How could they imagine that he—a middle-aged Jew with a beard and side curls, who had been ordained as a rabbi, who had devoted all the days of his life to Torah and to divine service—could all of a sudden peddle icons and spread word of Jesus of Nazareth? No, even they couldn't be serious about that! So he thought, and he didn't even try to answer them. He just sighed quietly, wiped the sweat off his face, and sat without moving, sure that they wouldn't bring up such a notion again.

Later he realized he'd been mistaken. Those roommates of his had been very serious. Not daring to propose the idea outright, they had begun by alluding to it, joking about it. He had remained silent and, contrary to their expectations, hadn't jumped up from his seat as though he had been scorched. So they had begun to broach the subject directly, insisting that he not even try another livelihood, even if one presented itself. He, of all people, was in just the right position to turn the greatest profit from peddling the "gods." No one else could approach his success. "For every god you sell, you'll clear a thousand percent profit."

"And the Cubans love to buy gods." "Especially from you, Rabbi Joseph, who looks so much like the bastard, pardon the comparison." "You'll see how eager they'll be to buy from you." "And they'll pay whatever you ask." "Listen to me, Rabbi Joseph, just try it! You'll see! They'll sacrifice everything they have for you! People who don't even need a god will buy one from you!" Thus his roommates urged him to become a god peddler. They couldn't stand to see him half-starved, in total distress, bereft of the slightest prospects. And they really did believe that selling the gods would solve his problems.

The more persistent they became, the more pensive he grew. He didn't answer them, for what could he say? Could he cut out his heart and show them how it bled, how every word they uttered made a sharp incision in it, tearing at it painfully? How could they understand what he felt if they didn't know how he'd been trained, what his position had been in the old country? He was consumed with self-pity. The world had stuck out its long, ugly tongue at him. Rabbi Joseph, so diligent a pupil that he'd been hailed as the prodigy from Eyshishok, was now supposed to spread tidings of Jesus of Nazareth throughout the world?!

He couldn't resign himself to his lot. Every day, in the blue, tropical dawn, he dragged himself through the narrow streets of Old Havana, offering his labor to one Jewish-owned factory after another, promising to do whatever it would take to earn a pittance. He was rejected everywhere. How could they let a venerably bearded Jew work in a factory? Who would dare holler at him? How could they prod him, ordering him around as necessary? "How could someone like you work in a factory?" "In the Talmudic academy of Volozhin, did they teach shoe making?" "Rabbi, you're too noble to work here." They looked at him with pity, not knowing how to help.

"Why? Wasn't the great Rabbi Yokhanan a shoemaker?" he asked, pleading for mercy. "That was then, this is now."

"And what about now? Wouldn't Rabbi Yokhanan still need to eat?" That was what he wanted to cry out, but he couldn't. He was already too discouraged. The unanimous rejections tortured him more than the constant hunger. And the charity, the sympathy, offered by all became harder to bear. It wouldn't have humiliated him had it not been for the presence, in a far-away Lithuanian town, of a wife and three small children who needed to eat. "Send some money, at least for bread." Thus his wife had written to him in a recent letter. And the word *bread* had swelled up and grown blurry from the teardrop that had fallen on it from the eye of a helpless mother.

Joseph recalled the words from *The Ethics of the Fathers*: "If I am not for me, who will be for me?"

"I must harden myself. I must find work!" He called out these words, forcing himself onto the street. Pale, thin, with a despairing mien, he posted himself at a factory door, glancing around helplessly, hoping to catch sight of the owner. From among the workers, a middle-aged Jew ran up to the door and pressed a few pennies into his palm. Joseph froze. His eyes popped out of his head; his mouth gaped open. The couple of cents fell from his hand. Like a madman, he ran from the factory. Late that night, when his room-mates returned, he pulled himself off his cot, stared at them momentarily, and said, "Children, tomorrow you will help me sell the gods." They wanted to ask him what had happened, but, glimpsing the pain in his eyes, they could not move their tongues.

Binding both packages of gods together, he left between them a length of rope to place on his neck, thereby lightening the load. He had only to hold onto the packages with his hands, lest they bump into his sides and stomach.

The uppermost image on his right side portrayed Mother Mary cuddling the newborn child, and the one on his left showed Jesus already grown. Between the two images he himself looked like the Son of God. His eyes were larger than life, and his face was paler than ever. Deep, superhuman suffering shone forth from him, a reflection of the pain visited on Jesus of Nazareth as he was led to the cross.

The day was burning hot. Pearls of sweat shone on his mild, pale face, and his clothes stuck to his tortured body. He stopped for a while, disentangling his nightmarish thoughts, slowly removing the rope from his neck, straight-ening his back racked with pain, and scraping away the sweat that bit into his burning face. He wiped tears from the corner of one eye.

He saw, far off, the low wooden cabins in the next village. In the surrounding silence, from time to time, there came the cries of the village children. Feeling a bit more cheerful, he slowly loaded his body with the two packages of gods. Trembling, he strode onward, onward. He was noticed first by the lean, pale children playing in the street. They immediately stopped their games and stiffened in amazement. The tropical fire in their black eyes burst forth as they caught sight of him. Never had they seen such a man.

"¡Mamá, mamá, un Jesús viene!" "A Jesus is coming!" Each started running home. "¡Mira! ¡Mira!" The children's voices rang through the village.

From windows and doors along the road, women leaned their heads out, murmuring excitedly to one another: "¡Santa María!" "¡Qué milagro!" "¡Dios mío!" They all whispered in astonishment, unable to turn their straining eyes away from the extraordinary man.

Joseph approached one of the houses and pointed to the image of Jesus, mutely suggesting that they buy a god from him. But the hot-blooded tropical women thought he was indicating how closely the image resembled him. Filled with awe, they gestured that he should enter. "¡Entre, señor!" said each one separately, with rare submissiveness. He entered the house, took the burden off his neck, and seated himself on the rocking chair they offered him. Looking at no one, he began untying the gods. No one in the household dared to sit. Along with some neighbors who had sneaked in, they encircled him and devoured him with their wide-open eyes.

"¿Tienes hijo?" "Do you have a son?" a young shiksa asked, trembling.

"I have two," he answered.

"And are they as handsome as you?" asked another girl excitedly.

"I myself don't know."

"¡Mira, él mismo tampoco sabe!" "He himself doesn't know!" A strange shame overtook the girls. They looked at each other momentarily, then burst into embarrassed laughter: "Ha ha ha! Ha ha ha!" Their hoarse guffaws echoed through the modest home.

"What's going on?" asked the mothers, glancing unkindly toward the man.

"Nothing!" said the girls, embracing each other, then repeating ecstatically, "¡El mismo tampoco sabe! ¡El mismo tampoco sabe! Ha ha ha! Ha ha ha!" Their suffocating laughter resonated as each tucked herself more closely into her girlfriend's body.

"And what's your name?" One of the girls tore herself from her friend's embrace.

"José . . ."

"What?" asked several of the women in unison.

"José . . ."

"José, Jesús!"

The village women began to murmur, winking more than speaking.

One of the shiksas was unable to restrain herself: "And what's your son's name?"

"Juan . . .

"Juan, Juan," the shiksas began to repeat, drooling. Embarrassed, they pushed each other into the next room, wildly, bizarrely. There was a momentary silence. Those watching were still under the spell of what had taken place. Joseph, however, was out of patience.

"Nu, ¿compran? Are you going to buy or not?" he asked, raising his eyes, filled with the sorrow of the world. He could say no more in Spanish, but no more was necessary. Every woman purchased a god from him by paying an initial installment—from which he already cleared a handsome profit—and promising the rest later.

Home he went, with only the rope. All the gods had been sold. He had never felt so light, so unencumbered. He had no packages to carry, and a hope had arisen within him that he would be forever free from hunger and want.

Later he himself was astonished at how he had changed, at how indifferently he could contemplate Jesus's beard. He went to a Cuban barber and had his blond beard trimmed in the likeness of Jesus.

"Your mother must have been very pious!" said the barber to him, with great conviction.

"How can you tell?"

"When she conceived you, she couldn't have stepped away from the image of Jesus."

"Perhaps." Joseph was delighted.

How could he act this way? He didn't know. The Christian women, his customers in the villages all around, waited for him as Jews await the Messiah. They worshiped him, and he earned from them more than he could ever have dreamed.

They had no idea who he was. He never told them he was a Jew, and he still wondered how he could deny his Jewish background. He learned a little Spanish, especially verses from the New Testament, and spoke with the peasant women like a true santo, a saint. Once, when a customer asked him, "¿Qué eres tú?" "What are you?" he rolled his eyes to the heavens and started to say, drawing out his words, "What difference does it make who I am? All are God's children."

"And the *judíos?* The Jews?" asked the women, unable to restrain themselves.

"The judíos are also God's children. They're just the sinful ones. They crucified our Señor Jesús, but they are still God's children. Jesús himself has forgiven them." He ended with a pious sigh.

"And do you yourself love the judíos?"

"Certainly."

"¿De veras?" "Really?"

"¿Y qué?" "What of it?" He put on a wounded expression and soon conceded, "My love for them isn't as deep as for the Christians, but I do love them. A sinner can be brought back to the righteous path through love, as our Señor Jesús said."

"¡Tiene razón!" "He's right!"

"¡Y bien que sí!" "And how!"

"¡Es un verdadero santo!" "He's a true saint!" All the women drank in his words.

"Have you yourself seen a real Jew?" Their curiosity couldn't be sated.

"Yes, I have."

"Where?"

"There, in Europe."

"What did he look like?"

"Just like me."

"Really?!"

"Yes, indeed."

"¡Si él lo dice, debe ser verdad!" "If he says it, it must be true." The peasant women winked at each other, and their faces grew intensely serious, as if in a moment of great exaltation. Joseph fell silent, engrossed in his thoughts. He let the peasant women examine some sample gods. For now he simply took orders, which he filled by mail. In the meantime, he took stock of his situation, how much money he had in the bank, how much he was owed, and how many more thousands he would earn in the coming year if business improved by just 50 percent. "Who needs to worry?" A smile lit up his face as he felt these words in his heart: "I give thanks and praise to Thee, almighty God, who hast given Jesus unto the world."

A new god peddler showed up in the same area. Day in and day out, he dragged himself from one village to the next, stopping at every home. He scraped the scalding sweat off his face and neck as he knocked, trembling, on the hospitable Cuban doors.

"¿Compran algo?" "Will you buy something?" he asked, gesturing broadly. Solidly built mothers and passionate, well-formed daughters looked at him with pity, comforting him and caressing him with the softness of the Spanish tongue and the gentleness of their big, velvety eyes. They gladly offered him a handout but shook their heads at his gods. "I'm sorry." He got the same answer almost everywhere.

"¡Compra y no lamentes!" "Buy and don't be sorry!"

"You're right!" answered the women, with a slight smile. He stood with his distressed face and heavy heart, looking at the peasant women, unable to understand why they were so stubborn.

A few children gathered around him. They stared at his earnest face, carefully touched the frames of the unveiled images, and began playing with them. "Tell your mother to buy a santo," he said, caressing one of the children. The child stopped laughing. His glance passed from the god merchant to his mother. It was hard for him to grasp what was happening.

"How sweet you are," said the mother, affectionately embracing her now serious child.

"I have a child just like him in the old country," said the god merchant, about to burst into tears.

"¡Mira, parece una mujer." "He's acting just like a woman!" The peasants were astonished to see the shiny tears forming in the corners of his eyes.

"Should a man cry?" "And he's supposed to be the breadwinner for a wife and children!" "How funny!" A few girls, unable to restrain themselves, laughed in his face. Ashamed, he glanced at their widely smiling eyes, felt his own helplessness, and went away. His feet had grown heavier and his grasp of events slighter. Nonetheless, arming himself with courage, he went from village to village. He knocked on every door and humbly showed his wares: "¡Compren!" "Buy something! If you help me, God will help you. And I sell very cheap!"

But he seldom came across a customer interested in his low prices. Almost everyone was waiting for the santo, the holy peddler, who bore a great likeness to God Himself. They dismissed the new god merchant out of hand: "I don't need any." "I'm very sorry." "We've already bought some from someone else." He already knew all their answers by heart.

"Are gods the only thing to peddle?" Such was the bitter question he asked his fellow immigrants every day.

"Do you know of something better? Food isn't about to fly into your mouth. And what are you going to do with the gods you've already bought?"

"¡Hay que trabajar!" "You've got to work!" exclaimed one of his countrymen, eager to show off his Spanish.

"But my work is in vain!"

"Right now your work is in vain, but it will pay off in time," said his friends, trying to console him.

"In time, in time!" he muttered nervously, not knowing at whom.

It had grown dark in the middle of the day. The clear, tropical sky had suddenly clouded over. Waves of heat rose from the ground, and the air became closer and denser. At any moment buckets of rain could fall. Campesinos, riding into town, became uneasy lest the storm catch up with them. So they pushed back their gritty straw hats, their *tijanas*; fastened the palm-leaf baskets full of fowl on one side of their saddles; secured the cans of milk on the other side; and urged the horses on with all their might. "¡Pronto!" "Faster!" "¡Pronto!" "Soon there'll be a deluge!" "You'll get soaked with all your gods in the middle of the field." The riders took pity on the poor foot traveler as they dug their spurs ever more deeply into the sides of their horses. But he scarcely moved his feet, hammering his steps out heavily. It was already past noon, and he hadn't sold a single god.

Arriving at the next village, soaked to the bone, he caught sight of an open door leading into a home full of people. Sneaking in, he put down his pack of gods in a corner behind the door. As he started removing his wet clothes from his even wetter body, he heard a woman speaking: "Here's five dollars; send me a San Antonio like that next week." "And send me a *Jesús by the Well*." "I'll take a San Pablo. Take three dollars in the meantime, and I'll pay the rest later." "Make sure you don't forget to send me a Santa María." "And I want a *Mother with the Son*." The women shouted over each other.

He could hardly believe his ears. He thought he was dreaming one of his sweet nightly dreams, in which he saw himself amid circles of peasant women ripping his godly wares out of his hands. He had believed that such good fortune was possible only in a dream, but here it was happening for real. "What can this be?" He wondered why he hadn't yet looked into the opposite corner of the room, and he took a few steps toward it.

He stopped in his tracks, stupefied. All his limbs began to shake.

He tried to hide his surprise, for never had he seen a man who looked so much like Jesus. "So that's it!" he murmured to himself as he watched Joseph rolling his eyes from time to time toward heaven, blessing the peasant women as a rebbe blesses his Hasidim. "Aha!" He was astonished at the reverence the village women bestowed on the stranger. "No, no, I could never become such a showman!" He stepped off to one side to keep Joseph from noticing him.

His last bit of hope had run out. "Y tú, ¿de dónde vienes?" "And where have you come from?" The peasant women were surprised to see the new god peddler after Joseph had left.

"From Santo Domingo."

"You've just gotten here?"

"No, I'm just about to leave."

"Did you see our Jesusito?"

"You mean the *vendedor*, the seller of the gods?"

"Yes. Doesn't he look just like Jesús?" asked the peasant women, offended.

"Like Jesus? But he's a judío, a Jew!" These words came flying out of his mouth with unusual force.

"¡Mentira! ¡Mentira!" "That's a lie! A lie! You yourself are the judío, and a dirty one at that!" cried the peasant women in unison, pale with emotion.

"¡Palabra de honor!" "I give you my word of honor that he's a judío!"

The new god peddler couldn't restrain himself when he realized what a terrible impression the word *judío* made on them. But his claims were all in vain. The village women still didn't believe him. He couldn't make them understand. "¡No, no puede ser!" "No, it can't be!" "¡Vamos, vete de aquí!" "Come on! Get out of here!" They couldn't stand to hear his words any longer.

He fell silent and left the house but not the village. He sought out some young men and bought them a round of drinks. As he sipped black coffee by the white marble table, he told them that the god peddler with the face like Jesus's, who overcharged their mothers for the pictures they bought from him, was a Jew, a descendant of the ones who had crucified Jesus.

"¡No hable boberías!" "Don't talk nonsense!" "¿Cómo es posible?" "How can that be?" "¡No me lo diga!" "Don't tell me." The young men didn't want to believe him. As their stubbornness grew, so did his. Finally, he told them of the first Jewish commandment. He left twenty-five dollars with the owner of the café and swore that the money was theirs if he had been lying to them. The cash had the right effect. It was as though the young men had been touched by fire. The blood rushed to their faces, and they drank themselves into a stupor.

Joseph hadn't yet arrived at the first house in the village when a lad ran across his path. "¡Oiga!" Listen, sir, my mother wants to buy something." The boy breathed with difficulty, hardly able to utter these words.

"¡Bendito eres, hijito!" "Blessed art thou, my son!" Such was Joseph's gentle answer.

"¡Por aquí es más cerca!" "This way is shorter!" said the little goy as he strode over the field, with Joseph trailing behind him.

Soon they were far, very far, from the village. The boy had already pointed out that "right over there" was their house. Although Joseph saw no house "over there," he still suspected nothing, assuming that his eyes were not as keen as the little goy's.

"Oiga, santo, ¿tú eres judío?" "Listen, Your Holiness, are you a Jew?"

The earth had suddenly brought forth, before Joseph's eyes, a robust young Cuban. Joseph gazed in surprise. For once his quick tongue failed him. When he finally could say something, it was too late. He was already splayed on the ground, with several goyim pinning down his legs; one held his head and two his arms. He screamed bloody murder, thrashed with his feet, pulled with all his might, but to no avail. They were stronger and did what they had to.

When they found out that he was indeed a Jew, they left him lying there, half-naked in the middle of the field. Every one of them spat in his face, hollered "Judío!" and ran to the village to tell of this wondrous thing.

The village women refused to believe even their own children. And for a long, long time they wouldn't patronize the new god merchant, for they hoped that Jesús would come back. But Joseph never returned.

GUATEMALA

Kindergarten

VICTOR PERERA (1934–2003)

When Rites: A Guatemalan Boyhood *first appeared in 1986, critics immediately celebrated its engaging lyricism and touching honesty. This story from that collection, originally written in English, is reminiscent of Isaac Babel's "The Story of My Dovecot." The autobiographical narrator describes in an openly unsentimental fashion a child's first encounter with anti-Semitism. The plot involves two apparently unconnected murders: that of Jesus Christ and another of the narrator's favorite maid. Perera died in Santa Cruz, California. He was also the author of* The Cross and the Pear Tree *(1995), among other works.*

MY EARLIEST IMAGES are geometrical: the narrow bars of the bedstead that I amazed everyone by squeezing through one windy night when I was frightened by a sheet flapping on a clothesline and wanted my mother; the perfect rectangle of Parque Central, with its octagonal tiled benches, encircled fountains, checkered flagstones. And across the way the twin towers of the cathedral, housing a dark mystery of candles and painted idols that would forever be barred to me.

In my pedal car, I explored the limits of my universe, always certain that beyond our doorstep and the park's four borders lay unnamed terrors. I was especially fond of a wooded labyrinth in the park's northern end, a dark, sinuous place where I could act out my heroic reveries unseen by Chata, the Indian girl with long braids and sweet-smelling skirts who looked after me. To my five-year-old's eyes, Chata seemed a rare beauty; she dressed in the vivid, handwoven huipil blouse and skirt of her region and had unusually fine olive skin. Chata was a spirited and mischievous young woman who let me eat forbidden sweets from street vendors and who would gently tease me into fondling her firm round breasts under the thin blouse.

I made friends in Parque Central, the year before my second branding. The first I can recall was Jorge, an idiot boy with gray drooping eyes that did not disguise his sunny nature. I liked Jorge because he was affectionate—indeed, he was little else—and disarmed my budding defenses by hugging me uninhibitedly and stroking my face. Jorge taught me to touch another without shame or ulterior motive, and for this I am forever indebted to him. I grew to love Jorge and had begun to interpret his grunts and noises into a modest vocabulary when he stopped coming to the park. Chata found out from his *china* that Jorge had been placed in a home.

That year I acquired my first heroes, the platoon of uniformed guards who marched past every afternoon on their way to the *palacio*. I would follow them the length of the park, beating my hands to the beat of the drum, pumping my legs as high as I could to their stride. At the curb I would stop and mark time until they turned the corner and disappeared.

Chata had an admirer, a tall Indian laborer named Ramiro, who courted her in the afternoons and on weekends, when Chata would take me to the park. Ramiro wore a straw hat and leather shoes and used to flash a gold tooth when he smiled or smirked. Chata kept Ramiro on tenterhooks, encouraging his advances and then rebuffing him with a toss of her head, or mocking his confusion with a whinnying giggle that appeared to goad and arouse him. He looked at her at times with a cold, hungering menace that I recognized even then as lust. I disliked and feared Ramiro, but I never dared to intrude on their lovers' play or their frequent spats in the park. Instead, I would retaliate by making Chata admit, when she tucked me into bed at night, that I was her favorite.

I was some weeks short of five, and small for my age, the first time Chata took me to school and abandoned me in the hands of a tall, gaunt woman with hard eyes and a pursed mouth. Her name was Miss Hale, and I detected from her accent that she was foreign.

"Aren't we a little small to be starting school?" she said, in slow, badly slurred Spanish. I understood this to be a taunt, which, on top of my desertion by Chata, brought tears to my eyes. I feared and distrusted Miss Hale all the more when I realized that this was the exact reaction she wanted and that my tears had placated her.

The room she led me into was musty and dim. I was presented to my classmates, most of whom seemed strange to me, and very large. Even their names, Octavio, Gunter, Michel, Loretta, had a foreign ring. From my earliest consciousness I had known I was a foreigner in this strange place, Guatemala.

Now, in the kindergarten room of the English-American School, I felt an alien among aliens.

"My mother says you are a Jew." It was Arturo, a dark, thickset boy with hooded eyes and hairy legs below his short trousers. Within a week, he and Gunter, a tall blond boy with smudged knees who made in his pants, established themselves as the class bullies. We were at recess, which meant I could play with my new friends, plump-cheeked Grace Samayoa and Michel Montcrassi, who was French and wore sandals on his stockinged feet and a round blue cap. There was a fountain in the patio with goldfish in it and a rising nymph with mossy green feet who poured water from her pitcher. In each corner of the patio (Mother said the school had once been a convent) was a large red flowerpot, with pink and white geraniums. I sensed the question was critical and I must reply with care.

"Yes," I said.

"My mother says the Jews killed Christ."

Now this was a trickier question. Who was Christ? "They did not," I said, but all I could be certain of was that I, at least, had not killed Christ— whoever he was—because I had never killed anyone, at least not knowingly.

Then I remembered stepping on a cockroach once and stomping on ants in the kitchen. Maybe I had killed Christ by accident.

"Prove it," Octavio said.

I told him I would ask Father about it and give him a reply the next day.

That night I asked Father why I was a Jew. He hoisted me up by the armpits, sat me on his knee, and told me a long and complicated story about God, the Bible, and a Jew named Moses. When I asked if it was true that the Jews had killed Christ, he frowned and said the Romans had done it. He said I should pay no attention to Arturo.

When Arturo approached me next day, Father's story had gone clear out of my head. All I remembered was that the Romans had done it.

"The Romans killed Christ," I said.

"Who are the Romans?" Arturo asked.

I said I wasn't sure but would ask Father and let him know.

When I asked Father in the evening, he was reading a newspaper. He said the Romans did it and that was that, and I was to pay no heed to Arturo. Father was not in a talkative mood, and I did not press the matter. But I was confused, and I feared my next encounter with Arturo.

Several days passed, and Arturo did not mention the Jews and Christ. I dared hope the whole subject had been forgotten. In the meantime, my friendship with Michel grew. He let me call him Coco, which was his nickname, because his head was round and hard like a coconut; even his curly blond hair resembled a coconut husk. Coco was as much a foreigner in the school as I was. He was Protestant, and the bigger boys mocked his French accent and played catch with his cap.

Grace Samayoa was a little shy of me, although she liked me to tell her stories I'd made up in the labyrinth. Now and again she gave me an approving smile when I answered Miss Hale's questions correctly—and once she let me stroke her hair. Grace Samayoa was the most attractive female I knew next to Chata and my mother. But Grace was also my own size, which made her a challenge. I longed to hug her.

One afternoon Chata failed to pick me up at school. That morning Ramiro had followed us to school, as usual, although they had quarreled in the park the day before, when he had caught her flirting with a young chauffeur.

"He's following us. Don't turn around," I recall Chata saying, glancing behind her without turning her head. They were the last words of Chata's I would ever hear.

It had grown dark outside and my knees were cold when Father finally came for me, after closing the store.

"Chata has gone away," was all he would say. "We will get you another china."

After dinner I went into the kitchen and I wormed the truth out of Clara, the cook. She said that Chata and I had been followed by Ramiro. After she deposited me at the school, he waylaid Chata a block away and gave her "siete puñaladas en el mero corazón" ("seven knife stabs in the very heart"). I accepted Clara's story on faith, not at all concerned that her description matched word for word the title of a popular song. I stamped about the house, pumping my legs high like the palace guards and chanting the song title aloud: "Sie-te Puiia-ladas en El Mero Corazón. Sie-te Puiia-ladas en El Mero Corazón." The resonance of the phrase, its hard metric beat, gave Chata's disappearance a finality I could comprehend.

The fuller import of Chata's death did not dawn on me until the following day, when I was taken to school by her older sister, Elvira, whose braids were neither as long nor as glossy as Chata's and whose skirts did not smell half as good.

In the days that followed, Chata's violent death and Arturo's hard questions got mixed together in my dreams, and my apprehension grew that Chata had been murdered because of me, and because I was a Jew.

Unlike her younger sister, Elvira was a practicing Catholic, and one Sunday afternoon she sneaked me into the cathedral across from the park.

"You must pray to Our Lord," she whispered, pointing to the pale naked statue, with bloodied ribs and thorns on his head, that hung with arms outstretched from the front wall, in the same place where the Ark would stand in our synagogue; only this place was a lot bigger and scarier.

When I balked at reciting the paternoster she had taught me, Elvira rebuked me, "You must pray to Our Lord to be forgiven for your ancestors' sins against him. That way you can go to heaven, even if you're not Catholic."

Choking back tears, I mumbled the paternoster, not for myself so much but for Chata, who Elvira said had been punished for her sins.

During recess one noon, Arturo again brought up the Jews and Christ. This time Gunter was with him, and there was something in his face I had not seen here before. Gunter's blue eyes never looked right at yours.

"My mother says all Jews have tails and horns," Arturo said, with an accusing look. Now this I knew was absurd, because I had seen myself in the mirror.

"They do not," I said.

"Jews have bald-headed pigeons," Gunter said, with a smirk.

I flushed because this was true—at least I did, Father did and Uncle Mair, and Mr. Halevi at the Turkish baths, but not Señor Gonzales and the others there that day—their pigeons weren't bald . . . But then, what business was it of Gunter's anyway?

"It's none of your business," I said. My face was hot.

"My mother says Jews are the devil," Arturo said, and he gave me a shove.

Gunter called the other boys over and said, "Look at the Jew who killed Christ." Then they all gathered behind him and Arturo and stared at me.

"Leave him alone," called a thin, furry voice from the back. "He's not the devil." It was Coco.

"You keep still, dirty Frenchy," Gunter said.

"Dirty Frenchy, dirty Frenchy," chorused the other boys. Someone snatched the beret from Coco's head, and they all stomped on it, one by one.

"Let's look at his bald-headed pigeon," Gunter said, turning toward me, without looking in my eyes.

I was growing frightened now, but not of Gunter, whom I suspected to be the instigator of all this. I feared the mob.

"He killed Christ," Gunter said in a rising voice, and the group behind him grew tighter. Arturo shoved me again, harder. Torn between fear and anger, I wanted to punch Gunter in the face. But Gunter was a head taller than I, and out of reach.

I stretched to my full height. "At least I don't make in my pants," I said, and I looked Gunter straight in the eye.

He made a grab for my suspenders, and I swung at his face. But Arturo held me fast, and then all the other boys fell on top of me. I kicked and scratched and defended myself, but they were too many. When they had stripped off all my clothes—except my shoes and socks—they stepped back to look at me.

"He lost his tail," Arturo said, almost in relief.

"But he has a bald-headed pigeon," Gunter said. A giggle that was unlike any sound I had ever heard from a boy, or anyone else, came out of his face.

I turned toward the wall. My chest ached from the effort to hold back tears. Several of the boys had drifted away, as if they wished to distance themselves from the two leaders.

Silence, except for the trickle of the fountain and the heaving of my chest. Coco came forward and offered me his crushed beret so I could cover myself.

More boys moved away, and I saw that the girls had all gathered at the far end of the patio, behind the fountain—all except Grace Samayoa. She sat on the rim of the fountain and stared at me.

"Don't look," I said to Grace Samayoa, and I turned to one side. But she kept on looking.

Then Grace Samayoa said, "I hate you," and she walked toward the girls at the far end of the patio.

I covered myself with Coco's cap, and I cried. I cried at the top of my lungs until Miss Hale came. She cleared everyone from the patio and told me to get dressed.

The following year I was left back in kindergarten. Miss Hale and my parents agreed I was underage for the first grade.

Bottles

■ ■

ALCINA LUBITCH DOMECQ (b. 1953)
Translated from the Spanish by Ilan Stavans

Alberto Manguel, the celebrated Argentinian-born Canadian translator and editor, once divided writers into two categories: those who perceive a single corner of the world as their entire universe, and those who wander everywhere in the universe looking for a place called home—the particularists and the universalists. This novelist and storyteller unquestionably belongs to the first group. Her novel The Mirror's Mirror: or, The Noble Smile of the Dog *(1983) established her as a postmodernist in the tradition of Italo Calvina and Jorge Luis Borges, and* Intoxicated *(1988), her memorable collection of tales from which "Bottles" is taken, immediately elevated her to the level of master of the short story genre. A surrealist examination of motherhood, this tale has as protagonist a woman alienated from herself, a robot-like creature trapped in her own corner of the universe.*

MOM WAS TAKEN away, I don't know exactly where. Dad says she is in a nice place where they take good care of her. I miss her . . . although I understand. Dad says she suffered from a sickening love for bottles. First she started to buy them in the supermarket. All sorts of bottles—plastic and crystal, small and big. Everything had to be packed in a bottle—noodle soup, lemon juice, bathroom soap, pencils. She just wouldn't buy something that wasn't in one. Dad complained. Sometimes that was the reason we wouldn't have toilet paper or there wouldn't be any salt. And Mom used to kiss the bottles all day long. She polished them with great affection, talked to them, and at times I remember her saying that she was going to eat one. You could open a kitchen cabinet and find a million bottles. A million. I hated them, and so did my sister. I mean, why store the dirty linen in a huge bottle the size of a garbage can?

Dad says Mom didn't know anything about logic. I remember one night, after dinner, when Mom apologized and left in a hurry. An hour later she returned with a box full of wine bottles. Dad asked her what had gotten into her. She said she had been at the liquor store, and she immediately started to empty every single bottle into the toilet. All the wine was dumped. She just needed the bottles. Dad and I and my sister just sat there, on the living room couch, watching Mom wash and kiss those ugly wine bottles. I think my sister began to cry. But Mom didn't care. Then Dad called the police, but they didn't do a thing. Weeks later, we pretended to have forgotten everything. It was then that Mom began screaming that she was pregnant, like when my sister was born. She was shouting that a tiny plastic bottle was living inside her stomach. She said she was having pain. She was vomiting and pale. She cried a lot. Dad called an ambulance, and Mom was taken to the hospital. There the doctors made x-rays and checked her all over. Nothing was wrong. They just couldn't find the tiny plastic bottle. But for days she kept insisting that it was living inside her, growing; that's what she used to say to me and my sister. Not to Dad anymore, because he wouldn't listen to her, he just wouldn't listen. I miss Mom . . . She was taken away a month later, after the event with the statue in the living room. You see, one afternoon she decided that the tiny bottle wasn't in her stomach anymore. Now she felt bad because something was going to happen to her. Like a prophecy. She was feeling that something was coming upon her. And next morning, before my sister and I left for school, we found Mom near the couch, standing in the living room. She was vertical, standing straight. She couldn't walk around. Like in a cell. I asked her why she wouldn't move, why she wouldn't go to the kitchen or to my room. Mom answered that she couldn't because she was trapped in a bottle, a gigantic one. We could see her and she could see us too, but according to Mom, nobody could touch her body because there was glass surrounding it. Actually, I touched her and I never felt any glass. Neither did Dad or my sister. But Mom insisted that she couldn't feel us. For days she stayed in that position, and after some time I was able to picture the big bottle. Mom was like a spider you catch in the backyard and suffocate in Tupperware. That's when the ambulance came for the second time. I wasn't home but Dad was. He was there when they took her away. I was at school, although I knew what was happening. That same day we threw away all the bottles in a nearby dump. The neighbors were staring at us, but we didn't care. It felt good, very good.

BRAZIL

Love

-- --

CLARICE LISPECTOR (1925–1977)
Translated from the Portuguese by Giovanni Pontiero

Perhaps the most complex story in this volume, "Love," collected in Family Ties *(1960),
is to Brazilian letters what Virginia Woolf's "The Mark on the Wall" is to English
literature: a meditation on feminine angst. During a tram ride, Anna, a happy housewife and mother, is thrown into existential despair when she confronts the face of a
blind man chewing gum. Like the narrator of Sartre's* Nausea, *Lispector's protagonist
is horrified by the dense fluidity of existence, which challenges the neat arrangements of
domestic life as well as her reflective consciousness. Lispector's* The Complete Stories
appeared in English in 2015. Benjamin Moser's biography, Why This Word *(2012),
follows her existential and aesthetic journey in minute detail.*

FEELING A LITTLE tired, with her purchases bulging her new string bag,
Anna boarded the tram. She placed the bag on her lap and the tram started
off. Settling back in her seat, she tried to find a comfortable position, with a
sigh of mild satisfaction.

Anna had nice children, she reflected with certainty and pleasure. They
were growing up, bathing themselves and misbehaving; they were demanding more and more of her time. The kitchen, after all, was spacious with its
old stove that made explosive noises. The heat was oppressive in the apartment, which they were paying off in installments, and the wind, playing
against the curtains she had made herself, reminded her that if she wanted
to she could pause to wipe her forehead and to contemplate the calm horizon. Like a farmer. She had planted the seeds she held in her hand, no
others, but only those. And they were growing into trees. Her brisk conversations with the electricity man were growing, the water filling the bank

was growing, her children were growing, the table was growing with food, her husband arriving with the newspapers and smiling with hunger, the irritating singing of the maids resounding through the block. Anna tranquilly put her small, strong hand, her life current, to everything. Certain times of the afternoon struck her as being critical. At a certain hour of the afternoon, the trees she had planted laughed at her. And when nothing more required her strength, she became anxious. Meanwhile she felt herself more solid than ever, her body become a little thicker, and it was worth seeing the manner in which she cut out blouses for the children, the large scissors snapping into the material. All her vaguely artistic aspirations had for some time been channeled into making her days fulfilled and beautiful; with time, her taste for the decorative had developed and supplanted intimate disorder. She seemed to have discovered that everything was capable of being perfected, that each thing could be given a harmonious appearance; life itself could be created by man.

Deep down, Anna had always found it necessary to feel the firm roots of things. And this is what a home had surprisingly provided. Through tortuous paths, she had achieved a woman's destiny, with the surprise of conforming to it almost as if she had invented that destiny herself. The man whom she had married was a real man; the children she mothered were real children. Her previous youth now seemed alien to her, like one of life's illnesses. She had gradually emerged to discover that life could be lived without happiness: by abolishing it she had found a legion of persons, previously invisible, who lived as one works—with perseverance, persistence, and contentment. What had happened to Anna before possessing a home of her own stood forever beyond her reach: that disturbing exaltation she had often confused with unbearable happiness. In exchange she had created something ultimately comprehensible, the life of an adult. This was what she had wanted and chosen.

Her precautions were now reduced to alertness during the dangerous part of the afternoon, when the house was empty and she was no longer needed; when the sun reached its zenith and each member of the family went about his separate duties. Looking at the polished furniture, she felt her heart contract a little with fear. But in her life there was no opportunity to cherish her fears—she suppressed them with that same ingenuity she had acquired from domestic struggles. Then she would go out shopping or take things to be mended, unobtrusively looking after her home and her family.

When she returned, it would already be late afternoon and the children back from school would absorb her attention. Until the evening descended with its quiet excitement. In the morning she would awaken surrounded by her calm domestic duties. She would find the furniture dusty and dirty once more, as if it had returned repentant. As for herself, she mysteriously formed part of the soft, dark roots of the earth. And anonymously she nourished life. It was pleasant like this. And this was what she had wanted and chosen.

The tram swayed on its rails and turned into the main road. Suddenly the wind became more humid, announcing not only the passing of the afternoon but the end of that uncertain hour. Anna sighed with relief, and a deep sense of acceptance gave her face an air of womanhood.

The tram would drag along and then suddenly jolt to a halt. As far as Humaitá she could relax. Suddenly she saw the man stationary at the tram stop. The difference between him and others was that he was really stationary. He stood with his hands out in front of him—blind.

But what else was there about him that made Anna sit up in distrust?

Something disquieting was happening. Then she discovered what it was: the blind man was chewing gum . . . a blind man chewing gum. Anna still had time to reflect for a second that her brothers were coming to dinner— her heart pounding at regular intervals. Leaning forward, she studied the blind man intently, as one observes something incapable of returning our gaze. Relaxed, and with open eyes, he was chewing gum in the failing light. The facial movements of his chewing made him appear to smile and then suddenly stop smiling, to smile and stop smiling. Anna stared at him as if he had insulted her. And anyone watching would have received the impression of a woman filled with hatred. She continued to stare at him, leaning more and more forward—until the tram gave a sudden jerk, throwing her unexpectedly backward. The heavy string bag toppled from her lap and landed on the floor. Anna cried out, the conductor gave the signal to stop before realizing what was happening, and the tram came to an abrupt halt. The other passengers looked on in amazement. Too paralyzed to gather up her shopping, Anna sat upright, her face suddenly pale. An expression, long since forgotten, awkwardly reappeared, unexpected and inexplicable. The Negro newsboy smiled as he handed over her bundle. The eggs had broken in their newspaper wrapping. Yellow sticky yolks dripped between the strands of the bag. The blind man had interrupted his chewing and held out his unsteady hands, trying in vain to grasp what had happened. She removed the parcel of eggs from the string, accompanied by the smiles of the passengers. A second signal from the conductor, and the tram moved off with another jerk.

A few moments later, people were no longer staring at her. The tram was rattling on the rails, and the blind man chewing gum had remained behind forever. But the damage had been done.

The string bag felt rough between her fingers, not soft and familiar as when she had knitted it. The bag had lost its meaning; to find herself on that tram was a broken thread; she did not know what to do with the purchases on her lap. Like some strange music, the world started up again around her. The damage had been done. But why? Had she forgotten that there were blind people? Compassion choked her. Anna's breathing became heavy. Even those things that had existed before the episode were now on the alert, more hostile, and even perishable. The world had once more become a nightmare. Several years fell away, the yellow yolks trickled. Exiled from her own days, it seemed to her that the people in the streets were vulnerable, that they barely maintained their equilibrium on the surface of the darkness—and for a moment they appeared to lack any sense of direction. The perception of an absence of law came so unexpectedly that Anna clutched the seat in front of her, as if she might fall off the tram, as if things might be overturned with the same calm they had possessed when order reigned.

What she called a crisis had come at last. And its sign was the intense pleasure with which she now looked at things, suffering and alarmed. The heat had become more oppressive; everything had gained new power and a stronger voice. In the Rua Voluntarios da Patria, revolution seemed imminent, the grids of the gutters were dry, the air dusty. A blind man chewing gum had plunged the world into a mysterious excitement. In every strong person there was a lack of compassion for the blind man, and their strength terrified her. Beside her sat a woman in blue with an expression that made Anna avert her gaze rapidly. On the pavement a mother shook her little boy. Two lovers held hands smiling . . . And the blind man? Anna had lapsed into a mood of compassion, which greatly distressed her.

She had skillfully pacified life; she had taken so much care to avoid upheavals.

She had cultivated an atmosphere of serene understanding, separating each person from the others. Her clothes were clearly designed to be practical, and she could choose the evening's film from the newspaper—and everything was done in such a manner that each day should smoothly succeed the previous one. And a blind man chewing gum was destroying all this. Through her compassion, Anna felt that life was filled to the brim with a sickening nausea.

Only then did she realize that she had passed her stop ages ago. In her weak state everything touched her with alarm. She got off the tram, her legs shaking, and looked around her, clutching the string bag stained with egg. For a moment she was unable to get her bearings. She seemed to have plunged into the middle of the night.

It was a long road, with high yellow walls. Her heart beat with fear as she tried in vain to recognize her surroundings; while the life she had discovered continued to pulsate, a gentler, more mysterious wind caressed her face. She stood quietly, observing the wall. At last she recognized it. Advancing a little farther alongside a hedge, she passed through the gates of the botanical garden.

She strolled wearily up the central avenue, between the palm trees. There was no one in the garden. She put her parcels down on the ground and sat down on the bench of a side path, where she remained for some time.

The wilderness seemed to calm her, the silence regulating her breathing and soothing her senses.

From afar she saw the avenue, where the evening was round and clear. But the shadows of the branches covered the side path.

Around her there were tranquil noises, the scent of trees, chance encounters among the creeping plants. The entire garden fragmented by the ever more fleeting moments of the evening. From whence came the drowsiness with which she was surrounded? As if induced by the drone of birds and bees. Everything seemed strange, much too gentle, much too great.

A gentle, familiar movement startled her, and she turned round rapidly. Nothing appeared to have stirred. But in the central lane there stood, immobile, an enormous cat. Its fur was soft. With another silent movement, it disappeared. Agitated, she looked about her. The branches swayed, their shadows wavering on the ground. A sparrow foraged in the soil. And suddenly, in terror, she imagined that she had fallen into an ambush. In the garden there was a secret activity in progress, which she was beginning to penetrate.

On the trees, the fruits were black and sweet as honey. On the ground lay dry fruit stones full of circumvolutions, like small rotted cerebrums. The bench was stained with purple sap. With gentle persistence, the waters murmured. On the tree trunk, the luxurious feelers of parasites fastened themselves. The rawness of the world was peaceful. The murder was deep. And death was not what one had imagined.

As well as being imaginary, this was a world to be devoured with one's teeth, a world of voluminous dahlias and tulips. The trunks were pervaded by leafy parasites, their embrace soft and clinging. Like the resistance that precedes surrender, it was fascinating; the woman felt disgusted, and it was fascinating.

The trees were laden, and the world was so rich that it was rotting. When Anna reflected that there were children and grown men suffering hunger, the nausea reached her throat as if she were pregnant and abandoned. The moral of the garden was something different. Now that the blind man had guided her to it, she trembled on the threshold of a dark, fascinating world, where monstrous water lilies floated. The small flowers scattered on the grass did not appear to be yellow or pink but the color of inferior gold and scarlet. Their decay was profound, perfumed. But all these oppressive things she watched, her head surrounded by a swarm of insects, sent by some more refined life in the world. The breeze penetrated between the flowers. Anna imagined rather than felt its sweetened scent. The garden was so beautiful that she feared hell.

It was almost night now, and everything seemed replete and heavy; a squirrel leapt in the darkness. Under her feet the earth was soft. Anna inhaled its odor with delight. It was both fascinating and repulsive.

But when she remembered the children, before whom she now felt guilty, she straightened up with a cry of pain. She clutched the package, advanced through the dark side path, and reached the avenue. She was almost running, and she saw the garden all around her, aloof and impersonal. She shook the locked gates and went on shaking them, gripping the rough timber. The watchman appeared, alarmed at not having seen her.

Until she reached the entrance of the building, she seemed to be on the brink of disaster. She ran with the string bag to the elevator, her heart beating in her breast—what was happening? Her compassion for the blind man was as fierce as anguish, but the world seemed hers, dirty, perishable, hers. She opened the door of her flat. The room was large, square. The polished knobs were shining, the windowpanes were shining, the lamp shone brightly—what new land was this? And for a moment that wholesome life she had led until today seemed morally crazy. The little boy who came running up to embrace her was a creature with long legs and a face resembling her own. She pressed him firmly to her in anxiety and fear. Trembling, she protected herself. Life was vulnerable. She loved the world, she loved all things created, she loved with loathing. In the same way she had always been fascinated by oysters, with that vague sentiment of revulsion that the approach of truth provoked, admonishing her. She embraced her son, almost hurting him. Almost as if she knew of some evil—the blind man or the beautiful botanical garden—she was clinging to him, to him whom she loved above all things. She had been touched by the demon of faith.

"Life is horrible," she said to him in a low voice, as if famished. What would she do if she answered the blind man's call? She would go alone . . . There were poor and rich places that needed her. She needed them. "I am afraid," she said. She felt the delicate ribs of the child between her arms. She heard his frightened weeping.

"Mummy," the child called. She held him away from her. She studied his face and her heart shrank.

"Don't let Mummy forget you," she said. No sooner had the child felt her embrace weaken than he escaped and ran to the door of the room, from where he watched her more safely. It was the worst look that she had ever received. The blood rose hot to her cheeks.

She sank into a chair, with her fingers still clasping the string bag. What was she ashamed of? There was no way of escaping. The very crust of the days she had forged had broken and the water was escaping. She stood before the oysters. And there was no way of averting her gaze. What was she ashamed of? Certainly it was no longer pity; it was more than pity: her heart had filled with the worst will to live.

She no longer knew if she was on the side of the blind man or of the thick plants. The man, little by little, had moved away, and in her torment she appeared to have passed over to the side of those who had injured his eyes. The botanical garden, tranquil and high, had been a revelation. With horror, she discovered that she belonged to the strong part of the world, and what name should she give to her fierce compassion? Would she be obliged to kiss the leper, since she would never be just a sister? "A blind man has drawn me to the worst of myself," she thought, amazed. She felt banished because no pauper would drink water from her burning hands. Ah! It was easier to be a saint than a person! Good heavens, then was it not real, that pity that had fathomed the deepest waters in her heart? But it was the compassion of a lion.

Humiliated, she knew that the blind man would prefer a poorer love. And, trembling, she also knew why. The life of the botanical garden summoned her as a werewolf is summoned by the moonlight. "Oh! But she loved the blind man," she thought with tears in her eyes. Meanwhile, it was not with this sentiment that one would go to church. "I am frightened," she whispered alone in the room. She got up and went to the kitchen to help the maid prepare dinner.

But life made her shiver like the cold of winter. She heard the school bell pealing, distant and constant. The small horror of the dust gathering in threads around the bottom of the stove, where she had discovered a small spider. Lifting a vase to change the water—there was the horror of the flower submitting itself, languid and loathsome, to her hands. The same secret activity was going on here in the kitchen. Near the waste bin, she crushed an ant with her foot. The small murder of the ant. Its minute body trembled. Drops of water fell on the stagnant water in the pool.

The summer beetles. The horror of those expressionless beetles. All around there was a silent, slow, insistent life. Horror upon horror. She went from one side of the kitchen to the other, cutting the steaks, mixing the cream. Circling around her head, around the light, the flies of a warm summer's evening. A night in which compassion was as crude as false love. Sweat trickled between her breasts. Faith broke her; the heat of the oven burned in her eyes. Then her husband arrived, followed by her brothers and their wives, and her brothers' children.

They dined with all the windows open, on the ninth floor. An airplane shuddered menacingly in the heat of the sky. Although she had used few eggs, the dinner was good. The children stayed up, playing on the carpet with their cousins. It was summer and it would be useless to force them to go to sleep. Anna was a little pale and laughed gently with the others.

After dinner, the first cool breeze finally entered the room. The family was seated around the table, tired after their day, happy in the absence of any discord, eager not to find fault. They laughed at everything, with warmth and humanity. The children grew up admirably around them. Anna took the moment like a butterfly between her fingers, before it might escape forever.

Later, when they had all left and the children were in bed, she was just a woman looking out of the window. The city was asleep and warm. Would the experience unleashed by the blind man fill her days? How many years would it take before she once more grew old? The slightest movement on her part and she would trample one of her children. But with the ill will of a lover, she seemed to accept that the fly would emerge from the flower, and the giant water lilies would float in the darkness of the lake. The blind man was hanging among the fruits of the botanical garden.

What if that were the stove exploding, with the fire spreading through the house, she thought to herself as she ran to the kitchen, where she found her husband in front of the spilled coffee.

"What happened?" she cried, shaking from head to foot. He was taken aback by his wife's alarm. And suddenly understanding, he laughed.

"It was nothing," he said. "I am just a clumsy fellow." He looked tired, with dark circles under his eyes.

But, confronted by the strange expression on Anna's face, he studied her more closely. Then he drew her to him in a sudden caress.

"I don't want anything ever to happen to you!" she said.

"You can't prevent the stove from having its little explosions," he replied, smiling. She remained limp in his arms. This afternoon, something tranquil had exploded, and in the house everything struck a tragicomedic note.

"It's time to go to bed," he said. "It's late." In a gesture that was not his but that seemed natural, he held his wife's hand, taking her with him, without looking back, removing her from the danger of living.

The giddiness of compassion had spent itself. And if she had crossed love and its hell, she was now combing her hair before the mirror, without any world for the moment in her heart. Before getting into bed, as if she were snuffing a candle, she blew out that day's tiny flame.

Inside My Dirty Head—The Holocaust

- -

MOACYR SCLIAR (1937–2011)

Translated from the Portuguese by Eloah F. Giacomelli

Prolific and prodigious, Scliar had a lighthearted style and an enchanting voice that recalls the art of Sholem Aleichem. But the tone in this extraordinary tale from the collection The Enigmatic Eye *(1989) is dark, ironic. As in Victor Perera's "Kindergarten," events are told from a child's point of view. At its center is an obsession with tattooed concentration camp numbers as a sign of personal identity and also a sense that, after the Holocaust, the world has been invaded by impostors. Compared with Szichman's "Remembrances of Things Future," the focus here is, in Joseph Brodsky's words, "the dance of the ghosts of memory." Scliar is also the author of* Max and the Cats *(1989) and* Kafka's Leopards *(2011). His* Collected Stories *appeared in 1999.*

INSIDE MY DIRTY head, the Holocaust is like this:

I'm an eleven-year-old boy. Small, skinny. And dirty. Oh boy, am I ever dirty! A stained T-shirt, filthy pants, grimy feet, hands, and face: dirty, dirty. But this external dirt is nothing compared to the filth I have inside my head. I harbor nothing but evil thoughts. I'm mischievous. I use foul language. A dirty tongue, a dirty head. A filthy mind. A sewer inhabited by toads and poisonous scorpions.

My father is appalled. A good man, my father is. He harbors nothing but pure thoughts. He speaks nothing but kind words. Deeply religious; the most religious man in our neighborhood. The neighbors wonder how such a kind, pious man could have such a wicked son with such a bad character. I'm a disgrace to the family, a disgrace to the neighborhood, a disgrace to the world. Me and my dirty head.

My father lost some of his brothers and sisters in the Holocaust. When he talks about this, his eyes well up with tears. It's now 1949; the memories of World War II are still much too fresh. Refugees from Europe arrive in the city; they come in search of relatives and friends that might help them. My father does what he can to help these unfortunate people. He exhorts me to follow his example, although he knows that little can be expected from someone with such a dirty head. He doesn't know yet what is in store for him. Mischa hasn't materialized yet.

One day Mischa materializes. A diminutive, slightly built man with a stoop; on his arm, quite visible, a tattooed number—the number assigned to him in a concentration camp. He arouses pity, poor fellow. His clothes are in tatters. He sleeps in doorways.

Learning about this distressing situation, my father is filled with indignation: Something must be done about it. One can't leave a Jew in this situation, especially when he is a survivor of the Nazi massacre. He calls the neighbors to a meeting. I want you to attend it, he says to me (undoubtedly hoping that I'll be imbued with the spirit of compassion. I? The kid with the dirty head? Poor Dad).

The neighbors offer to help. Each one will contribute a monthly sum; with this money Mischa will be able to get accommodation in a rooming house, buy clothes, and even go to a movie once in a while.

They announce their decision to the diminutive man, who, with tears in his eyes, gushes his thanks. Months go by. Mischa is now one of us. People take turns inviting him to their homes. And they invite him because of the stories he tells them in his broken Portuguese. Nobody can tell stories like Mischa. Nobody can describe like him the horrors of the concentration camp, the filth, the promiscuity, the diseases, the agony of the dying, the brutality of the guards. Listening to him brings tears to everybody's eyes . . .

Well, not to everybody's. Not to mine. I don't cry. Because of my dirty head, of course. Instead of crying, instead of flinging myself upon the floor, instead of clamoring to heaven as I listen to the horrors he narrates, I keep asking myself questions. Questions like: Why doesn't Mischa speak Yiddish like my parents and everybody else? Why does he stand motionless and silent in the synagogue while everybody else is praying?

Such questions, however, I keep to myself. I wouldn't dare ask anybody such questions; neither do I voice any of the things that my dirty head keeps imagining. My dirty head never rests; day and night, always buzzing, always scheming . . .

I start imagining this: One day another refugee, Avigdor, materializes in the neighborhood. He too comes from a concentration camp; unlike Mischa, however, he doesn't tell stories. And I keep imagining that this Avigdor is introduced to Mischa; and I keep imagining that they detest each other at first sight, even though at one time they were fellow sufferers. I imagine them one night seated at the table in our house. We're having a party; there are lots of people. Then suddenly—a scene that my dirty head has no difficulty devising—someone suggests that the two men have an arm-wrestling match.

(Why arm wrestling? Why should two puny little men, who in the past almost starved to death, put their strength against each other? Why? Why, indeed? Ask my dirty head why.)

So, there they are, the two, arm against arm; tattooed arm against tattooed arm; nobody has noticed anything. But I have—thanks, of course, to my dirty head.

The numbers are the same.

"Look," I shout, "the numbers are the same!"

At first, everybody stares at me, bewildered; then they realize what I'm talking about and see for themselves: Both men have the same number. Mischa has turned livid. Avigdor rises to his feet. He too is pale, but his rage soon makes his face and neck break out in red blotches. With unsuspected strength, he grabs Mischa by the arm; he drags him to a bedroom, forces him to go in, then closes the door behind them. Only my dirty head knows what is going on there, for it is my head that has created Avigdor, it is my head that has given Avigdor this extraordinary strength, it is my head that has caused him to open and shut the door, and it is in my head that this door exists. Avigdor is interrogating Mischa and finding out that Mischa has never been a prisoner anywhere, that he is not even a Jew; he is merely a crafty Ukrainian who had himself tattooed and who made up the whole story in order to exploit Jews.

So, once the ruse is exposed, even my dirty head has no difficulty in making Avigdor—and my parents and the neighbors—expel Mischa in a fit of fury. And so Mischa is left destitute, and he has to sleep on a park bench.

My dirty head, however, won't leave him alone, so I continue to imagine things. With the money Mischa gets from panhandling, he buys a lottery ticket. The number—trust this dirty head of mine to come up with something like this—is, of course, the one tattooed on his arm. And he wins in the lottery! Then he moves to Rio de Janeiro and buys a beautiful condo, and he is happy! Happy. He doesn't know what my dirty head has in store for him.

There's one thing that bothers him though: the number tattooed on his arm. He decides to have it removed. He goes to a famous plastic surgeon (these are refinements devised by my dirty head) and undergoes surgery. But then he goes into shock and dies a slow, agonizing death . . .

One day Mischa tells my father about the soap bars. He says he saw piles and piles of soap bars in the death camp. Do you know what the soap was made of? he asks. Human fat. Fat taken from Jews.

At night I dream about him. I'm lying naked in something resembling a bathtub, which is filled with putrid water; Mischa rubs that soap on me; he keeps rubbing it ruthlessly while shouting that he must wash the filth off my tongue and off my head, that he must wash the filth off the world.

I wake up sobbing. I wake up in the midst of great suffering. And it is this suffering that I, for lack of a better word, call the Holocaust.

APPENDIX

The Mythical Jew of Jorge Luis Borges

Emma Zunz

-- -- -- -- -- -- -- -- -- -- -- -- -- -- -- -- --

JORGE LUIS BORGES
Translated from the Spanish by Donald A. Yates

First published in September 1948 in the Buenos Aires magazine Sur, *later part of* The Aleph and Other Stories *(1942; included in its English translation in* Labyrinths, *1962), this story constantly surprises with its secret messages. It is a tale of revenge and theodicy, in which the protagonist challenges the code of ethics by taking the law into her own hands. While the word* Jew *and its synonyms never appear, the historic and linguistic context leaves no doubt as to the ethnic setting. The selection of the character's first name, Emma, is not arbitrary: the heroine is passionate and rebellious—like Jane Austen's Emma Woodhouse and Flaubert's Emma Bovary.*

RETURNING HOME FROM the Tarbuch and Loewenthal textile mills on the fourteenth of January 1922, Emma Zunz discovered in the rear of the entrance hall a letter, posted in Brazil, which informed her that her father had died. The stamp and the envelope deceived her at first; then the unfamiliar handwriting made her uneasy. Nine or ten lines tried to fill up the page; Emma read that Mr. Maier had taken by mistake a large dose of Veronal and had died on the third of the month in the hospital of Bagé. A boardinghouse friend of her father had signed the letter, some Fein or Fain from Río Grande, with no way of knowing that he was addressing the deceased's daughter.

Emma dropped the paper. Her first impression was of a weak feeling in her stomach and in her knees; then of blind guilt, of unreality, of coldness, of fear; then she wished that it were already the next day. Immediately afterward she realized that that wish was futile because the death of her father was the only thing that had happened in the world, and it would go on happening endlessly. She picked up the piece of paper and went to her room. Furtively, she hid it in a drawer, as if somehow she already knew the ulterior facts. She had already begun to suspect them perhaps; she had already become the person she would be.

In the growing darkness, Emma wept until the end of that day for the suicide of Manuel Maier, who in the old happy days was Emmanuel Zunz. She remembered summer vacations at a little farm near Gualeguay, she remembered (tried to remember) her mother, she remembered the little house at Lanus that had been auctioned off, she remembered the yellow lozenges of a window, she remembered the warrant for arrest, the ignominy, she remembered the poison-pen letters with the newspaper's account of "the cashier's embezzlement," she remembered (but this she never forgot) that her father, on the last night, had sworn to her that the thief was Loewenthal. Loewenthal, Aaron Loewenthal, formerly the manager of the factory and now one of the owners. Since 1916 Emma had guarded the secret. She had revealed it to no one, not even to her best friend, Elsa Urstein. Perhaps she was shunning profane incredulity; perhaps she believed that the secret was a link between herself and the absent parent. Loewenthal did not know that she knew; Emma Zunz derived from this slight fact a feeling of power.

She did not sleep that night, and when the first light of dawn defined the rectangle of the window, her plan was already perfected. She tried to make the day, which seemed interminable to her, like any other. At the factory there were rumors of a strike. Emma declared herself, as usual, against all violence. At six o'clock, with work over, she went with Elsa to a women's club that had a gymnasium and a swimming pool. They signed their names; she had to repeat and spell out her first and her last name; she had to respond to the vulgar jokes that accompanied the medical examination. With Elsa and with the youngest of the Kronfuss girls she discussed what movie they would go to Sunday afternoon. Then they talked about boyfriends, and no one expected Emma to speak. In April she would be nineteen years old, but men inspired in her, still, an almost pathological fear . . . Having returned home, she prepared a tapioca soup and a few vegetables, ate early, went to bed, and forced herself to sleep. In this way, laborious and trivial, Friday the fifteenth, the day before, elapsed.

Impatience awoke her on Saturday. Impatience it was, not uneasiness, and the special relief of it being that day at last. No longer did she have to plan and imagine; within a few hours the simplicity of the facts would suffice.

She read in *La Prensa* that the *Nordstjärnan*, out of Malmö, would sail that evening from Pier 3. She phoned Loewenthal, insinuated that she wanted to confide in him, without the other girls knowing, something pertaining to the strike, and she promised to stop by at his office at nightfall. Her voice trembled; the tremor was suitable to an informer. Nothing else of note happened that morning. Emma worked until twelve o'clock and then settled with Elsa and Perla Kronfuss the details of their Sunday stroll. She lay down after lunch and reviewed, with her eyes closed, the plan she had devised. She thought that the final step would be less horrible than the first and that it would doubtlessly afford her the taste of victory and justice. Suddenly, alarmed, she got up and ran to the dresser drawer. She opened it; beneath the picture of Milton Sills, where she had left it the night before, was Fain's letter. No one could have seen it; she began to read it and tore it up.

To relate with some reality the events of that afternoon would be difficult and perhaps unrighteous. One attribute of a hellish experience is unreality, an attribute that seems to allay its terrors and that aggravates them perhaps. How could one make credible an action that was scarcely believed in by the person who executed it, how to recover that brief chaos that today the memory of Emma Zunz repudiates and confuses? Emma lived in Almagro, on Liniers Street: we are certain that in the afternoon she went down to the waterfront. Perhaps on the infamous Paseo de Julio she saw herself multiplied in mirrors, revealed by lights, and denuded by hungry eyes, but it is more reasonable to suppose that at first she wandered, unnoticed, through the indifferent portico . . . She entered two or three bars, noted the routine or technique of the other women. Finally she came across men from the *Nordstjärnan*. One of them, very young, she feared might inspire some tenderness in her and she chose instead another, perhaps shorter than she and coarse, in order that the purity of the horror might not be mitigated. The man led her to a door, then to a murky entrance hall and afterward to a narrow stairway and then a vestibule (in which there was a window with lozenges identical to those in the house at Lanus) and then to a passageway and then to a door that was closed behind her. The arduous events are outside of time, either because the immediate past is as if disconnected from the future or because the parts that form these events do not seem to be consecutive.

During that time outside of time, in that perplexing disorder of disconnected and atrocious sensations, did Emma Zunz think *once* about the dead man who motivated the sacrifice? It is my belief that she did think once, and in that moment she endangered her desperate undertaking. She thought (she was unable not to think) that her father had done to her mother the hideous thing that was being done to her now. She thought of it with weak amazement and took refuge, quickly, in vertigo. The man, a Swede or Finn, did not speak Spanish. He was a tool for Emma, as she was for him, but she served him for pleasure, whereas he served her for justice.

When she was alone, Emma did not open her eyes immediately. On the little night table was the money that the man had left. Emma sat up and tore it to pieces as before she had torn the letter. Tearing money is an impiety, like throwing away bread; Emma repented the moment after she did it. An act of pride and on that day . . . her fear was lost in the grief of her body, in her disgust. The grief and the nausea were chaining her, but Emma got up slowly and proceeded to dress herself. In the room there were no longer any bright colors; the last light of dusk was weakening. Emma was able to leave without anyone seeing her; at the corner she got on a Lacroze streetcar heading west. She selected, in keeping with her plan, the seat farthest toward the front, so that her face would not be seen. Perhaps it comforted her to verify in the insipid movement along the streets that what had happened had not contaminated things. She rode through the diminishing opaque suburbs, seeing them and forgetting them at the same instant, and got off on one of the side streets of Warnes. Paradoxically, her fatigue was turning out to be a strength, since it obligated her to concentrate on the details of the adventure and concealed from her the background and the objective.

Aaron Loewenthal was to all persons a serious man, to his intimate friends a miser. He lived above the factory, alone. Situated in the barren outskirts of the town, he feared thieves; in the patio of the factory there was a large dog and in the drawer of his desk, everyone knew, a revolver. He had mourned with gravity, the year before, the unexpected death of his wife—a Gauss who had brought him a fine dowry—but money was his real passion. With intimate embarrassment, he knew himself to be less apt at earning it than at saving it. He was very religious; he believed he had a secret pact with

God that exempted him from doing good in exchange for prayers and piety. Bald, fat, wearing the band of mourning, with smoked glasses and blond beard, he was standing next to the window awaiting the confidential report of worker Zunz.

He saw her push the iron gate (which he had left open for her) and cross the gloomy patio. He saw her make a little detour when the chained dog barked. Emma's lips were moving rapidly, like those of someone praying in a low voice; weary, they were repeating the sentence that Mr. Loewenthal would hear before dying.

Things did not happen as Emma Zunz had anticipated. Ever since the morning before, she had imagined herself wielding the firm revolver, forcing the wretched creature to confess his wretched guilt and exposing the daring stratagem that would permit the justice of God to triumph over human justice. (Not out of fear but because of being an instrument of justice, she did not want to be punished.) Then, one single shot in the center of his chest would seal Loewenthal's fate. But things did not happen that way.

In Aaron Loewenthal's presence, more than the urgency of avenging her father, Emma felt the need of inflicting punishment for the outrage she had suffered. She was unable not to kill him after that thorough dishonor. Nor did she have time for theatrics. Seated, timid, she made excuses to Loewenthal, she invoked (as a privilege of the informer) the obligation of loyalty, uttered a few names, inferred others, and broke off as if fear had conquered her. She managed to have Loewenthal leave to get a glass of water for her. When the former, unconvinced by such a fuss but indulgent, returned from the dining room, Emma had already taken the heavy revolver out of the drawer. She squeezed the trigger twice. The large body collapsed, as if the reports and the smoke had shattered it, the glass of water smashed, the face looked at her with amazement and anger, the mouth of the face swore at her in Spanish and Yiddish. The evil words did not slacken; Emma had to fire again. In the patio the chained dog broke out barking, and a gush of rude blood flowed from the obscene lips and soiled the beard and the clothing. Emma began the accusation she had prepared ("I have avenged my father and they will not be able to punish me . . ."), but she did not finish it, because Mr. Loewenthal had already died. She never knew if he managed to understand.

The straining barks reminded her that she could not yet rest. She disarranged the divan, unbuttoned the dead man's jacket, took off the bespattered glasses, and left them on the filing cabinet. Then she picked up the telephone and repeated what she would repeat so many times again, with these and with other words: *Something incredible has happened . . . Mr. Loewenthal had me come over on the pretext of the strike . . . He abused me. I killed him . . .*

Actually, the story *was* incredible, but it impressed everyone because substantially it was true. True was Emma Zunz's tone, true was her shame, true was her hate. True also was the outrage she had suffered: only the circumstances were false, the time, and one or two proper names.

Death and the Compass

JORGE LUIS BORGES
Translated from the Spanish by Donald A. Yates

Included in Ficciones (1944) *and translated into English in* Labyrinths (1962), *this masterful detective story, constructed with esoteric symbols, is an homage to Edgar Allan Poe's "The Murders in the Rue Morgue." The unnamed metropolis in which it is set could be Amsterdam, where an important group of converso families, including that of Baruch Spinoza, lived in the seventeenth century. And indeed, the unraveling of the mysterious death of three Jews in three different cardinal points of the city is based on the idea that geometry is a tool for achieving knowledge of God, a theory proposed in* Ethics.

For Mandie Molina Vedia

OF THE MANY problems that exercised the reckless Discernment of Lönnrot, none was so strange—so rigorously strange, shall we say—as the periodic series of bloody events that culminated at the villa of Triste-le-Roy, amid the ceaseless aroma of the eucalypti. It is true that Erik Lönnrot failed to prevent the last murder, but that he foresaw it is indisputable. Neither did he guess the identity of Yarmolinsky's luckless assassin, but he did succeed in divining the secret morphology behind the fiendish series as well as the participation of Red Scharlach, whose other nickname is Scharlach the Dandy. That criminal (as countless others) had sworn on his honor to kill Lönnrot, but the latter could never be intimidated. Lönnrot believed himself a pure reasoner, an Auguste Dupin, but there was something of the adventurer in him, and even a little of the gambler.

293

The first murder occurred in the Hôtel du Nord—that tall prism that dominates the estuary, whose waters are the color of the desert. To that tower (which quite glaringly unites the hateful whiteness of a hospital, the numbered divisibility of a jail, and the general appearance of a bordello) there came on the third day of December the delegate from Podolsk to the Third Talmudic Congress, Dr. Marcel Yarmolinsky, a gray-bearded man with gray eyes. We shall never know whether the Hôtel du Nord pleased him; he accepted it with the ancient resignation that had allowed him to endure three years of war in the Carpathians and three thousand years of oppression and pogroms. He was given a room on Floor R, across from the suite that was occupied—not without splendor—by the Tetrarch of Galilee. Yarmolinsky supped, postponed until the following day an inspection of the unknown city, arranged in a placard his many books and few personal possessions, and before midnight extinguished his light. (Thus declared the tetrarch's chauffeur, who slept in the adjoining room.) On the fourth, at 11:03 a.m., the editor of the *Yidische Zaitung* put in a call to him; Dr. Yarmolinsky did not answer. He was found in his room, his face already a little dark, nearly nude beneath a large, anachronistic cape. He was lying not far from the door that opened on the hall; a deep knife wound had split his breast. A few hours later, in the same room, amid journalists, photographers, and policemen, Inspector Treviranus and Lönnrot were calmly discussing the problem.

"No need to look for a three-legged cat here," Treviranus was saying as he brandished an imperious cigar. "We all know that the Tetrarch of Galilee owns the finest sapphires in the world. Someone, intending to steal them, must have broken in here by mistake. Yarmolinsky got up; the robber had to kill him. How does it sound to you?"

"Possible, but not interesting," Lönnrot answered. "You'll reply that reality hasn't the least obligation to be interesting. And I'll answer you that reality may avoid that obligation but that hypotheses may not. In the hypothesis that you propose, chance intervenes copiously. Here we have a dead rabbi; I would prefer a purely rabbinical explanation, not the imaginary mischances of an imaginary robber."

Treviranus replied ill-humoredly: "I'm not interested in rabbinical explanations. I am interested in capturing the man who stabbed this unknown person."

"Not so unknown," corrected Lönnrot. "Here are his complete works." He indicated in the wall cupboard a row of tall books: a *Vindication of the Kabbalah*; *An Examination of the Philosophy of Robert Fludd*; a literal translation of the *Sepher Yezirah*; a *Biography of the Baal Shem*; a *History of the Hasidic Sect*; a monograph (in German) on the Tetragrammaton; another on the divine nomenclature of the Pentateuch. The inspector regarded them with dread, almost with repulsion. Then he began to laugh.

"I'm a poor Christian," he said. "Carry off those musty volumes if you want; I don't have any time to waste on Jewish superstitions."

"Maybe the crime belongs to the history of Jewish superstitions," murmured Lönnrot.

"Like Christianity," the editor of the *Yidische Zaitung* ventured to add. He was myopic, an atheist, and very shy.

No one answered him. One of the agents had found in the small typewriter a piece of paper, on which was written the following unfinished sentence:

The first letter of the Name has been uttered.

Lönnrot abstained from smiling. Suddenly become a bibliophile or Hebraist, he ordered a package made of the dead man's books and carried them off to his apartment. Indifferent to the police investigation, he dedicated himself to studying them. One large octavo volume revealed to him the teachings of Israel Baal Shem Tobh, founder of the sect of the Pious; another, the virtues and terrors of the Tetragrammaton, which is the unutterable name of God; another, the thesis that God has a secret name, in which is epitomized (as in the crystal sphere that the Persians ascribe to Alexander of Macedonia) his ninth attribute, eternity—that is to say, the immediate knowledge of all things that will be, that are, and that have been in the universe. Tradition numbers ninety-nine names of God; the Hebraists attribute that imperfect number to magical fear of even numbers; the Hasidim reason that the hiatus indicates a hundredth name—the Absolute Name.

From this erudition Lönnrot was distracted, a few days later, by the appearance of the editor of the *Yidische Zaitung*. The latter wanted to talk about the murder; Lönnrot preferred to discuss the diverse names of God;

the journalist declared, in three columns, that the investigator, Erik Lönn-rot, had dedicated himself to studying the names of God in order to come across the name of the murderer. Lönnrot, accustomed to the simplifications of journalism, did not become indignant. One of those enterprising shop-keepers who have discovered that any given man is resigned to buying any given book published a popular edition of the *History of the Hasidic Sect.*

The second murder occurred on the evening of the third of January, in the most deserted and empty corner of the capital's western suburbs. Toward dawn, one of the gendarmes who patrol those solitudes on horseback saw a man in a poncho, lying prone in the shadow of an old paint shop. The harsh features seemed to be masked in blood; a deep knife wound had split his breast. On the wall, across the yellow and red diamonds, were some words written in chalk. The gendarme spelled them out . . . That afternoon, Treviranus and Lönnrot headed for the remote scene of the crime. To the left and right of the automobile, the city disintegrated; the firmament grew and houses were of less importance than a brick kiln or a poplar tree. They arrived at their miserable destination: an alley's end, with rose-colored walls that somehow seemed to reflect the extravagant sunset. The dead man had already been identified. He was Daniel Simon Azevedo, an individual of some fame in the old northern suburbs, who had risen from wagon driver to political tough, then degenerated to a thief and even an informer. (The singular style of his death seemed appropriate to them: Azevedo was the last representative of a generation of bandits who knew how to manipulate a dagger but not a revolver.)

The words in chalk were the following:

The second letter of the Name has been uttered.

The third murder occurred on the night of the third of February. A lit-tle before one o'clock, the telephone in Inspector Treviranus's office rang. In avid secretiveness, a man with a guttural voice spoke; he said his name was Ginzberg (or Ginsburg) and that he was prepared to communicate, for reasonable remuneration, the events surrounding the two sacrifices of Aze-vedo and Yarmolinsky. A discordant sound of whistles and horns drowned out the informer's voice. Then the connection was broken off. Without yet rejecting the possibility of a hoax (after all, it was carnival time), Treviranus found out that he had been called from the Liverpool House, a tavern on the rue de Toulon, that dingy street where side by side exist the cosmorama and the coffee shop, the bawdy house and the Bible sellers. Treviranus spoke with the owner. The latter (Black Finnegan, an old Irish criminal who was immersed in, almost overcome by, respectability) told him that the last person to use the phone was a lodger, a certain Gryphius, who had just left with some friends. Treviranus went immediately to Liverpool House. The owner related the following. Eight days ago Gryphius had rented a room above the tavern. He was a sharp-featured man with a nebulous gray beard and was shabbily dressed in black; Finnegan (who used the room for a purpose Treviranus guessed) demanded a rent that was undoubtedly excessive; Gryphius paid the stipulated sum without hesitation. He almost never went out; he dined and lunched in his room; his face was scarcely known in the bar. On the night in question, he came downstairs to make a phone call from Finnegan's office. A closed cab stopped in front of the tavern. The driver didn't move from his seat; several patrons recalled that he was wearing a bear's mask. Two harlequins got out of the cab; they were of short stature and no one failed to observe that they were very drunk. With a tooting of horns, they burst into Finnegan's office; they embraced Gryphius, who appeared to recognize them but responded coldly; they exchanged a few words in Yiddish—he in a low, guttural voice; they in high-pitched, false voices—and then went up to the room. Within a quarter hour, the three descended, very happy. Gryphius, staggering, seemed as drunk as the others. He walked— tall and dizzy—in the middle, between the masked harlequins. (One of the women at the bar remembered the yellow, red, and green diamonds.) Twice he stumbled; twice he was caught and held by the harlequins. Moving off toward the inner harbor, which enclosed a rectangular body of water, the three got into the cab and disappeared. From the footboard of the cab, the last of the harlequins scrawled an obscene figure and a sentence on one of the slates of the pier shed.

Treviranus saw the sentence. It was virtually predictable. It said,

The last of the letters of the Name has been uttered.

Afterward, he examined the small room of Gryphius-Ginzberg. On the floor was a brusque star of blood; in the corners, traces of cigarettes of a

Hungarian brand; in a cabinet, a book in Latin—*Philologus Hebraeo Grae-cus* (1739) of Leusden—with several manuscript notes. Treviranus looked it over with indignation and had Lönnrot located. The latter, without remov-ing his hat, began to read, while the inspector was interrogating the contra-dictory witnesses to the possible kidnapping. At four o'clock they left. Out on the twisted rue de Toulon, as they were treading on the dead serpentines of the dawn, Treviranus said, "And what if all this business tonight were just a mock rehearsal?"

Erik Lönnrot smiled and, with all gravity, read a passage (which was underlined) from the thirty-third dissertation of the *Philologus: Dies Judaco-rum incipit ad solis occasu usque ad solis occasum diei sequentis.*

"This means," he added, "'The Hebrew day begins at sundown and lasts until the following sundown.'"

The inspector attempted an irony.

"Is that fact the most valuable one you've come across tonight?"

"No. Even more valuable was a word that Ginzberg used."

The afternoon papers did not overlook the periodic disappearances. *La Cruz de la Espada* contrasted them with the admirable discipline and order of the last Hermetical Congress; Ernst Palast, in *El Martir*, criticized "the intolerable delays in this clandestine and frugal pogrom, which has taken three months to murder three Jews"; the *Yidische Zaitung* rejected the hor-rible hypothesis of an anti-Semitic plot, "even though many penetrating intellects admit no other solution to the triple mystery"; the most illustrious gunman of the south, Dandy Red Scharlach, swore that in his district simi-lar crimes could never occur, and he accused Inspector Franz Treviranus of culpable negligence.

On the night of March 1, the inspector received an impressive-looking sealed envelope. He opened it; the envelope contained a letter signed "Baruch Spinoza" and a detailed plan of the city, obviously torn from a Baedeker. The letter prophesied that on the third of March there would not be a fourth murder, since the paint shop in the west, the tavern on the rue de Toulon, and the Hôtel du Nord were "the perfect vertices of a mystic equilateral triangle"; the map demonstrated in red ink the regularity of the triangle. Treviranus read the *more geometrico* argument with resignation and sent the letter and the map to Lönnrot—who unquestionably was deserving of such madnesses.

Erik Lönnrot studied them. The three locations were in fact equidistant.

Symmetry in time (the third of December, the third of January, the third of February); symmetry in space as well ... Suddenly he felt as if he were on the point of solving the mystery. A set of calipers and a compass completed his quick intuition. He smiled, pronounced the word *Tetragrammaton* (of recent acquisition), and phoned the inspector. He said, "Thank you for the equilateral triangle you sent me last night. It has enabled me to solve the problem. This Friday the criminals will be in jail, we may rest assured."

"Then they're not planning a fourth murder?"

"Precisely because they *are* planning a fourth murder we can rest assured."

Lönnrot hung up. One hour later he was traveling on one of the Southern Railway's trains, in the direction of the abandoned villa of Triste-le-Roy. To the south of the city of our story flows a blind little river of muddy water, defamed by refuse and garbage. On the far side is an industrial suburb where, under the protection of a political boss from Barcelona, gunmen thrive. Lönnrot smiled at the thought that the most celebrated gunman of all—Red Scharlach—would have given a great deal to know of his clandestine visit. Azevedo had been an associate of Scharlach; Lönnrot considered the remote possibility that the fourth victim might be Scharlach himself. Then he rejected the idea ... He had very nearly deciphered the problem; mere circumstances, reality (names, prison records, faces, judicial and penal proceedings) hardly interested him now. He wanted to travel a bit; he wanted to rest from three months of sedentary investigation. He reflected that the explanation of the murders was in an anonymous triangle and a dusty Greek word. The mystery appeared almost crystalline to him now; he was mortified to have dedicated a hundred days to it.

The train stopped at a silent loading station. Lönnrot got off. It was one of those deserted afternoons that seem like dawn. The air of the turbid, puddled plain was damp and cold. Lönnrot began walking along the countryside. He saw dogs, he saw a car on a siding, he saw the horizon, he saw a silver-colored horse drinking the crapulous water of a puddle. It was growing dark when he saw the rectangular belvedere of the villa of Triste-le-Roy, almost as tall as the black eucalypti that surrounded it. He thought that scarcely one dawning and one nightfall (an ancient splendor in the east and another in the west) separated him from the moment long desired by the seekers of the Name.

A rusty wrought-iron fence defined the irregular perimeter of the villa.

The main gate was closed. Lönnrot, without much hope of getting in, circled the area. Once again before the insurmountable gate, he placed his hand between the bars almost mechanically and encountered the bolt. The creaking of the iron surprised him. With a laborious passivity, the whole gate swung back.

Lönnrot advanced among the eucalypti, treading on confused generations of rigid, broken leaves. Viewed from anear, the house of the villa of Triste-le-Roy abounded in pointless symmetries and in maniacal repetitions: to one Diana in a murky niche corresponded a second Diana in another niche; one balcony was reflected in another balcony; double stairways led to double balustrades. A two-faced Hermes projected a monstrous shadow. Lönnrot circled the house as he had the villa. He examined everything; beneath the level of the terrace he saw a narrow venetian blind.

He pushed it; a few marble steps descended to a vault. Lönnrot, who had now perceived the architect's preferences, guessed that at the opposite wall there would be another stairway. He found it, ascended, raised his hands, and opened the trapdoor.

A brilliant light led him to a window. He opened it: a yellow, rounded moon defined two silent fountains in the melancholy garden. Lönnrot explored the house. Through anterooms and galleries he passed to duplicate patios, and time after time to the same patio. He ascended the dusty stairs to circular antechambers; he was multiplied infinitely in opposing mirrors; he grew tired of opening or half-opening windows that revealed outside the same desolate garden from various heights and various angles; inside, only pieces of furniture wrapped in yellow dust sheets and chandeliers bound up in tarlatan. A bedroom detained him; in that bedroom, one single flower in a porcelain vase; at the first touch the ancient petals fell apart. On the second floor, on the top floor, the house seemed infinite and expanding. *The house is not this large*, he thought. *Other things are making it seem larger: the dim light, the symmetry, the mirrors, so many years, my unfamiliarity, the loneliness.*

By way of a spiral staircase he arrived at the oriel. The early evening moon shone through the diamonds of the window; they were yellow, red, and green. An astonishing, dizzying recollection struck him.

Two men of short stature, robust and ferocious, threw themselves on him and disarmed him; another, very tall, saluted him gravely and said: "You are very kind. You have saved us a night and a day."

It was Red Scharlach. The men handcuffed Lönnrot. The latter at length recovered his voice. "Scharlach, are you looking for the Secret Name?"

Scharlach remained standing, indifferent. He had not participated in the brief struggle, and he scarcely extended his hand to receive Lönnrot's revolver. He spoke; Lönnrot noted in his voice a fatigued triumph, a hatred the size of the universe, a sadness not less than that hatred.

"No," said Scharlach. "I am seeking something more ephemeral and perishable, I am seeking Erik Lönnrot. Three years ago, in a gambling house on the rue de Toulon, you arrested my brother and had him sent to jail. My men slipped me away in a coupé from the gun battle with a policeman's bullet in my stomach. Nine days and nine nights I lay in agony in this desolate, symmetrical villa; fever was demolishing me, and the odious two-faced Janus, who watches the twilights and the dawns, lent horror to my dreams and to my waking. I came to abominate my body. I came to sense that two eyes, two hands, two lungs are as monstrous as two faces. An Irishman tried to convert me to the faith of Jesus; he repeated to me the phrase of the goyim: All roads lead to Rome. At night my delirium nurtured itself on that metaphor; I felt that the world was a labyrinth, from which it was impossible to flee, for all roads, though they pretend to lead to the north or south, actually lead to Rome, which was also the quadrilateral jail where my brother was dying and the villa of Triste-le-Roy. On those nights I swore by the god who sees with two faces and by all the gods of fever and of the mirrors to weave a labyrinth around the man who had imprisoned my brother. I have woven it and it is firm: the ingredients are a dead heresiologist, a compass, an eighteenth-century sect, a Greek word, a dagger, the diamonds of a paint shop.

"The first term of the sequence was given to me by chance. I had planned with a few colleagues—among them Daniel Azevedo—the robbery of the tetrarch's sapphires. Azevedo betrayed us: he got drunk with the money that we had advanced him, and he undertook the job a day early. He got lost in the vastness of the hotel; around two in the morning he stumbled into Yarmolinsky's room. The latter, harassed by insomnia, had started to write. He was working on some notes, apparently, for an article on the Name of God; he had already written the words: *The first letter of the Name has been uttered.* Azevedo warned him to be silent; Yarmolinsky reached out his hand for the bell that would awaken the hotel's forces; Azevedo countered with a single stab in the chest. It was almost a reflex action; half a century of violence had taught him that the easiest and surest thing is to kill . . . Ten days later I learned through the *Yidische Zaitung* that you were seeking in Yarmolinsky's writings the key to his death. I read the *History of the Hasidic Sect*; I learned that the reverent fear of uttering the Name of God had given rise to the doctrine that that name is all powerful and recondite. I discovered that some Hasidim, in search of that secret name, had gone so far as to perform human sacrifices . . . I knew that you would make the conjecture that the Hasidim had sacrificed the rabbi; I set myself the task of justifying that conjecture.

"Marcel Yarmolinsky died on the night of December third; for the second 'sacrifice,' I selected the night of January third. He died in the north; for the second 'sacrifice,' a place in the west was suitable. Daniel Azevedo was the necessary victim. He deserved death; he was impulsive, a traitor; his apprehension could destroy the entire plan. One of us stabbed him; in order to link his corpse to the other one, I wrote on the paint shop diamonds: *The second letter of the Name has been uttered.*

"The third murder was produced on the third of February. It was, as Treviranus guessed, a mere sham. I am Gryphius-Ginzberg-Ginsburg; I endured an interminable week (supplemented by a tenuous fake beard) in the perverse cubicle on the rue de Toulon, until my friends abducted me. From the footboard of the cab, one of them wrote on a post: *The last of the letters of the Name has been uttered.* That sentence revealed that the series of murders was *triple.* Thus the public understood it; I nevertheless interspersed repeated signs that would allow you, Erik Lönnrot, the reasoner, to understand that the series was quadruple. A portent in the north, others in the east and west, demand a fourth portent in the south; the Tetragrammaton—the Name of God, JHVH—is made up of *four* letters; the harlequins and the paint shop sign suggested *four* points. In the manual of Leusden I underlined a certain passage: that passage manifests that Hebrews compute the day from sunset to sunset; that passage makes known that the deaths occurred on the *fourth* of each month. I sent the equilateral triangle to Treviranus. I foresaw that you would add the missing point. The point that would form a perfect rhomb, the point that fixes in advance where a punctual death awaits you. I have premeditated everything, Erik Lönnrot, in order to attract you to the solitudes of Triste-le-Roy."

Lönnrot avoided Scharlach's eyes. He looked at the trees and the sky, subdivided into diamonds of turbid yellow, green, and red. He felt faintly cold, and he felt, too, an impersonal—almost anonymous—sadness. It was already night; from the dusty garden came the futile cry of a bird. For the last time, Lönnrot considered the problem of the symmetrical and periodic deaths.

"In your labyrinth there are three lines too many," he said at last. "I know of one Greek labyrinth that is a single straight line. Along that line so many philosophers have lost themselves that a mere detective might well do so too. Scharlach, when in some other incarnation you hunt me, pretend to commit (or do commit) a crime at A, then a second crime at B, eight kilometers from A, then a third crime at C, four kilometers from A and B, halfway between the two. Wait for me afterward at D, two kilometers from A and C, again halfway between both. Kill me at D, as you are now going to kill me at Triste-le-Roy."

"The next time I kill you," replied Scharlach, "I promise you that labyrinth, consisting of a single line that is invisible and unceasing." He moved back a few steps. Then, very carefully, he fired.

The Secret Miracle

JORGE LUIS BORGES

Translated from the Spanish by Harriet de Onís

This tale, also from Ficciones *(1944; included in its English translation in Laby-rinths, 1962), recalls Ambrose Bierce's "An Occurrence at Owl Creek Bridge," which takes place during the American Civil War. Suspending the pace of nature, the two are dazzling visions of death in which the protagonists are allowed to return to their past sub specie aeternitatis. But a religious element is added here: Jaromir Hladik, a Czech playwright and translator of Kabbalistic literature, imprisoned by the Nazis in Prague, whose intellectual plight recalls that of Kafka, asks God, before dying, for enough time to finish a drama he has begun. Borges's ending is troublesome: Can a miracle, in the biblical sense, be truly secret? Other possible conclusions have been suggested. In one, the manuscript of Hladik's* The Enemies *is found in a rare book room of a New York City library.*

And God had him die for a hundred years and then
revived him and said:
"How long have you been here?"
"A day or a part of a day," he answered.

—KORAN, II, 261

THE NIGHT OF March 14, 1943, in an apartment in the Zeltnergasse of Prague, Jaromir Hladik, the author of *Vindication of Eternity*, the unfinished drama *The Enemies*, and a study of the indirect Jewish sources of Jakob Böhme, had a dream of a long game of chess. The players were not two

persons but two illustrious families; the game had been going on for centuries. Nobody could remember what the stakes were, but it was rumored that
they were enormous, perhaps infinite; the chessmen and the board were in
a secret tower. Jaromir (in his dream) was the firstborn of one of the con-
tending families. The clock struck the hour for the game, which could not
be postponed. The dreamer raced over the sands of a rainy desert and was
unable to recall either the pieces or the rules of chess. At that moment he
awoke. The clangor of the rain and the terrible clocks ceased. A rhythmic,
unanimous noise, punctuated by shouts of command, arose from the Zeltnergasse. It was dawn, and the armored vanguard of the Third Reich was
entering Prague.

On the nineteenth, the authorities received a denunciation; that same
nineteenth, toward evening, Jaromir Hladik was arrested. He was taken
to an aseptic white barracks on the opposite bank of the Moldau. He was
unable to refute a single one of the Gestapo's charges; his mother's family
name was Jaroslavski, he was of Jewish blood, his study on Böhme had a
marked Jewish emphasis, his signature had been one more on the protest
against the Anschluss. In 1928 he had translated the *Sepher Yezirah* for the
publishing house of Hermann Barsdorf. The fulsome catalog of the firm
had exaggerated, for publicity purposes, the translator's reputation, and the
catalog had been examined by Julius Rothe, one of the officials who held
Hladik's fate in his hands. There is not a person who, except in the field of
his own specialization, is not credulous; two or three adjectives in Gothic
type were enough to persuade Julius Rothe of Hladik's importance, and he
ordered him sentenced to death *pour encourager les autres*. The execution
was set for March 29 at 9:00 a.m. This delay (whose importance the reader
will grasp later) was owing to the desire on the authorities' part to proceed
impersonally and slowly, after the manner of vegetables and plants.

Hladik's first reaction was mere terror. He felt he would not have shrunk
from the gallows, the block, or the knife but that death by a firing squad was
unbearable. In vain he tried to convince himself that the plain, unvarnished
fact of dying was the fearsome thing, not the attendant circumstances. He
never wearied of conjuring up these circumstances, senselessly trying to
exhaust all their possible variations. He infinitely anticipated the process of
his dying, from the sleepless dawn to the mysterious volley. Before the day
set by Julius Rothe, he died hundreds of deaths in courtyards whose forms

and angles strained geometrical probabilities, machine-gunned by variable soldiers in changing numbers, who at times killed him from a distance, at others from close by. He faced these imaginary executions with real terror (perhaps with real bravery); each simulacrum lasted a few seconds. When the circle was closed, Jaromir returned once more and interminably to the tremulous vespers of his death. Then he reflected that reality does not usually coincide with our anticipation of it; with a logic of his own he inferred that to foresee a circumstantial detail is to prevent its happening. Trusting in this weak magic, he invented, *so that they would not happen*, the most gruesome details. Finally, as was natural, he came to fear that they were prophetic. Miserable in the night, he endeavored to find some way to hold fast to the fleeting substance of time. He knew that it was rushing headlong toward the dawn of the twenty-ninth. He reasoned aloud: "I am now in the night of the twenty-second; while this night lasts (and for six nights more), I am invulnerable, immortal." The nights of sleep seemed to him deep, dark pools in which he could submerge himself. There were moments when he longed impatiently for the final burst of fire that would free him, for better or for worse, from the vain compulsion of his imaginings. On the twenty-eighth, as the last sunset was reverberating from the high barred windows, the thought of his drama, *The Enemies*, deflected him from these abject considerations.

Hladik had rounded forty. Aside from a few friendships and many habits, the problematic exercise of literature constituted his life. Like all writers, he measured the achievements of others by what they had accomplished, asking of them that they measure him by what he envisaged or planned. All the books he had published had left him with a complex feeling of repentance. His studies of the work of Böhme, of Ibn Ezra, and of Fludd had been characterized essentially by mere application; his translation of the *Sepher Yezirah*, by carelessness, fatigue, and conjecture. *Vindication of Eternity* perhaps had fewer shortcomings. The first volume gave a history of man's various concepts of eternity, from the immutable Being of Parmenides to the modifiable Past of Hinton. The second denied (with Francis Bradley) that all the events of the universe make up a temporal series, arguing that the number of man's possible experiences is not infinite and that a single "repetition" suffices to prove that time is a fallacy . . . Unfortunately, the arguments that demonstrate this fallacy are equally fallacious. Hladik was in the habit of going over them with a kind of contemptuous perplexity. He had also composed a series of expressionist poems; to the poet's chagrin they had been included in an anthology published in 1924, and no subsequent anthology inherited them. From all this equivocal, uninspired past, Hladik had hoped to redeem himself with his drama in verse, *The Enemies*. (Hladik felt the verse form to be essential because it makes it impossible for the spectators to lose sight of irreality, one of art's requisites.)

The drama observed the unities of time, place, and action. The scene was laid in Hradcany, in the library of Baron von Roemerstadt, on one of the last afternoons of the nineteenth century. In the first scene of the first act, a strange man visits Roemerstadt. (A clock was striking seven, the vehemence of the setting sun's rays glorified the windows, a passionate, familiar Hungarian music floated in the air.) This visit is followed by others; Roemerstadt does not know the people who are importuning him, but he has the uncomfortable feeling that he has seen them somewhere, perhaps in a dream. They all fawn upon him, but it is apparent—first to the audience and then to the Baron—that they are secret enemies, in league to ruin him. Roemerstadt succeeds in checking or evading their involved schemings. In the dialogue, mention is made of his sweetheart, Julia von Weidenau, and a certain Jaroslav Kubin, who at one time pressed his attentions on her. Kubin has now lost his mind and believes himself to be Roemerstadt. The dangers increase; Roemerstadt, at the end of the second act, is forced to kill one of the conspirators. The third and final act opens. The incoherencies gradually increase; actors who had seemed out of the play reappear; the man Roemerstadt killed returns for a moment. Someone points out that evening has not fallen; the clock strikes seven, the high windows reverberate in the western sun, the air carries an impassioned Hungarian melody. The first actor comes on and repeats the lines he spoke in the first scene of the first act. Roemerstadt speaks to him without surprise; the audience understands that Roemerstadt is the miserable Jaroslav Kubin. The drama has never taken place; it is the circular delirium that Kubin lives and relives endlessly.

Hladik had never asked himself whether this tragicomedy of errors was preposterous or admirable, well thought out or slipshod. He felt that the plot I have just sketched was best contrived to cover up his defects and point up his abilities and that it held the possibility of allowing him to redeem (symbolically) the meaning of his life. He had finished the first act and one or two scenes of the third; the metrical nature of the work made it possible for him to keep working it over, changing the hexameters, without the manuscript in front of him. He thought how he still had two acts to do and that he was going to die very soon. He spoke with God in the darkness: "If in some fashion I exist, if I am not one of Your repetitions and mistakes, I exist as the author of *The Enemies*. To finish this drama, which can justify me and justify You, I need another year. Grant me these days, You to whom the centuries and time belong." This was the last night, the most dreadful of all, but ten minutes later sleep flooded over him like a dark water.

Toward dawn he dreamed that he had concealed himself in one of the naves of the Clementine Library. A librarian wearing dark glasses asked him, "What are you looking for?" Hladik answered: "I am looking for God." The librarian said to him, "God is in one of the letters on one of the pages of one of the four hundred thousand volumes of the Clementine. My fathers and the fathers of my fathers have searched for this letter; I have grown blind seeking it." He removed his glasses, and Hladik saw his eyes, which were dead. A reader came in to return an atlas. "This atlas is worthless," he said, and he handed it to Hladik, who opened it at random. He saw a map of India as in a daze. Suddenly sure of himself, he touched one of the tiniest letters. A ubiquitous voice said to him, "The time of your labor has been granted." At this point Hladik awoke.

He remembered that men's dreams belong to God and that Maimonides had written that the words heard in a dream are divine when they are distinct and clear and the person uttering them cannot be seen. He dressed: two soldiers came into the cell and ordered him to follow them.

From behind the door, Hladik had envisaged a labyrinth of passageways, stairs, and separate buildings. The reality was less spectacular; they descended to an inner court by a narrow iron stairway. Several soldiers—some with uniforms unbuttoned—were examining a motorcycle and discussing it. The sergeant looked at the clock; it was 8:44. They had to wait until it struck nine. Hladik, more insignificant than pitiable, sat down on a pile of wood. He noticed that the soldiers' eyes avoided his. To ease his wait, the sergeant handed him a cigarette. Hladik did not smoke; he accepted it out of politeness or humility. As he lit it, he noticed that his hands were shaking. The day was clouding over; the soldiers spoke in a low voice as though he were already dead. Vainly he tried to recall the woman of whom Julia von Weidenau was the symbol.

The squad formed and stood at attention. Hladik, standing against the barracks wall, waited for the volley. Someone pointed out that the wall was going to be stained with blood; the victim was ordered to step forward a few paces. Incongruously, this reminded Hladik of the fumbling preparations of photographers. A big drop of rain struck one of Hladik's temples and rolled slowly down his cheek; the sergeant shouted the final order.

The physical universe came to a halt.

The guns converged on Hladik, but the men who were to kill him stood motionless. The sergeant's arm eternized an unfinished gesture. On a paving stone of the courtyard, a bee cast an unchanging shadow. The wind had ceased, as in a picture. Hladik attempted a cry, a word, a movement of the hand. He realized that he was paralyzed. Not a sound reached him from the halted world. He thought, "I am in hell. I am dead." He thought, "I am mad." He thought, "Time has stopped." Then he reflected that if that was the case, his mind would have stopped too. He wanted to test this; he repeated (without moving his lips) Virgil's mysterious fourth eclogue. He imagined that the now remote soldiers must be sharing his anxiety; he longed to be able to communicate with them. It astonished him not to feel the least fatigue, not even the numbness of his protracted immobility. After an indeterminate time, he fell asleep. When he awoke the world continued motionless and mute. The drop of water still clung to his cheek, the shadow of the bee to the stone. The smoke from the cigarette he had thrown away had not dispersed. Another "day" went by before Hladik understood.

He had asked God for a whole year to finish his work; His omnipotence had granted it. God had worked a secret miracle for him; German lead would kill him at the set hour, but in his mind a year would go by between the order and its execution. From perplexity he passed to stupor, from stupor to resignation, from resignation to sudden gratitude.

He had no document but his memory; the training he had acquired with each added hexameter gave him a discipline unsuspected by those who set down and forget temporary, incomplete paragraphs. He was not working for posterity or even for God, whose literary tastes were unknown to him. Meticulously, motionlessly, secretly, he wrought in time his lofty, invisible labyrinth. He worked the third act over twice. He eliminated certain symbols as overobvious, such as the repeated striking of the clock, the music. Nothing hurried him. He omitted, he condensed, he amplified. In certain

instances he came back to the original version. He came to feel an affection for the courtyard, the barracks; one of the faces before him modified
his conception of Roemerstadt's character. He discovered that the wearying
cacophonies that bothered Flaubert so much are mere visual superstitions,
weakness and limitation of the written word, not the spoken . . . He concluded his drama. He had only the problem of a single phrase. He found
it. The drop of water slid down his cheek. He opened his mouth in a mad-
dened cry, moved his face, dropped under the quadruple blast.

Jaromir Hladik died on March 29 at 9:02 a.m.

ACKNOWLEDGMENTS

The new edition of this anthology benefited from the assistance of Daniel Canizares, Derek García, and Saúl Grullón. *Muchas gracias* to my editor, Elise McHugh, for her sustained devotion to this project; to Lauren Gladu at Amherst College for her administrative support; to John W. Byram, director of the University of New Mexico Press, for his unflagging enthusiasm; to Peg Goldstein for her wonderful job in copyediting; and to Frederick T. Court-right for helping to secure all the permissions.

I gratefully acknowledge permission to reprint the following works:

"Jesus" by Pinkhes Berniker, translated by Alan Astro. From *Yiddish South of the Border: An Anthology of Latin America Yiddish Writing*, edited by Alan Astro. © 2003 by University of New Mexico Press. Reprinted by permission of the translator.

"The Closed Coffin" by Marcelo Birmajer, translated by Sharon Wood. © 2008. Reprinted by permission of the author and the translator.

"Death and the Compass" by Jorge Luis Borges, translated by Donald A. Yates, from *Labyrinths*, © 1962, 1964 by New Directions Publishing Corp. Reprinted by permission of New Directions Publishing Corp. UK, Commonwealth, and European rights for extracts from *Labyrinths: Selected Stories and Other Writings* by Jorge Luis Borges reprinted by permission of Pollinger Limited on behalf of the Estate of Jorge Luis Borges.

"Emma Zunz" by Jorge Luis Borges, translated by Donald A. Yates, from

Labyrinths, © 2007 by New Directions Publishing Corp. Reprinted by permission of New Directions Publishing Corp. UK, Commonwealth, and European rights for extracts from *Labryinths: Selected Stories and Other Writings* by Jorge Luis Borges reprinted by permission of Pollinger Limited on behalf of the Estate of Jorge Luis Borges.

"The Secret Miracle" by Jorge Luis Borges, translated by Harriet de Onís, from *Labyrinths*, © 1962, 1964 by New Directions Publishing Corp. Reprinted by permission of New Directions Publishing Corp. UK, Commonwealth, and European rights for extracts from *Labryinths: Selected Stories and Other Writings* by Jorge Luis Borges reprinted by permission of Pollinger Limited on behalf of the Estate of Jorge Luis Borges.

"Celeste's Heart" by Aída Bortnik. Translation © 1989 by Alberto Manguel, care of Guillermo Schavelzon & Asociados, Agencia Literaria, www.schavelzon.com. First published in *Toronto Life Magazine* 23, no. 12 (August 1989).

"Temptation" by Salomón Briansky, translated by Moisés Mermelstein. From *Yiddish South of the Border: An Anthology of Latin America Yiddish Writing*, edited by Alan Astro. © 2003 by University of New Mexico Press. Reprinted by permission of the translator.

"Asylum" by Ariel Dorfman, originally published in *Playboy*. © 2008 by Ariel Dorfman. Used by permission of the Wylie Agency LLC.

Excerpt from *Cláper* by Alicia Freilich, translated by Joan E. Friedman. © 2002. Reprinted by permission of the University of New Mexico Press.

"Camacho's Wedding Feast" from *The Jewish Gauchos of the Pampas* by Alberto Gerchunoff, translated by Prudencio de Pereda. English language translation © 1955 by Abelard-Schuman Inc.; renewed © 1983 by Harper & Row, Publishers Inc. Reprinted by permission of HarperCollins Publishers.

"Genealogies" (excerpt) by Margo Glantz. From *Genealogies*. © 1991. Translated by Susan Bassnett. Reprinted by permission of Profile Books Limited.

"The Conversion" by Isaac Goldemberg, translated by Hardie St. Martin. © 1985. From *Play by Play*. Reprinted by permission of Persea Books and Isaac Goldemberg.

"Papa's Friends" by Elisa Lerner, translated by Amy Prince. ©1991. Reprinted by permission of the author and the translator.

"Love" by Clarice Lispector, translated by Giovanni Pontiero, from *Selected Cronicas*, © 1984 Editora Nova Fronteiro; translation © 1992 by Giovanni Pontiero. Reprinted by permission of New Directions Publishing Corp. UK/Commonwealth rights for "Love" by Clarice Lispector reprinted by permission of Carcanet Press Limited.

"Bottles" by Alcina Lubitch Domecq. From *Intoxicated*, translated by Ilan Stavans. © 1988. First published in *Albany Review* 11 (Winter 1989). Reprinted by permission of the author and the translator.

"In the Name of His Name" by Angelina Muñiz-Huberman. From *Enclosed Garden*, translated by Lois Parkinson Zamora. © 1988. Reprinted by permission of Latin American Literary Review Press and Angelina Muñiz-Huberman.

Chapter 1 from *Like a Bride/Like a Mother: Two Novels* by Rosa Nissán, translated by Dick Gerdes. © 2005. Reprinted by permission of the University of New Mexico Press.

"Solomon Licht" by Yoyne Obodovski, translated by Moisés Mermelstein. From *Yiddish South of the Border: An Anthology of Latin America Yiddish Writing*, edited by Alan Astro. © 2003 by University of New Mexico Press. Reprinted by permission of the translator.

"Kindergarten" by Victor Perera. From *Rites: A Guatemalan Boyhood*. © 1985. Reprinted by permission of Victor Perera and the Watkins/Loomis Agency.

"A Man and His Parrot" by José Rabinovich, translated by Debbie Nathan. From *Yiddish South of the Border: An Anthology of Latin America Yiddish*

Writing, edited by Alan Astro. © 2003 by University of New Mexico Press. Reprinted by permission of the translator.

"In Honor of Yom Kippur" by Samuel Rollansky, translated by Alan Astro. From *Yiddish South of the Border: An Anthology of Latin America Yiddish Writing*, edited by Alan Astro. © 2003 by University of New Mexico Press. Reprinted by permission of Alan Astro and the Estate of Samuel Rollansky.

Excerpt from *The Enigmatic Eye* by Moacyr Scliar, translated by E. F. Giacomelli. Translation © 1988 by Eloah Giacomelli. Used by permission of Ballantine Books, an imprint of Random House, a division of Random House LLC. All rights reserved.

"The Invisible Hour" by Esther Seligson. From *Indicios y quimeras*. © 1988. Translated by Iván Zatz. Reprinted by permission of the Estate of Esther Seligson.

"A Nice Boy from a Good Family." Extract from the book *Los amores de Laurita*, Editorial Sudamericana, Buenos Aires 1984. © Ana María Shua, 1984. Reprinted by arrangement with Literarische Agentur Mertin Inh. Nicole Witt e. K., Frankfurt am Main, Germany. Translation reprinted with permission of Andrea Labinger.

"Xerox Man" by Ilan Stavans. From *The Disappearance: A Novella and Stories* (TriQuarterly, 2006). © Ilan Stavans, 2005. Reprinted by permission of the author.

"Innocent Spirit" by Alicia Steinberg, translated by Andrea Labinger. © Alicia Steinberg 2012. Translation © Andrea Labinger 2012. *Su espíritu inocente* was published in a single volume together with *Músicos y relojeros* in 1992. Reprinted by permission of Andrea Labinger and the Estate of Alicia Steinberg.

"Remembrances of Things Future" by Mario Szichman, translated by Iván Zatz. © 1993. Reprinted by permission of the author.

"The Bar Mitzvah Speech" by Salomon Zytner, translated by Debbie Nathan. From *Yiddish South of the Border: An Anthology of Latin America Yiddish Writing*, edited by Alan Astro. © 2003 by University of New Mexico Press. Reprinted by permission of Debbie Nathan and the Estate of Salomon Zytner.

SELECT BIBLIOGRAPHY

The following list of titles provides a source for further reading and research. A useful resource is "Latin American Jewish Literature," in Oxford Bibliographies (www.oxfordbibliographies.com). Section I, including the most authoritative works in the field (a number of which I cite in the introduction), serves as historical, sociological, and literary context; section II is a catalog of related movies; and section III is devoted to the work of Jewish Latin American writers, including those in this book and others.

I

Agosín, Marjorie, ed. *Passion, Memory, and Identity.* Albuquerque: University of New Mexico Press, 1999.

Aizenberg, Edna. *Books and Bombs in Buenos Aires: Borges, Gerchunoff, and Argentine-Jewish Writing.* Hanover, NH: University Press of New England, 2002.

Astro, Alan, ed. *Yiddish South of the Border: An Anthology of Latin American Yiddish Writing.* Albuquerque: University of New Mexico Press, 2003.

Avni, Haim. *Argentina y la historia de la inmigración judía (1810–1950).* Buenos Aires: AMIA/Comunidad Judía de Buenos Aires/Hebrew University of Jerusalem, 1983.

Barr, Lois Baer. *Israel Unbound: Patriarchal Traditions in the Jewish Latin American Novel.* Tempe: Arizona State University Center for Latin American Studies, 1995.

Beller, Jacob. *Jews in Latin America.* New York: Jonathan David, 1969.

Cohen, Martin A., ed. *The Jewish Experience in Latin America: Selected Studies from*

317

the Publications of the American Jewish Historical Society. 2 vols. Waltham, MA: American Jewish Publication Society/Ktav, 1971.

DiAntonio, Robert F., and Nora Glickman, eds. *Tradition and Innovation: Reflections on Jewish-Latin American Writing.* Albany: State University of New York Press, 1993.

Elkin, Judith Laikin. *Jews of the Latin American Republics.* Chapel Hill: University of North Carolina Press, 1980.

Elkin, Judith Laikin, and Gilbert W. Merkx, eds. *The Jewish Presence in Latin America.* Boston, MA: Allen and Unwin, 1982.

Elkin, Judith Laikin, and Ana Lya Sater, eds. *Latin American Jewish Studies: An Annotated Guide to the Literature.* Fairfield, CT: Greenwood Press, 1990.

Feierstein, Ricardo. *Cien años de narrativa judeoargentina: 1889–1989.* Buenos Aires: Milá, 1989.

———. *Cuentos judíos latinoamericanos.* Buenos Aires: AMIA, 1990.

Foster, David William, ed. *Latin American Jewish Cultural Production.* Nashville, TN: Vanderbilt University Press, 2009.

Gardiol, Rita M. *Argentine Jewish Short Story Writers.* Ball State University Monographs 32. Muncie, IN: Ball State University, 1986.

Gitlitz, David M. *Secrecy and Deceit: The Religion of the Crypto-Jews.* Albuquerque: University of New Mexico Press, 2002.

Goldemberg, Isaac, ed. *El gran libro de la América judía.* San Juan: Editorial de la Universidad de Puerto Rico, 1999.

Grosser Nagarajan, Nadia, ed. *Pomegranate Seeds: Latin American Jewish Tales.* Albuquerque: University of New Mexico Press, 2005.

Kaufman, Edy, Yoram Shapira, and Joel Barroni. *Israeli–Latin American Relations.* New Brunswick, NJ: Transaction Books, 1979.

Lesser, Jeffrey, and Raanan Rein, eds. *Rethinking Jewish-Latin Americans.* Albuquerque: University of New Mexico Press, 2008.

Lieberman, Seymour B. *The Jews in New Spain: Faith, Flame, and Inquisition.* Coral Gables, FL: University of Miami Press, 1970.

———. *The Inquisitors and the Jews in the New World.* Coral Gables, FL: University of Miami Press, 1974.

Lindstrom, Naomi. *Jewish Issues in Argentine Literature: From Gerchunoff to Szichman.* Columbia: University of Missouri Press, 1989.

Lockhart, Darrell B., ed. *Jewish Writers of Latin America: A Dictionary.* New York: Garland, 1997.

Muñiz-Huberman, Angelina, ed. *La lengua florida. Antología sefaradí.* Mexico City: Fondo de Cultura Económica-UNAM, 1989.

Sable, Martin H. *Latin American Jewry: A Research Guide*. Cincinnati, OH: Hebrew Union College Press, 1978.

Sadow, Stephen A., ed. *King David's Harp: Autobiographical Essays by Jewish Latin American Writers*. Albuquerque: University of New Mexico Press, 1999.

Senkman, Leonardo. *La identidad judía en la literatura argentina*. Buenos Aires: Pardés, 1983.

Senkman, Leonardo, Ricardo Feierstein, Isidoro Niborski, and Sara Itzigson, eds. *Integración y marginalidad: Historia de vidas de inmigrantes judíos a la Argentina*. Buenos Aires: Milá, 1985.

Sheinin, David, and Lois Baer Barr, eds. *The Jewish Diaspora in Latin America: New Studies on History and Literature*. Latin American Studies 8. New York: Garland, 1996.

Shua, Ana María. *El pueblo de los tontos: Humor tradicional judío*. Buenos Aires: Alfaguara, 1995.

Shua, Ana María, and María Dias Costa, eds. *Cuentos judíos con fantasmas y demonios*. Buenos Aires: Grupo Editorial Shalom, 1994.

Sofer, Eugene. *From Pale to Pampa: The Jewish Immigrant Experience in Buenos Aires*. New York: Holmes and Meier, 1982.

Sosnowski, Saúl. *La orilla inminente. Escritores judíos argentinas*. Buenos Aires: Legasa, 1987.

Stavans, Ilan, ed. *Tropical Synagogues: Short Stories by Jewish-Latin American Writers*. New York: Holmes and Meier, 1994.

————, ed. *The Oxford Book of Jewish Stories*. New York: Oxford University Press, 1998.

————, ed. *The Scroll and the Cross: 1,000 Years of Hispanic-Jewish Writing*. New York: Routledge, 2001.

————, ed. *The Schocken Book of Modern Sephardic Literature*. New York: Schocken Books, 2005.

Toro, Alfonso. *La familia Carvajal*. 2 vols. Mexico City: Editorial Patria, 1944.

Vieira, Nelson H. *Jewish Voices in Brazilian Literature: A Prophetic Discourse of Alterity*. Gainesville: University Press of Florida, 1995.

Weisbrot, Robert. *The Jews of Argentina: From the Inquisition to Perón*. Philadelphia, PA: Jewish Publication Society, 1979.

Winsberg, Morton. *Colonia Baron Hirsch: A Jewish Agricultural Colony in Argentina*. Gainesville: University of Florida Press, 1964.

Zivin, Erin Graff. *The Wandering Signifier: Rhetoric of Jewishness in the Latin American Imaginary*. Durham, NC: Duke University Press, 2008.

II

Burman, Daniel, dir. *Lost Embrace* (2004).

Burman, Daniel, Alberto Lecchi, et al., dirs. *18-j* (2004).

Carnevale, Marcos, dir. *Anita* (2009).

Hamburger, Cao, dir. *The Year My Parents Went on Vacation* (2009).

Jusid, José Luis, dir. *The Jewish Gauchos* (1975).

Ripstein, Arturo, dir. *El Santo Oficio* (1974).

Shifter, Guita, dir. *Like a Bride* (1993).

Springall, Alejandro, dir. *My Mexican Shiva* (2007).

Szifrón, Damián, dir. *Wild Tales* (2015).

III

Absatz, Cecilia. *Feigele y otras mujeres*. Buenos Aires: Ediciones de La Flor, 1976.

———. *Té con canela*. Buenos Aires: Sudamericana, 1982.

———. *Los años pares*. Buenos Aires: Legasa, 1985.

———. *¿Dónde estás, amor de mi vida, que no te puedo encontrar?* Buenos Aires: Espasa Calpe/Seix Barral, 1995.

Aguinis, Marcos. *Refugiados. Cronica de un palestino*. Buenos Aires: Planeta, 1976.

———. *La conspiración de los idiotas*. Buenos Aires: Emecé, 1980.

———. *Carta esperanzada a un general: Puente sobre el abismo*. Buenos Aires: Sudamericana/Planeta, 1983.

———. *La gesta del marrano*. Buenos Aires: Planeta, 1991.

———. *Asalto al paraíso*. Buenos Aires: Planeta, 2002.

———. *La matriz del infierno*. Buenos Aires: Planeta, 2004.

Aridjis, Homero. *1492. Vida y tiempos de Juan Cabezón de Castilla*, 1985. Translated by Betty Ferber as *1492: The Life and Times of Juan Cabezón of Castile*. New York: Summit Books, 1991.

Barnatán, Marcos Ricardo. *Los pasos perdidos*. Madrid: Rialp, 1968.

———. *El laberinto de Sión*. Barcelona: Barral Hispanova, 1971.

———. *Gor*. Barcelona: Barral, 1973.

Behar, Ruth. *An Island Called Home: Returning to Jewish Cuba*. Photographs by Humberto Mayol. Newark, NJ: Rutgers University Press, 2007.

———. *Traveling Heavy: A Memoir in between Journeys*. Durham, NC: Duke University Press, 2013.

Birmajer, Marcelo. *Ser humano y otras desgracias*. Buenos Aires: Ediciones de La Flor, 1997.

———. *Historias de hombres casados*. Buenos Aires: Alfaguara, 1999.

————. *No tan distinto*. Buenos Aires: Grupo Editorial Norma, 2000.

————. *Nuevas historias de hombres casados*. Buenos Aires: Alfaguara, 2001.

————. *Ultimas historias de hombres casados*. Buenos Aires: Seix Barral, 2004.

————. *El Once: Un recorrido personal*. Buenos Aires: Aguilar, 2006.

————. *Historia de una mujer*. Buenos Aires: Seix Barral, 2007.

————. *Tres Mosqueteros*, 2001. Translated by Sharon Wood as *Three Musketeers*. New Milford, CT: Toby Press, 2008.

————. *La despedida*. Buenos Aires: Grupo Editorial Norma, 2010.

Blaisten, Isidoro. *El mago*. Buenos Aires: Ediciones del Sol, 1974.

————. *Dublín al sur*. Buenos Aires: Sudamericana, 1980.

————. *Cerrado por melancolía*. Buenos Aires: Editorial de Belgrano, 1981.

————. *Cuentos anteriores*. Buenos Aires: Editorial de Belgrano, 1982.

————. *Anti-conferencias*. Buenos Aires: Emecé, 1983.

————. *A mí nunca me dejan hablar*. Buenos Aires: Sudamericana, 1985.

————. *Carroza y reina*. Buenos Aires: Emecé, 1986.

Borges, Jorge Luis. *Collected Stories*. Translated by Andrew Hurley. New York: Viking, 1999.

————. *Selected Essays*. Edited by Eliot Weinberger. New York: Viking, 1999.

————. *Selected Poems*. Edited by Alexander Coleman. New York: Viking, 1999.

Borinsky, Alicia. *Cine continuado*, 1997. Translated by Cola Frazen and the author as *All Night Movie*. Evanston, IL: Northwestern University Press, 2002.

————. *The Collapsible Couple*. Translated by Cola Frazen and the author. London: Middlesex University Press, 2002.

————. *Dreams of the Abandoned Seducer*. Translated by Cola Frazen and the author. Lincoln: University of Nebraska Press, 2002.

————. *Frivolous Women and Other Sinners*. Translated by Cola Frazen and the author. Chicago, IL: Swan Isle Press, 2002.

————. *Mean Woman*. Translated by Cola Frazen and the author. Lincoln: University of Nebraska Press, 2002.

————. *Las ciudades perdidas van al paraíso*. Buenos Aires: Corregidor, 2003.

————. *Low Blows: Snapshots*. Translated by Cola Frazen and the author. Madison: University of Wisconsin Press, 2007.

Bortnik, Aída. *Guiones cinematográficos*. Buenos Aires: Centro Editor de America Latina, 1981.

————. *Primaveras*. Buenos Aires: Teatro Municipal General San Martín, 1985.

————. *Domesticados*. Buenos Aires: Argentores, 1988.

Bortnik, Aída, and Luis Puenzo. *La historia official*. Buenos Aires: Ediciones de la Urraca, 1985.

Calny, Eugenia. *La madriguera*. Buenos Aires: Instituto Amigos del Libro Argentino, 1967.

———. *Las mujeres virtuosas*. Buenos Aires: Instituto Amigos del Libro Argentino, 1967.

———. *Clara al amanecer*. Buenos Aires: Crisol, 1972.

———. *La tarde de los ocres dorados*. Buenos Aires: Maymar, 1978.

Cony, Carlos Heitor. *A verdade de cada dia*. Rio de Janeiro: Biblioteca Universal Popular, 1963.

———. *Pessah: A travesia*. Rio de Janeiro: Civilizacao Brasileira, 1967.

———. *Sôbre tôdas as coisas*. Rio de Janeiro: Civilizacao Brasileira, 1968.

———. *O ventre*. Rio de Janeiro: Civilizacao Brasileira, 1971.

———. *Pilatos*. Rio de Janeiro: Civilizacao Brasileira, 1974.

———. *Quase memória: Quase-romance*. São Paulo: Companhia das Letras, 1995.

———. *O piano e a orquesta*. São Paulo: Companhia das Letras, 1996.

———. *A casa do poeta trágico*. São Paulo: Companhia das Letras, 1997.

———. *O burguês e o crime e outros contos*. Edited by Maura Sardinha. Rio de Janeiro: Ediouro, 1997.

———. *O harém das bananeiras*. Rio de Janeiro: Objetiva, 1997.

———. *Matéria de memória*. São Paulo: Companhia das Letras, 1998.

———. *Informação ao crucificado*. São Paulo: Companhia das Letras, 1999.

———. *O indigitado*. Rio de Janeiro: Objetiva, 2001.

———. *A tarde da su auséncia*. São Paulo: Companhia das Letras, 2003.

———. *A revolução dos caranguejos*. São Paulo: Companhia das Letras, 2004.

Costantini, Humberto. *De dioses, hombrecitos y policías*, 1977. Translated by Toby Talbot as *The Gods, the Little Guys, and the Police*. New York: Harper & Row, 1983.

Cozarinsky, Edgardo. *Vudú urbano*, 1985. Translated by Ronald Christ as *Urban Voodoo*. Introduction by Susan Sontag. New York: Lumen, 1990.

———. *The Bridge from Odessa*. Translated by Nick Caistor. London: Harvil, 2004.

———. *The Moldavian Pimp*. Translated by Nick Caistor. London: Harvil Secker, 2004.

———. *Museo del chisme*. Buenos Aires: Emecé, 2005.

———. *Tres fronteras*. Buenos Aires: Emecé, 2006.

———. *Maniobras nocturnas*. Buenos Aires: Emecé, 2007.

———. *La tercera mañana*. Barcelona: Tusquets, 2010.

———. *Diario para fantasmas*. Barcelona: Tusquets, 2012.

Darío, Rubén. *Canto a la Argentina*. Buenos Aires: Libro Amigo, 1935.

Dorfman, Ariel. *Viudas*, 1981. Translated by Stephen Kessler as *Widows*. New York: Random House, 1983.

———. *La última canción de Manuel Sendero*, 1982. Translated by George R. Shrivers as *The Last Song of Manuel Sendero*. New York: Viking, 1987.

———. *Heading South, Looking North: A Bilingual Journey*. New York: Farrar Straus & Giroux, 1998.

———. *Feeding on Dreams: Confessions of an Unrepentant Exile*. Boston, MA: Houghton Mifflin Harcourt, 2011.

Eichelbaum, Samuel. *El viajero inmóvil y otros relatos*. Buenos Aires: Paidós, 1969.

Feierstein, Ricardo. *Cuentos para hombres solos*. Buenos Aires: Instituto Amigos del Libro Argentino, 1957.

———. *Cuentos de rabia y oficina*. Buenos Aires: Stilcograf, 1965.

———. *El caramelo descompuesto*. Buenos Aires: Editorial Nueva Presencia, 1979.

———. *Mestizo*, 1994. Translated by Stephen A. Sadow as *Mestizo*. Introduction by Ilan Stavans. Albuquerque: University of New Mexico Press, 2000.

———. *La logia del umbral*. Buenos Aires: Galerna, 2001.

Fihman, Ben Ami. *Mi nombre Rufo Galo*. Caracas: Monteávila, 1973.

———. *Los recursos del limbo*. Caracas: Monteávila, 1981.

Freilich, Alicia. *Cláper*, 1987. Translated by Joan E. Friedman as *Cláper*. Introduction by Ilan Stavans. Albuquerque: University of New Mexico Press, 1998.

Fuentes, Carlos. *Cambio de piel*, 1967. Translated by Sam Hileman as *A Change of Skin*. New York: Farrar, Straus & Giroux, 1968.

———. *Terra Nostra*, 1975. Translated by Margaret Sayers Peden as *Terra Nostra*. New York: Farrar, Straus & Giroux, 1976.

———. *La cabeza de la hidra*, 1978. Translated by Margaret Sayers Peden as *The Hydra Head*. New York: Farrar, Straus & Giroux, 1978.

Gerchunoff, Alberto. *Los gauchos judíos*, 1910. Translated by Prudencio de Pereda as *The Jewish Gauchos of the Pampas*. New York: Abelard-Schuman, 1955. Revised edition with an introduction by Ilan Stavans. Albuquerque: University of New Mexico Press, 2007.

———. *Cuentos de ayer*. Buenos Aires: Ediciones America, 1919.

———. *La jofaina maravillosa: Agenda cervantina*. Buenos Aires: Biblioteca Argentina de Buenas Ediciones Literarias, 1922.

———. *La asamblea de la bohardilla*. Buenos Aires: Manuel Gleizer, 1925.

———. *Historia y proezas de amor*. Buenos Aires: Manuel Gleizer, 1926.

———. *El hombre que hablo en la Sorbona*. Buenos Aires: Manuel Gleizer, 1926.

———. *Pequeñas prosas*. Buenos Aires: Manuel Gleizer, 1926.

————. *Heine, poeta de nuestra intimidad.* Buenos Aires: Babel, 1927.

————. *Los amores de Baruj Spinoza.* Buenos Aires: Babel, 1932.

————. *El hombre importante.* Montevideo/Buenos Aires: Sociedad Amigos del Libro Rioplatense, 1934.

————. *La clínica del Dr. Mefistófeles: Moderna milagrería en diez jornadas.* Santiago de Chile: Ercilla, 1937.

————. *Entre Ríos, mi país.* Buenos Aires: Futuro, 1950.

————. *Retorno de Don Quixote.* Prologue by Jorge Luis Borges. Buenos Aires: Sudamericana, 1951.

————. *El pino y la palmera.* Buenos Aires: Sociedad Hebraica Argentina, 1952.

————. *Argentina, país de advenimiento.* Buenos Aires: Losada, 1952.

Glantz, Margo. *Las genealogías,* 1981. Translated by Susan Bassnett as *Genealogies.* London: Serpent's Tail, 1990.

————. *El rastro,* 2002. Translated by Andrew Hurley as *The Wake.* Willimantic, CT: Curbstone, 2005.

Glickman, Nora. *Uno de sus Juanes.* Buenos Aires: Ediciones de la Flor, 1983.

————. *Mujeres, memorias, malogros.* Buenos Aires: Milá, 1991.

Goldemberg, Isaac. *La vida a plazos de Don Jacobo Lerner,* 1980. Translated by Roberto S. Picciotto as *The Fragmented Life of Don Jacobo Lerner.* New York: Persea, 1976. Revised edition with an introduction by Ilan Stavans. Albuquerque: University of New Mexico Press, 2008.

————. *Hombre de paso/Just Passing Through.* Translated by David Unger and Isaac Goldemberg. Hanover, NH: Point of Contact/Ediciones del Norte, 1981.

————. *Tiempo al tiempo,* 1984. Translated by Hardie St. Martin as *Play by Play.* Hanover, NH: Ediciones del Norte, 1983.

————. *La vida al contado.* Hanover, NH: Ediciones del Norte, 1992.

————. *La vida son los ríos.* Lima: Fondo Editorial del Congreo del Peru, 2005.

Goldemberg, Isaac, and José Kozer. *De Chepén a La Habana.* New York: Editorial Bayu-Menorah, 1973.

Goloboff, Mario. *Entre la diáspora y octubre.* Buenos Aires: Stilcograf, 1966.

————. *Caballos por el fondo de los ojos.* Barcelona: Planeta, 1976.

————. *Criador de palomas.* Buenos Aires: Bruguera, 1984.

————. *La luna que cae.* Barcelona: Muchnik, 1989.

————. *El soñador de Smith.* Barcelona: Muchnik, 1990.

————. *The Algarrobos Quartet.* Translated by Stephen A. Sadow. Introduction by Ilan Stavans. Albuquerque: University of New Mexico Press, 2002.

————. *La pasión según San Martín y otros relatos.* La Plata, Argentina: Ediciones al Margen, 2005.

Lerner, Elisa. *Vida con mamá*. Caracas: Monteávila, 1975.

———. *Una sonrisa detrás de la metáfora*. Caracas: Monteávila, 1977.

———. *Yo amo a Columbo*. Caracas: Monteávila, 1979.

———. *Carriel para la fiesta*. Caracas: Blanca Pantín, 1997.

———. *En el entretanto*. Caracas: Monteávila, 2000.

Levinson, Luisa Mercedes. "El abra," 1967. Translated by Sylvia Lipp as "The Cove."
In *Short Stories by Latin American Women: The Magic and the Real*. Edited by
Celia Correas de Zapata. Houston, TX: Arte Publico Press, 1990.

Lispector, Clarice. *Perto do coraçao salvagem*, 1944. Translated by Giovanni Pontiero
as *Near to the Wild Heart*. New York: New Directions, 1990.

———. *Laços de familia*, 1960. Translated by Giovanni Pontiero as *Family Ties*, Aus-
tin: University of Texas Press, 1972.

———. *A maçâ no escuro*, 1961. Translated by Gregory Rabassa as *The Apple in the
Dark*. New York: Alfred A. Knopf, 1967.

———. *A legião estrangeira*, 1964. Translated by Giovanni Pontiero as *The Foreign
Legion*. New York: New Directions, 1992.

———. *A paixão segundo G. H.*, 1964. Translated by Ronald W. Souza as *The Passion
According to G. H.* Minneapolis: University of Minnesota Press, 1988.

———. *Uma aprendizagem ou O Livro dos Prazeres*, 1969. Translated by Richard A.
Mazarra and Lorri A. Parris as *An Apprenticeship, or The Book of Delights*. Aus-
tin: University of Texas Press, 1986.

———. *A hora da estrêla*, 1977. Translated by Giovanni Pontiero as *The Hour of the
Star*. New York: New Directions, 1991.

———. *Soulstorm*. Translated by Alexis Levitin. New York: New Directions, 1988.

Lubitch Domecq, Alcina. *El espejo del espejo, o La noble sonrisa del perro*. Mexico
City: Joaquín Mortiz, 1983.

———. *Intoxicada*. Mexico City: Joaquín Mortiz, 1984.

Muchnik, Mario. *Mundo judio: Crónica personal*. Barcelona: Lumen, 1984.

Muñiz-Huberman, Angelina. *La morada interior*. Mexico City: Joaquin Mortiz, 1972.

———. *Tierra adentro*. Mexico City: Joaquin Mortiz, 1977.

———. *La guerra del unicornio*. Mexico City: Artifice, 1983.

———. *Huerta cerrado, huerto sellado*, 1985. Translated by Lois Parkinson Zamora as
Enclosed Garden. Pittsburgh, PA: Latin American Literary Review, 1988.

———. *De magias y prodigios*. Mexico City: Fondo de Cultura Económica, 1987.

———. *De cuerpo entero* (autobiography). Mexico City: UNAM-Ediciones Corunda,
1991.

———. *Dulcinea encantada*. Mexico City: Joaquin Mortiz, 1992.

———. *Las confidentes*. Mexico City: Tusquets, 1997.

————. *El mercader de Tudela.* Mexico City: Fondo de Cultura Económica, 1998.

————. *La sal en el rostro.* Mexico City: Universidad Autónoma Metropolitana, 1998.

————. *Conato de extranjería.* Mexico City: Trilce, 1999.

————. *Trotsky en Coyoacán.* Mexico City: Instituto de Seguridad y Servicios Sociales, 2000.

————. *Molinos sin viento.* Mexico City: Aldus, 2001.

————. *Cantos treinta de otoño.* Mexico City: Verdehalago, 2005.

————. *La burladora de Toledo.* Mexico City: Planeta, 2008.

————. *La tregua de la inocencia.* Mexico City: Consejo Nacional para la Cultura y las Artes, 2008.

Nissán, Rosa. *Novia que te vea.* Mexico: Planeta, 1992.

————. *Hisho que te nazca.* Mexico: Planeta, 1996.

————. *Like and Bride/Like a Mother.* Translated by Dick Gerdes. Introduction by Ilan Stavans. Albuquerque: University of New Mexico Press, 2003.

Orgambide, Pedro. *Aventuras de Edmundo Ziller en tierras del Nuevo Mundo.* Mexico City: Nueva Imagen, 1984.

Pacheco, José Emilio. *Morirás lejos.* Mexico City: Joaquín Mortiz, 1967.

————. *Las batallas en el desierto,* 1981. Translated by Katherine Silver as *Battles in the Desert and Other Stories.* New York: New Directions, 1987.

Perera, Victor. *The Conversion.* New York: Little, Brown, 1970.

————. *Rites: A Guatemalan Boyhood.* San Diego, CA: Harcourt Brace Jovanovich, 1986.

————. *The Cross and the Pear Tree: A Sephardic Journey.* New York: Alfred A. Knopf, 1995.

Portnoy, Alicia. *La escuelita,* 1981. Translated by the author as *The Little School.* London: Virago, 1988.

Rawet, Samuel. *Contos do imigrante.* Rio de Janeiro: L&PM, 1956.

————. *Os Sete Sonhos.* Benfica, Brazil: Olive Editor, 1967.

————. *O terreno de uma polegada quadrada* Benfica, Brazil: Olive Editor, 1969.

————. *Viagens de Ahasverus.* Benfica, Brazil: Olive Editor, 1970.

————. *Eu-tu-êle.* Rio de Janeiro: Jose Olympio, 1972.

————. *The Prophet and Other Stories.* Translated by Nelson H. Vieira. Introduction by Ilan Stavans. Albuquerque: University of New Mexico, 1998.

Rozenmacher, Germán. *Cabecita negra.* Buenos Aires: Jose Alvarez, 1963.

————. *Los ojos del tigre.* Buenos Aires: Galerna, 1967.

————. *Cuentos completos.* Buenos Aires: Centro Editor de América Latina, 1971.

————. *Réquiem para un viernes a la noche.* Buenos Aires: Talia, 1971.

Rozitchner, León. *Ser judío.* Buenos Aires: Ediciones de la Flor, 1967.

Satz, Mario. *Luna*. Barcelona: Noguer, 1976.

———. *Tierra*. Barcelona: Noguer, 1978.

———. *Sol*. Translated by Helen Lane. Garden City, NY: Doubleday, 1979.

———. *Marte*. Barcelona: Barral, 1980.

Scliar, Moacyr. *O exército de um homem só*, 1973. Translated by Eloah F. Giacomelli
as *The One-Man Army*. New York: Ballantine, 1986.

———. *A balada do falso messias*, 1976. Translated by Eloah F. Giacomelli as *The Bal-
lad of the False Messiah*. New York: Ballantine, 1987.

———. *O carnaval dos animais*, 1976. Translated by Eloah F. Giacomelli as *The Carnival of the Animals*. New York: Ballantine, 1986.

———. *Os deuses de Raquel*, 1978. Translated by Eloah F. Giacomelli as *The Gods of
Raquel*. New York: Ballantine, 1986.

———. *O centauro no jardim*, 1980. Translated by Margaret A. Neves as *The Centaur
in the Garden*. New York: Ballantine, 1985.

———. *Os voluntários*, 1980. Translated by Eloah F. Giacomelli as *The Volunteers*.
New York: Ballantine, 1988.

———. *A guerra no Bom Fim*. Porto Alegre: L&PM, 1981.

———. *Max e os felinos*, 1982. Translated by Eloah F. Giacomelli as *Max and the
Cats*. New York: Ballantine, 1989.

———. *A estranha nação de Rafael Mendes*, 1983. Translated by Eloah F. Giacomelli
as *The Strange Nation of Rafael Mendes*. New York: Harmony Books, 1987.

———. *Os melhores cantos de Moacyr Scliar*. Edited by Regina Zilberman, 1984.
Translated by Eloah F. Giacomelli as *The Collected Stories*. Introduction by Ilan
Stavans. Albuquerque: University of New Mexico Press, 1999.

———. *A condição judaica: das Tábuas da Lei à mesa da cozinha*. Porto Alegre:
L&PM, 1985.

———. *O olho enigmatico*, 1986. Translated by Eloah F. Giacomelli as *The Enigmatic
Eye*. New York: Ballantine, 1989.

———. *Minha mãe não dorme enquanto eu nõ chegar e outras crônicas*. Porto Alegre:
L&PM, 1995.

———. *A majestade do Xingu*. São Paulo: Companhia das Letras, 1997.

———. *Histórias para (quase) todos os gostos*. Porto Alegre: L&PM, 1998.

———. *A mulher que esceveu a Bíblia*. São Paulo: Companhia das Letras, 1999.

———. *Os leopardos de Kafka olho enigmatico*, 2000. Translated by Thomas O. Bee-
bee as *Kafka's Leopards*. Lubbock: Texas Tech, 2011.

Seligson, Esther. *Otros son los sueños*. Mexico City: Editorial Novaro, 1973.

———. *La morada en el tiempo*. Mexico City: Artífice, 1981.

———. *Sed de mar*. Mexico City: Artífice, 1987.

Shua, Ana María. *Soy paciente*, 1980. Translated by David William Foster as *Patient*. Pittsburgh, PA: Latin American Literary Review Press, 1997.

———. *Los amores de Laurita*. Buenos Aires: Sudamericana, 1984.

———. *Casa de geishas*. Buenos Aires: Sudamericana, 1992.

———. *El libro de los recuerdos*, 1994. Translated by Dick Gerdes as *The Book of Memories*. Introduction by Ilan Stavans. Albuquerque: University of New Mexico Press, 1998.

———. *La muerte como efecto secundario*. Buenos Aires: Sudamericana, 1997.

———. *Como una buena madre*. Buenos Aires: Sudamericana, 2001.

———. *Historias verdaderas*. Buenos Aires: Sudamericana, 2004.

———. *Quick Fix: Sudden Fiction*. Translated by Rhonda Dahl Buchanan. Buffalo, NY: White Pine Press, 2008.

———. *The Weight of Temptation*. Translated by Andrea G. Labinger. Lincoln: University of Nebraska Press, 2012.

———. *Without a Net*. Translated by Steven J. Stewart. Brooklyn, NY: Hanging Loose Press, 2012.

Stavans, Ilan. *On Borrowed Words: A Memoir of Language*. New York: Viking, 2001.

———. *The One-Handed Pianist and Other Stories*. Evanston, IL: Northwestern University Press, 2006.

———. *The Disappearance: A Novella and Stories*. Evanston, IL: Northwestern University Press, 2007.

———. *Return to Centro Histórico: A Mexican Jew Looks for His Roots*. Newark, NJ: Rutgers University Press, 2011.

———. *El Iluminado*. Illustrations by Steve Sheinkin. New York: Basic Books, 2012.

Stavans, Ilan, and Marcelo Brodsky. *Once@9:53am*. Buenos Aires: La Marca Editores, 2011.

Steinberg, Alicia. *De músicos y relojeros*, 1971. Translated by Andrea G. Labinger as *Musicians and Watchmakers*. Pittsburgh, PA: Latin American Literary Review Press, 1998.

———. *La loca 101*. Buenos Aires: Ediciones de la Flor, 1973.

———. *El espíritu inocente*. Buenos Aires: Pomaire, 1981.

———. *El árbol del placer*, 1986. Translated by Andrea G. Labinger as *The Rainforest*. Lincoln: University of Nebraska Press, 2006.

———. *Cuando digo Magdalena*, 1992. Translated by Andrea G. Labinger as *Call Me Magdalena*. Lincoln: University of Nebraska Press, 2001.

———. *La selva*. Buenos Aires: Alfaguara, 2000.

Szichman, Mario. *Los judíos del Mar Dulce*. Buenos Aires: Galerna/Síntesis, 1971.

———. *La verdadera Crónica Falsa*. Buenos Aires: Centro Editor de America Latina,

1972.

———. *A las 20:25 la señora entró en la inmortalidad*, 1981. Translated by Roberto S. Picciotto as *At 8:25 Evita Became Immortal*. Hanover, NH: Ediciones del Norte, 1983.

———. *Las dos muertes del general Simón Bolívar*. Caracas: J. A. Catalá/El Centauro, 2004.

Tiempo, Cesar (Israel Zeitlin). *El becerro de oro*. Buenos Aires: Paidós, 1973.

———. *El ultimo romance de Gardel*. Buenos Aires: Quetzal, 1975.

———. *Mi tío Sholem Aleijem y otros relatos*. Buenos Aires: Corregidor, 1978.

———. *Manos de obra*. Buenos Aires: Corregidor, 1980.

Timerman, Jacobo. *Preso sin nombre, celda sin número*, 1981. Translated by Toby Talbot as *Prisoner without a Name, Cell without a Number*. New York: Alfred A. Knopf. 1981.

Vargas Llosa, Mario. *El hablador*, 1988. Translated by Helen R. Lane as *The Storyteller*. New York: Farrar, Straus & Giroux, 1989.

Verbitsky, Bernardo. *Café de los angelitos*. Buenos Aires: Siglo XX, 1950.

———. *Una pequeña familia*. Buenos Aires: Losada, 1951.

———. *Villa miseria también es América*. Buenos Aires: Kraft, 1957.

———. *Un hombre de papel*. Buenos Aires: Jorge Alvarez, 1966.

———. *Etiquetas a los hombres*. Barcelona: Planeta, 1972.

Viñas, David. *Los dueños de la tierra*. Buenos Aires: Losada, 1958.

———. *Dar la cara*. Buenos Aires: Centro Editor de América Latina, 1967.

———. *En la Semana Trágica*. Buenos Aires: Jorge Alvarez, 1966.

———. *Jauría*. Mexico: Siglo XXI, 1979.

CONTRIBUTORS

PINKHES BERNIKER (1908–1956), born in Belarus, helped start the first Yiddish newspaper in Cuba, *Dos Fraye Vort*.

MARCELO BIRMAJER is the author of *Three Musketeers*, as well as *El Once*, a travelogue through the Jewish neighborhood of Buenos Aires.

JORGE LUIS BORGES (1899–1986) is the author of *Ficciones*.

AÍDA BORTNIK wrote the screenplay, together with Luis Puenzo, of *The Official Story*, which won the Oscar for Best Foreign Film in 1987.

SALOMÓN BRIANSKY (1902–1955) immigrated to Bogotá in 1934. He published three volumes of fiction.

ARIEL DORFMAN is a poet, essayist, playwright, novelist, activist, and professor of literature at Duke University. He is best known for his play *Death and the Maiden*.

ALICIA FREILICH, an essayist and newspaper columnist born in Caracas, Venezuela, is the author of *Cláper*.

ALBERTO GERCHUNOFF (1884–1950) was an influential columnist and man of letters, as well as one of Borges's mentors. He wrote *The Jewish Gauchos of the Pampas*.

MARGO GLANTZ wrote *Las genealogías*, about her immigrant family in Mexico.

ISAAC GOLDEMBERG is the author of *The Fragmented Life of Don Jacobo Lerner*.

ELISA LERNER is a Venezuelan writer and diplomat.

CLARICE LISPECTOR (1925–1977), a Ukrainian-born Brazilian writer, is the author of *Family Ties, The Passion According to G. H.,* and *The Hour of the Star*.

ALCINA LUBITCH DOMECQ, born in Guatemala in 1953, is the author of *The Mirror's Mirror: or, The Noble Smile of the Dog*. She lives in Israel.

ANGELINA MUÑIZ-HUBERMAN was born in 1936 to Spanish parents in France and immigrated to Mexico at a young age. She is the editor of anthologies of Sephardic literature and the author of *Enclosed Garden*.

ROSA NISSÁN is the author of *Like a Bride*, which was made into a movie, and *Like a Mother*.

YOYNE OBODOVSKI, a Yiddish writer, first lived in Argentina and then in Chile before settling in Israel in 1965. He wrote satiric sketches of Jewish immigrants.

VICTOR PERERA (1934–2003), a Guatemala-born journalist, wrote *The Cross and the Pear Tree: A Sephardic Journey*.

JOSÉ RABINOVICH (1903–1977), originally from Bialystok, immigrated to Argentina. He switched from writing in Yiddish to writing in Spanish. He wrote *El violinista bajo el tejado* (The Fiddler under the Roof).

SAMUEL ROLLANSKY (1902–1995), a cultural impresario, wrote a daily column for *Di Yidishe Tsaytung* in Buenos Aires.

MOACYR SCLIAR (1937–2011) is best known as the author of *The Centaur in the Garden*.

ESTHER SELIGSON (1941–2010) wrote on Kabbalah and Jewish mysticism.

ANA MARÍA SHUA is the author of *The Book of Memories*.

ILAN STAVANS is the Lewis-Sebring Professor in Latin American and Latino Culture at Amherst College.

ALICIA STEINBERG (1933–2012) is the author of *Musicians and Watchmakers*.

MARIO SZICHMAN, an Argentine journalist born in 1945, is the author of *At 8:25 Evita Became Immortal*.

SALOMON ZYTNER (1904–1986) was a Labor Zionist who immigrated to Uruguay. He wrote short stories, which are collected in three volumes published between 1955 and 1974: *Der gerangl* (The Struggle), *Di mishpokhe* (The Family), and *"Tsvishn vent" und andere dertseylungen* ("Within Four Walls" and Other Stories).